DIFFERENT SIDES

By Phil Chapman

and

Adam Lewis

Chapters.

Prologue

1 England 1936
2 Berlin Olympics 1936
3 Spain
4 Paris 1938
5 Hamburg 1938
6 Berlin   1939
7 General Harrer
8 Stalingrad Otto Witzell
9 France
10 Almira France Portugal Morocco
11 Marseille
12   Paris
13 Gun Running to the Macquis
14 Hamburg 1945
15 Scotland   and North Atlantic

Epilogue

Prologue by Adam Lewis

I was on the move again. The house is sold. I have packed nearly everything from my two floors of accumulated mismatched furniture and memorabilia. The removal company has taken everything into storage. My next house is still waiting for the sellers to vacate. They are full of apologies which they appear to struggle to sound sincere about.

I am neither bothered nor worried. I have decided to take a sort of working holiday and visit some places in Scotland. I will be heading up the M6 later today with a short detour into Liverpool to see an old friend for a beer or two and hopefully a trip into Chinatown for a decent Chinese meal, if he's up for it.

The motivation for all of this came when I was emptying my loft. Old books which should have gone to the charity shop, and papers which should have been binned or burnt a long time ago and, bound up in a couple of old suitcases, a partial history of family tales.

A story I had written years before, ten percent a history lesson and ninety percent anecdotes lacking cohesion, and direction, not certain what it was trying to tell.

My friend Phil lives in Liverpool, and as he was on my way, sort of, and a quick phone call told me he could put me up for a few days; plan not hatched yet, but looking promising in the incubator.

 I spent a couple of days with Phil. I showed him the contents of the two suitcases.

He took the suitcases, all the notes, the maps, the stories, and put it all together, the way I should have done it years back.

Things were a bit different then. I'd been too close, and too involved, with the people to be objective enough to tell a story, that let the truth shine through the intrigue, and the family allegiance.

I put his name first on the cover as he did the work. I provided the research and the notes and the basics of the story and the opening pages in the first chapter which all started at Alec's funeral.

Alec was my uncle, the youngest of seven Lewis brothers. He got the last rites at the age of twelve, when the poor boy's heart decided it didn't want to keep going anymore. The vicar from St James on hearing the news, from the flower ladies at the church, immediately came to visit. The doctor, on his daily check-up, was just leaving, and after a brief word, the doctor left, and a solemn faced reverend entered the house gingerly. My grandmother was less than five feet tall weighed about six stone had nine children and was the daughter of Swiss Catholic missionaries. Nobody in their right mind was not intimidated by her. Protestant vicars would require more than God on their side if they upset her. Today was different. Alec, the baby of the family was not well and today she would take any help from any direction she could get.

Alec had the bed to himself. It was probably the only time he had done so. Grandmother got the reverend a chair from the living room and sitting kneeling and between cups of tea he spent an hour praying for Alec's survival or, in a worst case scenario, a safe passage to heaven.

Alec always reckoned, it must have been the vicars fine words, rather than the truth, but whatever it was, he survived the night, and then the following day, then the week, and the next week, and on the Sunday after Alec attended church possibly for the first time ever since his christening and gave thanks to God, to the vicar, and to whoever else was instrumental in keeping him alive.

Having done it this once no one is ever certain if apart from the obligatory family gathering for weddings, funerals, and christenings, if he ever felt the need to step foot inside a church again.

He got to fifty three when he finally went into the chapel at the cemetery. His heart had lasted forty one years without any further assistance from either the priesthood or the medical profession.

Landican cemetery is a cold place. Middle of summer outside the cemetery the sun is cracking the flags. The second you enter those gates, at the junction in the road, the temperature seems to drop. It's mostly open ground apart from a few stunted trees and neatly trimmed hedgerows, around the original plots. There is little protection against the wind. It matters little whichever direction it's coming from there is always a chill factor. To protect those still alive from rapidly joining the ones they have come to say goodbye to, there are big cast iron radiators in the chapels. In all the times I've been there I've never noticed any sign of warmth. With a service lasting twenty minutes filing in through one set of doors and then out again with a production line burial system doesn't lend itself to keeping the place warm or the breathing visitors comfortable.

Uncle Alec had a good turnout. Grand dad and grandma had gone a few years back. His brother, Frank, had died in the second world war. The rest of the family had made it. Even Uncle Alan had got here. He was on a zimmer and walking badly now. I hadn't seen him for at least ten years. He was the second eldest two years younger than my father. So that would make him sixty seven now give or take a couple of months. He still had a head of hair which made him appear younger than his years and though typical of the family not tall maybe only five feet six he held himself very straight even when not relying on the zimmer.

Alec was buried in the family grave with nan and granddad and one of my young cousins who had lasted less than a year.

It was an early funeral, the pubs were still closed and as cold as it was people, who hadn't seen their friends or relatives since the last funeral, hung around talking to each other, and we left them to it.

Prior arrangements had been made, and we followed our plan, and having arranged early access went to the pub, near Alec's house, for tea and sandwiches, before opening time.

I drove two of the brothers, Arthur and Bert, while my sister squeezed their wives into her car and took the scenic route at a dawdle. It wasn't that they hadn't been invited, but the start would just be the brothers and two sisters. No others for the first half hour. They had business to sort. Given Alec's increasing age and medical condition, a will would have been a good idea. Like a lot of things tomorrow will do. Perhaps it was his way of having the final laugh.

Alan had been driven over by a friend who waited outside while the family adjourned.

"You not going in?" He asked me.

"I'm a nephew." I told him. "The brothers and sisters will have a short while alone I'll join them when the rest arrive."

"I take it then that Alan is your uncle."

" Yes."

"How do you do my name is Steven. I am a friend of your Uncle Alan's. I guess that you're his brother Adam's son."

"Yes My dad is Adam, his dad was Adam, I am Adam, they have a history, first born of each generation is Adam my second name is Frank. Named after my uncle who died in the war."

"Who if I remember correctly is buried in Rome."

"He is. You couldn't have known him though you aren't old enough."

"Alan tells me lots about his family. I know he likes you. The boy who went to Grammar school then university, the clever one."

"I'm not so clever. I've not got round to doing the things I wanted to do or kept the promises I made to myself. Which sounds a bit maudlin I know, but you get reminded every time there's a funeral that immortality has a place only in fairy tales."

"There is always time. What you have to do is make the time that you have to get the things done that you want to do."

"Please don't misunderstand me I'm neither sad nor unhappy it's at times like these that I'm reminded of the fact that I'm quite privileged. I have no commitments, no dependants, and a well-paid job, and I've never had to struggle or work hard in my life. I am a lucky man."

The pub door opened and I could see my father beckoning me to come in. "I'm assuming that the invitation applies to us both but just in case if you will hold on here until I speak to father. I will wave you over if the free for all is starting. Oh and try to stay out of any fights or arguments if you can. If you interfere you'll end up fighting them all and I kid you not. It wouldn't be a Lewis family drinking session without at least one fight. I have to mind my father he won't fight but he will try to stop it."

"What about you?"

"Without trying to sound either arrogant or superior No one will fight with me they might be Lewis but none of them are that stupid."

Father was waiting just inside the pub doorway. He always did as much as he could at the family gatherings. Mum had died two years ago and it gave him something to do rather than sitting alone and lonely.

"Your Uncle Alan would like to talk to you see if you can find the time to chat to him. I don't know what he wants but he has asked me to ask you to speak to him."

"Will do, has he said when?"

"No. Just try to sort something out with him before this afternoon. He won't stay over tonight. I think he's looking for maybe a visit and a probable stayover at his place. When and if it fits for you."

Whatever dad was saying to me wasn't in dad's normal way of talking.

"Dad you're going around this what are you not saying?"

"Alan never married and I have met his friend before and I think he, nodding towards Steven, "plays by both sets of rules".

Father turned instantly, probably embarrassed by his own unproven suspicion, and went back to the bar. I beckoned Steven over just as the wives and my other cousins had arrived along with the brothers in law.

The family pretty well had the whole of the lounge bar. And they were getting noisier and a lot more boisterous. Alan and Steven had got themselves a corner table. Alan's zimmer was at his side. Perhaps an opportune moment to speak to him before the noise became too loud to have any chance of quiet conversation.

"Adam sit you are looking well. And more like your father than when I saw you last must be nearly ten years now probably not since mother died." We shook hands he still had a grip like your hand had been shut in a drawer.

"You've filled out what you doing with yourself?"

I'm a building surveyor. I've Been working for her majesties government for about eight years now."

" Civil servants can end up soft and podgy from flying a desk you're too solid for that."

"I still climb, mostly in the summer and play rugby in the winter"

"Position?"

"Hooker."

Figures. Like it?

"I'll get a couple more seasons. Recovery times are getting longer now. Bodies as I'm sure you know can only take the pounding for so long."

"Too right. It's done you good though, so don't push it for longer than you should. Your body will tell you when to stop listen to it. It's been programmed by someone who's a lot cleverer than you and I." My sister brought a plate of sandwiches over , nodded to Alan while ignoring Steven and me completely. Not much change there then.

"I'm moving house." He suddenly said. "And I want you to come and see me in my old place before I move. Which is in about two weeks or two months depending on who turns up for work and when, so we haven't got too long to sort this out."

"Sort what out ?" I asked.

"I don't want to go into too much detail now. Time for that when were in somewhere quieter without possible interruptions. Can you get some leave say a week? Another family bereavement maybe could help. Death nearly always gets some sympathy."

"Probably wouldn't be a problem, my desk is clear enough I can get cover for my job in a couple of days and I still have twenty five plus days holiday to take this year."

"That's a lot."

"I carried some over from last year."

"Good that s settled then. Will you have a drink with me on it?"

"Yes."

"Steven will you go to the bar for us please?"

"Adam what do you want?"

"Bitter please."

"The rugby players drink."

"I'll have my usual please Steven."

Steven left us alone.

"Steven is my minder. He takes care of me even when I don't need to be taken care of. He's a good man. And sometimes he can be a like an old woman. He will not bother you. You can be assured of that. Even though my brother may have said something to you don't worry."

I was stuck for anything to say.

"Don't reply. There is no need for conversation on the subject."

"Does the jug of beer still go around after a game?"

"Yes, if the game was good and we didn't win by too much or rub their noses in it."

"Not a lots changed then?"

"I didn't know you played."

"When I first joined the army I was a lot younger than a lot of the old hands. I was very quick, so they put me on the wing and periodically, in the middle of a fight, a rugby match would break out. When it did and the ball was mine, I had to run like hell with it and maybe score. I developed a technique of a hand off that if timed properly would do damage. Effectively the opposing player broke his own nose on my hand off. They banned me in the end totally unjustified of course. So, I took up hockey. It wasn't too long before I got banned from that. Illegal use of the stick. I returned better than I got. One officer said I'd done more damage to his regiment than the Germans had done in the first war, an exaggeration of course, but one, which to be honest, I was quite proud of."

The drinks arrived

"Thank you Steven."

One pint of bitter, a large scotch, and what turned out to be lemonade.

 "Steven is teetotal handy having a driver that doesn't drink."

"Plan on staying a week if you can" said Alan. He passed me a business card. " I've written my home address on the back. ignore the front that's my business address telephone at home is on the back with the business one on the front. During the day if you don't get me at one you will normally get me at the other.

Any problems the business one has an answerphone message machine thing on it. But we don't do problems only solutions.

Now I must mingle say hello to all and in an hour or so I shall be off. It's a two and half hours to drive from here to our home. I like to get there in the daylight. When you see where we live you'll realise what I mean. If I don't see you before I leave I will hopefully see you soon." We shook hands and again with Steven

 "Safe journey home. I hope to see you soon."

Alan did as he said he would do mingled with the family. The noise eventually quietened till there was just a couple of us left. The pint, that Alan had bought me, was nearly flat now. Dad was nearly ready to go and as the eldest brother he had stayed the course and seen them all off home. He paid the bill at the bar for the food and we left. First time I had ever been to a Lewis do when there wasn't a fight. Thinking about it though the main culprit was in a box now about four foot underground and as we left the pub it started to rain.

"The soil will sink down tonight." Dad said. "I'll get the bus up to cemetery tomorrow and finish back filling it. The diggers will have left the excess there."

" Do you want a lift?" I asked

"No thanks I'll be alright." Perhaps he wanted a moment alone at the graveside. His mum, dad and youngest brother, were all together now. I could see no point in pursuing the transport discussion there was nothing to be gained by it. I took him home and then did the same for myself.

Two weeks later, and I'm on my way to Alan's house in the Peak district. I passed a large stone mill wheel, on a plinth, that signified that I was in the national park. I counted the miles from there. A hump backed bridge, go slowly, a single track sharp left hand turn, and a steep rise off the road, up a narrow gravel track, to a steel gate. There is a cattle grid. Only open gate if no herds of anything about. Close the gate. One point two miles of single track, go slowly again, heifers regularly loose, and walking like they own the place.

Two storey Stone house with slate roof on right hand side of lane. Turn in. Park on concrete and wait to get out of car. Dog is okay if someone is there to greet you but has been known to be a bit over protective.

As I expected Alan's instructions were perfect even down to the dog that came bounding and barking from a kennel near the side door.

The barking had brought a lady o out from inside the house. I wound down the window.

" Bandit quiet." She called and the dog sat down at the side of the car.

"I'm Adam." I shouted.

" Then come in. Bandit friend" she said, "He'll be fine now." I carefully opened the door not wanting to hit the dog with it and as I got out and started to walk towards the house he came towards me and put his head next to my knee.

"Good boy," she said "He must know you're family"

"He's a big border collie, isn't he?"

"He's a Scottish one. They seem to be bigger from up there. Maybe it's because the snow's deeper." I assumed she was joking but I didn't laugh in case it wasn't supposed to be funny.

"I'm Katarina," she told me "Steven's mother. I will make you a drink what would you like, tea, coffee, or a beer?"

"Coffee will be fine please."

"Good." She said. "Then I shall join you. Alan and Steven are still at the office. They will be back about six; which will give you time to sort out your stuff. I have organised the guest room for you. It has an en suite so you won't be disturbed through the night. Not that anything much goes on here after dark."

We had our dinner. Steven and his mother had retired upstairs. The house was split into two separate units. Katarina and Stevan had the upper floor, Alan and I were on the ground. We sat outside wrapped up in top coats and woolly hats and bottles of beer to keep us hydrated. Fresh air was Alan's drug of choice.

"It's why I live here." He told me. " I think I'll miss this place more than I realise when I leave." We sat quietly for a short while enjoying the silence.

"Now why you're here. I want you to write a book for me. I want to have it written as though I'm telling you a story. Imagine we are sitting down in the pub, or on the verandah, as we are here, having a cup of tea or a beer, bottle of wine, whatever you think, and I'm telling you tales about my life. I want you to write it down then edit it and turn it into a biography. I've tried doing it myself but I get too factual too much information and even I'm getting bored with it."

"But why me? I've never written a book before in my life."

"Because you know the family. To a certain extent, it's to put the record straight, or straightish, in my opinion. Think for a minute and tell me have you ever heard a Lewis say I think I made mistake. I got that wrong sorry."

I knew he was right without having to think for too long.

"I'm not looking for apologies or to apologise or anything as silly as that. It's just me wanting to explain things that have happened to me, in my time, that became formative. I'm no different to anyone else. I don't feel superior in any way whatsoever. But I would like to tell it how it happened, from my point of view.

Then add to your family knowledge, you have a degree and more importantly, as I understand, you've actually got a master's now in modern political history. Perfect as far as I'm concerned. You know what to put in, and what to leave out. I have read your dissertation by the way. Your dad sent it over to me last year when I got this idea into my head. It's good groundwork for what I need from you. The other important thing, as well, is you know the family as well as anyone. I reckon that the relevant bits will be in the book and the dross will be removed."

"So is this a book about us our family."

" Not really there's maybe some relevant bits, but that's for you to decide. It needs one person with an objective mind to process all the stuff I'm going to give you and turn it into a book."

"Why?"

"Because I want to, and for the first time in my life, I have to admit, I actually can't do it. But I can sit here and tell stories and I have reams of notes and reports that you can have unlimited access to. Many years ago, I was an instructor and trainer in the army. I kept notes about everything to use as an aid de memoire and a reference to learn from. They may be useful in many ways. I often wrote down conversations, or my version of a conversation, which as we know is different possibly from someone elses, but as just about all the others are dead now, it shouldn't make too much difference, but we'll see.

The good thing as well is I will pay you for writing it. It's a job of work and if it's good enough to publish you will share in any income that it generates if it produces any at all. The object is to write it down and tell the story that I want . Publishing or making money isn't the exercise for me. Heaven knows I have enough for my needs. It's just something I want to get done."

When Alan had finished we sat for a short while saying nothing. He knew I was letting the idea float around inside my head.

"Right, let's have another beer and I'll start you off."

He took the tops of two more bottles. Gave me one and started to tell me stories.

"They call it head hunting now. Someone is picked to do a job. They have a talent, or may, given the right training, become suitable, for useful gainful employment. When we did head hunting it was a different ball game. Sometimes it was alive and with the rest of the body when we brought it in. Often it was in a state of no longer functioned and no longer fit for purpose. Then job done onto next. That was how Alan started to tell me the story of how before the war he was trained and prepared for jobs that at the time were only possibilities but someone higher than his boss had the wisdom to see what a useful tool might be created with some careful planning and preparation. Thereafter, Alan became responsible for a part of the training and development of others.

CHAPTER 1   June 1936

By Phil chapman

"The colonel wishes to see you in his office as soon as you can sir."

"Very good corporal tell him I'll be with him by next Tuesday."

"Sir?"

"A joke corporal. I will lock my office and be with him, a couple of minutes after you."

"Yes sir."

Captain Peter Cameron, loosely attached to the Royal Artillery at Woolwich, but at this time working out of a two storey timber building on Salisbury Plain, scooped up the papers on his desk, slipped them into the bottom drawer, and locked the whole unit via a nonstandard locking system in a very secure piece of military office furniture.

He pulled the office window tight shut and drew the curtains. He might be on the upper floor, but old habits die hard. He took his hat and his stick, and having locked the office door behind him, walked along the black painted uncarpeted corridor, towards the wooden staircase, at the far end of the building. The floor board to the left of centre by Toby Watson's door, last office on the right creaked. Another old habit had him avoid the offending board and enabled him to steer a silent passage along the landing to the stairs. Walking tight to the right hand side of the staircase he made it to the bottom, no noise. Stealth was something he liked to practise purely, he suspected, for his own pleasure, but maybe just in case.

The colonel's office, the inner sanctum, was accessed only by getting passed the nco who was duty clerk. I was told to tell you to knock and go straight in sir

Peter did as directed, then shut the door behind him.

The colonel seated behind his desk is working his way through a small sheaf of papers and initialling them as he scans through them.

"Come in Captain. Sit down, these are for you. I'm just checking what I'm giving you so I know you've got what you need." He initialled the last sheet.

"How's your German? still good I assume."

"I read it fluently and conversation wise I'm ok depending on which part of Germany I'm talking to."

"Berlin."

"It'll be Fine there sir with Berliners."

"Splendid. We can't budget for everyone, but we thought you were the right person. Got a job for you. Suit you down to the ground.

You will travel as part of the British Olympic team to Berlin as an administrator and adviser. There's over two hundred athletes, numerous coaches, trainers, medics, travel organisers, and hangers on. You shouldn't have any problems in blending in with them if you need to, and as there's so many, it shouldn't be too difficult in avoiding any direct contact or work."

"Got that sir. And?"

"We want you to go snooping around. You'll be there for around a month and you'll need to take someone with you another fluent German speaker who can always mind your back."

"Understood sir."

"Got any ideas who ?"

"Sergeant Lewis is ideal."

"You don't want another officer?"

"I'd prefer Lewis his German is better than most as is his French. He is also the most able man I know if I ever needed back up at any time I would pick him before anyone else."

"Are you sure ?"

"I am sir."

"Tell him he's going with you. You have plenty of time to get yourselves sorted the games start officially on the first of August, that gives you nearly four weeks, but you'll need to be there well before then.

There will be a man I assume a man but nevertheless someone from MOD will be here in the next couple of days to give you a briefing before you leave.

This is between you me. Sergeant Lewis is only on a need to know. No one else is to hear about any part of it. When we had that meeting last year with the MOD and those other government chaps, it seems we started a little thought process going in their heads. They have taken on board our original concerns and rather than get left behind in what's going on in the rest of the world, they wish us to continue, with a monitoring brief, or whatever description you wish to attach to it. Captain don't get caught doing anything illegal. I can tell you now you won't get any help from anyone this side of the English Chanel."

" I understand"

"Good, as of now you are on you are on someone else's time. What's on your desk?"

"I've been watching what's going on in Spain sir."

"And"

"In my opinion there will be a war and a bloody one at that."

"Do we have people on the ground?"

"We do."

"Pass it on to someone else to keep an eye on it whilst you're away."

"There isn't anyone here sir. Most of it is in Spanish, and I'm the only Spanish reader here, and I only read it . I don't speak it very well. All the others are in country, keeping a closer eye on things."

"Send me a memo I get a feeling with what noises I'm hearing from the MOD, and his majesties government, we won't have any difficulty getting some extra staff here, to cover these sort of things. Don't get flowery, succinct memo, tell us what we need, ask for more than we actually need, and we might get what we want."

"Will do sir."

"These papers are what I have as a brief, come personnel requirement, there's not a great deal in there, for so many sheets, but have a read, and file it wherever you want. I have a set, so it can go in the fire, but make certain it goes somewhere safe. Good luck. I'll see you when you're back."

Peter Cameron returned to his office, read the bumf that Colonel Williams had given him, and then put them with the sheaf of papers from the desk drawer put them all into a card board folder he tied and wax sealed the whole parcel and left it along with his desk and office keys with the duty officer.

"Where is sergeant Lewis supposed to be according to duty roster?"

"He's running a course out on the plain."

What course?

"He's running a three day Escape and evade should finish by tonight. He's probably letting them run for bit. He lets them get tired. Lot easier to pick up then. A bit of fox and hound chasing on first day then when they're knackered he moves in. It's a low level first run around he won't be hard on them really wants to see how fit they are and then when they're all back he'll do a debrief another hour or so he will normally finish around midnight."

"How does he know where to find them?"

"He says the terrain does the work for him. When they're tired and they're feet are sore the inclination is to move downhill because it's easier. And as he pointed them off in one particular direction, the average person, on a first time exercise doesn't normally double back."

"What if they do?"

"That's where he waits for them if he thinks they're any good. But he sends a team around into a semi-circle to watch and wait."

"How many has he got out?"

"Four trainees six pursuers."

"When he's back take him off duty roster until further notice. Colonel's orders. Check if you wish Lieutenant. I probably would. You'll have to cancel any other courses after this one, unless there's anyone else to run them."

"I don't think so sir. Unless some of the chasers are any good. He's training them at the same time as instructors."

"Tell him my office 0800 tomorrow morning. He and I are on other duties, as of now. Have the file locked up in my section please, only to be taken by me, or again on Colonel's orders."

"Yes sir."

At two minutes to eight Captain Cameron arrived at the top of the stairs. Standing outside his door in uniform, smart, clean shaven, and standing loosely to attention was, as ordered, Sgt. Alan Lewis.

"Good morning Alan."

"Good morning sir."

"Jolly good you got my message then."

"Yes sir."

Peter opened the office door. "Come in grab a seat."

"Thank you sir."

"Have you breakfasted?"

"No Sir."

"Ok you can do that later after I've briefed you."

"Sir?"

"I know you are fluent in German and French as well as English. How come?"

"My mother taught me German and French before I went to school. My mother was a Swiss national before she married my father. She holds dual nationality now. Her English wasn't very good, when I was young, and father being at sea all the time resulted in my learning German and French from her."

"It's the fact that you speak both. I'm interested in."

"Mother was born and lived in Bern. Bern is bilingual French and German. Mother's parents were Catholic missionaries. She learnt her German as Swiss German. Which is a slightly different dialect. Her father though spoke more like people who spoke German in Germany, so you could understand her better so she tells me. My German seems I can understand Germans Swiss and Dutch though I don't speak Dutch I get a bit of an understanding when I'm hearing it. Her parents took her on their missionary journeys until they died from malaria in Nigeria. This is how mother met father. Father, who was first mate on a cargo boat, rescued her when they were picking up a load in Lagos. She was trying to get away from there to get back to Switzerland. She was having a problem with some locals, which father, with some assistance from a couple of deck hands with sjamboks, sorted out. Dad spoke a little French basically enough to understand she needed help. Then not wishing to leave her to the mercy of the people who she'd been having trouble with he brought her back to England.

They got married and when dad came home they made babies. One every couple of years or so. I spoke more German and French than English at home, until I went to school which obviously was in English. But I still speak with mother mostly in German. Mother will often put all three languages in the same sentence. Conversations can keep you on your toes at home."

"Those little extra bits are missing from your file here. It doesn't effect anything but it does explain to me how it happened."

"What doesn't it effect sir?"

"We're off to Berlin to the Olympics. We're going as technical advisers for the modern pentathlon shooting specialists. There may well be some other things we have to do but until I know what they are I'm as in the dark as you are about it. There is a chap or a chapess going to brief me at some stage before we go. I don't as yet have a departure time or how long we'll be away for. I do know that the games start in about a month so we'll definitely be there before then. That's it for now I'm sorry to say. I don't have any other info available. I've taken you off normal duties so my advice is get a travel warrant and take a couple of days leave and let's say back here in seven days. But leave us a contact address if it isn't home and that way we can send a telegram or the local bobby if we need you back early which is at this time doubtful."

"Thank you sir."

"Get yourself fed and then away, and I'll see you back here again in a week."

Talbot Conway, senior admin officer at the ministry of defence, which meant, as it was supposed to, absolutely nothing to anyone; arrived at just after ten am, two days after Alan had gone on leave. No one knew if there was anyone higher up the system than him. They knew there were permanent secretaries and a government minister but there was a theory; suspected but never actually established; that if he couldn't get his own way he would by-pass everyone and go direct to the prime minister. There were stories that this had happened in the past but if someone knew for definite no one had ever confirmed it. He arrived in, a very smart government officials for the use of, Humber saloon car with two assistants, one was the driver, who remained in the vehicle, while the other carried Mr Conway's briefcase. He also went first and opened doors.

Peter's door was open and ready for his visitor.

"Captain Cameron, I believe. You look like your photograph. Novelty in that I suppose. Mind you your still young. I meet some chaps and their ID picture was one they got at university twenty years previous. They assume it makes them look younger when all it does is get a list of problems at a border crossing." He took the briefcase and walked past Peter. "

Thankyou Martin. Wait in the car with Richard. Shut the door Cameron and get yourself comfortable if it's possible. They didn't splash out on luxury here did they?" Captain sat himself down while Mr Conway took Captain Camerons similar rickety seat behind the desk.

"Sorry old son I need your desk. I believe I may be taking my life in my hands here. Is this all the furniture they gave you when you got here?"

"This is what turned up on day one and it's been here as it has since then sir." Cameron realised he had to be careful this man wasn't some low level delivery boy with a folder of instructions. Any man who comes with two bodyguards and newish Humber and calls him Cameron is way up the food chain. Time to take note and listen carefully.

"Do you know that the USA has had a war plan for every country in the world including the UK? It gets updated on a regular basis as information etc. comes available. The one thing I can tell you is that since 1927 the USA has not updated the possibility of fighting a war with us. As they no longer think that we will ever fight against each other, which apart from it only being nine years ago, amongst other things I find it, quite reassuring.

We had that meeting last year and your colonel intimated that you had been monitoring western Europe and down to and including Spain. So, I have decided to send you on a cheap recce for us to have a snoop around Germany and see what stinks . The Olympics are coming up there will be all sorts happening. Your part of a, long term, ongoing programme, that just about every country in the world runs.

I will make it clear we have been playing this game like every other major player since time began. Governments have been making decisions, about huge numbers of issues, knowing information, that the man on the street will never be aware of. The question asked why did they do that is only known to a select few, because it would compromise our friends and allies, if privileged information got into the wrong hands, or worse possibly, the source of the intelligence. There is a Jewish issue our belief is that Hitler is trying to get them all out of Germany. I'm not certain how he's thinking he will succeed but the theory is that he is about to try. He has removed all of the Jewish athletes, from his teams, and has managed to create a level of paranoia, in other nations teams, to the point that they have not selected Jewish athletes themselves. Hitler is frightening the free world, as we would describe ourselves, whilst certain other countries seem to be aligning with him. The situation seems at the moment just about balanced. I'm interested in how long it will remain so, and what the hell we have to do when it tips. We, and a lot of our allies, with some justification, are monitoring the situation very carefully."

Conway had removed a number of sheets of paper from his briefcase while he was talking.

"What are you been working on?"

"I've been monitoring goings on in Western Europe but currently keeping a close eye on Spain as a part of my duties here and also overseeing various parts of the officer training program."

"Continue with the Spanish part."

"It's going to get bad there if Franco gets going. An elected government seems to be on its way to hell in a handcart."

"We too are thinking along the similar lines. Our belief is that the shape of Europe as we know it is about to change. Hell in a handcart is an interesting phrase. It won't be instant, but like you we think it's going to happen. We need to be ready. We need friends and partners in Germany. Go there make friends in high places and low places, where ever you can you aren't alone we've been on it for a while but you're a military man perhaps military people will find you interesting to talk to. I assume your colonel told you that you'll be on your own if it goes awry?"

" Yes he did mention that ."

"Don't let it happen. It'll set the whole programme back.

War costs money it's a high investment project and realistically if you don't put enough money into it you will lose. Our military forces are at an uncomfortable low, in my opinion, and putting an army together takes time and effort and funds. The powers that control the purse would prefer to be at peace with Europe; but there are more than a few of us who believe that another war, size not yet known, is on the cards, and if we get involved it's going to have to be a very small one, for us to come out of it in one piece, given our current man power and investment levels."

"I've noticed that enlistment is lower than it's been for a couple of years now. As you are aware I'm a loose part of the officer training here. My real brief is to sort the really useful people, from the also rans. I run people with extra talents ,linguists, experienced travellers, people with extensive knowledge of other countries, preferably unmarried and extremely fit. My staff will train them in how to do all the necessary stuff with guns, knives, and explosives before they go into the field. And to be perfectly honest talent has been getting thinner on the ground."

"You are sadly confirming what we've been thinking for a while. Who's going with you?"

"A Sergeant instructor. Speaks fluent German and French teaches combat and weapons."

"Married?"

"No don't even think he has a girlfriend."

"Age?"

"27"

"Trust him?"

"With my life."

"Let's hope it doesn't come to that. How come he's not with you today?"

"Colonel said it was a need to know brief for him."

"Would he have said the same if you were taking an officer with you?"

A moments thought and, "I suspect not."

"He's your back up and you just said you'd trust him with your life."

"Yes."

"Then don't keep him in the dark, he may need to make decisions on what information he has. If he doesn't know what's going on, his decision may be the wrong one."

"Understood."

"Where is he now?"

"I gave him some leave so I didn't have to explain why he wasn't invited to the meeting."

"Well done . A bit of devious diplomacy won't do any harm. But a shift in policy now, keep him informed. Your colonel isn't running this, I am. I put you here, and I put the colonel here. I have been running what goes on here, since we opened this department. The Colonel is my mouth piece, sometimes I think I pull the strings that make him walk too. I am not normally rude about senior officers, and if it ever gets repeated you will be out on your ear, but here I had to have someone of sufficient rank to be in charge, but one malleable enough not to want to be in control. Do you understand?"

"Yes sir."

"From now on you are in my department along with your man Lewis. I hope you picked the right one."

"I think so sir."

"When you've trained people a few have come to me. I have been putting possibles in here for a while. We have also been watching you, and how you operate. I won't tell you which ones, but two of your students were actually your assessors, both came back as favourable, so hence first go . Let's see if we can make it work.

I have a large number of people in the field, all over Europe especially, but all over the world is nearer the truth. It's not privileged information just about every country in the world has spies in every other country in the world. It's been going on probably since Roman times, after prostitution it's probably the next oldest profession. Sometimes it goes ok, sometimes it's a waste of time and money. Your brief is purely military. Talk to people see, what's going on. It's befriend Generals, and high rankers, go to dinner, don't spend lots of money you won't get it back. You will get a food allowance but it won't stretch to champagne and caviar. We know there are issues with the Jewish people, and everyone who doesn't align with Mr' Hitlers view and concept of what might be considered to be a good German. This includes Negroes, Romany's, foreigners who aren't sparkling white, ideally blonde and beautiful, not that he fulfils those criteria. Put that to him might end up like the fastest ever disappearing act ever.

You should also be aware that you may find that you are being considered in exactly the same way. They may see you as someone they could find useful to them. Sometimes that will be even better, they may start offering trading, material hoping to extract knowledge from you."

"Are there any rules of engagement sir?"

"Have you read The Art of War by Master Sun?"

"Never even heard of it."

"An extremely interesting book. If you can get your hands on a copy. Have a read of it. I expect you will find it interesting and informative. When you have read it you will come out of it with the knowledge, that everything you thought you knew, now could be false, and the likelihood is that if the rest of the world has read it then all our knowledge is suspect. It's a bit like an invitation to a paranoia party, and some sort of weekend away in the country get together, with Genghis khan, et al, courtesy of Agatha Christie. Death is almost certain for, to, and by whom. Who knows? Essentially It's about deviousness, subterfuge, deceit, confusion, and any other adjective that you might want to throw at it. It's theme is essentially about knowing your enemy. That's your brief and your starting point. Things will develop as time goes on. Don't get caught don't get into trouble. With you, we are at a sticking our toe in the water stage at this time, what we need is accurate information, infinitely better than a lot of guessing. There'll be enough of that if things go wrong. Avoid diplomatic problems don't get pissed and incapable and stay out of police stations and jail. You will be beaten. Questions?"

"How do I contact you?"

"I will find you when your back and debrief you."

"What if I need to contact someone urgently?"

"The embassy. They won't have a clue who you are and they may try to fob you off. Insist on speaking to the military attaché and use the code, that's in your briefing notes, for whatever day it is. There are seven, one for every day of the week. Memorise them. Your briefing notes, which I have sorted out for you, are these on your desk. There's not very much in them but they will need burning before you leave here. Anything else?

"No I don't believe there is I assume everything is covered in these papers."

"I doubt it but if we know about it I would hope so. Good luck. Don't forget to brief your sergeant fully and let him know he's been promoted to lieutenant. It'll look better when he's snooping around. Young lieutenants can appear irritatingly interested and a bit nosey, because they're still learning. Sergeants are way cleverer than that, so any questions and he's a new fresh junior officer not too bright but don't lay it on too thick, the people you will be talking to, are a long way from being either naive or stupid.

I'll have the promotion docs sent to you as soon as possible. No uniforms, no weapons, definitely nothing more than a pen knife. Show up sometime with the team so they see who you are and so you know what's happening. Don't get so involved you miss the reason for being there. You didn't travel with the team as you were waiting for passports. All clear?

"At the moment, as mud sir."

"You'll be fine. If I didn't think you were any good you wouldn't be going."

A week later 0800 hours and Alan Lewis is standing outside Camerons office when the captain arrives.

"Good morning Alan."

"Good morning sir."

"Congratulations on your promotion to Lieutenant."

"Pardon sir"

Cameron shook hands with Lewis. "We'll have to get you a new uniform sometime, but we can start with a couple of pips for now on your sweater."

"How did this come about sir?"

"You have been promoted to second lieutenant and it's official the paperwork is in the office and if it hasn't already it will be gazetted. The man from the MOD decided you would be better off being an officer, as he figured, and he is almost certainly right, sergeants are too clever and probably too streetwise. So in theory you are a young new junior officer, so welcome aboard, and you will now have to eat in the officer's mess which is about as spartan as this office, so you'll probably feel like you're slumming it at lunchtime, when I take you down there."

CHAPTER 2 1936 BERLIN OLYMPICS

Alan managed to borrow a couple of small suitcases from the stores. Having spent the last ten years packing his kit into a small back pack or Bergan and carrying that wherever he need to go, carefully folding shirts suits and shoes and underwear was an alien task. His new uniform was still in a cutting room somewhere. But that was of little matter as it was on this job surplus to requirement. Trying to be certain that he had the right clothing was the issue as since he joined the army he had probably never worn anything other than military issue kit.

A knock on his door and Captain had arrived.

"Ready Alan?"

"As near as I'll ever be sir. Will you just have a quick gander through my kit please?"

"Certainly. Open up the cases. Alan put the cases on the bunk and flipped the catches open."

The captain quickly looked through the kit. "You're worrying unnecessarily Alan. Nothing wrong and nothing missing as far as I can see. And it all looks in very good condition."

"Most of it isn't new. It's never been worn much; I'm surprised it still fits me."

"Well our transport is waiting, the Colonel's organised a lift to Woolwich, then someone from there will take us to the station."

Tired and aching and ready for sleep, Cameron and Lewis have managed to get a room in a shared bungalow at the Olympic village. The train carriage had a bumpy journey, during the Dover to Ostend crossing, on the overnight ferry. Normally the crossing would take just over an hour but that night took longer than planned due to the stormy conditions. Then everything else lost its planned timed sequence and seemed to take twice as long. It didn't but it did feel that way. Buses had been full or non-existent which is probably why the ones that turned up, were overflowing, and in the end they did the final leg in a taxi. Neither of them cared what time it was and having got access to a bed each they grabbed a couple of hours sleep.

They are lodging with two male coaches from the swimming team, so should be able to avoid any unnecessary contact. The other coaches are at the training pool which saves small talk that asks questions that they can't answer. Their brief is only to be contacted by the Olympic team if there is a problem that can't be solved. Which gives them no job to do unless there is something of a catastrophe. Perfect. Today they need to sort out transport and find out how to get around without relying on the team buses or spending a fortune on taxis. They have shaved and washed earlier in the communal bath house and were just dressing for the day out.

Then a knock on the door. Alan looked at the captain who shrugged his shoulders who knows? Alan was dressed, lying on his bunk bed. He checked his fly after pulling his braces over his shirt. He opened the door just as the young man, in Hitler youth uniform, was about to knock again.

"I'm sorry sir. Is this Captain Cameron's room?"

"It is. Do you wish to speak to him?"

" I am to give him this letter sir."

" Should I pass it to him or do you need to hand it personally?" Alan opened the door fully to allow the youngster to see in. He looked at Peter Cameron. "Very good sir. Thank you. I was told to give it to the older man. I'm sure now that I've seen him that will be okay." Alan took the letter, his thank you to the boy lost as he hurriedly turned and walked quickly away.

A smiling Alan passed the letter over to Peter

Here we are sir.

Peter opened the letter

"We have been invited to spend an afternoon with some German officers who would be interested in saying hello and I suppose trying to pump us for information about anything that they think might be useful."

"When ?"

"Today."

"They're not hanging round then."

"Opening ceremony is on Saturday. So, maybe they're thinking we might be too busy shortly."

"Where are we meeting them as I assume they're not coming here?"

"We have been invited to join them at one of the Olympic shooting ranges, which is actually the one that wil be used for the pentathlon, where they are putting the final touches and measuring etc. they figure it might be a working, saying hello, and welcome to Germany, lunch type chat."

"Do you believe them sir ?"

"Not a bloody word Alan but let's go see."

"Where is it?"

"I Haven't got a clue you may have to go in search of the young short sighted delivery boy who thinks I'm old. Perhaps a young man like you will get more from him." He laughed there was less than two months between them but Alan was the elder.

"There must be an admin block or at the very least an office hereabouts."

Alan grabbed his jacket "I'll go see".

There were a lot of the uniformed youngsters about. Alan spotted the young man who delivered the letter.

An about turn and back at the bungalow

"It's around an hour and a half, to two hours, depending how fast you drive."

"Sounds like an Irish country mile to me."

"Is there a telephone number on the letter?"

Peter checked the letter.

"No"

"We know it's a shooting range. So, let's figure someone here in admin will know."

"Are you going to try that young man again?"

"Let's see what we can do."

The young man was not in sight but finding out the admin office was just a couple of minutes' walk along the road, Alan headed for it. The admin office had a bench seat and a counter with an open hinged flap top. Fortunately, Alan was the only customer. An older man behind a roll top desk suggested Alan should take a seat for a minute and he would make a call for him.

Five minutes later and Alan was back at the bungalow.

"They're sending a car. A cold lunch will be available there for us, so we don't need to rush, but dress smartly, I have been informed."

"Once more unto the breech dear friends. We've got time for a coffee let's get a map of this place, from the admin man, and find out where the main canteen is, or if there is somewhere else to eat as well. We're going to need to find our way around, as I don't see us being invited out for all our meals."

Right on time a black sedan arrived at the bungalow. A very smartly dressed corporal sprang from the driver's seat, moved quickly around the car, and opened the rear door. Cameron and Lewis were ready outside. They looked, with interest, at the car then each other. Right hand drive, top range limousine, Cameron looked at Alan and commented. " Whatever else we'll learn I know not. But that driver knew exactly which bungalow we are in. they know were here Alan and I suspect they know more about what we want than we do."

Before they took off, the corporal looked into his rear view mirror at his two passengers.

"Journey time should be about two hours. If you wish a stop, or something to drink, please let me know. I have water, beer and schnapps in the front. The beer will be frisky from the bouncing along the road. We are in General Harrer's vehicle. I am his personal driver. If I get his vehicle wet with beer, he will not be happy. If you want a beer we must park and open the beer outside. The car is a Tatra made in Czechoslovakia. As you can see it is right hand drive and to add to this it has to be driven very carefully or it will go anywhere it decides it wants to. I have to concentrate."

Cameron leaned forward, head over the seat. "We will manage to go without drinking for a couple of hours corporal. Thank you for the offer but please carry on."

"Very good sir."

As expected it was just on two hours when the black car pulled into the parking area at Ruhleben. As the corporal parked the vehicle he looked to the rear.

"Timing seems to be perfect sirs as luncheon is just being served." He jumped smartly out of the vehicle and opened Cameron's door.

"We have had some rain sir but fortunately the sand has absorbed most of it though I expect that you will find some damp patches about. There are a number of army personnel here sir, as well as Olympic games people. I don't see General Harrer at the moment but his adjutant, Captain Witzell, is talking to the lady in the black coat and hat. The one with her back to us. He has noticed your arrival, and he has just signalled, that he will be with you in a minute. If you will excuse me sir, I shall make certain that the General's car is ready for when he might need it. Ah, he is here, the well-built officer, who has joined at the front of the queue."

"Thank you corporal. I shall join the others in the food queue. I suspect following General Harrer's lead might be considered less than polite as a guest."

"You may be right sir but it is not for me to comment."

"Perhaps you will talk to the General's adjutant Alan, while I get us something to eat." Cameron moved away, as the young officer finally extricated himself from what appeared to be a one way conversation. He moved quickly across the sandy ground focused directly on Alan, so no one might catch his eye, he hoped. He extended his hand and a solid man's grip shook hands with Alan.

"Herr Lewis or Lieutenant if you prefer. I don't mind if we don't at this time know each other well enough to use first names unless you are happy to do so." The Germans handshake was firm the greeting warm and friendly. His English was slightly lumpy and uncertain, Alan replied in German.

"I am perfectly happy with first names and speaking in German

"Good, thank you.my name is Otto Witzell. You were listed in the team list as Sergeant Lewis Alain. We found you eventually or we worked it out. When we got the team lists of course we checked everyone out and you and Captain Cameron were added on at the end. We were a little surprised until we found that Captain Cameron is with Mr Conway who is part of your governments security advisers.

I therefore suspect that you and I are in similar positions. Basically we are bodyguards for our senior officer. In your case a Captain, in mine a General. That is in no way to diminish your responsibility to your captain, you are, at the end of the day, in a foreign country, and as a consequence, your job in theory is a lot more difficult than mine. Nothing detrimental is going to happen, and as we are all friends here, hopefully it will remain so."

"I'd hate to think that any antagonism or aggravation should occur sir. I certainly have no desire to do anything other than my job as an advisor to the British team."
"Well whatever your job is here Alan I hope you enjoy your stay. I am not aware of every decision my general makes and every reason but he has invited you over today for a visit for a reason I must admit I'm not privy to. I must tell you though that my general is a jovial, friendly man and also a wonderful actor. As nice as he appears he has never forgiven the British and hates losing but especially to England. In Southwest Africa his family had large investments there and they lost a great deal of money and standing when the British moved in, But he hides his distaste for everything that isn't German and behaves like a good host, so that all runs smoothly. His family are the only thing that he loves as much as the fatherland and on them he dotes. Fortunately, for us all, there is no malice in my general. He was my father's adjutant, and he is a planner, and an academic, rather than a fighting man. As generals go, in intelligence, his forte, has always been planning and strategy, he is a desk man rather than going out and collecting. Activity is for the younger person as far as he is concerned. He's perfectly happy for others to make a name for themselves. He would have to tow a much stricter party line if his aim was to get much higher than the General

he already is. That and his family would make life more difficult for him."

Alan, other than nod, as Otto was talking, made no comment to what he had said. He did, to a certain extent, feel out of his depth with these people. Going form training prospective officers to a place numerous rungs up a ladder was going to take more than a couple of days to acquire the confidence and relaxed attitude of what was now becoming his peer group. He was quite surprised and at a loss to understand why Otto had given him so much unsolicited information about his boss.

"Here he is now." General Harrer was on his way through the small crowd which opened up to let him through. Closer up, Alan could see a round faced round bodied man highly polished jackboots jodhpur type trousers and a Wehrmacht jacket slightly testing the button stitching. He moved nimbly for a man of such shape and though his face appeared a tad florid, there was no sign of breathlessness in his speech.

"And whom do we have here Captain Witzell?"

"This is Alan Lewis sir, with the British Olympic team. He is here as a civilian, though he is a lieutenant in the British Army."

"Ah you are the man we couldn't find where you were coming from. Well, it's nice to meet you lieutenant. And what part are you here to observe. I'm not aware that there is anything the British team are involved in that could be of interest to the military."

"Modern pentathlon Herr general."

"You do the modern pentathlon?"

"No. Not at all sir. I am a weapons instructor. Just here in case of anyone requiring any advice. Which given the quality of our chaps, I don't really believe my services are likely to be required."

"What about the pistol shooting?"

"We have not entered any competitors for the pistol competition sir."

"Do you not have any shooters in your team?"

"No sir, for some unknown reason the only shooters are in the pentathlon."

"Then we must organise a contest. We have just completed the measuring for the twenty-five-metre pistol shooting range, so a test is in order next. And what better way to test it than a competition. I've just been talking to Captain Cameron who is still waiting to get served in the food queue. I assume he is the senior officer, so, I shall suggest a small competition. What do you think lieutenant?"

"I think, with all due respect sir, that that decision is down to Captain Cameron. But I must tell you that we haven't brought any pistols with us."

"We are at an Olympic shooting range lieutenant. If we can't find a suitable pistol for you to use here, it would be embarrassing for the whole of our organisation. Have no fear a proper pistol will be found for you and some extra cartridges to at least try it out. You can be assured we don't want you to win but we want you to be confident you weren't cheated. I shall speak to your Captain to invite him to our competition. You of course Otto will be our competitor. It would be an unfair contest to put in an Olympic shooter against the lieutenant."

With that he smartly about faced and made his way back towards the small group of officers who were chatting to Cameron, now finally nearing the front of the food queue.

Captain Witzell leaned his head towards Alan. "I can assure you of one thing Alan. He won't think of cheating you, but he will be overjoyed if I win and as miserable as sin if in way you do. Have you shot target pistols much at all?

"I've shot pistols Otto many times, but not usually target pistols. I shoot mostly Webley revolvers. Standard British army issue pistol. Whatever that hits, leaves a hole in, or gets knocked over."

The general had spoken to Cameron just as he was leaving the food queue carrying what looked like enough food for a platoon. He motioned with his head to Alan to join him.

"It looks like I'm being summoned. If you'll excuse me? I guess that the competition is on."

Alan made his way over to Cameron as the general was leaving. They walked a short distance off towards an empty table and a couple of wooden seats. Cameron had got various sausages and a number of different looking breads.

"The man serving the food said he would bring us fresh coffee as soon as it was brewed. General Harrer tells me he is an intelligence officer and possibly, listening to him, a lot cleverer than he initially wants to appear. He has intimated, that if his Captain wins the shooting contest, he will probably confirm his position as his adjutant come personal assistant. He tells me that he was adjutant to the captain's father, who was a General during the first world war and he, according to Harrer, still has a voice inside Germany and a following. Might be worth noting him for some extra research. Could give us a better idea into who pulls what strings."

" I take it then that you don't want me to win this competition?"

"No. Though I think you should come a very close second. we are having carrots dangled in front of us, and we are being tempted to do things, possibly to see how flexible we are at creeping around or how we can be manipulated to suit a certain purpose, or of course we could be being treated to genuine German hospitality, to encourage us to look favourably, in our assessment, of what we see hear or are shown. Failing that of course we could be being led up the garden path like a couple of dim donkeys. Let's stay aware and careful."

"I need to shoot second if I am to make certain of not winning, but making it look like I am at least making a serious attempt. But first things first sir. Can we eat?

The variety of breads and sausages, Cameron had managed to put together, though not typical British fare, Alan was quite used to the different textures and tastes, having parents used to cosmopolitan cooking had taught him to eat anything that was designated edible.

The man who promised the fresh coffee had delivered and as they were finishing their lunch, Otto joined them.

"Food satisfactory?" he asked more out of politeness, too late to do anything about it, if it wasn't.

"Perfectly adequate thankyou Otto. Filled the gap without bloating me. Wouldn't want to be shooting with too much in my belly."

"Excellent so you are ready to practice then?"

"No sense in waiting any longer. If you are ready let's get on with it. What are we shooting?"

"We can test the set-up we have just completed. The twenty five metre rapid fire system is currently in place but we could do it at your own speed rather than rapid fire if that's better for you?"

" What do you think Otto?"

"Whichever you wish to play Alan."

"You have set it up Otto so let's go with your choice of contest, but I get to go after you if that's agreeable?"

"Ok five rounds of five shots one three and five at our own speed. Two and four rapid fire."

"Do we have turning targets?"

"Of course. We'll set them as standard eight seconds for round two and six seconds for round four. But first you must at least shoot a pistol you will find that shooting twotwo a lot different to thirty eight stoppers. We have a pair of new Walther target pistols at our disposal. They are the models that we have been using for years. Walther have made a new model for us to shoot with, in this year's Olympics, so there is no problem about us using these."

Otto put five cartridges into a magazine and loaded the Walther. He passed it to Alan who lined the target up and fired five steady shots into the paper silhouette of a standing man. One had gone outside the target rings; the rest were in the rings but not scoring many. Otto had loaded another magazine with another five shots. "You are certainly right. There is hardly any kick from the twotwo." The second five were reasonably close to centre and after another magazine load Alan felt he'd had enough practice to give it a go.

The noise of the shooting had attracted a reasonable sized crowd of spectators. Cameron was fairly close and General Harrer was very clearly at the front and watching intently as his champion had given instruction and advice to Alan. They had got themselves into the area near to the shooting bays. Some of the army personnel were on the steps that were on the right side of the shooting range, while behind the range was a tiered sitting area, and there a number of others had taken advantage of the available space.

"We appear sir to have an audience." Alan remarked. "I wonder who they'll be rooting for?" Alan had partially wandered back in to English making the comment mostly to himself.

"Rooting. Forgive me Alan rooting?"

"Supporting Otto Just another word for supporting"

"Then I may have a home team advantage."

"I'd be surprised if you didn't"

"Ready to go?"

"Yes let's get it done before I forget what you've taught me."

Otto had a box of fifty cartridges. He split them half each. Alan did at the same time as Otto put five cartridges into each of his two magazines. As he was firing second he put the pistol down and stood back. They had taken alternate shooting bays . Otto had taken number two so Alan took number four. Peter Cameron had been given a pair of binoculars so he could act as Alan's spotter. There was a civilian Alan assumed spotting for Otto as he was one of the few who were close up not in uniform. He was the one who signalled to the two officials who were sitting at a table above another short set of steps just on the left hand side of the range. His target turned and Otto lifted his pistol aimed, fired and rest then lift aim fire rest, until he had completed his five shots. Cameron could see their opponent's target and added up the score. Alan then did almost the same not as quickly as Otto and a score three less than Otto's forty two. Otto managed thirty five on the first rapid fire exactly the same as Alan. Round three Alan pulled one back on his three deficit with a forty two to forty one. The second rapid fire one again produced a draw at thirty two apiece. Alan was two shy going into the last round. The crowd were extremely well behaved they were playing very fairly there was no noise at any time apart from the scores and the sound of pistol shots. Otto shot forty four and Alan settled for the same which brought then, a huge cheer from the crowd and a very big smile on the face of General Harrer. Otto shook Alan's hand.

"You are a very good shot lieutenant Lewis for a man who has never shot target pistols before. If you train yourself on thirty -eights and forty-fives then perhaps I too may get better by doing the same. Thank you for the competition."

"You are very welcome and may I compliment you on a good score and congratulations on your win it is deserved."

A small number of army officers were waiting patiently for Otto to finish his conversation with Alan. Not so General Harrer he couldn't wait any longer.

"Very well done Captain, excellent shooting and you too lieutenant you were very close, a good competition tested the range out too. What more could we ask for?"

"Thank you sir. The better man won."

"You are generous in your praise lieutenant; so I shall be generous too. First I shall have the pistols boxed and sealed and a letter given to you saying that they have been given to you by me. Which will allow you to take them out of Germany with you, when you go home, which I suppose, will be after the end of the games. Secondly to reward Captain Witzell, I shall confirm to the High Command that he is my personal assistant and adjutant." There was a small round of applause from the congratulating officers who now had even more to speak to Otto about. Alan thanked the general for his present and slipped out of the gathered group to join Cameron, who too had, a huge smile on his face, reason not quite known, thought Alan, but as everyone else was smiling, maybe it was infectious.

The luncheon team had packed up their equipment but Cameron had manged to get his hands on some leftover bread and sausage. "We have a two hour journey back to the village Alan, Get some food down you. You ate at lunchtime but I know what you normally eat and you scrimped somewhat."

"As I said sir I didn't want a belly full of food these breads can sit heavy in the gut. As much as I enjoy them they can feel like you've been loaded."

Otto wandered over to them as they were finishing off the extras that Cameron had wangled.

"We have a refreshment tent at the other side of the carpark where I would like to buy you a beer Lieutenant. You too are welcome of course Captain."

Cameron was happy to leave Alan with his new friend and perhaps he might if circumstances permitted take up the offer later during their stay if they met again. In the meantime he would trade some gossip with the others as they still had to get themselves back to the village sometime before the canteen shut.

"Franz." Otto shouted across to the man who had been his spotter. "Are you going back to the village today?"

"After I've finished here in about thirty minutes maybe a little longer"

"Can you take our guests with you?"

Of course, I only have the guns and the ammunition to take back."

"You have your transport. I'm sure Franz would be happy to entertain you while I have a quick beer with Alan. That is with your permission Captain."

"Granted. Enjoy your beer gentlemen. I shall see if I can be less than a hindrance to Franz."

On the other side of the carpark a small marquee had been erected. There was, what was almost certainly, only a temporary bar. A couple of trestle tables various bottled beers and spirit bottles glasses and towels and dish cloths. The smell of alcohol and cigarette smoke hung in the air inside.

"We could get drunk on the fumes," Otto continued. "If you grab that table near to the entrance Alan I will get us some beers."

Otto came back with a tray. He was overtaken by a waiter who hurriedly wiped the table carefully keeping any slops away from either of the chairs. Otto passed a glass of beer to Alan and a schnapps.

"Thank you for the competition lieutenant, Your very good health." "Likewise and the same to you."

They touched glasses and Otto sank his spirit in one Alan sipped it, never having drunk it before, and believing that if it was good enough to drink, it was better to savour it.

Otto picked up his beer and continued. "You must come to the General's house and visit. Frau Harrer will welcome you as she always does, when I bring a friend with me. We could go and shoot some deer and get fat on venison and enjoy ourselves in their garden. The general's wife is very pretty. They have two children. The girl is in her early twenties and studying medicine at university in Berlin. The young man who is nearly twenty now is learning how to manage the estate. He is very handsome, and I must admit he is becoming a very dear friend."

There was a change in Otto's demeanor as he spoke of his general's son. It was as though there was an excitement and fascination in what he was thinking. Alan was, obviously, not privy to his thoughts, but his wistful look, when he spoke of him, made him think that there was something more brewing under the surface.

"As I said earlier, you are a very good shot lieutenant Lewis. You managed to shoot a couple behind me, which allowed me to win, and more importantly a rise in estimation of my General's trust in me. As you know he has, as a result of this win, confirmed my position as his personal assistant, and adjutant. Until today I was on a provisional posting and even though it has been nearly a year, I could easily have been moved at a moment's notice. Confirmation of my position, should allow me to rise up through the ranks, without having to spend long times in humdrum positions, and odd places to further my career, It also has the advantage of easy access to shooting in the Black forest with the general's son."

"I'm pleased it'd all worked so well for you today."

"As we spoke earlier about our relative positions, in many ways, mine is not dissimilar to yours, Lieutenant you having been seconded to Captain Cameron who is working for Mr. Conway from the MOD. I'm not certain exactly what your job is nor Captain Cameron's, but we do know what Mr. Conway does, so I suspect, at some point, after your return to England, you will meet up with

Mr. Conway and be debriefed. You look at me as if you are not aware of what I'm talking about, so you are either, as good an actor as my jovial general, or you are actually here to mind the members of the Olympic team, and if so you are neglecting your duty by sitting here drinking schnapps and beer listening to me waffling on" He laughed. "Come, one more for the road, as they say, as I too must get back to business. He signaled the waiter. He signaled two plus two.

"I'll pay." said Alan. "No Herr Lewis the very least I can do is buy you some drinks. I will still owe you. I am in your debt. As I've told you, not a position I enjoy, but what you did for me earlier on today I will always be grateful for." Alan shrugged his shoulders saying nothing was his best option.

"I could conceivably accuse you of cheating. An accusation I couldn't possibly prove. It would beg the question; what advantage could have been gained for the second person to fire if they lost. I believe there are times, Herr Lewis, when winning is important; coming first is imperative. For whatever reason today, I think coming second for you, was more important, unusual, but extremely interesting.

Four drinks arrived. two beers, two schnapps. "Your very good health Herr Lewis. Hopefully we will meet again." They touched glasses, sat in silence for a short while, then Otto stood quickly, shook Alan's hand and left.

Franz did as he said he would and dropped Peter and Alan back at the Olympic village. They spent the next couple of days familiarizing themselves with their surroundings and making contacts with the management of the British team to get them into the opening ceremony on Sunday the first of August and then transport back to Ruhleben for the Shooting on the fourth.

Though initially, they were considered to be a couple of hangers on, when they realised that they were military, and had been at the testing of the range, and knew the officials there, someone woke up to the fact that they might be of some use. That then got them access to transport and to be seen to keeping up essential appearances, got them where they needed to be. And where they needed to be, was at Ruhleben, on day three of the Modern Pentathlon. It was busy, which was hardly surprising, Alan and Peter were trying to look like they were supposed to be there when they heard a voice shouting "Herr Lewis. Lieutenant Lewis." Franz, who had driven them back to the village was pushing his way through the crowd towards them. "I thought I would find you here" Franz said when he got over to Alan and Peter standing with the shooters from the British team. "This is the letter form General Harrer and here are the pistols. There is no ammunition with them but even though they were hardly used they have been cleaned, checked and reoiled with preservation oil so they will require a cleaning again before you fire them. They are very nice pistols; I must admit I am quite envious. But now I'm sorry to say, you must forgive me, I am a part of the management group here, and I have work to do." He shook hands with Alan and disappeared back into the crowd. No one was taking any real notice of them, until Franz had shown up with the letter from the general and the boxed Walther pistols, after which their credit rating went through the roof. Unfortunately, it had little effect on the outcome of the competition. The shooting section in the end was won by a competitor from the USA with a perfect rapid- fire score of two hundred from twenty shots. the highest British competitor scored one hundred and eighty-seven very credible, but amazingly only thirteenth place.

From a British Olympic team point of view even though they didn't have an official position with them, someone managed to get them into the general officials list, which got them onto the transport back to the UK. After a month away they reported back to Woolwich barracks in order to get a lift back to Salisbury.

"Good job you reported back here." the duty office informed them. "The powers that be have got you a new office. Same shoddy furniture different location, the man said, Sir. The second message was and I quote, "Saves me going to Salisbury to speak to you. I believe his name is Mr. Conway."

"That makes sense" Cameron replied. "Where do we sleep?"

"I have a double room for you in the main building sir"

Well we're off there now, via the mess, we're tired and hungry. Food and rest we'll be fine tomorrow."

I hope so sir as Mr. Conway left a third message he will be here at 0900 tomorrow morning.

At exactly 0900 hours, Talbot Conway arrived.

Good morning, Captain, and to you too Lieutenant Lewis. So, gentleman tell me, how did it go?

Alan left Peter to do the talking and running through everything that had happened while they were away.

"Anything to add to what Captain Cameron has said Lieutenant?"

"I would only add sir that they knew exactly who we were and all about us. It was as if our details had been sent in advance."

"They were. I did say I'd try not to get you killed Cameron, but by the same token, I didn't want to send you two over there and not get anything achieved . So, I decided to drop some hints.

The Germans have a contact in our department, who we use to send messages to them via him. We're not exactly certain who he works for, it may be both countries but it is handy having someone we can feed stuff to, knowing it will get to where we want it to go. I let it be known that you were looking to make friends and contacts for future development. Let them know that we'd promoted sergeant Lewis to second lieutenant, to make it look better. Worked well didn't it?"

CHAPTER 3   SPAIN   1937

Captain Cameron and Lieutenant Lewis had got themselves comfortable in their office with the Royal Artillery at Woolwich. Cameron spends his days working his way through reams of paperwork, while Lewis, who having been given his own desk, was then sent back to Salisbury Plain to supervise officer training instructors. While Cameron was monitoring the Spanish civil war and trying to stay on top of what Germany was doing or more importantly what it might do, Lewis had assumed Captain Cameron's role as officer in charge of assessing prospective and potential specialist operatives for, small team, one off projects.

Cameron was left to occupy his time reading reports, assessing their value and usefulness, and then sending them to the right person he hoped. No one outside of his office knew what the reason for his being there was, and on occasions he had had similar thoughts himself.

One Tuesday morning, without warning, Talbot Conway arrived.

"How good is your Spanish Captain?"

"I read it fine sir. I don't speak it often enough to be fluent and the same with listening to it."

"To be perfectly honest Cameron, a trait I'm neither totally familiar with nor famous for, but I don't have anyone else. I want you to go to Spain and find out why some people have not been heard of for a while. I can put you in touch with a couple of people who will go down there with you, and they can do all the talking for you. They aren't military or fighting types; just people who blend in and observe and report. Do I assume that you will want Lewis with you?"

"He doesn't speak Spanish either, and I don't think he reads it."

"He's there for other reasons. You may need someone who's good at damaging people. According to my information he's top dog you can take him, and he can have any weapons he wants, as long as he can hide them and carry them."

"Yes sir. I'll send for him."

"You don't need to. I've already done it. I phoned Colonel Haslet at Salisbury before I left the office. By now he should be on his way down here."

"When do we go?"

"I've left one of the office wallahs to organise something that's quick easy and works. As soon as I know, I'll let you know. But it won't be long. Get Lewis to go to the armoury and get what he wants. I'll instruct Colonel here to assist. Any issues get straight on to him. Questions?"

"Names, photographs, location, funds."

Conway took a large envelope from his briefcase and gave it to Cameron. "I'll bring anything else I get over with the travel plan. Anything else?"

"At the moment no sir."

Cameron was still reading through the papers that were in the envelope, when Lewis arrived.

"By Jove Alan you've got here quick."

"Colonel organised a car sir, Seems someone's in a hurry."

"They certainly seem to be. Let's not waste any time then. Your job first is to get yourself armed with whatever you want. Mr. Conway said you have to be able to carry it and if necessary hide it. You're brief is to provide armed response when and if needed."

"Armoury then sir."

Cameron locked his office, and they headed over to the main building.

A corporal, carrying a rifle, standing just inside the door, barred their way.

"Duty officer please corporal."

"He's in his office sir."

"Well go and get him. Tell him Captain Cameron wishes to speak to him. Don't worry. No one will get past lieutenant Lewis you can take my word on it. Now hurry up man I don't have a lot of time and certainly none to waste."

   The corporal was completely thrown off line and decided not to argue crossed quickly across the hallway to the Office door, knocked, opened it, and walked partially in, so he could still keep an eye on Cameron and Lewis, as they waited by the main door.

Cameron couldn't hear the conversation but not long after he had opened the door, out came an artillery captain, carrying his stick, and putting on his cap.

"You are duty officer today Captain."

"I am. And you are?"

"Cameron and Lieutenant Lewis we are based in a little office in the annex. We keep ourselves to ourselves, but today we require use of some of your equipment."

"And what might that be?"

"Alan, your turn."

The artillery man looked at Alan like he was a junior officer come no mark.

"Three pistols, ideally all the same, my choice when we get to see what you've got, and two hundred rounds of ammunition. I may, when I see what's down there, might add a bit." The artillery man laughed.

"On who's orders?"

"Mine." said Cameron. "If you can't authorise it, get your Colonel now. I don't have time to waste. Told your corporal that." The captain's cheeks started to redden. Cameron looked at the corporal. "Corporal get your colonel now, before I get irritated, and let Lieutenant Lewis off his leash."

"I'm going." said the Captain. "Stay here corporal any problems shoot them."

"Yes sir."

Corporal stood quickly to attention and Alan took his rifle off him.

"I'll give it back after corporal. Don't want anything silly happening. Could spoil my day and wreck yours completely."

The artillery Captain was coming out of his office as Colonel Livingstone was coming down the long flight of stairs from the top floor. "What 's going on here gentlemen.?" He shouted.

"Cameron and Lewis sir presuming that Mr. Conway had been in touch."

"By god, he's not hanging around on this is he? He spoke to me but thirty minutes ago. I expected this to be sometime this week not instantly."

"Lieutenant Lewis was in Salisbury early this morning sir. And Mr. Conway spoke to me just over an hour ago. There is certainly a rush on."

"What are you wanting from us Captain?"

"Weapons and ammunition sir, and anything else that catches Lewis's eye sir."

"Captain," to his OOD..

"Sir."

"Take them down to the armoury and give them anything they want. As long as they sign for it. It will be approved."

"Yes Sir."

"Captain, Lieutenant, Have a good trip."

"Thank you sir. And thank you for your help."

"If you will follow me please gentlemen. The man in charge here can be difficult. He is CSM White. Been here for a long time. Thinks he owns the place."

"That chalky White still here then?" Alan asked.

"I believe some people have been known to call him by that nickname lieutenant, not normally to his face."

"He'll be fine Captain."

The heavy steel door to the armoury was unlocked but stiff to open. The hinges squeaked as it opened. Saved having a bell or a buzzer to let the person inside know there was a visitor.

There was no one visible behind the counter.

"Come on chalky get out here we're in a hurry."

"I'd recognize that voice anywhere that's you Sgt Lewis isn't it?"

"Sadly, no you old bugger. They made me a lieutenant. You'll have to be nice to me now."

"Army's gone to the dogs. That to stop you abusing officers, made you join the club, did they?"

"Just get out here you useless old piece of derelict lard."

The two captains were sensibly staying out of the conversation.

A side door just visible above the counter top, already open but opened a little further and out came company sergeant major Douglas White.

"Just thinking about you is enough to spoil my lunch but seeing you again is enough to make a man sick. Ah! a redeeming feature, Captain Cameron. Good day sir still got the millstone hanging around then sir?"

"Hello Douglas. Not changed much have you?"

"Can't improve on perfection sir."

"No, You've not changed at all have you?" Cameron was laughing the artillery captain didn't have a clue as to what was going on but nevertheless had to tell the CSM the reason for their visit.

"Sergeant Major, Colonel's orders are to give these officers whatever they ask for." Cameron leaned over towards Alan. "Be nice to him Alan, I think we need him."

"He doesn't know how to be nice to anyone Mr. Cameron. Yorkshire people and Merseysiders all the same sir and he's both. You're not from there are you sir?"

"No Dougie, Carshalton in Surrey."

"Exactly what I mean sir. Officer country, not scabby Merseysiders from Yorkshire sneaking into the army via the back door."

"Douglas as much fun as this is we're in a hurry."

"Fire away Alan, What do you want?"

"Three semi auto pistols, all same calibre, but small enough to go in a pocket, plus three extra magazines and two hundred rounds."

"Haven't got them. Can do two Beretta model 34's or three Colts but they're bigger." Could do two Berettas and a Walther, but the Walther is a 32 not 38."

"Can you do two Walthers with spare magazines and a hundred rounds of each?"

"Yes."

"Sign on the dotted line sir we have a deal. How long Dougie?"

"Ten minutes."

"Sorry to hassle you matey. It's good seeing you again but this has been sprung on us, and we need to be ready."

While Alan was talking Dougie had been filling in the register of weapons leaving the armoury. "I assume you don't want holsters?"

"No thank you. Put it all in a duffle bag please. Anything new that might be of interest?"

Douglas had a think for a moment,

"Nothing that will go in a pocket. Some new heavy stuff but we're not carrying much here. It's all quiet really. Too bloody quiet in my opinion."

"We're done then," Alan told him. "It's with you now."

"Give me a few minutes out the back and I'll get the gear. I still need to put the serial numbers in. Then you can go."

The sergeant major was done in less than ten minutes. Cameron signed the register. Dougie shook hands with them.

"Come back safe you two. Alan congratulations on your promotion. It's not before time."

"Thanks Dougie we'll have a beer when we're back."

"Just make certain you get back."

Alan grabbed the duffle bag and left Cameron to thank the Artillery Captain and follow him out.

"You obviously know those two men then sergeant major."

"Yes sir. We supply them with weapons and ammunition when they want it."

"They said they.ve been in the annexe for a while."

"Probably have. They work for a man named Conway sir. What Mr. Conway does doesn't get talked about. But I do know that part of that work is a specialist course of officer training on Salisbury plain. The not long ago sergeant, now Lieutenant Lewis teaches people how to kill other people in a variety ways and how to get away after. That is possibly where they are going now given what he wanted to take with him."

The artillery captain left it at that. Whatever they shared between them had nothing to do with rank or position. What linked them was respect for each other. The captain filed it into his knowledge bank. He didn't think he was going to get any more useful information from his armourer at this time but possibly in the future a pleasant chat might let him in to somewhere.

Back at their office, Cameron checked with the duty corporal if there had been any calls, but so far nothing.

Alan followed Cameron into the office. "What's the job and what do we know about it Sir?"

"According to Mr. Conway some people are missing and haven't reported in for a while."

"Where are they?"

"Spain."

"It's quite big Spain isn't it sir or is there a Spain I don't know about?"

"I don't think that we've got all the information yet. With what we've got so far it will be easier to find the needle in the haystack."

"I can only assume that Mr. Conway is up to his usual stuff and feeding us what he wants to." Alan felt a need to say it even though Cameron was equally aware of Mr. Conway's habits. "Given that he's organised an any weapons you want, implies to me that he expects us to be either threatening, or shooting something, sometime, somewhere. And chucking us into a country, itself in the middle of a civil war, does nothing to dispel my fears about that."

"I wouldn't argue against that Alan. Let's have another look at what he sent over. I only managed a quick once over, before you arrived. There might be more in there than I got the first time."

Cameron emptied the envelope carefully on to his desk and started separating off the contents. He put the Spanish pesetas to one side and looked again at the two photographs of the missing persons.

"One lady and one gentleman. Names on back. Not much else. No idea when they were taken and doesn't have much info in the notes we've got either." Cameron passed them over to Alan. Alan gave them a quick look, shook his head. "We know there's more. There has to be. we'll have to wait for Mr. Conway."

Cameron started to put it all back into the envelope. "Let's get some food while we can. Knowing what normally happens it'll be another rush somewhere and nothing to eat or drink. Do you want to lockup the guns?"

"No. I'll carry them with me. Dougie 'll go ape shit if I don't mind them, though I can't see anyone trying to rake them from me here."

It is debatable, if it hadn't been for the artillery captain arriving when he did, if they would have managed to get anything to eat in the mess. As Lewis hadn't ever been in there, and Camerons meals were always brought over by his corporal clerk, neither were known, and not having artillery stamped on their forehead, there was a certain reluctance to feed them. As they were late, and most had been fed they settled for sausage and chips for lunch.

"And jolly good it was. My compliments to the chef." Cameron replied when the waiter enquired if he had enjoyed his lunch.

"We are pleased sir. If you wish to have luncheon in future sir, will you be good enough to order ahead. Cookie would be happier, and if cookie's happy we'll all be happy sir. Thank you, and I will pass on your compliments."

The steward brought over a pot of tea and when Alan was doing the dishing out Cameron suddenly asked him out of the blue. "So what did Dougie mean when he said

'Merseysiders sneaking into the Army via the back door in Yorkshire'? Didn't make any sense to me."

"It's a long tale but I'll try and be quick." Alan took a mouthful of tea and having checked who and how many were still in the mess.

"I have told this once before to a friend, so I do remember how it goes. When I first started school I used to get picked on because my English wasn't very good and they used to call me the foreigner. I've been fighting since I was 5 years of age. When I was 6 some kid started a fight and I tried to smash his head through a glass window in the classroom. I got six of the best. Hurt like hell it did. Never knew if it was for beating the kid or trying to smash a school window. He started it and I got the cane. Didn't seem fair so I thumped in the park one weekend. He told teachers when we got into school on the Monday. They said tough, nothing to do with us. He never bothered me again. And the others left me alone as well. Next school all started again I was thirteen when I got expelled from the senior school for fighting. The problem was I kept winning. The big boys and the hard cases were getting a beating so they kept picking on me and trying to beat me. I kept beating them so school solved problem by moving me out. When dad was next home from sea he decided to take me to his mums in Sheffield or just outside Sheffield. He'd asked his sister at Pontefract but she said she had no room, so Granny took me in at her cottage.

Granny was the head teacher at the local village school where she lived and her influence got me into a decent school in Sheffield where she knew some of the staff and they kept me in line and from then on, I have to be honest, I thrived. Most times I would get the bus to and from school but occasionally she would pick me up if she were going shopping in town. Granny had a 350 cc Triumph motor cycle. Single seat with a parcel rack on the back she use to carry the shopping on. When she wanted to carry a passenger she would put a cushion on the rack and a while back before I got there she'd had some footrests bolted onto the frame, one either side, not strong enough for standing on, but perfect to keep her passengers deet for getting into the back wheel or trailing behind. Sometimes the passenger would be obliged to carry a shopping bag with groceries in it on others when there was no shopping you hung on while granny went quicker. To stay warm you would hold granny around the waist and put your hands in grannies coat pocket. Granny had holes in her pockets and sometimes your hands would go right through and inside the coat. I was between fourteen and fifteen when I learnt all about the birds the bees and lady's body parts and how to ride a motor buke. I don't think what we did was legal but I didn't complain and it's too late to do anything about now. I was at the cottage when granny did the shopping on her way home from school one day. A horse and trailer with a lot of hay and stuff on got stuck across the road. Horse was alright. Trailer got damaged when granny hit it but not badly. Motor bike lost some paint off the tank. Granny died. I did the ID on granny. It was just two days before my sixteenth birthday, granny left half of her estate to dad and the other half to Dad's sister who as I said lived in Pontefract. She left the motor bike to me. The one I've still got at Salisbury. I went up to see my auntie before the funeral, because I'd never met her or her husband. She didn't know me and didn't want to. So I tried to join the army. I had become instantly lonely. I'd left school and now I'd lost my best friend. Kings Own Yorkshire Light Infantry I thought would be a good idea with my track record. The man on the desk there told me I wasn't old enough. 'Comeback when you're eighteen'. I'll be back when I'm eighteen I told him. 'We'll see' he said 'people change their minds' I said I'll be back so I will be.

Dad left Blue Funnel, bought a fishing boat with the money he'd been left and asked me to crew for him . Adam my elder brother had a job in the flour mills. Arthur brother number three was too young, and at that time and still at school. So I crewed for dad for a bit less than two years. Then on the day after my eighteenth birthday I rode motor bike up to Pontefract and joined KOYLI. That was 1925 . I signed on for 12 years. Mormally7 full time and 5 in reserves. As a sergeant instructor they kept me full time and the rest is history sir as for most of them I've been with you."

" But you signed on again."

"Yes this year 37 started it all again. It's five more now. It seems because we work for Mr Conway normal rules and regulations don't always apply."

"Thank you Alan what an extraordinary start you've had in life. I am certainly in awe of your perseverance. I'm glad your with me and not against me. I think we better get back now." Alan drank the remains of his tea now less than warm.

Shortly after returning to their office Talbot Conway phoned.

"Cameron good. I've caught you. Is Lewis with you?"

"Yes sir."

"Excellent, I will be with you in half an hour."

As usual Conway arrived in his normal rush. Cameron and Alan waited patiently in their office knowing only that Mr. Conway was on his way, and he would be there when he arrived. Which today turned out to be less than twenty minutes.

"Right gentlemen some more reading material." He put two small cases on Cameron's desk. "My travel man at the office has come up with a plan. It is provisionally approved, and just needs ministerial approval, and then we can go. There is no commercial flight, I can get you on, with sufficient flexibility to make it cockup proof. So, the plan is we are looking at the possibilities of developing a future route, London to Barcelona, when the war is over. We are therefore, hiring an aeroplane and crew and along with British Airways and with the authority of the British government looking to link up with French Aviation companies for a joint venture. We are going to fly the route, plan stops, and cost the whole thing out at our expense, and then pass on the information to the French Government, with the idea of the aforementioned future joint venture.

As it's a commercial operation, and has no political issues attached, the French surprisingly have quickly approved the idea, with the proviso of a French pilot being with you in the aeroplane, when you survey the route. I think this is best we're going to get. In point of fact, I'm not certain that we could actually do it any better by any other way." I am also totally certain that the French are neither naive nor stupid and that they are almost certainly aware that there is more to this than we are telling them. They will wash their hands of any knowledge of anything if it goes wrong and at some time in the future they will ask a favour in return, which we will be obliged to repay. I can tell you that just about every country in Europe has some interest n what is going on in Spain, but all of them are stating categorically, that they are in no way involved. Complete pack of lies I can assure you. So, fingers crossed we just keep bashing along as we are, but don't start revealing plans along the way, then no one can think about objecting to anything. All clear?"

"Then we are flying there and back. Is that what you are telling us Sir?"

"That's exactly what I'm saying, and we know when you get there where the first place to look is, as we have the location now of the properties that the family own. We found which address their parents were at, and I sent a senior police chappie around to speak to them. It was slightly more difficult than it sounds. The parents were down at a house in the West country. If I'd sent anything less than a chief super he probably wouldn't have got in let alone an answer. Now we have a list and a probable order of likely locations. It's moving better than I hoped for a couple of hours ago. We are still involved with some finger crossing but it does I'm happy to say look like it's going in the right direction." Conway looked at his watch. "I hope now to get the OK to go. I have an appointment with the minister in half an hour. By that time, he says he should have received the go ahead from his French counterpart. Questions be quick."

"French francs sir we have some psetas but no francs We will get receipts when we can sir."

"Your interpreters will have any funds you need; they can draw it from finance before they leave the office. They will give you any amount you need. We are not on a limited budget but don't get silly with it. You need to be dressed in civvies. You're away for a couple of days. Minimum stuff. A couple of soft bags, passport, and whatever Lewis got from the armoury. I will be giving you a couple of small cases to carry. You're to look like business people not military on a job. Understood?"

"Yes sir."

"Now I must go. I will phone you tomorrow morning as I am leaving my office. You should be ready to leave as soon as I get there. We can talk in my car on the way.

"We'll be ready sir"

At 0800 hours the following morning, Conway arrived to pick up Cameron and Lewis. There had been little extra information received overnight and most of the journey was quiet and relaxed in the back while Richard negotiated the early morning rush.

There was a fair amount of traffic about the airport. Parking the car wasn't too much of a problem though. A policeman about to tell Richard you can't park there sir was shown a government warrant card by him and after a smart salute, he guided them carefully into the space he'd originally aimed for.

Cameron took the holdalls from the boot when Alan grabbed the duffle bag.

"Will you stay with the car please Richard? Martin will come with us. I assume Martin, that you know whom we are looking for?"

"I do sir." The four of them moved slowly, but smoothly through the crowded main building. Not having arranged an exact meeting point it was about Martin spotting the ladies minder no easy task in the crowd if they were sitting down and facing the other way. It was made easier by Martin towering over most others and in the end it was the ladies minder spotting Martin that got everyone together. "Marcia Johnson and Pamela Thomas were the two lady interpreters. Middle to late thirties slim well-dressed looking like they were going on holiday. A shoulder bag come handbag, a suitcase each, low-heeled shoes, calf length skirt, warm knee-high coat, and small soft trilby style hat with a matching colour scarf. They looked different but the same. Conway emceed the introductions and followed up with a quick briefing.

"It's a British Airways De Havilland plane, more than enough seats so you've got the whole plane as you will have an extra British pilot and a French one from Paris. There isn't any requirement to tell anyone what you do for a living, and then one might prefer to lie anyway. You have a short while before you need to board, I would suggest you get to know what you need to know about each other. And do take care of yourselves. Any questions?" Two shaken heads and two "no sir's" and Conway turned and left, with Martin leading, and the second minder tucking himself in behind. Cameron watched as Conway's minders shepherded him.

Whatever he was and where in the system he was Cameron didn't really know, but what he did know was he got the same level of protection normally accorded to senior members of parliament.

Cameron took the lead. "It might not be easy, but let's see if we can find a table, or somewhere out of the way, so we can have as near a private discussion as we can."

They were in luck. A group leaving on a flight before theirs was ready, vacated a couple of tables at the window wall, that gave them a view of the planes in front of the main building.

"That looks like our plane parked there looking at the markings." Cameron said as he took a seat. Lewis sat with his back to the wall facing into the building.

"Do you want to change seats with me?" Pam asked.

"Alan likes to see what's going on in the room," Cameron replied for him, he was right. Alan's job was watch and mind "If you'll sit next to Alan please Marcia, Pamella and I'll share plane watching. Which one of you worked with Melinda?"

"Me mostly, I think, though you did on the odd occasion didn't you Marcia?"

"I did she replied but not very often we didn't really get on that well. One problem was grammar school verses her private education. Which is really strange given how far to the left she is politically."

"She was in many ways a mixed-up kid really." Pam had rejoined the conversation. "I'm not certain if it was as clear cut as one school or another, though it certainly could have been a contributary factor. Her parents didn't help, father is in the House of Lords when he turns up in England, mother is landed gentry as well, ancient family with lots of very old money. Melinda's early years were at the very least the creation and ongoing development of a spoilt child. Even by the standards of the rarified atmosphere of that elevation of education she was a horror show."

"what about her brother?" Alan was happy leaving Cameron to do the talking.

"A wastrel, a prodigal son, Kicked out of so many schools, behaved so badly, even his parents prestige and money couldn't help him in the end. Met him once, nice as pie, because he was trying to bed me, rest of the information is gossip naturally, but most of it has been confirmed by Melinda at one time or another."

Do either of you know anything about Melinda's husband?"

Marcia didn't but Pamela continued.

"He's a left-wing activist, name of Miguel and we think Fonsi, but we're not certain of the exact surname. He is we are told well known around the Barcelona area but often uses a different last name; for a reason we are unsure of. Probably what started all the friction in the first place. Melinda's family were dead set against the marriage and couldn't stand him because he had too many aliases. This needless to say had Melinda digging her heels in and marrying him anyway. He's a Republican, which didn't sit well either with her parents and her leaning towards the left as well will have only exacerbated the hostility. I wouldn't be surprised if that didn't tip the scales in them returning to England, probably feeling they could control things better from here."

"Excuse my interruption" said Cameron. That unfortunately may be a lot nearer the truth than we realise but right at this moment there is something happening on what we think is our plane. Are we all ready?" Cameron moved the seats as he passed Pamela her bag and led the way to the departure gate. Marcia linked Alan's arm as they headed towards the gate.

"We look a bit more like a couple now." she said as she leaned her head into his shoulder to whisper in his ear.

Cameron and Pamela were at the exit and waving at Alan to join them.

"This is Mr. Lewis and Miss Johnson?" the man at the gate was asking Cameron when Alan and Marcia arrived.

"Yes."

"This is all your luggage you are taking?" the gateman asked.

Another yes from Cameron.

"Your office have been in touch and cleared everything with management here. Have a good flight." He waved them through.

The engines were warming as they walked across from the building.

Cameron introduced himself to a pilot standing by a short flight of steps. They boarded; a ground crew person took away the steps. The door got shut. He spoke as they seated themselves.

"Good morning everyone my name is Patrick Sinclair; I am one of your pilots today. It won't get any warmer than this, there are blankets to wrap yourselves up in. Try and stay warm, it's hard work getting warm in here when you've got cold. Believe me I know. We will stop at Paris and take on some fuel there, and then up again when we have spoken to the airport staff and picked up our French pilot. They are monitoring everything that's happening with the war going on. Paris is a long way from Spain, but we have a flexible flight plan that can change to suit conditions, on the ground, in the air, or with the weather. Airplanes are expensive but more importantly neither Bertie, who's the other pilot, nor I are in any rush to change our jobs for a set of angel wings. He'll be in the front taking care of business, I'll be with you in the back. If it was Paris and back there would just be one of us but this is a let's see if we can make it work. If you're feeling sick there's bags and buckets in the box behind you. Let's hope it isn't too bumpy this morning. Okay?"

Cameron gave him a nod. He gave a tap on the cockpit door.

"Time to roll Bertie." He sat himself down at the back and the engine noise increased as they started to move towards the runway. Marcia's gloved hand found Alan's hand she snuggled into him, pulled the blanket around her shoulder and fell asleep.

Her head popped out once, from under the blanket, during the two and a quarter hours of flying time and then again, as the wheels touched the Paris airport runway with a bit of a bump. She was still holding Alan's hand.

"I'm sorry." she said, "that must have been uncomfortable for you."

"I've been in worse places Alan replied "but I am keen on moving a bit. I've been colder as well. How are you doing?"

"Can you see my feet, I think they might have fallen off or they're frozen?"

"Wiggle your toes. When we take off next time take your shoes off and wrap your feet in a blanket."

"Are you sure?"

"Yes the blood will have a chance to circulate better. Ladies shoes are generally too tight as it helps to keep them on."

"You seem to know a lot about ladies shoes." She laughed. "Do you have a secret?"

"No, I have a mother and two sisters."

"I shall take your advice then."

Bertie taxied the plane after it had landed while Patrick briefed his Passengers. It was near lunchtime now and years of experience had taught Cameron and Lewis to eat and sleep whenever you got the chance.

"Welcome to Le Bouget. Bertie will park us up somewhere and we will refuel and will go and get an update on weather and activity around our destination. If one of you gentlemen would like to accompany me and perhaps the other might stay with the ladies. There is nothing unsafe about the place, but it will be handy if we can all find each other when we're ready to leave again. Stretching your legs is a good idea, as well as food, drink, and toilet."

"I'll go with Patrick if you will stay with the ladies please Alan."

"Of course."

Shortly after that Bertie switched off the engines and Patrick opened the side door.

"Bear with me a moment please and I will find a set of steps." He slipped quickly out of the side door and disappeared towards the main building, returning a minute or so later pushing a small set of steel stairs on wheels. When the headroom is less than five feet getting in and out of an aircraft is a potentially hazardous undertaking especially when you can't feel your feet, Marcia just about managed it without any real problem. Pamela had no problem at all.

"I can't feel my feet yet." Came from Marcia.

"I took my shoes off." replied Pamela.

"What a good idea. That accounts for the smell anyway."

"Ooooh you witch. I'll get you back for that." They were laughing and it all seemed quite normal.

By this time Bertie had got out of the aircraft. He said a quick hello and went off to organise a refuel.

"I'm not certain of our time scale." Alan was saying to Pamela and Marcia but as they are unlikely to leave without us and food drink and toilet was mentioned I figure we should head over to the main building and see what we can find. Agreed?"

"First I need to warm my feet; so, I need a minute or two before I'm ready to go. It isn't very warm here and thin shoes and stockings do not a warm foot make."

"Agreed, me too." Said Pamela, "What are you thinking Marcia a quick clothes change?"

"Yes but just the bottom half."

"Where?"

"In the plane."

They climbed back inside, shut the door and emerged a few minutes later wearing tweed trousers, thick woolen socks, and well-polished black leather laced ankle boots.

"Now that is sensible footwear. I need my duffle bag before we go. Get your handbags unless you don't need them."

"You might know about ladies shoes and boots, mon ami, but you don't seem to know much about the contents of a lady's handbag." Marcia said as she retrieved the two handbags and Alan's duffle bag. Knowing what he had in his duffle bag he was surprised she made no comment about the weight.

They headed for the terminal hoping that somewhere inside was food and drink available. Toileting could always be managed if one was discreet.

The building wasn't exactly heaving, but it was busy, lots of aircrew and many different uniforms about the main area with travelers sitting, waiting, most seats taken as they were at Croyden. If they could find a café perhaps there would be some seating there not because they needed to sit but because they needed to eat and trying to eat a meal standing up is an unnecessary chore.

"Before we go rushing off into anything fancy," Alan asked. "Did Mr. Conway give you any money to cover expenses or buy food or accommodation etc. because he's extraordinary tight with us when he sends us out?"

"Don't worry." Pamela replied. "He said he hadn't given you much just some psetas and a few francs. We have cash and traveller's cheques. He is well known for being slow to part with money and as we work full time for him we refused to go unless money was in hand before we left. I believe the urgency of this job may well have motivated him to not mess about too much and I hope we've got more than we need and that in itself is unusual."

"Halleluiah," from Alan,, "We did three weeks in Berlin last year living on handouts and our savings. I don't know what he's given Peter but if it's anything like last year it won't be much."

"We're not even certain who's job this is Pamela continued We don't know if we are here to translate for you and Peter or you are here to protect us when we try to find Melinda and her brother.

My guess is it's both He tends to throw the ingredients into the pan light the gas and let it cook. Trusting that if he's got it right it'll work. And there is Peter now with Patrick and I assume our French pilot.

"Glad we spotted you. This is Gaston he is our French chaperone to get is through everywhere we hope." Peter made all the introductions. "He has also kindly invited us for lunch as they have a canteen here for their staff."

"We need to find Bertie." Alan said to Patrick.

"That's already done Bertie will know what to do. As I said earlier on this is a normal day job for us, so we sometimes manage to scrounge a bite here when we can."

During lunch Bertie arrived told us he'd filled up with fuel, had the mechanics check engine oil, said hello to 'Gaston and then proceeded to eat everything he could get his hands on and his mouth around.

"The plan," Patrick told us is to fly to Claremont Ferrand this afternoon and after checking everything there fly to Perpignan. This is as it stands at the moment, but it will probably end up being tomorrow. This means we will stay in Claremont tonight. This may add in what appears to be an extra day, but it will have you in Spain early enough the following day, for you to speak to the people you need to speak to.

The flight to Clermont was as uneventful as could be hoped for. Gaston was a bonus he got everyone into staff accommodation as this was an appraisal flight with the countenance of the French government therefore assistance should be offered and then provided.

They found a restaurant near to the airport which was easily accessed via a local single-decker bus every half hour on the dot.

Pamela paid for the meal with one of Conway's travelllers cheques and though the beds were relatively primitive they were warm and come the following morning when the airport was fully open and operational coffee croissants and crepes filled the overnight stomach gap.

There was a flight of three hours to Perpignan, where they refuelled and sat down together for a plan discussion.

They refuelled the plane and had the mechanics check everything over. Perpignan to Reus flight was 190 miles in each direction making a total distance of 380 miles. Assuming no problems, detours, or unforeseen issues. The plane fully fuelled with passengers had a range of 450 miles. Therefore, in theory there was enough fuel to go there and back if, for any reason, there wasn't any fuel available in Reus. Given that there was a war going on, and the republicans were flying planes on bombing raids, they would probably be unlikely to want to part with any fuel for a return flight for us. All agreed.

Up until this discussion started Gaston had been happy to come along as a very useful assistant but the talk about war possible extra passengers was making him feel that this was not a part of his original brief and possibly something he was not certain he should be included in.

"So how come we are flying in to Reus rather than main airport at Barcelona? Surely a more logical place to land as it has all the transport links and facilities needed. Reus is new, undeveloped, and comparatively primitive in contrast."

Pamela gave him the ladies talk. "Two reasons. First, if we can establish a link here, fees will be cheaper, and future development could be tailored to suit our purposes, and secondly, we are hoping that our employees may be at their home which is on a farm not too great a distance from the airport. Hence Reus rather than any of the others.

"Yes that makes sense and a better reason for being refuelled here rather than trusting to luck at the other end. But why do we need to pick up your staff as well?"

"Our employees here have been doing the doing survey work for the company and as we are here we thought it would be lovely to see them and then if they wanted to return with us we could pop them into the two spare seats we have. As there are six passengers and eight seats our friend Melinda and her brother could easily fit in behind us and then we could all fly back together with the survey info and our survey of the possibilities of this new route. We all know routes require planning and testing both for finance and making sure that passenger numbers can make it all work. Well, they've been doing the on the ground surveys testing passenger numbers which is all going slightly awry now with the war going on that currently we are no longer getting an accurate figures that are representative of what a commercial requirement might actually be." Gaston was nodding his head, not certain if it was because he understood exactly where

Pamela was coming from and what she was saying or if it was because if he nodded his head enough times she might stop and let him ask a question. "So do you understand what a good idea this is we get out our employees stuck in a war zone and at the same time we complete a practical flight test from London to Paris to Reus. Which will give your government and your airline all the info required to do Paris to Reus or any of the other airports we have used. Everyone's a winner Gaston."

"I don't think I'm allowed to cross into Spain on this trip they told me to go no further than Perpignan. "

"Oh, right well then what if you wait here at Perpignan and we'll pick you up on the way back"

"I think that is what I have to do. I don't speak Spanish anyway so I cannot be helpful there."

"Well don't worry we speak Spanish. Is there somewhere you can stay here at Perpignan?"

"There is staff accommodation as always for pilots."

"Well, that sorts your bed and sleeping out. We'll leave you money for food and some wine, and you have your overnight bag?"

"Yes."

"Then that's sorted. Wonderful, that wasn't so difficult was it?"

"No Madame."

Poor Gaston, Alan was thinking, he'd been squeezed into a corner, and bamboozled with information overload, that meant absolutely nothing, and then he agreed to it. It didn't matter what Pamela was employed to do by Conway; she was definitely worth her salary.

After landing they reported to the admin building. As they thought there was no fuel available, and they shifted the plane over towards the end of the main runway. There was the possibility that a daytime bombing raid might occur, but choice normally was to come at nighttime. The hope that as a passenger aircraft it might be clearly visible to any nationalist planes during daylight hours was no guarantee of safety and the advice was to park it up wherever they were happy with and as long as it wasn't in the way it was their responsibility alone. Fingers crossed and common sense might tell you not to sleep in it but away from it.

Yes they could hire a car for some money. American dollars preferred. Just for a short journey down the road at a cost of ten dollars for the hire and ten dollars towards the fuel. Some might even come back if there was no damage and not much fuel used. Not too unreasonable given petrol was at a premium. Pamela was carrying some US dollars someone was thinking ahead again.

Patrick and Bertie would clearly be minding the aeroplane, while the other four climbed aboard the bright red Plymouth and headed off to find the farm.

The directions had been confirmed by one of the men at the airfield. He was a member of the local militia. He didn't know the owners, but he told them that the farm house was not visible from the road but was a good distance inside the property. It can't be missed as soon as you seen the lines of olive trees on the left-hand side you are near the entrance, which has a wooden gate between two concrete gate posts. The directions from the man at the airport were perfect. When Cameron turned into the drive, although the gate was closed, the padlock and chain were hanging loose at the side, showing obvious signs of having been chopped through.

Alan decided that perhaps this was a good time to remove the guns from his duffle bag. They were all loaded and ready to go but now it was time to make them even more ready. He passed the Walthers to Cameron and put a Beretta one in each side pocket of his jacket. Neither Marcia nor Pamela seemed even the slightest bit bothered; they were half watching the procedure, made no comment, but kept a careful eye all around. Cameron decided to say nothing. Alan never said anything anyway. Alan opened the gate then shut it again after Cameron had driven through. The road was crushed gravel packed down by years of traffic, rutted in part, and potholed occasionally, but not a difficult one to drive even when faced with a steep hill, the car took it easily which as they crested showed in front of them the house, where they hoped they might find Melinda and her brother Simon.

Cameron took the drive down the hill slowly. It gave warning to the people if there were people inside that they had visitors; it also gave Alan a chance to look the place over to assess what he could see that could be happening.

"I'm happy driving in slowly," Cameron said, "We're not trying to attack the place, so I want to go gently not intimidate anyone." He was more talking to himself than any of the others in particular. Pamela leaned from the back into the front seat.

"Melinda doesn't know either of you two, so my suggestion is, as long as nothing happens when we get down there Marcia and I will get out and go to the front door and see who's inside. We are not unhappy about doing this and you can keep an eye front and back for us ok. Alan asked. "Are you sure you don't want me to come with you?"

"Yes, but if you get out first, and let us out, you will be outside, and although you'll be more exposed, you won't be any worse off than us and you won't be restricted by the vehicle."

Cameron slowly drove towards the front of the building. He turned the vehicle to the right which allowed him to see directly through his window. "There is some movement of shadow inside the ground floor front window to the left of the front door. No curtain movement, but a slight shade shift that made me think something, or someone, caused it.

"Okay so someone is home lets go knock. If you will let Marcia and me out please Alan."

Alan climbed out and walked around to other side to let the ladies out. His hands went into his pockets and stayed there watching for anything untoward. Before they got up the front steps the main door opened and out came a man carrying a rifle. Alan recognized him as Simon instantly from the photograph. He was unshaven as lightly chubbier than he expected. His face and lower arms visible below the rolled-up sleeves showed a tanned and weathered look. His shirt and trousers looked like they needed a wash.

"Simon! It's me Pamela nice to see you."

"I'm sorry. Who the hell are you?"

"Pamela Thomas. A friend and a colleague of Melinda's. In point of fact, we all work for the same organisation."

"Now I remember you. We met once a long time ago. Why are you here?"

"To find out what goes on and see why you've disappeared off the work sheet."

"Who are these two?" He waived his rifle towards the car.

"They are fellow workers."

"Melinda is inside with her husband, and her son. Bring your friends in. it'll get warm even though it's only late April it'll get hotter than this."

Marcia signalled to Cameron and Alan to join them. Cameron wound up his window and they headed inside.

"It isn't any cooler in here." Simon said, "but inside you won't burn in the sun. People round here avoid going out too much, you end up red, then brown, then old before your time, and gnarled like the olive trees we grow here. If they weren't a warning to what the sun can do to your body I don't know what is. I'm Simon and you are gentlemen?"

"Peter Cameron and Alan Lewis how do you do?" Cameron and Alan shook hands.

"Take a seat guys I shall take the ladies to Melinda she is out the back and was feeding her little one when you arrived. I'll get you some coffee, or tea if you prefer, when I check with them in the back room."

Neither Alan nor Cameron sat down. But kept themselves standing and alert.

A few minutes later Marcia returned with Simon.

"Tell them what you know Simon. These are the people who will get us out of here. We both know Conway does not deal with amateurs. And we've got this far let's see if we can get it all the way."

"It's like some western movie, but it's real and not in any way funny. We're holed up here, sort of, we're not getting bothered by anyone, at the moment, because they're doing someone, somewhere else. Melinda is in her bedroom in the back of the house. She has a three-month-old son, Her husband, Miguel, is in bed. He has a gunshot wound to his upper chest, right shoulder, he has been treated by a doctor; the bullet went right through, does not appear to have done any damage, other than two holes, unsurprisingly, however he is not comfortable, and in some pain. We got him treated about a week ago but other than keeping it clean and changing the dressing now and again there's not been anything else we can do. He is able to walk. He is young and strong, so we are lucky in that respect.

If it's possible we are more than happy to go back to the England but there would have to be the four of us.

Melinda won't go obviously without her baby and also her husband. And me as well. Tell me what is the problem with the numbers?"

"The plane will only carry eight passengers, and we will be nine," Marcia told him.

"When it's nine we will be in France in Perpignan. We're out of here and out of the war zone, not a problem." Alan had joined the conversation. "I can travel back on my own, making my way through France is not any sort of a problem for me. Let's get the job done. Do you have a vehicle here?"

"Yes. We have a four-seater car."

"Will it start and run to Reus airport ok?"

"Yes it normally starts and runs fine. Father bought an Austin, so it's got a starting handle as well, but we've never needed to use it

"Then we will load you all into it and drive to Reus. How long will it take for you to get ready?"

"I can go as I am."

"You will need clothing for the flight, and everything for the baby and Melinda. It will get cold. Let's get moving; we will just chuck it all in and make it work. Take essentials only though, and only enough for two days. Do you drive?"

"I can. But I was thinking we have a baby, and Miguel, both of whom will need some support."

"Where is your car?"

"Out behind the house, it has enough room for us plus a driver.

If you will drive their car Peter, I'll take our ladies, and the Plymouth Alan suggested and when you get to the airfield we'll cover you while you head straight for the plane; drop everyone off and then get them into the plane. We hopefully will get airborne quickly in case someone there decides to finish the job on Miguel off."

Cameron knows to leave the security to Lewis and is happy to go with his plan.

"Right Simon show me the car and then help everyone else to get going. The quicker we get out of here the better. Marcia will you do whatever you can with Pamela and Melinda please. Alan here's the keys to the Plymouth." Aalan took the keys and glanced at the rifle.

"Does the rifle work Simon?"

"Don't know I've never fired it. It was given to Miguel after he was shot to protect himself. I don't know if he ever fired it either."

"May I have a look? Do you have any bullets?"

"I don't know anything about guns. I was just walking around with it pretending."

Alan was checking it over. "You would have either had to hit them with it or thrown it at them it doesn't have any bullets these are blanks and no firing pin either."

"Is that what they gave it to Miguel to protect himself?"

"Yes. Fine friends they turned out to be."

Alan chucked it ion the settee. He wasn't going to need a club. He didn't want to get that close to any opposition.

Simon, Melinda, her baby, and her husband went out the back way into the car. Silmon locked the house, though he knew it would almost certainly be vandalized and empty, if they ever got back here. Marcia and Pamela got into the Plymouth, and they led the way back to the road. Alan put his gun between his legs and drove gently.

Cameron, he knew would have to take it carefully with Melinda in the front seat and Miguel's wound showing signs of fresh blood before they'd even started.

At the gate he got out to open it. Marcia slid across and drove out and parked just far enough away to let Cameron out. Alan made the gate look locked it might give the illusion of still being occupied.

"I can drive this." Marcia said, save your credentials being blown off by accident from a bump in the road."

"Are you sure?"

"You mean if I can drive?"

"No. If your trying to save my credentials." Alan took the front passenger seat. Pamela had a little giggle. They overtook Cameron and led the way back to Reus airfield. As they neared the airport Marcia slowed and then stopped. Cameron tucked in behind. Alan got out and went back to check the passengers in Cameron's car.

"We arranged with the pilots to start the engine as soon as they saw   the car coming back. I reckon just before the airport stop and hold out of sight for just a couple of minutes and then follow us in. By that time, we'll be ready to get your passengers aboard. Cameron gave him a nod, and they continued on.

Their plane was parked up at the far end of the runway. Outside the main building there were now two military type vehicles and a number of men in some sort of uniform lounging around in chairs. They were outside the building but in the shade. When the Plymouth arrived nothing happened, and no one moved. When the Austin showed there was a spontaneous flurry of activity, and some of the men jumped into one of the vehicles and headed towards the plane. Bertie was outside and Patrick had the engines running. As arranged they had started them as soon as they saw the red vehicle coming through the gates.

Marcia had backed the car towards the plane blocking the view of Melinda and family as they scrambled aboard. Alan stood and waited both Berettas now in his hands but hidden behind his back.

Marcia shouted, "Is everyone in? Pam get in cover us from door. Mr. Cameron?"

"I'm covering you and Alan dear." She looked around to find Cameron also armed with two pistols and like Alan in his hands hidden behind his back. She just stood there with her hand hanging onto her shoulder bag.

"Why don't you get aboard Marcia?" Cameron asked

"You don't think these morons are going to speak kings English do you Peter. We'll be lucky if they understand Spanish properly. I'm here to talk but be ready please guys I reckon with what information I've got this far from Melinda is they don't want to kill them because they are British nationals, but her husband is on their list for execution. If they get caught in a cross fire and die accidentally, just in the wrong place at the wrong time, and the same will apply t us all.

The small military truck was nearly here when it made its turn as they suspected it would and blocked the line of the plane. Four men jumped out from the tailgate carrying rifles. The driver, his window already open, half pointed his rifle through the window. One man, their assumed leader, as Marcia had said speaking in Spanish.

"We are here to arrest the man Miguel Fonsi."

"Do you not speak English? Marcia asked. Certain that at best his English would be limited.

"No speak English. The man in office said you speak Spanish."

"I do but my friends don't."

"Fonsi has escaped from custody; and he is wanted for crimes against the state."

"He was freed." Marcia told them, "and pardoned, no case to answer".

"I am still going to arrest him. When he goes to court, and a judge tells us to let him free, he will go free. But my orders now are to arrest him and deliver him to our station in Barcelona. He is wanted by the state. My job is to bring him in. Thank you for bringing him here. Now you must step back and allow us to take him. Or we will be obliged to arrest you too, for withholding an escaped prisoner. You understand Senora?"

"No. I do not."

"It is simple Senora give him to us, or you all get arrested."

"It's showtime Alan"

Marcia her hand still on her bag, shot him through the hand bag and he hit the ground as Marcia turned towards the other three. They had hardly made a move not realizing that their officer had been shot, and still looking in Marcia's direction, died when Alan shot them. The driver didn't know what to do and he wasn't quick enough to do anything but die Cameron's single shot through the window hit him in the head.

"I'll move the truck," said Alan, "you get on the plane and I'llsend it off down the road at the rest of them". Alan dragged the dead driver out, did a a quarter reverse turn which headed it towards the main building. He jammed the driver's rifle onto the accelerator as he jumped out. The vehicle was heading towards the main building. Even more activity was now taking place; but this time it was panic and chaos, Cameron pulled Alan into the airplane as Patrick had started to move. Bertie got the door shut right and flopped back into his seat.

"Stay on the floor guys" Bertie said "wait till Patrick has us up and away before you move. you'll be safe enough down there. You lot don't mess about do you?"

Two hours later Patrick landed at Perpignan airport. Pamela had a look at Miguel's wound and gave it a clean and plugged the holes and redressed it using the first aid kit that the airplane carried.

Bertie was surprised it had anything in it. In all the years he'd been flying he never ever seen one used.

Before they left the aircraft Bertie called a meeting.

"While you were collecting passengers, Patrick and I had a discussion about the flight back to England. We have eight seats and nine people plus pilot. We are not carrying any significant weight of luggage. And we don't have anything close to our maximum range to fly. If one person is happy to sit on the floor for the journey Patrick and I are quite prepared to fly all of us back. Obviously when we get to Paris Gaston will be leaving us and then we will have enough seats and won't be breaking any British civil aviation rules when we land there. Are we ok with this?"

"More than happy." Said Alan, "and I will take the floor if no one minds. I found the takeoff quite exhilarating."

"It's the landing we need to worry about. Heavy breaking and you'll be up the front with Patrick or me. We don't wat that so we need to jamb you behind the e back seats, but we can pad it out with a cushion or two. Okay with this?"

"Got to be better than hitching a ride home."

"Good then let's get some food sorted. Hopefully, Gason has found a place, not too far, where we can eat and relax. I'll get the mechanics to check it all over so grab your valuables and everything that you don't want to be seen or found, and tomorrow morning we'll get the weather report and go to Clermont. Refuel there and tomorrow night if it's a slow one we'll be in Paris or if it goes well and it's quick we'll be back in London."

Sitting in the restaurant later on Marcia leaned into Alan.

"I said, when we first left a short while ago, we looked like a couple. We should have dinner together sometime away from the madding crowd and talk about nice things rather than how many have you shot today then Mr. Lewis."

"I seem to remember you shot the first one. I wondered why your bag was so heavy."

"It was the easiest way to get it done. I reckoned telling you what to do might have not worked, but Conway told us you knew what you were at, so I knew I cloud get one shot off, and you and Peter would get the others. Pam would have been ready on the plane as well if it got into a fire fight. But no more of this dinner and some friendship maybe if we get on well enough. We live lonely lives I suspect Mr. Lewis. I have been working for Mr. Conway for nearly ten years; it pays well but has limited fun opportunities. Friends in the same boat understand the job and forgive the sudden disappearances. It goes with the territory. Think about it. I do a great lamb roast, if you want to eat in. Now I've said that, stone cold sober, and I am going to get steaming on a bucket of wine. Do me a couple of favours. Keep my glass filled and make certain I get back to the airport and to bed please."

They got away from Perpignan early and headed for Clermont Ferrand. Pam was helping Melinda. Marcia had a hangover. Gaston kept quiet and went with the flow. Miguel was supported by Simon, Cameron sat next to Patrick. Bertie had the joystick, and Alan was comfortable and slept all the way To Clermont, wondering if he should take up the offer of a lamb roast sometime in the future.

They got crepes and coffee at Clermont, Pamela checked Miguel's wound again. It was bleeding a bit but not excessively.

At Paris Gaston left them, he hugged everyone, some with gallic passion, fragile others gently, and took away a sheaf of papers and information regarding feasibility of flying Paris to Reus as a regular flight.

Alan took Gastons seat. Marcia was well sobered up. Melinda was surprisingly sweet, given her previous reputation. Simon said they had changed when their parents left. They both realised that they were not particularly pleasant people. Melinda had changed with the marriage and the baby. Simon did so because he felt he ought to, but didn't know why as yet, other than he knew he needed to take care of his sister and her husband until he was better.

They landed at London and sat. Pamela left the plane and headed to the main building entrance. She showed her id and was let inside. She came out after ten minutes or so and beckoned everyone off the plane. The pilots joined them while ground crew moved the plane to a hanger for a service check over and refuel.

A customs officer showed them all into a private VIP type of lounge.

The curtains, on the windows, were closed. The officer asked that they remain so please. Would they like anything to eat or drink?

"Tea, coffee, sandwiches, hot water to feed baby."

It took an hour for Conway to arrive. He came in with both Martin and Richard. He looked around at everyone and for the first time ever they saw Conway smile like he meant it.

"I have outside some transport for you all. There is a car for Cameron and Lewis to Woolwich. Miss Thomas and Miss Johnson a vehicle to take you to your homes. Take tomorrow off back in the office day after and debrief then. I have a car to take Simon, Senor Fonsi Melinda, and child to a private hospital, location as private as the hospital. We can get your injury sorted there and you, Melinda, and baby can get checked. You can come along for the ride Simon.

Cameron and Lewis I will debrief you tomorrow I will come to Woolwich. I will phone first Cameron, about midmorning. Well done everyone and thank you. Now let's get going, pick up your bags, customs are bypassed, Martin clear the way for them please."

Pamela and Marcia had been sitting talking to Melinda and the extended family. Cameron and Lewis gave them a wave before they left. Simon mouthed Thank you.

Outside, by the side of the building, there were four Humber government cars. The three front one's with liveried chauffeurs and presumably it was Conways at the back. Martin pointed to the front car ladies first just tell him where you want to go and he will drop you off there. Before they left they hugged Cameron and Lewis. Marcia
whispered 'lamb roast' turned and walked away.

"Gentlemen, second car, bags in boot please. His orders are Woolwich, he knows where he's going."

Ninety minute s later Cameron and Lewis are back at Woolwich.

"Do you think there's any possibility we can get something to eat sir?"

"Let's go to the pub we can get something there."

"I'm carrying four pistols and one hundred and ninety six rounds of ammunition." Alan reminded him.

"You'll be alright you can't leave them here and chalky won't be in the armoury at this time."

They headed for the red lion. It was early and quiet. They could have something with chips, beef pie, eggs, or sausages; midweek was never the full menu.

They'd settled for sausage and chips, and in walked Douglas. He spotted them picked up his pint and wandered over.

"Good evening gentlemen, are you working or have you finished?"

"Finished two hours ago, job done. Have a seat Dougie."

"Thank you Mr. Cameron I will." Dougie saw the duffle bag on the floor between Alan's legs when he took the seat next o Alan.

"Glad to see you're minding the goods Alan."

"Nowhere to leave them, we reckoned nobody was going to try and take them in here but just in case I have one loaded in my pocket."

"Seriously?" Douglas had asked but knew Alan was telling the truth.

"Most definitely."

"Do you want something to eat? We've just ordered." Cameron asked.

"No thanks, I've got food ordered at mess. I'm having Just a quick beer, then grub, and bed. We've got a delivery coming early tomorrow. Might be some interesting bits in it. Some new stuff you could do me a favour and have a look over it and see what you think. I would also suggest that keeping a piece each would be a good idea. Add somethings to come out of the end of them, lost or damaged in a shootout is not unusual. They'll go down as not repairable as a box of broken pieces in our spares box."

"Thank you Douglas," Alan said, "owe you another."

"Not at all. You never know when you might need something other than a service pistol. It's no good standing in a queue when someone's trying to inflict serious damage on you."

"We have a debrief tomorrow morning shall we come over after lunch?" Cameron asked.

"Perfect, I'm just hiding for twenty minutes, and my meal will be done soon so I'll see you tomorrow. Nice to have you back. Long may it continue."

Douglas swallowed his pint quickly and left.

"And we go and get a present each as well. Isn't that nice?"

"Are you going to take him up on his offer?" Cameron asked.

"I am. You can't hide a Webley in your pocket. Marcia and Pam proved that yesterday. I wondered why they both had big handbags with shoulder straps exactly the same, We know why now."

Mr. Conway's secretary phoned to let them know he was on his way. "Good morning gentleman. My personal thanks for what you managed in the last couple of days.

Cameron it will be on your record.

Lewis I've put a second pip on your shoulder. Not a dramatic increase but might get you a bit more attention in the short term.

Any problems Cameron?"

"Nothing we couldn't deal with sir. We had a bit of luck that they were at the first address we had. Once we were there, they were happy to get away. I think Pamela and Marcia were the motivators for that. I am not convinced they would have been so ready to follow us had the ladies not been there with us."

"There was some shooting I'm told"

"Five dead sir brought it on themselves."

"Details please."

"They wouldn't accept that Miguel Fonsi was a free man, and having shot him once, were keen to finish the job, Miss Johnson did for one Lieutenant Lewis did for three and I shot the driver blocking our take off with their vehicle. Lewis moved their truck and then sent the vehicle off in the direction of the remaining opposition and we got the hell out of there."

"Any problems with pilots?"

"None sir, both very professional, didn't appear to be bothered at all. The French chappie was happy enough going along for the ride."

"Use them again?"

"After their performance, no hesitation, can't speak for the French man though."

"No interest in the French pilot. How were Misses Johnson and Thomas?"

"Again, couldn't have done it without them. They were the catalyst that got it all moving both with Melinda and family, and sweet talking the French pilot into doing what we wanted."

"Anything to add Lewis?"

"No sir."

"Thank you again. No doubt I will be in touch at some time in the future. Nobody knows anything about this, nor are they ever to. You stay here for now Cameron and back to Salisbury Lieutenant."

"I have some weapons to return sir, and I said I would have a look at what the armoury has arriving today for future reference."

"I assume you are dealing with sergeant major white."

"Yes sir."

"Tell him I said hello. Douglas used to do some work for me many years ago. When Captain Cameron picked you to go to Berlin with him I spoke to Douglas; what he said was enough to confirm your position. Make you r own way back to Salisbury when you've done what you need to do. We shall no doubt speak again."

After lunch, pre-ordered from the officers mess, Cameron and Lewis headed down to the armoury to keep the promise to sergeant major White. The corporal on the main door did not query their right to be there and presumably the OOD was in his office and if he had known they were there would have acted the same.

"Come through the flap and look at what I wanted to show you."

In the backroom known to some, as Dougie's domain, was his desk, numerous weapons, boxes of ammunition, nuts, bolts, gun parts, books, papers, and service manuals. A small bench with a couple of vices also held more tools, oils, grease, and an overflowing ashtray, below a wall sign saying, 'no smoking'.

On the floor, near a Windsor chair, was a rough wooden case, with a top obviously skewed and loose.

"Have a look in that box Alan take it out it isn't loaded."

Alan lifted the lid. Inside wrapped in a cloth was what appeared to be a big rifle.

"What have we got here Dougie?"

"It's called a Bren gun. It's going to replace your namesake the Lewis gun. Magazine sits on top; based on a Czechoslovakian light machine gun. They've been testing them for about three years maybe even a bit longer. The story is Enfield will make them under license. That's just one of a few samples as I understand but they've shot more than fifty thousand rounds through them over the last few years, and they don't have any nasty habits. They tell me that they are going to start making them later this year. What do you reckon?"

"Either I'm getting stronger or it's lighter than the Lewis. How heavy is the magazine."

"It's in the grease proof roll in the bottom of the box. Specs say its lighter when loaded the sheets are on the table. Always depend on how much ammo your carrying and if you got a spotter with you who can do the mule work as well.

They wanted to replace the Vickers with it, but that's not going to happen. It comes with a bi pod and an optional tripod and as good as it's supposed to be I can't see it taking the Vickers' place."

Alan had passed the Bren over to Cameron.

"Will it shoot like a rifle?" Cameron asked.

"It's supposed to. I think I'd give it a couple of goes from the hip first it is heavier and I'm sure if you're strong enough there's no reason why you shouldn't. Cartridge are standard issue so kick shouldn't be an issue, but it comes with a bipod or a tripod and a folding side handle. If they've done that then there's been a reason. Any way that's what I wanted to show you. Let's put the returns away what did you break?"

"One of each replied Lewis and we shot nearly two boxes of ammo."

"Give me the two full boxes back, two guns, and two spare mags. I'll put the broken bits in the spares box." Dougie told them. "Keep the duffle bag till you find somewhere safe for your storage. Which one did you use Alan?"

"The Beretta and Captain had the Walther."

"You'll have no problem finding Ammo for them, though the 32ACP is more usual than the 38ACP there should always be plenty around for topping up supplies."

"Thanks Dougie Do you fancy a beer later?"

"Don't laugh or I'll regret telling you. Sorry I can't. I go ballroom dancing tonight with the missus. We do one night a week and to be honest I really enjoy it."

"Good on ya Dougie." Alan said, "if you're enjoying it, it's got to be worth doing. I'm back at Salisbury from tomorrow. So, another time it'll have to be."

Cameron and Lewis headed back to their office.

"Do we eat in or out?" Cameron asked. "We will only get the same offers as last night if we go to the Lion."

"I know and to be honest I don't fancy travelling anywhere else. Shall we eat in the mess then?" was Alan's suggestion.

Cameron and Lewis decided it was too late to order now so they wandered over to the mess for their evening meal.

The steward got them a table and a seat each

"It's chef's special tonight sir."

"What's that?" asked Cameron.

"Sausage, chips, and green beans, sir." Perhaps it was tiredness, or the delayed tension relief at the end of a job, but whatever it was Cameron and Lewis had a fit of the giggles.

"I'm sorry sir. Did I say something funny?"

"No private, just a coincidence, couldn't have planned it better myself."

"Very good sir do you want anything to drink?"

"No thank you."

The young private was feeling uncomfortable. Two officers, he didn't know, couldn't stop giggling. He felt like he was being laughed at and didn't know why.

Cameron thought he should reassure him he was looking worried

"Don't worry young man it's been a hectic couple of days, and it always seems to be sausage and something."

CHAPTER 4   1938   PARIS

"I remember asking you last year Cameron how good was your Spanish? This time is, How good is your French?"

"My answer is pretty much the same sir. I can get by in French, if they speak slowly. It's a lot better than my Spanish. I read both without any problem but not living with the constant conversation it's got very rusty."

"If I said I want you to go to France and do something similar to what you did in Germany with a view to not being there just a month but staying and developing a plan I've been thinking about for a while then I don't believe I need to ask this question. Who would you take with you?"

"Lieutenant Lewis."

He stayed just over an hour, left Cameron with a lot of papers, some French francs, sign here please, and an obscure brief as to what he was to do and achieve.

'During the Great war the criminal elements of Paris were one of the few groups who managed to maintain some degree of survival and some even increased development. Go and find them and befriend them as you did in Berlin and at the same time make friends with anyone in authority. How you do it is up to you.'

On Friday morning Cameron and Lewis were on their way to Paris. They arrived and reported, as instructed, to the office of the military attaché, at the embassy. An officer elderly stiff backed clipped moustache almost a cliché with an included limp like an old war wound spoke to Cameron at the counter, before the two of them disappeared behind closed doors, to see another staff man, while Lewis was left at the front desk, sorting out paperwork, with another younger and probably lower ranked assistant attaché, more Greek than Aristotle and more camp than a boy scout jamboree. When finished, he found a seat in the public side, not having got an invite through to the inner workings.

Cameron eventually returned, carrying a small bundle of papers, and what turned out to be a primitive hand drawn copy of a Michelin road map.

They left the embassy and headed out into the street. They talked as they walked.

"The chaps here, at the embassy, have found us some accommodation. Important thing is it's cheap. They have paid the rent for food and accommodation for two months in advance, but that, I've been informed, is all that they have been told to do. They won't provide us with any further financial assistance. As I expected, it was difficult enough to get them to even give us some worthwhile advice. The ones I've spoken to are more concerned about their personal careers than actually doing what the buggers are paid to do, and I guess they see us as unlikely to advance them up the diplomatic ladder with our project. The army chaps appear to be perfectly functional and doing what they're paid for, but the others see us outsiders as an unwelcome distraction;

and to be honest, I think they see us as something seedy and dodgy rather than useful."

They crossed a couple of roads and carefully avoided the French drivers who seemed intent on trying to kill pedestrians. Cameron was reading the map Alan had a backpack as well as a suitcase.

"I don't think it's much further now. What they've turned up is a small guest house. It normally caters for foreign seamen or immigrants, and often used by the heavies, who might be looking for a base, with few if any questions asked."

"Are you serious?"

"Unfortunately, I am. But they assure me that it is clean and safe. I don't see how the two statements fit together, but we are booked in, and it's paid for. I am told that reasonable quality lodging is usually expensive here but factoring in last year's Exposition has increased it to an even greater degree and even though the festival has clearly finished, prices are still at a premium."

They arrived at a four-storey, terraced building, after a couple of turns off the main road. There was little definition as to where if any pavement started or finished and given the distance between the houses any vehicle managing to negotiate the litter, and accumulating rubbish, would almost certainly be driving on one side pavement if not both.

 The solid timber glassless door was shut. There was a semi-circular fan light above the door. To the right of the door is another half round topped window. A line of similar topped windows ran vertically to the underside of the overhanging roof above. The rendered walls looked reasonably tidy, the windows were clean, and the outside appeared to be well maintained. There was a passage down the side of the house almost the same width as the street. Alan reckoned if the inside was as well maintained as the outside perhaps the embassy people might be right in their assessment of the building and fingers crossed whoever ran it. The ground floor window curtain was drawn so impossible to see inside. In the absence of a knocker all they could do was bang on the door. Once was enough a voice from inside called "A moment", and quite soon after that, the door was opened by a lady wearing a long loose cloak, and a headscarf. "Can I help you?"

Alan did the honours. "Madame I believe we have a room booked for a couple of months by the British embassy."

"You do. Please come in. I was told you were coming today. I'm glad you have arrived as I have cooked enough food for you as well as the others who are staying. You will need the food to give you the energy, as you are on the top floor. There is no lift to the penthouse suite and also fortunately neither of you are too tall not to be able to stand up straight for most of the space available. If you start to make your way up to the top, I shall get some papers and follow right behind you. Should you get there well before me please wait. I shall bring the keys to the room. The door will be locked."

Alan and Peter waited for only a moment when the manager lady arrived. She was carrying a large foolscap book and a bunch of keys.

She unlocked the door and walked in. The room was basic and smelt clean, like a cheap private hospital ward. A combination of bleach and disinfectant. One wall had a decent-sized opening window with a single curtain. There was a double wardrobe and two single beds with a washbowl and water jug on a table between them.

"The embassy has paid for you for eight weeks from today. The bedding has been changed and gets changed every fortnight. There are a few rules. No women in the house this is gentlemen only. No rowdiness and no drunkenness. Meal times are six to seven, morning and evening. My name is Fatima. I manage the property on behalf of my employer. I need to see some identification and you need to sign the register. Any problems speak to me." Alan and Peter completed the formalities and were given two keys each.

"One is the front door the other is for your room. Please don't lose either, it will be expensive to change the locks, and the embassy will not be happy to get a bill. Do you need any advice?"

Peter was just about following the talk. "Alan. You answer please"

"No madame. Not at this time. Thankyou. But I think that we will be seeking advice before too long if that is okay?"

"If I can, I will help. Evening meal will be ready at six o'clock. I will see you downstairs then. Just follow your nose and the dining room is at the end of the hall. The ground floor front room is mine. If I am in there it is because I am asleep. Unless the house is on fire please don't wake me up, my days are very long."

Alan and Cameron spent the weekend walking around the immediate area to get a feel for their location and to learn where all the places they might need for a longer term stay. They had found a laundry, one recommended by Fatima, a tobacconist a couple of public telephone kiosks, a post office and the nearest bank. They bought Michelin map and started to expand their range.

Cameron was learning to talk and follow conversation again. Speed is always an issue and just the simple spoken instruction to slow down with a hand signal at the same time and communication becomes easier.

A few days of chaperoning from Alan and Cameron was confident enough to try it on his own and while Alan took the rougher areas and those around the red light district Cameron worked his way around the commercial district and the government buildings. He had the map as a confidence booster on which he made notes as to what buildings were for possible future reference. The process was time consuming, but it had the benefit of both of them becoming familiar with the streets and people of Paris.

Gay Paris wasn't so gay. When it rained it was just as grey and gloomy as every other big city anywhere else in the world. The wind had got up. The rain wasn't exactly coming sideways yet if the low pressure didn't move then it would eventually. Eith er the wind or the rain needed to stop preferably the rain though as the street cafes would still feel damp and uninviting. Alan did not enjoy trying to find places where he could listen to conversation. Here in what was the slightly occasionally poor area of Paris a bar had too many unknowns. Finding someone to chat to was easy enough, especially if you were to buy them a drink, but what he wanted to do was eavesdrop and get a feel for what was going on in the city. Opinions expressed may tell you nothing other than a persons bigoted opinion but sometimes a snippet might prove useful. Someone selling something not too legal may just drift into a bar.

When it rained though the bars normally would lose all but the hardened drinkers, most of whom by midafternoon would be incapable of putting a coherent sentence together.

Alan was getting an idea about who and where the minor criminal element were and where they hung out. The small-time fences and thieves doing odd bits of trading in certain bars almost in full view of everyone watching. Then given the fact that most of the ones watching were generally of the same persuasion, with the same employment, it was hardly surprising that nobody appeared to be bothered. Alan would drink the occasional glass of wine or a beer but mostly he settled for coffee. He was continually conscious of spending money but as he was being fed by the government he thought maybe some investment from himself might be okay as long as it didn't get out of hand by too much.

It was on one such occasion when in one of his regular bars he managed to buy a bicycle, paint still damp, and a bit sticky, but should be ok to ride as long as you don't get too close to the crossbar with your trouser legs. This also gave him an in at the bar where previously he was looked on as known, but considered as potentially suspect, he was now one of the boys and though he was Swiss not French, he was ok; he also seemed keen on possibly buying other things, depending on what, and how much. When someone tried to steal his bicycle from outside the bar one afternoon, people also realised it was not a good idea to get in the wrong side of the man.

Midweek and after a rainy morning the sun was making a half-hearted attempt at warming up the wet streets of Paris in an area that separated the haves form the have nots. A car pulls up outside the bar. The car a black Citroen with a long bonnet very newish, not cheap, four doors, not a normal car for the clientele that generally frequented here. Alan had just arrived and ordered a coffee. Some of the tables are outside; a couple of them occupied by individuals, but the remainder free. Alan looked quickly at the car and took the number. The driver of the car spotted whomever he was meeting and strolled over to the table. Alan being nosey and not knowing either of the two men took his coffee and sat at an empty table not too near but within earshot of them. The car driver sat sideways on to Alan looking into the bar from the street. He was medium height about the same as Alan, but stockier build, slight paunch, about forty years of age. He wore a nicely tailored dark blue suit, polished shoes, clean white shirt and multi coloured striped tie. The car driver called over the waiter and quietly gave him his order.

The waiter went inside and came out with the manager. They came over to Alan's table and asked Alan if he would be good enough to come into the bar for a moment as they needed to discuss something in private.

"Monsieur I am sorry to ask you to join us in here but there is going to be a problem outside you are not part of the problem and are not involved."

"I don't understand." Alan told him.

There is going to be a fight Monsieur, and my advice is to stay in here and keep your head down when it kicks off. It will happen and just then it did. The driver of the car shot the other man at the table.

The manager and Alan were only just inside and a couple of feet away from the two men talking. The weapon was silenced, but then at exactly the wrong time, all had gone quiet outside, and Alan being Alan recognized the sound of a silenced pistol. He had fired three quick shots, then got in his car, as did the other three people who had been sitting outside at different tables. They had obviously been aware of what was about to happen and when Alan looked back at how it was; they had actually surrounded the victim, and he would have been unable to escape before one of the others stopped him.

It had been set up for a hit, and the one good thing about it was that Alan had not been caught in the crossfire, and didn't end as collateral damage. "Thank you Monsieur." Alan said to the manager perhaps one day I may be able to repay the favour. When will the police arrive do you think?"

"Soon perhaps if I were you I would leave quickly now as you did not see anything because you were inside here having a coffee. You have no idea what it is all about."

Alan finished his coffee, and he made an unhurried exit from the bar into the street. A small crowd had gathered, then almost as quickly disappeared. Today he had not used his bicycle as the roads had still been wet and the cobbled streets made riding up and down hills an unnecessary dice with an accident and assuming he managed to negotiate it all safely the cycle would leave him soaked by the spray from the tyres, and the inadequate mudguards. No one made any eye contact when he left, and he walked slowly along the street up the hill. At the junction of Rue Rouet by the corsetry shop he turned left again and continued up the hill until he came to another turning where he made another left turn and having started a gentle walk for a few yards he checked behind him and got a move on. He made a couple more left turns got back to near the main road again took off his jacket folded it over his arm and rejoined the road that the bar was on. He was now maybe a couple of hundred yards from the bar and outside were two what looked like police cars though he hadn't heard them arrive and now what was an ambulance looking at the red cross on the side panel. Alan spent a short while looking in the window of a tool shop; not at anything in particular, but he was in no rush to get away. Anyone who has been a party to a crime is likely to make a swift exit anyone looking in a tool shop window is hiding in full view. When he left the café he was wearing a dark blue jacket and a dark tie. The jacket was over his arm the tie was rolled up in a jacket pocket. Another police car was coming along the road it passed him, and he caught its reflection in the shop window. He thought he would just go in enquire on the cost of a set of spanners for his bike. Not that he had any intention of buying any, but he could if questioned by the police unlikely as it was might be remembered by the shopkeeper. Job done no more to do wander slowly back to lodgings perhaps a change of bar for a while might be a good idea.

Up in their room before the evening meal, after Lewis had written down the car registration number and a complete description of the man who did the shooting, he filled Cameron in on the details of what had happened at the bar earlier on.

"What do you think it was all about?" Cameron asked

"I don't really know other than it was a hit, and it was well set up. The only problem that they had was me, and I was surreptitiously moved out of the way before anything happened. The target had been effectively surrounded by having three others in there around him. Whether he knew what was happening, or didn't, we'll never know. But possibly rather than killing an innocent bystander as well or a witness to the crime they had me invited inside or just in case the target realised what was happening and he did a runner and I was in the way, who knows. But out of the way inside I wasn't in the way and where I neither saw nor heard anything. Innocent foreign nationals shot in Paris could create investigations and become an unnecessary problem. Whereas let's say one criminal professionally removing another criminal might be considered as a good result for everyone and the file in the pending disposal tray. I am not suggesting there is any collusion but clean and simple is easily the better way.

"I get the feeling," Cameron said, "that what you are telling me is that you are taking what happened this afternoon as not so much as being a witness to murder or execution as more of a well-rehearsed lesson in how to deal with an insurmountable problem in a perfectly acceptable way."

"That's probably as near to the truth as it gets. It looked like it was well planned and maybe even used before but whatever it was it was slick, and it worked, and I will avoid the bar and the area for a while, but I will go back in a week or so and see if anything further develops. However, I did take the number of the car a black Citroen as well as a description of the shooter. It might be a good idea to see if there's anyone at the embassy who has a pal in the French registry and see who it belongs to. If we keep an eye on the newspapers we may get a bit more information on who got shot and then we can find out why. If Mr. Conway persists in his idea of getting involved with France's criminal elements then I want the odds when and where I can be stacked in my favour. Given what happened in Spain last year I'm reluctant to work any other way and if Conway pushes us to get involved then every lesson and trick in the book we learn can only be of benefit, and just to be an alarmist we have also learned how we could be quickly and simply surrounded by the wrong people in the wrong place and disposed of. That is a bonus lesson."

At that moment Fatima banged the dinner gong. Cameron instinctively looked at his watch.

"Let's eat I've had enough though t for food now I'm properly hungry."

"What's on the menu?"

"It's Tuesday," Cameron replied, "Chicken tagine with couscous."

Alan had spent the following week wandering about in other parts of lower middle-class working class areas. His cycle purchase had been a lucky find or someone elses unlucky loss. He was at worst though getting exercise and riding around Paris was a lot quicker or cheaper than either walking or taxiing. The criminal element seemed to consist mostly of prostitution, some illegal gambling, some protection rackets. The odd one out was the killing of the man at the bar a week back. No one was talking about it, no one mentioned it when Alan stopped off there, on his way back from his afternoon excursion.

Both the waiter and the bar manager nodded a hello but nothing else when he sat outside.

The weather had perked up a bit and the wind having dropped and the rain dried off Paris had to a certain extent started to return to its happier bouncy self. The waiter brought Alan a coffee.

"On the house Monsieur, welcome back, sorry, you had to rush your last coffee, manager sends his compliments and hopes to see you again whenever you wish.

'Thank you' was all Alan could say. It was unexpected but he got the feeling the line had been drawn under the episode now and whatever had happened was no longer of either interest or concern.

Cameron and Alan had been there nearly a month. When after dinner one evening they were sitting in their room. They were going through their accounts and trying to work out what they knew what had they learnt from there travelling around and conversations with others.

Camerons French conversation was developing very quickly and improving daily. Because of his understanding of French and having a large vocabulary it was only a matter of time, before his conversational fluency would improve. While Alan had spent his time talking to people on the street, Cameron had put on his best suit and spent time talking to anyone he could find who worked in any of the French government departments.

When Alan had suggested this, Cameron thought the idea preposterous. how was he going to get into conversation with French officials? Alan's answer had been to go to the embassy, speak to the military attaché, tell them not to mess about, that in the end we are working for the same government, and shortly you will be going back to London to file your report to members of the government, and if that report says the Embassy and staff in Paris need some sort of shaking up then you suspect that that is going to be the unfortunate outcome. So do me a favour and do yourselves one at the same time and get me into contact preferably with military and defence people so that I'm not wasting my time here. Cameron agreed and reckoned something had to happen, so he decided to give it a go and

It worked slowly at first, but as Cameron said, not before 'I'd squandered some money on food and drink with the wrong persons.' Then, out of the blue, the right one turns up. Cameron continued with his story.

"Importantly he offers to buy me lunch, happy to take me into his confidence, appearing to be interested in a posting to London where he thinks it could be a smart career move. Why? I asked him. 'For a number of years, it has been my responsibility to monitor defence spending of other European nations. Britain is comparatively low on the list certainly lower than France. Others have a normal spend typical of previous years, but Germany is rearming and there is a genuine fear in a lot of places that Hitler has a plan, and it won't be for the benefit of others.

At expo last year there was problems between the Germans and the Russians here in Paris Sabre rattling is taking place and in a number of other countries and given the political ideology of the loudest rattlers prospects for continuous peace seem bleak. Spain is in turmoil on our Southern border Germany is around the other end and making offensive noises. Some of the French government believe that Germany is their friend and ally. Trying to convince them otherwise is proving to be a difficult and insurmountable problem.'

"We discussed issues that i was both interested in and knowledgeable about but what this contact didn't have available was facts and figures he could show to prove his theories and his concerns. Every time he had shown superiors his ideas and projections their argument had been that it was supposition and just as easy to argue that it could be accounting and catch-up and alarming people unnecessary and counterproductive. He knew he was being fobbed off by his superiors but there was nothing he could do about it.

He promised me if he could get his hands on more concrete information he would contact the attaché at the embassy who he knew would then contact me. To keep his interest and motivation I said I would discuss the possibility of a n assisted move to London if a position could be found for him and his immediate family when he reported back to my department head."

Apart from this man little more had happened and when Cameron got together with Alan they both knew it was time to make some moves one way or another. They had been here a month and though they were making contacts and listening and learning they were limited in what they could achieve when they continually were supplementing the budget with their own funds.

Alan suggested to Cameron that he was getting short on his own money and thought Camreron must be in a similar situation.

Cameron could do no ore than agree with him. "I'm glad you brought this up Alan. We don't have an open-ended budget, so I don't really know what they expect us to achieve, if finance isn't forthcoming. Currently I think I'm bankrolling his majesties government, out of my own personal savings, which won't last for a great deal longer, unless we find some extra curricula employment, and I don't believe that's a viable solution."

"May I make a suggestion?"

"Of course."

"Go back to London and tell them if we don't get a decent level of funding, nothing is going to happen, and all the work we've done so far will be wasted."

"They'll laugh at me."

"Then you tell them we're on our way home, and we're resigning our commissions, and when the war starts as it will, they'll be trying to catch up again, and they'll be a country mile behind if they're lucky.

The talk in Paris is of a war in Europe. Not if but when. If the Parisians think it, why isn't anyone listening to them I wonder. My suggestion is to go back and wake them up."

"Now I ask you are you serious?" Cameron looked hard at Lewis when he asked the question. He too had a similar feeling, given what he had heard and witnessed, over the last couple of years.

"Yes I think war is inevitable. When? Who knows. We started this in Berlin and even then one felt something was going on. Jewish situation with the athletes and people being rehoused in camps which are more like prisons. Some of us know what's happening. We're telling others what's happening, but they are saying they think we're wrong or they're in denial."

"They're not proof that a war will happen."

"No, I know. But no one has done anything to stop what's happening. And what happens after that is; we've got away with that; now what else can we do? We know the Germans are rearming if they don't need to kill anyone, why are they rearming? Give someone a gun and ammunition and tell them not to play with it and how long does that last? Ok you don't need to threaten to leave or resign commissions that's face minus nose, but it isn't possible to carry out our brief without some money coming in and some idea as to what they really want us to do."

"Right, I'll leave tomorrow. I'll go down to the Embassy and let them know what's happening and get some travel vouchers off them."

While Cameron has gone back to London to raise funds Alan continues learning about where they are living. He has walked all around the area so he knows how to get from all the landmarks, such as the louvre, the arc de triomphe, the Eiffel tower, back to his residence and short cuts through alleys and side streets that only a pedestrian can get down. This allows him to time journeys on foot and occasionally with his cycle.

When he had a few days learning these he took his second hand bicycle and repeats what he knows and times everything he learns the routes that he would do in a car if he had one and steadily worked and learnt as much as he could as if he was a budding cab driver. He located other bars shops of interest. He found where the banks were the post office the red light district chatted to some of the working girls and was threatened by some heavies. Decided it wasn't either the time or a good idea to prove a point so let it be. But it was logged in his head as to who had threatened him and he was never happy being bullied by anyone when he was not at fault. The bully went on his list as did the bar come brothel to be sorted if need arose. Fatima provided some information as where to get his laundry done and whom to avoid in the street they were living in. she said most of everyone who lived in the immediate area were fine. Her employer owned a couple more guest houses in the street with similar working men rooms were available. None she hastened to add were as good a house as the one she kept. As Cameron wasn't eating at the house and the rent and food had been paid for in advance Fatima offered Alan Lunch if he wanted it. She was not in a position to make any reductions or extensions to their stay but if he wanted lunch and coffee there was no reason why that could not be accommodated. Given his now impecunious circumstances he accepted the generous offer which allowed him to spend his days learning his way around Paris on his bicycle and avoided any need to seek refreshment in any of the bars or cafes.

It was over a week later when Cameron returned.

"I'll keep it brief," he told Alan, "Otherwise it will be tomorrow before I finish. It was a very full week. I got a meeting with Talbot Conway. I explained to him what was happening. He was up to his usual tricks. He sent us over here with a loose brief to see what we'd make of it. It seems we didn't disappoint him. My going back was the right move and demanding some support it meant we'd established that there was enough to do to justify a probable project that needed helping. He got me a meeting with some secretary chap. Which I didn't have much hope about. How wrong could I be? Transpires, this man is linked to a number of MPs who are opposed to government paying lip service to Hitler. One of them is Winston Churchill and although I didn't get to meet him, I got the feeling that his opposition to what has been happening and the anti-appeasement stance he took is making him very unpopular with some, but extremely popular with others. The others have leaned on a few and we have a great deal more financial clout than we had before and a promise of extra staff when we need them and although the budget isn't huge, they have instantly repaid me everything I have so far paid out of my own money and also some to refund you. Which in itself appears to be a first. We are being taken seriously by some people, of that there is no doubt. We're back in business, Alan. And added to this is the embassy and we are on a different support level. They have been instructed to support us in any way they can within reason of course. But primarily they are to provide us with assistance when we need to communicate when we ask for advice if they know they are to tell us if we need any support transport or equipment etc. we get it if it's possible."

"Well done sir."

"We're a team again Alan slightly different but nevertheless a team. I can play the diplomat, and creep quite successfully, and you are the enforcer and doer, and now we have the opportunity to beef up our players when we need to. That alone makes me happier. If you hadn't pushed me a ten days back I'd still be sitting here trying to run this off my savings. Thankyou."

"You're very welcome sir and thank you for the honesty."

"It's good to be back, now let's go downstairs and eat."

While Alan continued with his journeys and being nosey around the low life and down and outs of which there was an abundance of in the poor areas, Cameron spent a couple of days talking to people at the embassy and establishing his needs and letting finally the right people know what he required. He thought it was all a bit vague and to a certain extent it was but all he had been given by Conway was a broad loose idea and if not an open ended budget at least enough to get the ball rolling.

He was asked where Lieutenant Lewis was and what he was doing. Why wasn't he with him here. Cameron told them. 'He is supposed to be a Swiss national. He doesn't want to be seen continually going in and out of the British embassy when he's a Swiss. If you want to see him organise a meeting outside in a café or a park or wherever you want'.

The following evening as Lewis returned to the guest house Fatima passed a letter to him.

"A young man from your embassy gave me this about an hour ago."

Alan opened it up and having read it showed it to Cameron.

It was from the assistant that had interviewed Alan when they had first arrived in Paris. He had been given the job of their embassy link person.

"His name is Graham." Alan told him.

"I don't remember him." said Cameron.

"You probably didn't see him. He was the young chap who came out to see me while you were inside talking to one of the others. He and I had finished our business before you came out from the back office."

"That explains it. What's he like?"

"Delicate, more diplomatic service than military. Which sounds rude about the diplomats but this chap isn't any hard assed nutcase. He's presumably bright and intelligent or something else which could be anything between Daddy can you get me a post in Paris or where the hell can we dump him out of the way?"

"Let's hope it's the first one, bright and intelligent" Cameron replied. "We don't need any more idiots on the team we can fill those positions."

He had proposed a meeting for tomorrow afternoon 'let's say around three' was the ask from the embassy man. 'That way I'm not trying to drink coffee on a full stomach or risking spoiling a perfectly good evening meal with too much gateaux'.

He'd suggested a café a short walk from the embassy with outside tables and cover inside if it was raining. 'It's on a corner with a red pull down shade and red parasols over the outside tables. You can't miss it if you're at the right corner. If you can't see it you're in the wrong place'.

"Do you know it Alan?"

Yes a bit upmarket from where I normally frequent. Let's hope it's not too busy, it is quite popular."

At two minutes to three Alan and Peter arrived at the café. Graham was already there. He had secured an outside table with three seats close to the front windows, well sheltered from the cool breeze blowing up the street by the building itself, the sun was hiding somewhere behind a grey sky which looked to promise rain but hopefully not before close of their business. Alan made the introductions and Cameron and he took seats.

"Are you ok Alan?" Graham asked.

"I like to have my back to a wall, " Alan replied "It comes with my job description"

"Then we must change. I have ordered a large pot of coffee and a cake. The staff are waiting for you to arrive and I expect it all to arrive shortly." They had changed seats and he continued with his briefing. The embassy has an account here and we do our external meetings. It is always crowded which I know in theory is asking for someone to eavesdrop on the conversation but we don't say anything that could create a problem and sometimes there are safety in numbers. We are surrounded by a lot of people here in a busy area with difficult parking and as you are doing now what I normally do and watching everything that is going on. We are as safe as can be guaranteed if one can ever guarantee anything one doesn't have complete control of.

The waiter arrived with a tray three cups and saucers a pretty looking cream and jam sponge cake three plates and forks and two large coffee pots one with thick black strong coffee and the other with hot milk. Graham signed the chitty for the waiter after he had carefully placed everything on the table.

"Do help yourselves gentlemen we shall indulge in the cake and leave the chat for a moment; one might easily spoil the other.

Graham sliced the cake into thirds and placed it into the plates.

He poured the coffees and as promised he let the mouth savour the taste as Cameron described it. 'Quite the most delicious cake'. When the second coffees had been poured Graham continued his briefing.

"In my case there are two files. One file contains a short list of prospective business es that might be in need of some investment and assistance. The list isn't particularly long and to be honest there is only one that might be suitable and I give you a warning there is the possibility of violent physical issues with all of them but the worst is also the most suitable for your purposes. They are short of manpower which is why they are in there and my advice is do what you are doing now watch carefully and keep your back to the wall. The second file is a brief description of an employment agency we shall call them. They can provide labour and assistance if you require some. Your best bet is to speak to them first because if you can do a deal with them you will have something to trade with your prospective business partners. They are well known; the embassy use them as do other embassies, and as I believe though I can't confirm it I believe the government here and the local councils use them I In what capacity I cannot tell you because I don't know. Don't misunderstand this. They provide general cleaning and office cleaning and gardening, fruit picking. They are well known for those things but they do other things that are not so well known. I can vouch for that as they have done work for us here when required. Which is as far as I'm going on that. I will tell you though that I would wholeheartedly recommend them without any reservations whatsoever. They have never let us down. I sound like I'm selling them to you and I possibly am insofar as I don't know any better than them that don't come with strings attached. I am their link at the embassy so I have dealt with them on more than one occasion. Mr Conway, though he hasn't had any direct dealings with them, knows about them. It was he who gave me the go ahead for us to get involved in your project. Mr. Conway I can tell you if you hadn't already realised has more fingers than any normal human and they are all in a variety of various sizes of pie. You are playing a game that none of us will own up to knowing anything about. Your original brief from Mr. Conway left you isolated and on your own. I can tell you nothing has really changed you are still on your own but you will get a limited amount of deniable back up from us if absolutely necessary. There will be nothing that can be proven and nothing that could attract political problems for any of us in the embassy. We have a couple of staff members who have been provisionally allocated to 'filling in' duties basically so they can drop in to assist you in an urgent situation. All understood so far?"

"The information for contacting the relevant people presumably is in the file?" Cameron asked.

"Yes."

"Are we likely to require any other info about them?"

"If you do you will have to find it yourself. What I've supplied is everything we have. If something relevant or important becomes known, we will be in touch again via your guest house. I will give you another piece of useful information. That guesthouse is extremely safe for reasons I need not go into at this time as they're not important. Should you leave there for any reason, let us know at the embassy immediately. Any other questions?" He asked as he took the two foolscap folders from his briefcase and passed them to Cameron.

"I don't believe there are thankyou Graham for your time and the cake and coffee."

"Then I shall beat it back to the office. I'm off on Sundays so you can get me six days a week, eight to six, if you need me. Outside those hours I'm difficult to find. Good luck with your projects gentlemen."

He shook hands quickly and was away. He did move very quickly and as if they had been left in the starting blocks he had gone from sight when Cameron and Lewis made their exit.

Cameron had picked up the two well wrapped folders both quite thin and light weight.

"Clever and bright" said Alan

"Yes thank goodness." Cameron replied "And I see what you mean about being fragile and a bit Greek. But if he's turned up with the info we need in those files I'll forgive him anything."

Later in their room they had opened the two files.

"What are your thoughts then Alan?"

"We seem to have two choices for each of the proposals either we say yes or no. The back up people is straight forward. If we need back up then there seems no alternative to the one suggested other than a potential problem as the others are criminal organisations and we are likely to be having to negotiate ourselves out of trouble all the time. The bar that has been suggested as a cover possibility is a totally different ball game. He is the sort of person who you would not want in your security set up as you would be renegotiating yourself out of trouble. We have to decide how close we want to fly to being outside the law. If we analyse what Conway asked us to do it was to find a way of getting involved with the criminal elements of Paris so that from the inside we could keep an eye on what was going on. Am I reading that as accurate?

"I think that pretty well sums it up. Given that should there be another war of whatever size, Conway seems to think that criminal elenemts might not be averse to working with us rather than against us for a price of course, and rightly, I think, believes that we need to know who we are possibly going to be dealing with or against before it kicks off because finding out during will be no easy task."

"Pretty much as I see it as well. At least I'm not missing anything." Alan replied. "When he sends us on these things he leaves us to get on with it. Here is the start. Here is your finish. Get it done, the middle bit is yours, don't get it wrong, if you do you're on your own. Nothing has changed, other than the location, from all the other times then."

"Sadly, I'm with you it is as I see it too." Cameron sounded resigned as to what they had to do ."Ok then tomorrow morning I will take a look at the bar Alan, while you get yourself organised to speak to our possible security people."

"Are you happy to do the bar? Would you not prefer the security team sir?"

"I'll do the bar first. You do security. It's more your game than mine, and when you do the bar they won't have seen you before. I could go in there a couple of times and do some groundwork. It won't do me any harm to get back on the sharp end again . I think I'm getting a bit soft and rusty and that means I could be more of a liability than useful."

"OK that's a plan."

"Right let's eat before Fatima threatens to give it to the dogs."

Graham had put a telephone number in the file. When we were ready, we should phone the number. We might just get a 'hello' or we might get a name. When we do, we were to ask for Charles. If we didn't get Charles, get a time for when we can speak to him. Do not discuss anything with anyone else. When you give your name, Charles will ask you a question. Give him the answer. He has the answer, because I have told him both the answer and the question. It doesn't matter whether Captain Cameron or Lieutenant Lewis call. Use your full name. No ranks are necessary. As neither of you two know Charles and he does not know you the question will confirm you are each talking to the right person.

Alan made the call and was quite surprised that the operator had been quick and he got Charles first go.

Who is calling please?"

"My name is Alan Lewis."

"What colour was the sky last night Monsieur Lewis?"
"I Don't know I was asleep"

Where do you live Monsieur Lewis"

Alan gave him the address of the guesthouse and Charles told him he would receive instructions for a meeting . Follow the instructions carefully. Don't get it wrong or we will need to start again which might not be convenient for anyone. The n the phone went dead. Alan hung up and returned to the guesthouse.

It was late morning; he'd taken a coffee with a street vendor on the way back from the telephone box. It was too early for a lunch break, though the thick black unsweetened coffee had filled a hole like it was a cup of pure treacle. He was keen to catch up with Cameron to trade notes and possibly Fatima could be persuaded to do some semolina crepes for lunch if she wasn't sleeping. Cameron he assumed would be a while at the bar. He would want to hang around for a short time to get a feel for the place. He wasn't going to learn very much by rushing in and out and as he pointed out he had been in the back ground for a while with the embassy dealings and the trip back to the UK. If he felt a need to get himself comfortable on the sharp end then Alan wholeheartedly agreed with him. Familiarity might, on occasions, breed contempt, but it also kept you alive; how you applied it was down to commonsense. They had a hiding place to leave each other messages. The files were hidden in the lining of Camerons locked suitcase. Alan checked for messages and as there were none he took out the file on the security people he was expecting to meet.

Information was scant. Obviously there was not going to be any information that could compromise anyone and it was mostly a written version of what Graham had said in the meeting at the café. It did add though that there were two principals that we would likely be dealing with. One was the man, Charles, who Alan had asked for on the phone to arrange the meeting and the other was Madame Almira.

According to the paperwork it basically said that Madame Almira was the commanding officer and ran the whole business, while Charles was the adjutant, come minder, adviser, enforcer and anything else that needed doing. Alan found that information quite interesting as he could see a description of roles closely resembling his own.

Alan was reading through the file on the bar when he heard a key go into their door. He knew it would be Cameron but he was still up and going towards the door just in case. As Cameron came in he had an envelope in his hand.

"Hello Alan. Letter here for you. I think it was just given to Fatima by some street coffee seller. She was holding it as I walked in and the only other person was a man pushing a barrow back up the street. Hope your morning was ok mine was interesting and I'm glad I'm here because it looks like rain again."

When Alan thought of Paris he had in his head Moulin Rouge, Eiffel Tower, beautiful French ladies, perfume, Galois cigarettes, coffee at al fresco cafes sitting in a wooden chair at a candlelit table, noise of traffic, hustle bustle night life, laughter and gaiety. It was as his father had a habit of saying "that's for other people son". Father was right again. It was raining yet again. Alan trying to shelter in a shop doorway, knowing he couldn't get out of the rain in case he missed his contact. Perhaps they too had taken shelter thinking along similar lines, knowing that should they miss the connection; nothing was lost for them.

A man pushing a wheelbarrow. The iron rim around the wooden spoke wheel and the heavy load made a clicking sound on the cobbles while his worn out boots slapped in the puddles as he struggled to deliver whatever to wherever. His head bent down trilby sort of hat dripping water from the brim onto his saturated trousers as he passed in front of the shop. He stopped the barrow dragged it into the gutter and stepped onto the pavement. It looks like he is delivering to the shop here. Alan moved to the side to let him pass.

"Monsieur Lewis. Don't say anything in my hat is an envelope I will take it off you take out the envelope smoothly and discreetly and place the envelope inside your raincoat. I shall put my hat back on and go. Do not open the envelope until you are back at your guest house." With that he took off his hat appearing to shake off the water. Alan took the envelope smoothly out and the man put the hat back on his head turned and walked away. Alan waited a while still pretending to shelter. The man and barrow had long disappeared and the street was completely empty of traffic and people. He had given it about five minutes and conveniently the rain let up. Not knowing if he was being watched or tailed he made a show of checking his watch again and then headed back to the guest house. It's only supposed to rain in Britain he was thinking. By the time he got back to the residence he knew his suit needed pressing and his raincoat wasn't waterproof. Cameron was sitting in the dining room with Fatima and got to the bottom of the stairs at the same time as Alan.

"Ok?" Alan passed the envelope to him.

"I need to change while you have a read sir." Alan headed upstairs he could hear his socks squelching still in his shoes even though he had emptied them into the street as he had come into the guest house. Cameron gave him time to go upstairs and get undressed not because he was bothered about seeing him naked that was a normal happening but because he was leaking water from just about everywhere like a broken drainpipe.

Alan had hung his wet clothes over a wooden maiden and a bucket underneath to catch the water as it ran off.

"Fatima said to bring your clothes down in the bucket. She will dry them for you. Do you want me to open this?" Cameron asked.

"Of course please go ahead" Alan was busily towelling his body trying to get dry and then dressed as quickly as possible before he reckoned he might freeze to death.

You are invited to a meeting with Madame Almira this evening. There is a route you are to follow. You are to leave here at five o clock and carefully follow the route as stated in this letter. You must memorise the roads and streets turnings and directions or you will not get to the right place and then you will miss your meeting."

"Is there a lot to memorise ?" Alan was dressed now but was still drying his hair even though it was probably no longer wet.

"No about five turnings and a couple of street crossings."

"Will you read it to me please" Cameron had got to turn two when Alan stopped him.

"A problem Alan?"

"The reason I have to remember it all is because it's down the back streets and alleyways where there is no lighting nothing that would work as a guide except there is a laundry en route. I think I could do it easily in daylight nighttime is another issue. I have homework to do.

The darkness was starting to wrap around him as he ventured further into the back streets. The afternoon deluge had stopped almost as quickly as it had started; but It had washed the streets clean and cleaned the air, though the smell of soot and coal fires would soon prevail. Here down the back streets cooking and other smells alternated and then mixed with commercial industrial processes. Alan could see light coming from a ground floor window. He could smell a laundry working. Perhaps he was actually in the right street after all. He tried to see through the grimy window a cursory wipe of the dust revealed little of the inside, he would have to trust his nose. It smelt like a laundry, so it probably was. He hadn't travelled either far or for long but in the darkness he was to a certain extent very isolated and seriously under powered. There was neither moonlight nor stars the grey sky was as darker grey as it could get. The wrong people now and he would be unlikely to be seen again. He followed the instructions as given to him turn right next corner and continue. It was getting even darker now the light from the window had affected his night vision he moved carefully and slowly pale hardly apparent shadows on the cobbles disguising the unevenness of the ground he walked. Another turn next corner on the right. He could hear a car ahead somewhere a sound but no vision yet; but it was sounding nearer the further he walked along the narrow street that had width wise diminished till it felt almost like a narrow alley. He came to another corner around which was the car he could hear.

"Monsieur Lewis." A voice, a tall man, thickset, "you can have a ride the rest of the way". The man opened the rear door to the car. "Madame is inside I shall be in the front we have a driver."

Alan bent forward to look into the car; a lady smartly dressed, he assumed, as she smelt fine, the interior light came on her coat was fur, her leather gloved hand stopped him when she placed it on his forehead, and as she did so, the big man behind him frisked him, very smoothly and quickly from his armpits to his crotch.

"Lift left leg please monsieur. Now the other one". He checked both down to the ankles.

"Thank you monsieur. He is clean madame."

"Thank you Charles."

"Come Monsieur Alain sit inside." The lady spoke like she was used to fur coats, good living, chauffer driven cars and giving orders. The car started, the interior light went out, they crept towards a corner, carefully negotiated it, and arrived out onto a brightly lit main street.

"I could of course have given you different directions and made them considerably easier for you to meet me here, but checking if you were being tailed is easier the way I sent you and it lets me know that you are a man of a certain calibre that is not necessarily intimidated by being alone in the dark in a hostile environment. You have also learned, since you have been here, how to find your way around Paris on foot and also how to follow precise instructions. For those reasons alone I might be prepared to do business with you. Now tell me what is it that you want from me. I shall listen we shall talk if we can do a deal very good then we shall have dinner and then see what else the evening has to offer."

"I'm not exactly dressed for dinner."

"You will be fine. It will be my treat, in my restaurant, no one will refuse you entry." She laughed it was a laugh that said no one would dare to refuse me entry.

"D'accord?"

"D'accord."

"Now while we cruise around Paris tell me what you want."

"I am a Swiss businessman."

"Ha." She laughed again. "And I am the pope, the head of the catholic church. Swiss businessmen do not walk around the back streets of Paris alone like you did. Your French is excellent you could even be mistaken for Swiss not French but Swiss. But we spoke in English and you went straight into it as if was natural which it is. You think in English and you are a lieutenant in the British army because when you wanted a meeting I had you checked out. Now truth, from now, or I kick you out of car and no free dinner. D'accord?"

"Agreed do you want to do it in English or French?"

"We do it in French. I can teach you a lot of things in French Alain. English never sounds sexy. Time for being honest with each other now continue."

"I am what you say I am but for our purpose I am a Swiss businessman. I could have dual nationality as my mother was and both of her parents were Swiss nationals. My mother having married my father is whatever she wishes to be depending on how well she is getting on with my father at any given time. I'm fluent in French and German and I could hold if I wanted to Swiss identity papers if I preferred to be here as a Swiss citizen rather than a British army officer. A contact of a friend of mine has suggested that you may be able to assist with temporary staff requirements that I may need during some of my personal business ventures. He says that you have a sufficient numbers of reliable employees for a variety of tasks, whether it be driving general labouring or muscle and backup. I am also told that a small retainer is payable on a monthly basis, I am told to keep the banking system between us open. That jobs are half up front and the balance on satisfactory completion. Rates and costs to be agreed where possible before anything is started, but emergencies will be billed and final fee will be fair but non-negotiable. How am I doing?"

"You have done your homework or copied someone else's homework. Is that it?"

"I'm probably not looking for fruit pickers or building labourers but if I find myself in need probably for some discreet ruthless reliable backup numbers dependant on circumstances but unlikely to get into double figures."

"Finished ?"

"For now. You're go."

"I'm thinking at the moment . Enjoy the view. Paris in the early evening, especially after rain, is quite pleasant, don't you think. You must have got very wet this afternoon; you have changed your clothes."

Alan smiled and simply nodded his head. He took her advice and looked out of his window before turning back inside. He did not know what the car was, it was quiet and comfortable, the purr of the engine suggested lots of available power and speed if required. She was looking to her left out of her side window the fur coat had opened enough to offer a glimpse of a stocking topped leg. Alan found the view of her leg more appealing than the pedestrians crossing this bridge over the Seine. She turned back into the car adjusting the open coat as she did so.

"Business first Monsieur Lewis."

"Forgive me please. That was unnecessarily rude of me. My apologies."

"Accepted you can, and will, repay me later. What else apart from the finances do you know of my business?"

"Only gossip and guesswork and what little unconfirmed bits of information were given to me. But I was told if we do a deal you will honour it. Which was enough to assure me of getting what I need."

"Like you Alain my family, and therefore me as well, are foreigners here in France. My family are from Morocco. In the early part of this century my father with many of his countrymen, and lots of others from Algeria, Tunisia, and many parts of North Africa provided France with a labour supply. Temporary immigrant labour for use as required. Sometimes abused which caused my father to adopt a battle plan shall we call it. Cut a long story short my father is possibly one of the biggest gangmasters in western Europe. He is back with my mother at their house in Morocco. Father saw an opportunity to make money, by organising a labour force . Before he came to France he was already very rich. His family were, and some still are, nomadic. But before the great war he settled down in Morocco and he sent us, that is my brother and I to school, which is why he bought the house and they stayed in one place, and then when we were older, he sent us to England to learn English, then he brought us here to France, to learn to speak French like a French person. We learnt French at home in Morocco. Science and arts are more often in French so we polished our language here. Did you know the first university in the world was in Morocco?" Alan shook his head. "You ask just about anybody in the world where the first university was; I doubt many would say Morocco. I now mind business in Paris for my father while my brother does the same in Marseille. We have lieutenants and people who manage other parts of the business as required. I add here that we are not in any way a criminal organisation and do not wish to be seen on the wrong side of the law. The important word in the last sentence is seen. We have many international business clients. We must also include some foreign embassies and departments of the French government to add to our credibility. I suspect that all your information came via your embassy and they will have picked this up and more information from others on the political stroke diplomatic grapevine.

Even though you are private enterprise you tell me and knowing your real employer and how you got to find out about me. I will make you the same offer that I reserve for my better clients. The costs as I've stated are not negotiable. My father has set the rates and the value he puts on people. As much as my father loves and respects me; doing cheap work is not good for either party and doing favours I would be back in Morocco and living in a tent in either the desert or the high Atlas. Do you have any more questions?"

I am looking to establish a base here. Something public like a bar or a small café that I might be able to buy into. A reason to go wandering about doing business not like a tourist but as a commercial enterprise. I am told that there is a man named Henri Murcia, who has a small bar that might be the sort of thing I am looking for. I am also aware that I am potentially doing business with members of the criminal community, reasons not secret but currently not specifically defined."

"Charles." she leaned towards the front seat.

"Yes Madame."

"Time to eat Do you know where Habiba or Farah are?"

"As far as I know Madame they will be at the restaurant later. There is a new show at Les Folies and I believe their friand Marianna is appearing. They did say that they hoped to meet you later."

"Tomorrow when you see monsieur Alain speak to him about Henri Murcia."

"Henri madame?"

She wandered off into Alan assumed Berber or Arabic. Alan knew neither.

"As you wish madame."

"Excellent let's all eat then. Are you hungry Alain?" She laughed again, of course you are. I have seen hunger in your eyes ever since I put my hand on your forehead, when you leaned into my car. Charles frisked you for weapons he said you only had one which seemed to try and hide away, you will not have understood as very few people outside Morocco speak Berber. It can make for discreet conversation when you don't wish others to understand."

"Being searched by other men has that effect on me."

She laughed. "Perhaps." And then she laughed again.

"Charles restaurant please." He spoke to the driver. "My driver is Moroccan and still learning French. All of my people speak Arabic and or Berber. When you hire a team from us you will always have more than one French speaker for direct conversation. Instructions to the rest will never be misunderstood in our own language." They sat in silence, each with their own thoughts. Alan feeling as though he was on ice, slippy, care required, is there a thin bit he might fall through? Alan was hungry she was right about that and possibly for more than food. The car purred and he wondered if the cat in the car purred as sweetly.

"Now we are here let us eat business is over now. Charles will speak to you tomorrow and at some time will give you a contract it doesn't need signing it will start when the retainer is paid into the Bank account and will finish if for any reason the retainer is not deposited."

The car stopped on the wrong side of the road. Charles moved around to the to the other side and opened the door for madame. Alan slid across the seat and followed Madame out and onto the pavement. Two doormen moved quickly towards the car and made certain madame was chaperoned up the three wide stone steps to the restaurant entrance where a third opened the door and allowed madame followed by Alan through. The warm atmosphere and the gentle noise of dining groups a pleasant shift in atmosphere from the external street hubbub of motor engines and car horns.

The maître d enquired. "Madame a table for how many ?"

"Two with a stretch to four when the others arrive."

"Any preference?"

"No though a corner if we can Luigi."

"I can move someone if you wish."

"Unnecessary. We can wait at the bar until one is available."

"That may be a while madame we are very full and just had a number of starts."

"Good, business is what we're about. We can eat in my apartment. Are you happy for me to order Alain?"

"Of course."

"Spiced lamb tagine boiled rice and flat breads and all the side dishes with olives and dips please for two. A bottle of my red. And a bottle of iced water. Have you seen Habiba or Farah?"

"No madame."

"They are expected. Let me know when they get here and, assuming they arrive, ask them what they want to eat and drink, and invite them to join us."

Charles had joined them with maître d.

"Thank you Charles. We are finished for the evening. But one last job. Monsieur Alain's companion at the guesthouse should be informed that he is in good hands and is unlikely to be back to the guesthouse tonight. If you will do that for me please and I will see you tomorrow."

"Very good madame."

"Do we have enough staff Luigi?"

"Yes Madame."

"Then have a pretty girl bring our food."

"Very good madame."

"Come Alain we shall eat upstairs."

Alan followed madame as she weaved her way through the diners, the occasional recognition, a swift hello, and a wish of bon appetit, she glided through the dining area to the far side of the restaurant. Next to the two way swing door, that was access to the kitchen, was a door with a "no entrance" sign which madame opened with her key. The door closer cut the dining area noise instantly. A carpeted staircase, a short flight to a half landing, then a turn and another flight to another landing and a door. Madame opened the door and inside switched on the light to the room.

"We are above the kitchens here," she explained, "The dining room is much higher, but my father thought it might be possible to have accommodation here, without losing the ambiance of the dining area. It seems to work, so not a lot to complain about."

"You live here?"

"I live in a number of places, but yes this is one of them. My father and the business have property in many places. When you walked in the dark streets this evening we knew you would be ok as our people kept an eye on you from the houses as we own many of them. It is where a lot of our people live; so although you weren't aware of it you were safer than you may have realised. I will tell you now that Henri is a different proposition. Charles will advise you but now as business is finished eating and drinking and entertainment is the menu now."

"I am amazed that there is hardly any sound from below or from outside. Your room here is very nicely done." Alan looked around impressed with the finish and the layout so very unlike what he was used to with army accommodation.

"There is a shower room through that door no doubt it will get used sometime before you leave. There is no need for a kitchen with a restaurant below so I only require somewhere to entertain a guest and to sleep. I find this perfectly adequate."

"I wouldn't argue with you, it feels perfect."

"You interest me Alain. When business is concluded I will usually treat my new client to a meal and some decent wine if I like them.

But you have intrigued me and interested me; but at this time I don't know why, but perhaps if you stay longer than my usual clients I will find out. My friends will be round later and we shall see what we shall see.

I think that maybe you are more than what meets the eye. What you see is what you get does not apply. What you see is what he wants to show you. I don't wish to flatter you but you are different things to different people. Fatima, the lady who runs the guest house, tells us that you are clean and respectable polite and always thank her for what she has done. Yet you are not in any way intimidated at the prospect off dealing with the criminal elements of Paris.

You were not afraid, or you didn't show fear, when you walked through the dark streets to meet us tonight. You, I'm sure, have a plan and I think that we are going to make it work as long as it does not do anything that will cause us grief or embarrassment then we will work with you.

A bell over the room door rang three short rings.

"Our food has arrived time to eat. Sit down on the mat and we shall see who brings our meal.

Habiba and Farah. Good evening. You made it then." Alan looked up from his place on the floor at two more beauties. "This is Alain he is eating with us tonight."

"Good evening Alain, I am Habib this is Farah ." They shook hands with Alain and kissed Almira on both cheeks.

Habiba smiled as she kissed Almira. "You were very lucky she said Luigi had sent that pretty young thing from Tunis with your meals. Fortunately we got here just in time. Poor thing looked quite sad when we took the food off her and chased her back to the kitchen."

"You two are wicked."

"We know. And we are hungry but not for food. But we will help you eat it all, as a favour, to speed things up. now sit down Almira and we shall serve you.

There is no substitute for perfectly cooked food. Alan couldn't ever remember if he had eaten anything that tasted as good as that meal and side dishes he'd just eaten. He had eaten just enough. The two meals had been shared between the four of them and a glass of red wine had been worthy accompaniment.

"Meal ok?"

"Exquisite."

"Good now shower time." Almira got up Habiba and Farah also and they pulled Alan off the floor and took him into the bathroom. Almira started the shower while the sisters started to take off Alan's clothes.

Almira said, "Don't help they know exactly what they're doing relax now and enjoy the moment." Alan now naked stepped into the large cast iron bath and the sisters started to wash him. When he was cleaned they patted him dry and then rubbed some scented oil and perfume onto his body.

"Time for you to lie down on my bed. Now be off with you while ready ourselves." Alan did as instructed and walked back into the room and lay down on the bed. He thought trepidation was a good word or apprehensive. Almira came back into the room. She had got dressed again and was wearing her fur coat.

"I have been playing with you since this afternoon and all evening Alain. We have entertained each other in different ways; throughout the circuitous journey here, the meal, each other's company, and now my sisters and I will do the final act and hopefully you will enjoy the grand finale." Alan had added panic to his list of words.

Habiba and Farah joined Almira. They danced their way across the floor listening to whatever sound was playing in their head. Just in front of Alan, Almira stopped, let the fur coat fall open, and then let it slide onto the floor behind her. She wore nothing but a pair of red stiletto shoes. Alan realised then, why Charles never referred to madame as either her or she.

Her two sisters removed their gowns revealing a distinct physical similarity.

"Part of what we are is a product of brilliant Moroccan medicine, and some surgery. My sisters and I are in many way what we consider to be as the best part of both worlds. We have all that anyone might need for a good time. This is an unusual opportunity to share it with all three of us. There are people who would fight and pay dearly for this Alan. And I can assure you we can't be bought. I can also assure you that when I say a good time I mean it."

While Amira was talking to Alan, who was slightly in awe, slightly frightened, Habiba and Farah slipped off their shoes, and climbed onto the bed. They got one each side of Alan, and moved in close, without actually touching him.

Madame was silently in control. Alan mesmerised, listened to Almira. She moved around slowly, body still swaying, in rhythm to the silent music, keeping time in her head.

"I hope you can embrace the moment. There maybe a little pain or no pain at all. There may be more pain than you wish, part of it could be neutralised with some pills, or some other medicinal drugs, of which I have a sufficient supply of. If you start down that path you become addicted to the drug and not the act. Habiba and Farah moved closer hands gently touching his skin finger nails slowly and gently scratching thin red lines about his body.

The act won't kil you, but I'm convinced that the drug is more addictive, and more dangerous, and in the end will leave you empty. His penis was responding to the physical contact. Habiba was gently biting his shoulder; he could feel the sisters rising to the occasion and he watched madame's dancing, swaying hips as she sensually moved in front of him.

Alan didn't know what to do or how to respond; his body was rigid his hands still by his side not moving afraid to break the spell; happy to be mesmerised by the experience.

" The pleasure my sisters and I can create is hopefully good enough in its own right not to require supplementing with foreign toxic substances. Should you wish to halt everything instantly because you can't take anymore. You need a safe word. Pick one."

"What's a safe word?" Came out in a croaky shaky voice.

"A word that when you say it will instantly stop what's happening."

"I don't know."

"My father's name is Brahim. If you say Brahim it will stop and you will be out of it. We might not, but let's see what happens." Madame leaned over the bed dangling a very ample breast just in front of Alans lips. Remember; smooth skin, gentle hands, soft lips, and a searching tongue, have no gender in the dark. She switched the switch at the side of the bed and the room was plunged into total darkness and Alan was plunged into a deep sea of sexual euphoria. It had pain, sweat, exchanges of personal body fluids, and his body violated like never before. No one mentioned Brahim.

Alan awoke. Sort of. He could hear noises, dishes, a person moving.

"Ah very good monsieur, you are awake. A late breakfast monsieur Alain." Alan recognised Charles's voice. His head was buried deep into the pillow and as yet he wasn't totally au fait with what was going on.

"Shall I open the curtains monsieur? It is a beautiful day."

"Whatever you think Charles." Alan was desperately trying to fathom out what was happening. He didn't remember drinking a lot last night but….

"How are you this morning monsieur Alain?"

"If when you walked in, you had told me I had died and gone to heaven, I probably would have believed you."

"I have crepes and coffee for starters to get your system up and running. Then anything else you want chef will do for you." Alan was starting to comeback slowly into the land of the living.

"Madame is out on business. I have a set of instructions to follow and some paperwork for you to take away. I have sent a further message to your companion at the guest house; so he is aware of your good health. Details have not been provided to him you can be assured of that; so anything you tell him or don't tell him is between you and him alone."

Alan was about to get out of bed until he realised that he was naked and didn't know where his clothes were. He sat up in bed and Charles pushed a tray on a carriage, that put a covered breakfast tray in front of him

"Charles excuse my embarrassment; can you see my clothes anywhere?"

"Madame has had them cleaned for you. I shouldn't think they will be much longer. I shall get you a dressing gown if they aren't ready. Careful with the dishes the plates are hot to keep the crepe warm."

Charles left Alan to eat his breakfast in peace. It was only when he looked at his watch on a table beside the bed that he realised that it was more lunch than anything else, now just after midday and for the first time ever, he is still in bed from the day before. Charles returned carrying towels and his clothes all cleaned and freshly pressed.

"Can I get you anything else to eat?"

"No thank you."

"Then a shower?"

"Yes please."

The shower was running Alan looked at his body in the mirror just before it steamed up. He was covered in lipstick, kisses, smears, nibbles. and bite marks just about everywhere.

"You may need some assistance in getting properly clean shall I organise some help for you?"

"The answer should be yes Charles, but I'm not certain I would be able to cope with any more physical contact. What doesn't wash off my body will eventually wear off, as long as I get my face clean, I'll settle for that."

"As you wish monsieur."

"Please call me Alain."

"My position here requires me to call you monsieur. I would prefer to keep it like that madame would not approve."

"I understand."

Later scrubbed clean Alan is drinking coffee and reading through the papers Charles had given to him.

"Madame has asked me to tell you what we know about Henri Murcia. The first thing, I should say is that his links to what madame would consider as unsavoury are confirmed. He is a dangerous man with a history of violence which he seems to have been able to get away with. As far as anyone knows he has never been charged with any criminal offence, methods 0f avoidance and reasons unknown. There is an ongoing business arrangement with Marcel, Henri's brother, who is almost without a doubt just as unsavoury as Henri but somehow has avoided being ostracised like Henri. It might help that he provides the restaurants and our workers fresh meat and vegetables which would be sufficient to make madame flexible, purely for business needs. Although, in truth both are just as dangerous and lethal as each other Marcel has a certain warmth and friendliness about him that contrasts with Henri the psychopath. Which might really be that he knows how to do business and make money better than Henri. So, don't be lulled into his charm; I can assure you he is just as likely to slit your throat as his brother is . Madame will not deal with Henri. If you are to link with him madame will only deal with you or one of your people direct links to Henri will not happen. The consequence of his psychopathic persona has left him without any real allies and he inevitably ends up working alone or with help from his brother when desperate. He is also getting older and slowing down a bit and some back up muscle might be a sound business move for him and if you can provide that with your people as a starter madame would certainly be happy to provide additional support and add to your people though as I've said without you or one of your men there will be nothing available."

"What caused the rift between them?" Alan asked "Or is that a taboo subject?"

"It was a long time back. Henri spoke to madame like he was hiring a common prostitute. He then became rude and abusive to madame, not a good idea, and then showing a complete lack of respect, he threatened madame. Had I and our driver not been close at hand it could have got messy. Madame is not afraid to stick a knife in someone but killing Henri though welcomed by some would have, almost certainly, occasioned an investigation. Any sort of scandal is not good for business. If madame had been hurt Henri would have spent a long time dying. Madame's father would have seen to that. So now you can see why Madame will not deal with Henri. Neither of them will forgive the other so a stalemate exists; which is ok if at least it remains like it is."

Alan let the information he was gathering file itself in his memory store. He would as he always did write it all down when he had a moment to do so.

"Madame says you are likely to be looking for muscle and back up to supplement your people. We have a number of men with military experience some were in the army and involved with Franco in Morocco and then Spain. The war for many of them was nothing to do with them and so they moved here. Some might consider them as unreliable deserters. If we send them to you to do a job you can be assured that they will not let you down. They are with us full time they do any jobs that need doing though when they do your type of work they do get a significant increase in their wage. Generally speaking they are the office cleaners, the gardeners, the rubbish removers, the street sweepers, fruit pickers. We take the menial tasks that others don't want. Brahim provides food and accommodation and a small wage that gives a person, and they are mostly men, as Karl Marx said, the dignity that is work, and at the same time a link and kinship with fellow Moroccans which provides a bond, security and safety."

Alan could see another source of information gathering that might need looking at again in the future.

"Our language is Berber sometime Arabic from anywhere in North Africa; occasionally French as I'm sure Almira will have said, which we learn because we live here, and it is also a part of our language at home in Morocco. If we have agreed a price half up front half on completion. You will get a bill we expect it to be paid. If it isn't paid we will come and take it. This is not a threat Monsieur it is the terms we do business by; and all I am doing is setting out the ground rules as I have done with all of our clients. We don't expect anyone not to pay if we did we wouldn't do business with them. Collecting payment is almost certainly a costly and time consuming idea that would attract possible unwelcome attention from others that we might not want to be involved with. Do you have any questions?"

"Not at this moment. If I think there is something I need an answer to how do I get in touch?"

"Come to the restaurant; speak to Luigi and ask him to find me. You ask me and if I can't answer I will find out and find you Okay?"

"Good enough for now. Perhaps I should now go and speak to my boss and tell him where we're up to."

"Would you like a lift?"

"I think the walk might do me good thank you Charles."

"You're very welcome monsieur."

Charles was right. It was a beautiful day. Alan was uncertain whether he was sorry he had missed most of it or if he should confess to Cameron what had happened since he saw him last. He arrived back at the guest house Cameron was drinking coffee and chatting to Fatima when Alan let himself in.

"Hello Alan, you're looking very smart, and your clothes have been washed and pressed . But by God man, you look worn out."

Fatima gave Alan a coffee, after which they moved upstairs to their room.

"So come on tell me what were you up to that took the bet part of twenty four hours."

"What I did last night would have me jailed in Britain. A plea of I did it for Britain, I don't believe would be accepted."

"Why ?"
"Probably because I would be unable to deny I hadn't enjoyed it."

"Pray continue."

"We are making progress. I have established a business link with a provider of manpower shall we call it. Now what we need is an ear to the ground and a way of making it all function.

 Sometime soon but not quite yet, I think you need to go back to England and speak again to Your pal Mr. Conway and ask for enough money to buy into a bar here in Paris."

Peter's mouth dropped open a bit at this proposal but he didn't say anything.

"It is cheaper than buying a tank and it will do things you can't get a tank to do. The possibilities of cheap access to useful businesses is limited; and buying into something that will not get us anywhere is useless. Just about every bar in Paris is a brothel or has a link to one and the one I'm thinking about is run by one man who as I have been told by our new business partners may be a prime candidate for a need for a provider of back up services, which we can provide. Are you with me so far?"

"Yes. So why doesn't someone else buy in to the business?"

"It seems no one likes him. Most are scared of him though he works alone, he has some unknown protection from some where or someone. This is apparently more lawyers than heavies as he has a reputation for sticking knives into people who get in his way rather than employing someone else to do it"

"Oh is that all. Sounds like a sweet little pussycat. Are you crazy?"

"Not at all I think he's ideal. He is a notorious, unliked, unloved criminal, without a friend or any significant physical back up. What we will provide him with is everything he might require without restricting anything he is already doing; and he will make money from us. He will be better off physically and financially with us and we will have a source of information that comes direct from inside the French parliament the councils and some of the embassies."

"Are you certain about all of that?"

"No but I see no point in not exaggerating the possibilities at this point."

"You're ahead of me here Alan. So you've got a plan. Tell me what you think and I will pick holes in it if necessary."

"It 's simple. Or I think it is. You get Mr. Conway to tell the embassy that they are going to buy via a third party of their choice, let's say twenty-five percent of a French business. They can do all the legal bits and satisfy themselves that it is legit. That way we are not having any money that is for buying the business coming through our hands. Therefore if anything changes they still have control and ownership of the property."

"Keep talking. Sounds fine up to now."

"It's a keep it simple. Let the admin guys do the admin we'll do the groundwork. It won't be instant, but it will, when it's finished with, have a resale value, when it might not be required any longer."

"It sounds too simple; like we're missing something. His brother keeps getting a mention, but he seems to be a different beast altogether."

Alan let his knowledge about Marcel Murcia wander around inside his head for a short while. Cameron could see him thinking about what he had said and left him to it.

"You know sir you may have a very good point. We have been looking at Henri and the bar and not taking enough notice of what part his brother may be playing in all of this. Do you think a word with Graham at the embassy might be a good idea before we go any further just in case there's something else that everyone might have missed?"

"I don't believe that another couple of days will make any real difference and unless I speak to Graham we won't know if there is something else and we therefore haven't been diligent enough. Even gossip might have some value so I'll pop down there first thing tomorrow morning."

"So can I leave that with you sir, that way you can go straight to the embassy without arranging a n outside meeting?"

"Of course let's keep it as we have it. It's working so far."

Just before lunchtime Cameron met Alan back at the guest house. "I have done the checking up on our man and reassuring ourselves that what we know is factually correct.

The bar is registered solely to Henri Murcia. His is the only name showing on the documents. However, it is believed that his brother, Marcel, is possibly, though more likely probably, involved in the same venture. They have interests in some other businesses. Nothing big, but they own a garage repair shop, and a butchers and fresh food suppliers. They don't have many employees . A man and boy in the garage a couple of drivers and some part timers who work in the food supplies. He supplies hotels and restaurants with small amounts of fresh produce when required, rather than retail sales, which confirms what Madame Almira told you.

Now like most bars and places of entertainment here, there is also a more lucrative trade in an attached brothel. The next part is totally gossip and unsubstantiated. This brothel is a little different from the norm as not only is there a range of females of varying ages but it seems to have a number of what we would describe as underage employees, though nothing ever shows up or is seen anywhere, the talk on the street is that you can get what you pay for, as long as you are prepared to pay for it."

"This is sounding like information we should have been told about at the beginning." Alan said.

"There's a reason hang on a second. This didn't come from Graham. When I asked Graham about Marcel I got invited into the back office where I met another chap. His name is Martin Baxter. I'd not seen before and he had been looking at different issues as his priority here is people trafficking and slave labour.

He works for our secret service and is liaising with the French government in their efforts to stop the trafficking and slavery. Marcel lives on the outskirts of the city here. He owns a large piece of farmland, split into a number of fields, on which standing, close to the road, is a large, detached house. The house has been converted into two semi-detached houses. There is one very small dwelling in which Marcel, a bachelor, lives; and on the other side there is a large property that is used as an orphanage. The fields are used extensively for food production.

Marcel runs a working farm there . He has pigs, chickens, ducks, and geese; which are all fenced off in separate areas with coups and pens. In the rest of the fields he grows vegetables. His produce supplies both the orphanage and the local restaurants and hotels, hence the need for a variety of birds. He also buys in produce, including animals, as he has a slaughter house and a butchery building just along the road from the farm.

The older children do some work in the fields and with the animals. Some are old enough to leave the orphanage but remain there as helpers and minders. Nothing in any way considered as illegal.

This is where it gets both factual and conjecture.

First the factual. The orphanage was investigated as a potential transit place for the movement of people. The young residents there are long term and not just temporary and passing through. There is a matron, who is a qualified nurse and a catholic priest. Both are full time and live in.

Both of them have been there over five years. Very few of the children are French. mostly they are North African or eastern European and consequently difficult to place. This is what attracted the investigation in the first place; as a lot of the trafficking comes from North Africa via Marseille. They did a random check on the children one day, and found they were all fit, healthy, and well fed. There was no need to go any further with the investigation our man's brief did not extend past trafficking and slavery. He did note one thing though they all seemed to be completely uninhibited and more than happy to be holding hands and touching each other.

Not in any rude or offensive way but as a show of affection or familiarity. He described it as more like an extended family than an institution. Having been to a number of orphanages, as part of his investigations, he thought it slightly unusual. Investigation closed.

Graham and I then took what we know and played with it. If Henri and Marcel are in business together. Marcel owns a building which is occupied by a charitable organisation that uses it as an orphanage. Though he is not involved in the running of it, he provides the food to the staff and the children. Henri has a bar and brothel of which the only link is that they are two brothers with two totally different business ventures. Then any thoughts of a crossover between them is tenuous at best or pure conjecture."

"It makes for interesting guessing games" Alan was back into thinking mode and Cameron left him to it having spent his time with Graham trying to confirm any of their guesswork.

"I think that's the answer then. He has no back up because he can't trust anyone who might have the knowledge as to how it all works; he has no organised gang, nor police protection, he has been a loner all the time probably because what he illegally sells would leave him open to blackmail and other potential problems. If as we believe he has a clientele that would not wish to see their names in the papers and linked to him. Consequently he is the sort that, in the event of scandal, is likely to be disappeared into the Seine, or somewhere else never to be heard from or seen again. And that maybe our way into the business. He needs a support group and we are in a position to provide it."

"I agree," said Cameron

"How do you want me to play it then?"

"Whatever way you think you can carry it off."

"What about, I am Louis Alain, a Swiss national, i have access to funds and muscle. If he wants to see what we have then If needs be we'll put together a back-up crew from the chaps at the embassy and I think I can get some people who look the part mostly from North Africa as long as we have a bit of time. We can at the moment do pretty much anything we need to do. We don't want the whole place, we just want a share with him, still in there, but with the same sort of back up, the other players have."

"Ok, you'll be busking though."

"I know. But it's no good trying to rehearse something we really don't know how he will react. I will however take my Italian friend with me."

"A good idea. We do need a base; and it's a perfect place for the gathering of information; and if war does happen then I can see it as part of the long term strategy to stop us being caught with our trousers down, a very poor unintentional pun I assure you. It will if nothing else provide us with a realisable piece of Parisian real estate and we are not trying to turn this into gangland power struggle so let's go gently through this and don't let it get out of hand. We don't have the muscle or power instantly handy to compete with the big boys all we need is a base to keep us with an ear to what is happening.

Alan nodded nothing more needed to be said.

"I'll go back again to the bar later just to see if going back there again will give us any more info."

"How did you get on?"

The barman is a man named Jacques. It isn't his real name. He is pleasant enough though I get the idea that he too is not one to be messed with. He is tied to the place. He is from Albania an illegal person. He did time in prison and should have been deported and now he hides in the bar a goes by the name of Jacques.

"There was a working girl at the bar when I got there and we got into conversation. Her name is Simone she was tired and a little inebriated. The alcohol had slurred her voice, she walked a little unsteady on heels maybe too high for her, Without the heels though she was tiny maybe five feet maybe an inch taller her shape dumpy but in the heels her proportions improved. I must be honest Alan, she smelt nice and I am lonely. It has been a long time since I had any contact of any sort with a woman. She hadn't been looking for work tonight but nevertheless she took the offer from me. We found a quiet area in an alleyway away from windows and doors she hiked up her skirt and grabbed me and as I entered her she leaned back against the building and lifted her leg for easier access. She knew exactly what to do, her stiletto heel locked me into her and she matched my body thrusts. It had been a while since I had enjoyed any physical contact with another person and it was over quicker than I'd hoped. She slipped her body out from between me and the wall took the two notes I was holding kissed me gently on the forehead and wished me Bon nuit and left me sorting out the fly buttons on my trousers. I felt like an idiot. I'm glad no one saw me. I'm thirty one years old and I was behaving like a seventeen year old virgin. But now here and away from the bar, in retrospect, it was a bit of daring fun. Can't imagine what Mr. Conway would think of the whole thing if he ever found out.

Alan left the guesthouse and walked the fifteen minutes or so to the bar. The late afternoon sun had warmed Paris up and the evening was dry and pleasant, no fear of overheating with a gentle walk and after nearly missing his turn, mesmerised by a film star wiggle he was unwittingly following, he turned the corner and arrived at Henri's bar. Standing outside was a lady who fitted Cameron's description of his amour from last night. She was smoking a cigarette.

This evening, she looked to be ready for business. she was too old to be working in the bright daylight, her skin powdered to improve her looks, but a face had seen too much life and where she had not powdered around her neck, and in the fleshy area above her bosom, signs of age showed mercilessly. But it would be dark soon and as

Alan got closer he could smell the soft perfume. She was washed and soaped clean. Some girls would squirt strong cheap perfume to disguise the smell of sweat. Simone may have been around longer than most working girls and seen it all but there was an obvious sense of pride in her attempts to look attractive.

"Are you Simone?"

"I am, and you are?"

"My name is Louis Alain. Would you be interested in doing some work for me?"

Feigning innocence she asked. "And what might a good looking young man like yourself require from a poor old French woman like me, I ask?"

"Perhaps some company, and a friendly knowledgeable voice to chat with."

"Are you going to buy me a drink?"

"Well I think that would a fine place to start?"

"Where shall we go?" she asked.

"Here is the best place for me," replied Alan. "I wish to discuss some business with the owner later on, so this would be the place to go."

"Does he know you are coming?"

"No, I would like you to contact him for me and tell him that I have a business proposition for him, that is really worth considering. But first a drink and some small talk."

Alan opened the door allowed Simone to go in first. "Ask the barman for a glass of red wine for me please, and whatever it is you have for yourself." He handed over a 100 franc note.

"It is early he may not have enough change."

"It is early. We may not need any change. Tell him to hold the change until we're finished for the night."

"D'accord."

They took a table at the far corner away from the door, and the bar.

The curtains had been closed earlier when the low lighting was switched on. Sitting in full view from the street was not always good for business, too much light inside showed the general decay and requirements for redecoration.

Habit had Alan sitting with his back to the corner he moved the table and slotted a chair between the table and the upholstered seating.

"You don't like the seats then Monsieur Alain?" Alan just shrugged his shoulders, his non-committal sort of answer saved explaining why.

"Jacques, the barman, says you may have to stay here till tomorrow, unless business picks up, it has been quiet for a couple of days; unless you wish to sample other delights that he has to offer."

"I'll sit and wait for now." Alan gave Jacques a nod acknowledging his message.

"Last night you were complaining, to my friend, about not having access to the upstairs. Why do you want the upstairs?"

"I'm getting to old to walk the streets I need to be sheltered, and in here I will be protected from some of the nutcases that seem to have landed in Paris."

"When wasn't there nutcases in Paris or any other city in the world?"

"It is getting worse and I need someone like Jacques the barman." Alan looked over to the bar. Because they were the only people in the bar Jacque had heard his name and immediately looked over he was obviously paying attention.

"Jacques who minds the bar, is very dangerous. He takes care of the girls as well who work here."

"What about the very young ones?"

"Are you interested in children?"

"No, I just like to know what's going on."

"Are you a policeman?"

"No I'm just a Swiss business man."

"You sound like an Englishman."

"You're the second person who's told me that."

"I bet the other one was a woman too."

"It may have been."

"Why don't you know, can't you tell the difference?"

"It was dark."

"That's what I mean English. Only the English would make it into a joke."

She had a look of triumph, when she said that as if there couldn't be any other explanation. Alan was reluctant to continue the discussion, figuring that there was little if anything to be gained by prolonging the debate, so he did his shoulder shrug end of, as far as he was interested.

"You were telling me about the young ones."

"I wasn't but you seem to know about them. The young ones never come here. They are picked up from where they live, travel to where they are to work, and then they take them back to where they live. They are minded carefully by other dangerous men. Who I don't wish to meet or know about.

Do you know where they live?

Yes

Where?

"I have no more to say, other than If I told you, Henri would kill me. If you want to know then you must ask Henri. I will not tell you anymore unless Henri says I can. You do not know him he has no worries about violence or beating people up. He has been frightening the others for years because they know if they don't get him if they try then he will kill them. He has done it on more than one occasion and I'm sure he is prepared to keep doing it as long as it suits him to do so."

"Then it is maybe time to have a chat to Henri. Will he be here this evening?"

"I don't know."

"Will you phone him for me, and ask him to meet me here tonight?"

"Here?"

"As I told you before I wish to discuss some business with him, that would be extremely beneficial to him."

"I shall phone him for you."

"Finish your drink first. Order yourself another, if you want one, and ask Jacque for a coffee for me please."

Simone was whispering on the phone and she had turned her back on Alan so he could not even guess at what the conversation was about.

"Henri says he will be here in about twenty minutes he says he will not be happy if you are messing him about."

"Why, I wonder, does he assume, I wish to mess him about. We shall see. Tell Jacque the coffee is good. If he would do me another please. I will be most grateful."

Alan sat patiently waiting for Henri. Simone was at the bar still whispering but now to Jacque. The only customer still was Alan the place had a deathly hush about it. Not quite twenty minutes, and Henri walked in. He looked at Simone who nodded towards Alan. As he walked over Alan stood up and offered his hand. Henri shook it and sat down in Simone's seat.

"What is it that you want Monsieur Alain?"

"I wish to buy into your bar Henri."

He laughed at Alan.

"You cannot afford to buy my bar. If you could afford to buy my bar you would not want to buy it. You would be too rich to bother with it. Why don't you buy yourself a nice car and go travelling around.

Simone tells me you were asking about the young fresh ones. I can let you hire a young girl, she could pretend to be your daughter, or your niece, she would make you feel like a young man again. If you don't want a girl, I can let you have a boy, you don't look much like a boy lover type, but who can tell these days, when it's not legal people hide the truth behind a façade as you would say.

I hire you one clean and free from any nasty diseases that make your dick hurt. HaHa, mon ami you must take your strange ideas, and put your mind to more useful things like drinking my wine and enjoying the company of my special young ladies."

"I still like the idea of buying into your bar."

"You do not listen to me monsieur. The answer is no."

"Name a price and we can discuss it further."

"Monsieur you are stupid."

Jacques and Simone are listening to the conversation but pretending not to. Alan knew he was irritating Henri but he hoped he knew what he was doing.

"You, Simone, get out of here, and go to work or I give you a smack."

"She is my guest." Alan informed him and Henri looked even more irritated if that were possible.

"Then you will have to pay me."

"Do I not pay the lady as she is providing the service? I know that you take a cut of the earnings. I know that the bar itself does not do well without the income from the ladies, and the youth that you have for rent. I know you have a garage and some fresh food that you buy and sell through the trade. I have probably more knowledge about you than even your own brother and his people; who I haven't even got around to yet, and importantly, I know that you don't have a great deal of available muscle. You have some but not as much as I can provide, as part of my buying into your bar."

"I have said the bar is not for sale."

"I don't want the whole bar, and I don't want any parts of your other businesses. I am only interested in the bar and the brothel."

"Monsieur I am getting annoyed with you."

"Then you will have to get your friends to come and help you throw me out."

"I have no friends. No one else have I ever needed."

The flick knife came out from under the table and opened a practised art, undoubtedly done many times before. Quick as lightning, it would have been about a hands length in front of Alan's face, but he had moved quickly backwards, in the seat and when he moved his hand came from under the table carrying the Beretta.

The first thought was thank you Dougie, the second was more practice needed old son which he muttered to himself. His thoughts went a touch further It was nearly too late for you that time. This man might be getting long in the tooth but he, as advised was extremely dangerous.

"You are very quick Monsieur." The knife disappeared almost as quick as it had arrived. "Why do you wish to do business with me? I am a liar and a criminal and a dishonest man. I might cheat you."

"Because I am an honest man, and I always tell the truth. If you try to steal from me or cause me any problems I will come back and kill you."

"And what if I kill you first eh?"

"Then my friends will come and kill you. The problem they have is they're not very good at it; sometimes it takes them days to get it done. The noise can be horrendous, until the vocal chords finally give up, and the mouth screams but no sound comes out but they find that entertaining too."

Henri had become extremely frightened; he was controlling his fear. He hoped his voice would remain steady and he knew that this man was telling the truth. He was right things weren't that good and he was short of man power. Jacque was a godsend and without him he would have to employ people at significantly more cost than he paid him. Add that to the possibility of another war in Europe and money in the bank was always going to be useful.

The real worry though was that this man knew too much. Most people put two and two together and made four. He had put them together and made seven because somehow he had found the secret hidden three.

"Perhaps I underestimated you. It is a good time for taking care of business. The streets are becoming an unsafe place for an old man like me. Foreigners are taking over places that we Parisians always owned, and there will be a war soon I fear, and business might drop off, money in the bank will be useful, but profits I suspect may not be as good as they are now."

"We will finalise details and shares when I see your proposal. What I want is all the information you can gather about this war you think might happen. I know you have your ear to the ground and I know you are part of the not so legal side of business here. I also know that you would benefit from a business partner who can provide enough muscle to maintain your position within your peer group. You may have underestimated me Monsieur Murcia but I, and my friends, have done our homework on you, and to a certain extent on your business and your competitors. We will make a deal. You will do well. I will provide the barman here with a Swiss passport. He will keep his job here. The lady and he will be my link back to you. She will put my share of the profit into a bank account the name and number will be provided when we have our agreement.

If anything happens to either of them I will take it personally. I will not kill you but I will send my friends around to do the job. What I deal in is information. I like useful information. I like to know who is doing what with who. Who is doing something that maybe should be kept a secret. That's where you come in. Your ear to the ground is better than mine, and for that I'm prepared to pay; by providing protection for your business. I will buy part of your business let's say one quarter you will provide information as you get it, and I will, if I think it's really worth it, will provide extra funds for you to use as you see fit. Details we will sort out. I am not trying to rob you, but I don't have a lot of time to mess about with minutiae. The bits and pieces will sort themselves out as we do business together. Shall we shake hands on it now?"

Henri Murcia had never in his life been this intimidated and frightened by anyone until today. He offered his hand. Alan shook it.

"We should have a drink." Henri had only partially regathered his composure but he could speak.

"I will have a coffee the wine is not to my taste."

"If you buy cheap wine Jacques will serve stuff like piss. We have fine wine at a price, permit me to treat you."

"Good wine, and I may drink too much, poor wine, I will stay sober. Coffee is easy to drug I know, but they, who have listened to our conversation, will want what I've proposed, and Jacques will get the Swiss passport I have promised him, so he will not drug me. I have two witnesses to our conversation and my people know where I am, and what I'm doing today. I will have a coffee to cement our deal. My handshake is good enough credit for you not to worry, but we will make it all legal, when the lawyers have had a look at it."

Henri knew he had been coerced into a deal but he also knew that his position within the hierarchy, and on the streets, was starting to decline. The others seemed to have backing from organised crime. Mafia, Cosa nostra, French gangs, all seemed to be moving into Paris; maybe this man would be both his benefactor and saviour. He also knew that running a brothel with youngsters was a dangerous game and maybe this man would give him an edge that would keep it going. He also knew what the war might bring. He had survived the first one when he had been in the military. He had survived trenches, foot rot, gas, and the Germans. He was in no mood to fight them all over again, but his feeling was that he might not have a choice in the matter and funds in his bank would be an escape route out of here, should the situation become too difficult to deal with. Still not happy with being forced into a sale he hadn't wanted, but he was nevertheless warming to the possibility that it had advantages that he hadn't previously considered. What he had to do now was extract enough money out of this pretend Swiss man to make it worth his while.

Simone was probably right when she reckoned he was English. Wanting to know about war and looking for a base here in Paris smacked of deviousness and subterfuge that would go beyond a criminal plan. Most of the people he knew would have just come along and shot him if he had refused to sell the bar if they wanted to take it over. But he didn't want the bar he wanted the information that could be extracted from the clients who indulged themselves in their personal pleasures. Up to now they had all lived in a level of harmony that allowed for business to flourish without major disruption that was all changing he needed to keep up.

He had work to do. His first job tomorrow was to speak to his tame lawyer friend and then his bankers sooner rather than later. This man had a plan and what he didn't want to happen was being further embroiled in a business venture that he wasn't in some control of.

Henri left the bar shortly after he had finished his discussion with Alan. He spoke to Simone and Jacques before he left a conversation that Alan was not able to hear and which was never relayed to him.

"My business is complete for now. I will assume there is change available." he said to Jacques. "So, share it between you two, and I will see you sometime in the few next weeks, when Henri has worked out how to fiddle more money out of me than he's entitled to."

"Do you not require further services from me?" Asked Simone.

"I think an early night is in order Simone. I may have to return to Switzerland tomorrow morning. Goodnight I will see you soon."

Cameron got some travel vouchers from the embassy. Let Graham know what had occurred during the meeting at the bar. Please be discreet Graham yes I know you will. He left Alan with some spare cash and retuned to Woolwich to speak to Mr. Conway.

Alan made a call to Almira's restaurant and had a long meeting with Charles. He needed to create a messaging service, a banking account, and a link that would allow Simone to pass both funds and messages to the restaurant. Charles accepted that as long as Henri wasn't going to be visiting he thought Madame would be ok with it. Alan did not expect to get the service for nothing and as his money was being minded by them he assumed there would be a charge. He left it with Charles to speak to Madame and contact him when he had an answer.

Three days after he left, Cameron was back. He arrived in the afternoon, which gave Fatima enough time to feed him that evening. Afterwards in their room Cameron told his tale.

"I explained how we came up with a plan and a bit of guesswork and then how you had negotiated a deal with Almira and a prospective one with Henri. I passed on the details of the finances that Madame Almira had provided, which he said was the same deal that the embassy had so that was no problem; but he did baulk when I spoke to him about the bar. He wasn't too keen on it at all but when I said it's cheaper than a tank he laughed. Though it was so funny he just said 'agreed buy it via the embassy. I shall instruct them to get on with it. We'll put it in your name Cameron'.

"I asked him to put it in your name as you had brokered the deal with both Henri and Almira. I assumed that you would manage to do a deal with Almira to bank for us, so I told him it could then all be managed by Almira's bankers, who could then manage any income we might get from the bar and offset it against any payment we might owe for their services."

When everyone wants a deal to happen it does. After agreement to accept Simone as the link between Henri's bar and Almira's banking with Charles managing it all. Their accountants keeps an eye on things and provide reports as and when requested. Then the whole thing runs as any business would with external investment.

The embassy lawyers worked a deal that didn't get Henri smiling or at least when he could be seen. They kept the paperwork at the embassy. Cameron and Lewis thanked Fatima for taking care of them and returned to England. Cameron went back to his desk at Woolwich. After more than a couple of beers with Cameron and Dougie White in the Lion that night, Lewis went back over to Salisbury to keep an eye the specialist training.

CHAPTER 5 1938   Hamburg

The call from Conway came at 08.15., on Thursday. Cameron was in his office. The one to Lewis was less than fifteen minutes later, and Alan was just leaving to follow an exercise on the plain, but he managed to take the call. Just as well. The colonel had a car to take him to Woolwich already organised as Talbot Conway had phoned him while Cameron was speaking to Alan.

Conway met them in Cameron's office.

"We have something for you to do, but we don't really know what it involves, or what it is all about yet. Details that you need are that General Harrer, I'm sure you remember him, has asked for a meeting with you two in Hamburg ASAP. That's all we have nothing else other than it comes from a very reliable source, who I deal with on a regular basis. If they say it's legit then it is. As usual any questions.

"Tickets, funds, weapons, cover story," from Cameron

"Story is you are on a couple of days holiday, which might extend. No weapons, funds and tickets are here in this envelope, receipts please, there is nil budget when we don't know what it's about. Civvy clothes, spare set, extra shirts and underwear, just in case your away longer than we think. Look smart remember this is a General we are dealing with even if he is a German he is a general. Got it?"

"Yes sir. I think so."

"Whatever it needs, if funds start running out, or you need to get in touch, there is a consulate in Hamburg; best bet is to make a visit there as soon as you arrive. Speak to the military attaché introduce yourself and don't let them fob you off. If there's a problem threaten them with me. The source for this, as I said, is extremely reliable, and a gut feeling tells me to get a good grip on it, dividends will follow."

Once again they caught the overnight Ferry and then trains. This time they continued on past Berlin to Hamburg. In Hamburg they found a cheap old fashioned hotel, with restaurant, not too far from the Reeperbaum. Then the following morning, while Cameron visited the consulate, Alan, as instructed, took his breakfast in a street café. Sit outside where you can be seen, unless it's raining.

Alan was sitting on his own at an outside table. He'd picked up a local paper and was slowly working through the news while doing the same to his coffee. He put another cigarette in his mouth when from behind the click of a lighter. Assuming the waiter was bringing him another coffee he thanked him for the light .and when a voice from the past sounded from behind.

"Good morning Herr Lewis how are you?"

"Otto. Good morning." Alan stood up. "You are looking well my friend. Strange to see you out of uniform. You wear a fine suit and look very smart, and you are looking very fit and healthy. Will you have breakfast with me?"

"I have eaten thank you. I will take coffee with you though."

The waiter had hovered as soon as he had seen the new arrival. A large pot of coffee was ordered, which arrived just before Alan's hot sausages with bread and butter.

"First things first thank you for coming. I hope the journey was not too tiresome."

"It was a rush but not any real problem."

"In case I haven't previously told you I will give you a short history lesson. Before the first world war my general was a young officer in the Wehrmacht. His family had lost a lot of money when they were kicked out of German South West Africa. The home estate was struggling and required investment. The issue was resolved by marrying into money. A marriage of convenience, money in return for a name and security. After the war and the birth of two children, his wife's parents walked out of Russia and made their way down to their son in law's house to live with their daughter and her family.

They invested their money into the farm and as a result the farm prospered from time, hard work and especially their investment.

Being Jewish they are now no longer wanted in Germany, and many are being rehoused in makeshift buildings and ex prisons.

They think, and we all agree with them, that America would be a good place to go."

"So, what do you want from me?"

"If I said a favour that would put me further in your debt. So, what I want to do is offer you a business proposition. I want you to get these five people to America, for which you will be paid a decent sum of money, and all your expenses."

"Why don't you do it?"

"Because neither my General, nor I, are in a position to do so, and to be perfectly honest, we don't trust anyone that we know with the job. Which is terribly sad and a condemnation of the people we would expect to be able to rely on."

"I can possibly get them to Britain; they could then sail to America reasonably easily from there."

"That is a start. How easy would it be to get from England to America?"

"I don't know, but I can find out. How long do I have?"

"Sooner the better."

"Where are they?"

"In the south. Their estate is on the outskirts of the Black Forest."

"Are they fit enough to travel?"

"Yes."

"I need names, dates of birth, where born, plus any information that would be needed for a passport or identity papers."

"I knew I had the right person, when I thought of you."

Otto handed Alan a sealed envelope. "What you need is in here, including current photographs. Also in there is a significant amount of money. Currency, we weren't sure of, so it's half in Swiss francs and half in US dollars. There is more when you need it."

"Good saves trying to do this sort of thing on a shoestring."

"Shoestring?"

"Just an expression means on the cheap, no budget."

"Yes I understand. The budget is significant and I believe I know you well enough to know you will not abuse your position."

Alan had slipped the envelope into his inside pocket.

"How did you know I was here? We have only just arrived."

"Our people keep an eye on what is going on whatever and wherever we need to. Ever since the games in 36 I have followed your career with interest. Perhaps I know more than you realise. I do know that you will get a promotion shortly according to talk at the MOD."

Alan stopped eating momentarily his mouth slightly open taken totally off guard. Otto laughed.

" You did not know. Perhaps, I've got it wrong. Please don't let this spoil your meal. I will let you eat in peace and remind you of the urgency of this business."

"Leave it with me."

"Until when?"

"It's Monday. Same time next Monday. wait here for ten minutes. If I'm not here by then, do the same every day after, until I have your answers. If I've not turned up it's because I don't know. I will see you when I've worked it out and have everything we need."

Alan had taken a nap in their room. He knew it would be nearer lunchtime before Cameron returned form the consulate. The y would not open until ten so a nap and a catch up on lost sleep was his best idea.

He came too instantly; his inside his head alarm button heard the key in the door. He put his fingers to his lips asking Cameron to not say anything.

"Lunchtime soon let's go for a walk." Cameron immediately picked up on what Lewis was about and he opened the door again as Lewis grabbed his jacket and his room key. They dropped the keys at reception and headed out.

"We must go for a walk somewhere noisier," said Alan, as they left the hotel and wandered outside into the street. Most of the locals were now at work or in school and the traffic was mostly commercial deliveries.

"You remember our German hosts at the shooting competition in 36?"

"Yes, General Harrer and Captain Witzel. They are in military intelligence attached to who knows what."

"Well, apart from what Mr. Conway said, do you know more than me?"

"That does depend Alan on what you know?"

"Absolutely nothing at all. When Conway spoke to us it was the first contact or anything since we left Berlin; until this morning."

"I don't have much, but odd bits of news get sent. I think it's only because of what occurred in Berlin, and now I'm included in the information group and it's now a permanent link, so if a name gets a mention, it lands on my desk back at Woolwich."

"Have you heard anything recently then?"

"No just normal chit chat."

"Who's providing the stories?"

"No one in particular, odd snippets of stuff, mostly unimportant troop or mechanized movements. Why?"

"I think we're being drip fed for some reason or another or possibly, we've been deliberately had information passed to us to keep us in the frame, and linked to the players, because I have received a business offer from Otto Witzell."

"Interesting."

"It is. His boss has a problem that he thinks we can solve better than they can."

"Even more interesting. How far are we walking by the way? You are going quite quickly."

"I wanted to see if we would be followed. Going the wrong way down a one way street means it has to be someone on foot or persons posted along a possible route. We look to be in the clear."

"Are you being serious Alan?"

"Yes. Because Otto was on edge when I spoke to him this morning. He was tense for some reason, and I don't know what it was."

"So, tell me what does General Harrer want?"

"He wants us to ship his family to America."

"Why doesn't he do it?"

"Exactly what I asked." They had arrived at a small, grassed area not unlike a village green, with a convenient wooden seat which they took. Privacy in full view as no one could get near to them and listen. "It happens that his wife's parents are Jewish, and the others will be considered Jewish by being blood relations. Anybody assisting in their escape, shall I call it, would be guilty by association, and that would include any members or friends of the General, if they helped in any way. He also adds that he doesn't trust any of them to know about any escape plan."

"You think the rumours we're hearing are true?"

"I don't think they're just rumours. I think some people know exactly what's happening but are not doing anything about it. If members of the intelligence corps tell me they're true. I'm not certain I am in any position to argue with them."

"It sounds like another rush job. Do you have a plan?"

"Yes, I think we can adapt the idea we had a while back of using Switzerland as a part of import export business that we played about with."

"How?"

"Don't know for definite yet. Need you to give the OK on it before I start but also I think it'll be a good exercise for us to practice something that we've planned and see how easy or difficult is to put it together."

"That in itself might be worth the effort."

"Another thing that comes out of this is that we might find more information as to what is going on with the Military here than we have up to now."

"OK, provisionally we can run with this, but we don't have a lot of money to play with."

"But we do. All expenses plus a stipend for us." That perked Cameron up. Not so much the stipend but the budget for the project.

"Sounds like the plan is going to work then. What do you want from me?"

"I want a plane, a cargo plane with eight seats to make a pick up from northern Switzerland of machine parts or machinery of some sort. Let's ask for broken machinery needing fixing being returned to the factory for repair which means not a lot lost if we don't bring it back."

"Sounds interesting go on."

"If we use a DC2 cargo plane, with s the extra seating there'll be enough room for everything and there's enough of them around not to attract too much attention."

"Next." Cameron was warming to this plan. Alan hoped everyone else would.

"I need two vehicles to get me out of Switzerland into Germany and then back in again. I'm thinking a decent size van and a biggish car. I need a driver for one of the vehicles who speaks German and who holds either ideally a Swiss passport or German."

"I could drive the second vehicle"

"When we're doing the job sir I need you here to keep track of what's happening and any last minute issues that might happen."

"Go on." Cameron didn't sound too happy about not taking part, but he knew Alan was right. This was get the job done not any old exercise on the plain.

"I want five Swiss passports, names and details, as in this envelope. Plus, another one for whoever is the second driver. One of the embassy or consulate guys will do, assuming he speaks German fluently, and can bang heads together if needed.

"What about you?"

"I have Swiss papers and passport that I got a while back when I used to do some odd jobs before I joined you sir." Cameron thought that's not on his record card, but this wasn't the time to pursue it.

"Why do we need the passports surely the German ones will be ok?"

"I don't think the parents have any passports, and all Jewish ones are now stamped with a 'J'. Add to this the fact that the Swiss police have made some sort of agreement with the Nazis, and they are not letting any Jewish refugees across the border."

"When?"

"I picked it up from my newspaper this morning. Just a column inch at the bottom of a middle page like it wasn't important and that's why there may be more urgency about this than meets the eye. I suspect that it is to stall any mass exodus and escape from Germany and possibly to stop their money from being accessible and going somewhere else."

"This is starting to gather speed and snowball. I think you are confirming what we have suspected for a while Alan."

"There is enough money in there to get it all started; and I want an itemized account for our client, the balance of the funds unused, and a costing for the use of plane, crew and fuel etc., to give to them. We only need costings for the transport including the cost of borrowing car and van and its conversion work that's in the envelope until we get confirmation from the client that it's a goer. I also need a time scale for how long it all might take to get ready assuming we get the go ahead."

"Do we have a time they want it doing?"

"As I understand it 'yesterday'. So soon as possible, there is an uncertainty of how things are progressing here and it's frightening a lot of people."

"I will go and see a pal of mine at the consulate. He was my commanding officer when I first left Sandhurst. He's here now which should make things move swiftly."

"That's handy let's hope everything else runs like that."

"We can walk back to the hotel now. I've finished talking unless you have anything to add."

"No nothing I can think of. It's straight forward. And I can't think that we're breaking any more than half a dozen international laws that would automatically get us a long term prison sentence wherever they try us."

Cameron went straight on to the consulate, while Alan, after a short discussion and eavesdropping on the hotel receptionist phone conversation, went to pick up a car that between them they had managed to hire for the duration of their stay.

He parked it in the hotel car park just as Cameron was returning.

"We have a budget. I don't see any point in walking around or penny pinching when we're in a rush."

"Totally agree." Camerom replied, "especially as I have to go to Berlin. Though cars not needed for that; train's quicker."

"Let's get back in the car for now and you can tell me then, how the meeting went."

"First off, as I said, I need to go to Berlin for the passports; our man has been working there for a while now. I have spoken to him on the phone and without going into details he knows what I'm after and he knows it's a priority. I won't get back until near the end of the week or a bit later. There have been some developments over last weekend while we were travelling. Something has happened that we don't know about, and progress is being assisted shall we say.

We are now almost a department." Which got a strange look from Alan. "I'm being a bit flippant. Mr. Conway, in his wisdom, and possibly sarcastic, is increasing our budget and I've been promoted to Major and you to Captain, so my heartiest congratulations Captain Lewis."

"And my I offer mine to you sir. I didn't know about yours, but Otto told me about mine. I didn't say anything then about it because I though t it was a joke"

"Well, it's no joke and we're also getting a couple of staff currently based here at the consulate. They will work here unless we want them; and we have priority. They are both German speakers. One of them, Joe is fluent in German while George's German is more like I was with Spanish as he is one of the French speakers here.

As you'd expect as they are with the military attaché, they are both servicemen and as it happens both army. Two totally different characters. One with a bad habit of head breaking that's Joe Porter, while George Robinson is a slightly younger one; he's an ex student who joined the officer Training Corps at university then left with a degree in French language and literature and then enlisted as a private, he says because he couldn't get a suitable job with his qualifications. I think I got all I was going to get at that. He's in artillery and took and passed the courses at Salisbury after you left to join with me. He's totally different from Joe, but Joe will be your second driver; he is competent when speaking German and if it has a steering wheel he can drive it."

"Right then while we're here in the car we need to check train times organise a meeting to get Joe and George, into our group or programme, up to speed anyway."

"Department," offered Cameron. Alan ignored it as Cameron had expected him to. He headed the car off in the direction of the train station. He'd had a drive around when he picked up the car so knew how to get fuel, buses, trains, consulate, and back to hotel.

Then later on when Cameron was on the way to Berlin. Alan went to the consulate as arranged and spoke to Joe and George about what they were doing in broad terms, without names or numbers. He arranged to return sometime tomorrow morning, in the meantime start looking at airports, border crossings and current staffing at those places. Do not discuss the job with anyone.

On the following Monday morning at 08.45 Alan has eaten breakfast and ordered a large pot of coffee. If Otto is on time he will be here in just over five minutes, by which time the coffee should be here and ready to drink. The budget was sufficient to generate some speed and urgency into the project, which was just as well, as news coming out of Germany, via the Embassy, suggested that relationships between various groups, and political factions was developing into meltdown. Civil war was on some people's minds, but Hitler had too much power, for that to happen, but something was about to break, and that, everyone was certain of.

About fifty yards down the street a black official looking vehicle stopped at the kerbside. Alan saw Otto climb out, from the driver's seat. He shut the door and locked it. He walked along the pavement to the café.

"Good morning Alan. I hope you bring me good news."

"Help yourself to coffee Otto. Would you like something to eat?"

"Again, I have already breakfasted thank you."

"I have in my pocket a list of instructions and a proposed plan. I do not wish to amend it or change it in anyway. Timing is critical and to make it work we must follow it carefully."

"Sometimes flexibility is needed."

"If I start with the idea that we have no flexibility people will assume that they must comply. If I start with the idea that we have certain times that we have to get close to.

Then flexibility will naturally create an unnecessary leaning towards failure."

"Understood."

"The plan will require five days. When we start there is no turning back."

"Again, I understand. What are you proposing?"

"Driving in two vehicles from the Farm into Switzerland and then a flight from there to England. I have not confirmed any onward travel yet from England to America."

"How are you going to get plane tickets?"

"I'm not. They will leave on a cargo plane with the addition of some seats and fly across France in a direct flight to the UK."

"From where to where?"

"You don't need to know. and I don't know yet, as my people haven't located a landing area in Switzerland. We will deliver a cargo to an airfield load it onto an aircraft and fly it to the UK. This provides the required paperwork for a flight in and out."

"What are you going to carry?"

"Nothing of any significant weight on the way out probably a large piece of machinery but not a heavy piece probably aluminium. I have asked that Frau Harrer is to organise that."

"Who is flying the plane?"

"You are asking too many questions that I don't have an answer to at this time; but be assured whoever I use will be a professional and competent. Currently all I have is a very basic plan. People dates and locations will be entered when I get the go ahead. The relevant details are in the envelope along with an account for what I have spent so far. The remainder of the money you first gave me I still have. Should you change your mind I shall return the balance minus two breakfasts and two pots of coffee. There is also a balance that I will need before I set the whole thing in motion. The five days will be two days to get it started, three days for the program and a favourable weather window. We can take responsibility for the first two. God oversees the weather so unless we've irritated the one in charge badly it should all go well.

We're not looking for publicity here, keeping it all quiet will help in just making sure that it works, Hence timing and location are critical. Have a read of what's in the envelope. I shall breakfast here again for a few days what you have there is a plan there are only two possible answers yes or no."

Otto finished his coffee took the envelope from the table and slipped it inside his jacket. "Thank you. I shall see you as soon as I have an answer."

By the time Otto had got to his car. Alan had drunk his coffee. He went into the café and paid the bill. Anyone watching would assume he might leave the same way, but he went through the café and out of another door into the side street, out of view from the front of the building. His hire car was parked another hundred yards or so at the end of the street. Only a short drive and he'd be back at the hotel and fault-finding of the planning with Cameron.

Later after dinner in a restaurant. Cameron suggested, "Shall we have a beer?"

"Let's have them here. There's a bar next door, then we don't have to go too far to get back to the hotel."

They were part way through their second beer when Alan spotted an unexpected face in the mirror.

"Good evening Major, and Captain Lewis, how nice to see you again.

My friends like your idea, Captain, and what has been done so far. They are very happy with it. My brief is to let you know that we await your instructions and coffee tomorrow morning at the same café would be my treat, shall we say same time?"

Alan nodded "Then I will wish you a good evening. Sleep well we all have work to do."

All Alan could do was smile. Otto Witzel appeared to know more about what was going on than they did. He knew exactly where to find them.

"I see what mean It's going to be easier to run with it than change the game now."

"I hope that Sergeant you've got me is as good a head breaker as a driver just in case it goes pear shaped."

"He should be ok. Apparently quite decent fighter as street fighters go."

Alan was at the café at 08.40 he'd ordered just a large pot of coffee. He faced down the street and waited for Otto to arrive. At 09 05 he decided that he had stayed too long and decided to leave. Going into the building to pay his bill and having drunk all the coffee he thought it might be a good idea to use the toilet. The waiter was on the telephone "Herr Lewis."

"Yes."

"A call for you." He passed it over.

"Alan Lewis."

"A small problem Herr Lewis" it was Otto, "There is more urgency than we thought. We have to move quickly as our man has notified others of your plan."

"Give me a name and I'll cut off the supply."

"I don't have a name. I have shut down the receiver here but that will be only temporary."

"How long is temporary?"

"I don't know."

"Ok, give me an envelope and we'll let it run."

"A man will meet you by your car up the road where you've parked it. Leave now and he will be there."

Alan paid the waiter, used the toilet, and left through the side door.

As he got to his car, and just as he opened the door, a man walking passed slipped a large brown envelope onto the front seat. He kept on walking; Alan was hoping it wouldn.t blow up, and because it didn't, he got into the car and drove off.

He took a leisurely roundabout route back to his Hotel. He wanted to know if he was being followed, he wasn't, but he knew also that if they knew what was going on, then they would know he would eventually return to his hotel.

"It's going pear shaped already." Alan told Cameron. "We need to get started. How long did they need for the plane?"

"You can have one within twelve hours they're on standby. All they needed to do was finish putting seats in. and they must have done that by now. It's a lot easier than stripping out a passenger carrier and making it cargo safe."

"Good. Let's play and bluff then Zurich."

"Zurich?"

"Not ideal but it's easier to disappear in a crowd sometimes."

"Ok."

"Anything else?"

"I need you to organise the vehicles and Zurich will be easier to do that. And I need money to cover everything we can think of plus some slush money in case palms need assistance in decision making. Get the plane there for Thursday

I'll let you know when I'm there; but the plane can sit waiting for its cargo, and no one should bat an eyelid, especially if it goes over a weekend. Make certain they don't leave or go on the pop. Fly me and Joe down to Zurich get an hotel as near to the airport as possible with twin room or adjoining rooms and decent parking."

"Anything else?"

"I've put some details of the type of van I want it's pretty standard so the additions I've asked for will be fairly simple and probably loads more but we can busk it on the way. I don't think we have much of a chance for it to run smoothly, but who knows I'm feeling this is a perfect exercise. One objective, concentrate, and apply oneself to job in hand. Application, concentration, objective achieved."

"Are you sure about this Alan? It's easy for me I'm not sticking my neck out and you're going to do a job with someone you've never worked with before who looks extremely capable and might be a complete waste of space."

"With a bit of luck all he'll have to do is drive a vehicle. We'll be fine. When you book the flights book them on our British passports.; I only want the Swiss to go in and out of Germany."

Although the original idea had been to fly to Zurich, Alan and Joe caught a train from Hamburg to Berlin, and then from Berlin to Zurich. With British passports there were no issues at the border crossing for them, but they weren't certain that everyone else had a straightforward journey, as some appeared to be taken off the train and escorted towards a police van.

 Cameron had got them a twin room in an hotel about five miles from the airport. It was a bit further up market than Alan expected but as Cameron pointed out close to airport, car park, but slightly over budget. Two out of three is good and everything has a price, stop worrying.

They had arrived in Zurich and a taxi from the train station to the hotel had got them into their room at a little after 1600 hours Thursday evening. They'd washed and changed and were thinking about the evening meal when the internal phone rang.

"Alan Lewis."

"Mr. Lewis there is a man here who says he has a car for you."

"I'll be right down thank you." Alan put the handset back in the cradle. "Our transport has arrived, let's go see."

There is a man wearing a chauffeur uniform standing by the desk. The clerk points us out and he turns and walks over to Alan.

Joe took the room keys to reception and followed Alan and the delivery driver.

They went out through the back of the hotel and there, in the parking lot, side by side, are their two vehicles. A large Luton van next to a medium sized car, that looks capable of carrying at least four comfortably.

"The car is an Opel sir. Nondescript was my brief, and these are all over the place; so, it'll blend in nicely."

Another car parked near the gate driver inside. Alan looks across to it. "Our transport back Mr. Lewis. I hope these will be satisfactory we didn't have a lot of time."

"Are they reliable?"

"Yes."

"Are they legal?"

"Of course."

"I'm going to Germany with them."

"Not a problem Mr. Lewis."

"Excellent. Someone will contact you when we've finished Thank you."

The delivery team left. Alan and Joe went over to the vehicles. "See what we've got in that van Joe while I have a look at the limo."

A survey of both vehicles found full tanks, tool kits, spare wheels, and working lights, Wipers, and brakes. "Looking good Joe with the limo let's see back of van."

"Plenty of room in here and plenty to tie stuff to."

"Any ropes about?"

"Bag of them under front seat."

"Good all seems right for us then." Alan climbed inside and checked the size of the peak, the part over the top of the cab. He'd asked for a solid wood panel to be fitted, and easily removed, and with a ladder that would give easy access and could then be stored inside the peak as well. All good he thought to himself. Not a lot of room but they were going to have to fit.

"Let's go eat, and then we can go for a walk, and I'll fill you in on what we're up to."

The hotel's empty car park said that there weren't many guests, and the restaurant agreed. They found a quiet table for two to one side and Alan decided to brief Joe again there. They had already had a chat about the job and the original plan had been for Alan to drive the car and Joe to drive the van. Alan looked at Joe and had a change of mind. He looked like a bodyguard and Alan Decided to swap vehicles and make him the chauffer.

"Do you have a black jacket with you or better a black suit?"

"I have a Navy blue suit very dark."

"That may do, actually it'll have to."

"What are you thinking?"

"I'm thinking that, compared to me, you look like a chauffeur and a bodyguard, and that may fit nicely. A hat would have been handy a pity we couldn't get the one off my driver."

"The other guy left his. It's still in there, I put it under the seat."

"Let's hope it fits."

"He looked about the same size as me, so, fingers crossed."

"I'll take all the luck I can get at this time, but a peak cap shouldn't under normal circumstances be difficult to get but tomorrow is not a day to go shopping but getting on with a job, Shops are shut at this time,, and we won't be here when they open I hope."

Breakfast finished and vehicles checked and ready to roll. They'd gone over the route the night before. They had roughly a three hour drive to the border. Then about an hour plus to the farm. They would stay close to each other until they got near the border then Joe would go ahead driving the limo and Alan would follow around ten minutes behind. They left at 07 00. Joe had packed his suitcase and put it in the van with Alan. The run to the border went as planned.

When Alan got to the crossing there was only one man about. He stopped and waited. The guard left his box slung his rifle over his shoulder and asked for papers. Alan showed him his Swiss passport and order for an engine he was picking up for repair. "You work over weekend?" The border guard asked.

"The engineers will start work on the work first thing tomorrow morning. Two men are getting it ready now for pick up, and we will all be back later as soon as we've loaded it."

"I will be here till five," said the guard. "What time are you coming back through?"

"I'll time it right. I can give you a lift down to the village save you walking."

The guard waved him through. Alan had a new plan. Hopefully they were ready to go. Joe gave a thumbs up from the roadside, where he'd stopped and then tucked in behind Alan, as they headed further into Germany and towards the Black Forest.

The notes he'd been given were spot on and exactly as stated the turn just around the bend after the junction had a right hand turn which Alan took. Joe tucked nicely in behind him and they drove up a shallow incline through a large copse of conifers which opened up into a piece of farmland where inside fenced fields either side if the road roamed numerous cattle the odd one looking to see what was driving through but most more interested in feeding, obviously comfortable, with noisy vehicles arriving at the residence, visible from here, maybe another quarter mile along the drive. The people in the house would see them coming the fences were low there were no hedges, and the drive was flat wide and arrow straight. It would be difficult to sneak in here from this direction in daylight and probably easily lit with a good light at nighttime.

The house a two storey building, once upon a time a well-built residence now looking a little forlorn and in need of decoration and some small amount of restoration. Three wide steps up to a double front door which opened as Alan was about to knock. The house had a central entrance with what looked like a room either side of the hallway and over to the right a pair of wooden double garage doors.

An elderly gentleman, short cut grey hair, clean shaven, very erect, waist coated, slim, flat belly, finely pressed trousers, highly polished shoes. All the hallmarks of well-disciplined, institutionalized, ex-military.

"Yes can I help you?"

"Frau Harrer is expecting me."

"And who shall I say is here?"

"Alan Lewis."

"If you will wait a moment, please sir."

The door closed. Alan heard the bolt engage. He wondered if the butler was carrying a gun or where the nearest was. Given what he'd seen of the man he wouldn't have been surprised.

The door unlocked, "please come in sir. Frau Harrer is expecting you. If you will follow me, please."

The butler opened a large wide door. "Frau Harrer. Mr. Lewis."

Alan recognized the lady from the photographs that he had got from Otto.

"Welcome Mr. Lewis." she offered a tiny hand. The lady was so small and delicate, she looked about the size of a young teen child. But her handshake was firm and belied her appearance.

"We await your orders," her voice was strong not loud but positive and confident.

"Are you ready to go?"

"Yes. We are ready."

"Where are the others?"

"They went to the workshop as soon as we saw you coming through the bottom gate."

"What about your butler?"

"He was my husband's batman. He is now our housekeeper. He will mind the house for my husband."

"Let's go to the workshop then and see what we've got."

Alan helped frau Harrer with her long coat and then followed her as she left through the French doors down a couple of steps and a short walk along the rear of the house to a large building hidden from view by the house itself.

A single door led into a spacious workshop and storage area, with attached garage. Alan noticed the garage doors and assumed they were the ones that led to the drive.

"I have a friend in the drive. Can he come in through the judas door?"

"Yes." The elder of the two men opened the door.

"His name is Joe give him a call. He might just get through the door." He did have a squeeze, but once in and the door shut, introductions made, Alan laid out the plan.

"The three ladies will go with Joe in the car. I will drive the van with the machine. What do we have?" The younger man took a tarpaulin off an engine.

"This sir."

"Can we move it?"

Yes sir quite easily. And it's even easier here sir. We can put it on a trolley with the tractor and then lift the trolley and the engine into your van."

"Good."

"Why do we need this sir?" The young man asked.

"That is our reason to be going into the airport with the van."

"Why?" The young man appeared to be the spokesperson. Alan was happy that they asked because then they knew, and nothing should be bothering them.

"So, we can fly you out. There are no direct flights to the UK, so we're going to fly you out in a cargo plane, non-stop overnight."

"Now we understand."

"Are we all ready, packed, small suitcase only, warm clothes, passports, money?"

"We are ready Herr Lewis."

"Right then let's get these doors open and I'll back the van in. we'll have a practice, and I'll show you what I have planned. We have about two hours to get this organised and then we need to be on our way. Perhaps some food if that might be possible frau Harrer, It will be a long day, and possibly a while before we all eat again."

"Certainly Mr. Lewis. What would you like?"

"Anything, hot, cold, warm, anything, and coffee, if that would be possible please. You all should eat too."

"We have brought some cold meats and bread with us, and bottles of water." "Keep them as emergency supplies for later or tomorrow."

"I shall ask Ludwig, our butler, to see what he has available."

"Something within the hour. Whatever fits for you."

"I shall speak to him as long as I am not needed here."

"No. Please do as you need to do."

Whilst frau Harrer organised a meal Alan and Joe showed the others how this was all going to happen. They worked through the next hour making certain what they each had to do and then they loaded the engine into the van making sure that it was well strapped down. The last thing they wanted was anything going wrong when all was going this well.

Alan's fear was that eventually something would go awry because plans always need to do so and the longer everything ran smoothly the later it would happen when it would be too late to fix it. Alan was hoping he was worrying unnecessarily.

Alan watched the children working. The girl was built very like her father, while the young man had all the features of his mother. He understood why Otto might find him attractive too, as compared to his sister he was quite attractive in a more feminine way. Perhaps Otto played two games with a choice of rules. Or possibly of course only one but a different one, maybe. Who cares he thought nothing to do with me.

These thoughts were going around inside his head when Frau Harrer returned "We have set a table on the lawn when you are ready Mr. Lewis"

"Excellent timing, we are ready thank you."

"Before we eat. Is there anything more I need to know Mr. Lewis about today?"

"If I tell you to do something it means I want you to do it. It is not opening a discussion on the rights or wrongs of any decision I have made. I may sound rude and abrupt but getting a perfect ending to the day is my sole purpose. Your safety, and the safety of your family is my only objective. Hopefully it doesn't come to that but just in case."

"I understand perfectly Mr. Lewis Thank you. Now let us eat."

The butler and Frau Harrer had laid a running buffet on a side table with seven cushioned chairs set around a large marble topped garden table. Frau Harrer sat down next to her mother. Henrich, the butler, made up two plates of cold food and served the two ladies while the rest served themselves. He disappeared inside before returning quite quickly with two large coffee pots from which he served coffee to all.

Henrich fussed around his ladies and made certain all three were warm and comfortable in the car with Joseph. The timing was for Joe to arrive at the border at five minutes to five just before the customs man was due to finish. And timing was critical Alan reckoned.

Alan is driving to the crossing. Joe is at the barrier. There are no other vehicles in front of him. The border guard is checking the papers when he sees Alan driving down the road towards them. He finishes quickly and waves Joseph and the ladies through. Alan stops at the barrier. He gets out of the van to open up the back to show him the engine strapped inside. The father and his grandson climb into the back just as the relief border guard comes out to see what's happening.

"I can give you a lift if you are ready?" Alan tells the guard wanting a free ride. "The men will sit in the back until I drop you off." Alan adds.

"Very good," replied the guard

He tells his buddy that he is off and will see him tomorrow morning when they change over and that the driver is giving him a lift down to the village.

He passed the other guard his rifle and climbed into the front.

Alan dropped him off about five miles down the road.

They then continued on their way. Not long after they caught up with Joe who had been driving gently down the road waiting for Alan. Their aim is to get to the airport around 2100 hours when it would be quiet and most of the day's business will have been done.

It's dark in the carpark, and even darker in the far corner away from the road and the rear doors to the hotel. Alan parked the van and left enough space for joe to slip the car tight against the hedge and next to the passenger door of the van. The ladies moved quickly and easily from the car to the back of the van. In the back of the van Alan put the ladder against the Luton peak, the part that goes over the cab, and removes the timber cover which has been clipped in place.

Inside are three places to lie down on the floor part and two more in the space above the bottom three.

"You will need to squeeze the suitcases in there with you. It takes approximately twenty minutes to drive to the airport and then there will be security check, and then about ten minutes to the plane. We'll say forty five minutes maximum in total. At no point should you make any noise unless you hear my voice talking to you and I will start the conversation by tapping four times on the panel like the start of Beethoven's fifth da da da daa. I will do this three times so there should not be any misunderstanding. Understood?"
 they all understood.

"Why are we still hiding we are out of Germany?"

"Because the passports have got you past the border, by rushing the guard and bribing him with a lift home, but they might not stand up to cross-checking with the government officers, when they have lots of time available, because they are holding you in a cell for example."

"Ah yes. That makes sense." The young man was still the spokesperson.

"Right are you ready to get into the top?"

"Frau Harrer first into the top far bunk. Mother furthest bunk in underneath. Ladies suitcases inside at either end. Granddaughter in middle. Grandson on top and father last on bottom. You will need to squeeze in the ladder and then hold the panel in place then clip it from the inside. Joe and I will mind the other two suitcases under the front seat.

Are you all ok? We will drive gently, just relax and everything will be fine."

I'll drive Joe have you got all your gear from the car?

"Yes."

"British passport this time. Major Cameron was going to travel with them, but we changed it at the last minute to maintain control of our options here. I'm going to fly you out with them, to make certain they're ok during the flight, and at the other end."

"Where will that be?"

"Whichever RAF base in England they land at. The two guys in the front will have enough to do with the flying."

Alan moved the van around and pointed it towards the exit while Joe got his suitcase checked over and hid stuff that he was taking with him that no one wanted the border guards to see.

"Passport handy?"

"In my pocket."

"Good when we go into the airport, if asked, you are going with the Engine back to England. When I leave with an empty van everything will look as it's supposed to."

The journey driven gently took a quarter of an hour; customs, when they saw the paperwork, looked quickly in the van, checked Joe's Passport, and waved them through.

After a short drive to the cargo area. The DC2, with its registration number on the side, was easy to spot and both the pilots were ready, waiting, fuelled, flight plans sorted, and ready to go.

Alan backed the van up to the side of the plane where the cargo side door was.

Pilots had opened up when they saw the van reversing. He tapped the morse for letter V on the hatch and after the third time told them to release the catches on the inside. The ladder was lowered into place and the two men climbed out; the suitcases were passed down before the ladies followed.

Frau Harrer looked at Alan and tried a smile, "I assume Mr. Lewis that we are here, and this is where we part company." Her voice was a little shaky and a touch croaky. She was maybe a little stressed from the confines of the box in the roof of the van.

"I'm sad," she said, "to be leaving Germany. I felt after Russia it was my home; but things are not as we had all hoped them to be. Perhaps another move and life will become less hazardous. My parents are too old to be constantly running away but I fear that if we don't run away our right to run could be in other people's hands; and I doubt that we can afford to allow that to happen. I will be eternally grateful to you. I suspect we will never meet again. Thank you are inadequate words. But all I can say on behalf of my family is thank you." There was a tear in her eye and her voice just held before breaking completely. she shook Alan's hand, turned and walked onto the plane. Her daughter held her hand as she stepped inside and walked towards the front and the seating area.

Joe and Alan moved the engine on a bogey and one of the pilots supervised it being strapped down into place. It's a heap of scrap Alan told him but if I take it out it may create a problem. Alan fixed the panel back in place again over the Luton peak.

He shook Joe's hand and wished them all bon voyage. He waited until the plane had started its engines and watched it taxi towards its takeoff and when he could no longer see it but was guessing that it had had enough time to leave he made his way to the exit. The customs men waved him through and figuring a good job well done possibly a small indulgence this evening as a personal bonus.

A quarter of an hour later he was parked up in the hotel car park next to the limo. He checked both vehicles to make certain nothing was left then went back inside the hotel, hoping beyond all reasonable hope that at nearly midnight that somehow food might be available. He got to his room with a bottle of whisky, lit a cigarette, and didn't enjoy the whisky on an empty stomach. Perhaps the indulgence could be postponed until tomorrow. In the end, he cleaned his teeth and went to bed. He was tired and hungry, but nevertheless, slept the sleep of the innocent.

Chapter 6 Hamburg Berlin

Two days later he was back in Berlin having travelled back on the overnight train. He must remember that going back through the border post again he could be recognised. He got another train back to Hamburg where Cameron picked him up at the station.

"How was it?" Cameron asked the second Alan got into the car.

"Went very well, given the length of time we had to plan it. Which could have been either good or bad. Kept it simple worked fine."

"How was Joe?"

"Good man like him a lot, probably really handy in a scrap but he sticks out like a sore thumb. You can't hide him he's too big and if you want to be discreet and unnoticed, a man built like a silver back gorilla, with you, is not the way. I know he's bodyguard material and a good at what he does as I've said, but if it's a need to be discreet then the choice is I'd personally would prefer to go alone it's a lot easier to blend."

"Understood."

"How's your young man?"

"After what you have just said I'm pleased you asked. Probably exactly what you're looking for, by the sound of it. Army sergeant doesn't fight much, unusual in itself, but reason is he was a regiment boxing champ, punches like a mule kick. According to his record, he's quiet, boring, uninteresting, but can shoot just about anything and everything, and hits what he aims at."

Cameron arrived back in the hotel carpark. "We need to think about making a move back to England Alan. We are pretty well finished here, and Mr. Conway is certainly going to want to debrief us over the job we've just done."

"Agreed let's go to consulate now, speak to this man George, and get some travel arrangements made and get back to Woolwich. We could all be on our way home from first thing tomorrow morning if George can be ready as well. You're right all we are going to do here is get bored and I'd sooner get bored at home."

That evening they decided to eat out again chose the same restaurant and then went for a beer in the same bar next door to the restaurant.

"No Otto tonight." Cameron said. "I wonder why he picked this far away from the beginning."

"That's the answer to the question I think. The distance made it easier to hide. The other thing is Ottos family is here. I remember him telling me when we were in Berlin. That's how he knew all the cafes and the bars, this is his home turf. We don't need to see him, job's done last thing needed now would be someone to make the right assumption and a link."

The following morning, they paid their hotel bill, the hire car, picked up George, and got a taxi to the railway station. Caught a train to Berlin and eventually via Calais and Dover got finally back to Woolwich, forty two hours after they started. They'd crashed out and gone to bed when Mr. Conway tried to phone them.

Cameron and Alan ordered breakfast for three from the mess, which saved trying to get George a seat in the sergeants mess as he was probably going to Salisbury when they found what time the daily truck would be going.

Mr. Conway arrived at 0900. Sergeant Robinson was in the outer office making his travel arrangements with the corporal clerk.

"I couldn't get hold of either of you yesterday. Why?"

"We were tired sir. We travelled for forty two hours with no real sleep. We got here went to sleep and we wouldn't hear the phone because we were ibn bed sir." Alan had said it, and it sounded like 'and don't argue with me Mr. Conway' voice.

"Perfectly adequate and understandable explanation Lewis. I do prefer no bullshit answers. Pity, a lot more people couldn't learn the meaning of succinct. Now to business. Yugoslavia. I think after talking to Frau Harrer that there's more going on there than we know about, as her husband General Harrer is there. And that makes me think Why a Military Intelligence General who specialises in tactics and strategic planning is in Yugoslavia? Did your interests extend as far east as Yugoslavia Cameron?"

"No sir. And why he's there, I haven't a clue."

"Neither have I but I bet it isn't a holiday. You need to get your thinking caps on and come up with an answer. You aren't alone. I have others working with the same brief. We need to find an answer if there is one. And if we can't I'm going to send you two back to Berlin to sniff around and find what stinks. I'll leave it with you for now gentlemen. Before I go, I have put on your records, the job you've just done. It will stand you in good stead next time I want to promote you. Well done, it was beautifully executed according to your passengers. Don't wait for me to contact you; if you have something interesting, get in touch and keep me posted on any progress you make." As he opened the office door to leave one of the twins moved aside to let him pass. They left the door open to allow Sergeant Robinson in, who was standing outside, presumably, having been refused entry by whichever twin it was.

"Come in George. That was Mr. Conway in case you haven't met him before. The man at the door has a twin brother. Don't mess about with either of them. I think you will end up in the tower via nearest hospital A and E.. Nothing to add to that really is there Captain?"

"No sir."

"What do you know about Yugoslavia sergeant?" Cameron asked, "as we need to find a reason for a German General to be visiting them."

"Not a lot sir, though they did start the war in 1914. Or helped it to get going at the least."

"Keep talking," Cameron was getting interested, "you sound like you know more than I do."

"One of the factions there killed an Austrian I think which mobilized the Germans as well as all their mates. We did it at school in history class. I did pay attention, but it was a while back."

"You certainly paid more attention than I did. What about you Captain?"

"I missed the Yugoslavia lesson sir either I was off sick or expelled. But I'm thinking thar when we were in Berlin in 36 Otto Witzel mentioned that when General Harrer was a young officer he was adjutant to Otto's father."

"Go on Captain."

"Did anyone ever follow up on it? I wonder because we thought at the time that although officially retired, he was still a man of distinction, with a voice still listened to in Germany"

"Go on, Captain I'm waiting for it."

"He was a German general, and I think he was in what we now call Yugoslavia during the Great War. If he was, Harrer would have been with him, and though it was a long time back he would be aware of the politics there, the friends and the enemies. Though I would add that changing sides in eastern Europe is not unusual and there may not be the predictability that one would assume. Which might explain the General's interest, or I could be guessing."

"what do you want to do about it?"

"In what way sir?"

"Shall I give Mr. Conway the information as we have it?"

"I think if we don't sir, we're neglecting our duty. Even if it's hopelessly inaccurate it's worth checking on."

"That's not quite how I meant it. Given what you remember and what we know is there anything further we can do that might confirm or debunk the info.

"We don't have any way to confirm the information that I'm suggesting might be of use. It's probably better checked by others with the required access. I'm confident enough in passing on what we've got hoping that someone somewhere else can fill in the blanks."

"Agreed. I'll try and phone someone and see if I can get a message to him.

If you will organise the coffees please Captain. Do you want coffee sergeant?"

"Yes please sir."

"Then three coffees it is."

Cameron eventually got through to Mr. Conway's office and left a message, asking him to phone when he could.

It was the day after. And when told of what they had come up with had a long chat with Cameron.

Cameron had pointed out that they didn't have access to either records or information easily accessible to others, and it was the only thing they could work out given what little contact they had with the Harrer family. At no point did frau Harrer say anything other than where her husband was.

Conway decided then to send Alan and George back over to Salisbury and Cameron to keep the office there open, going backwards and forwards himself to Salisbury, as and when he deemed it practical.

Conway also agree to adding ncos to the training programmes. He agreed with the idea that the more well trained specialists that were available the better. Alan increased his instructor team with men who were specialists indifferent fields, and he also broadened the course making it longer with a general teach everyone everything then when you see were their talents were improve that to an expert level.

Conway arrived at Salisbury in the middle of August 1939.

"I said to you last year that I might send you back to Berlin to have a sniff around. Half the world is doing the same thing, and I know there's people at the embassy who can give me information, but we all speak the same language, and you know what I want to know about and if anyone can find it I think it might be you two. No one really believes in the piece of paper Mr. Chamberlain brought back last year. Disappointingly it's one of those not worth the paper it's printed on.

In short if things remain as they are. Italy have aligned with Germany. Part of Czechoslovakian has gone. Austria was on side already. Bulgaria will likely follow them and possibly Romania. Albania has become a puppet of Italy. Therefore, if an alliance can be acquired, by Germany, with some in Yugoslav. Then it will only be Greece that stands in the way of controlling the whole of the eastern Medit. Some staff at the embassy in Berlin are getting uncomfortable. Add to all of that the Russians and the Germans are discussing a non-aggression pact. And no one but the Germans and possibly the Russians know where that one's going.

When I sent you to Berlin in thirty-six there was little if any likelihood of problems currently there is. I have removed the man who was slipping our friends information, and he now gets three meals a day and some exercise courtesy of his majesty. As far as I know there will be no one broadcasting your arrival in Berlin. But that doesn't mean they won't r know you're there you can be assured of that. Do take care; any problems get out; you don't have the benefit of the embassy and diplomat status; you are again on your own. For those reasons I'm giving you enough US dollars, Deutch marks, and British pounds to get away by any means possible. This is not for a jolly, it's emergency funds, I want you two and the change back again. Usual route trains to Berlin. I don't need to tell you how to do your job bur we know trains are full of people some of whom like to talk and give opinions as to what is happening. The mood of a country often a feeling only available when caught up in the crowd. Take care of your selves gentlemen."

There was no discussion Cameron and Lewis listened to Conway, they emptied the standard brown envelope onto Cameron's desk, split the contents between them, and got themselves ready to travel.

Cameron and Lewis managed to get themselves a twin room on the third floor of the Grand Hotel. They also decided it would be prudent to remain together, rather than split up, and go walkabout in different directions. The Grand was priced in budget, and close to the center of Berlin, or certainly close to where everything was taking place.

They had spent a couple of days chatting to people in bars and cafes and were starting to put together a jigsaw of pieces that didn't exactly fill them with joy.

They had learnt never to prod the conversation but to let people talk. Often the talker would want to prove an insight or a piece of knowledge that they felt would make a greater impression on the listener. Cameron and Alan were more than happy to let others lead the conversation especially if it was going in the right direction.

Their hotel was a short walk along the Wilhelmstrasse to the Wilhelmplatz was the hotel Kaiserhof across the from the Reich chancelry building. They used the square a central point for their observations and would go through it a couple of times a day as their hub.

They stopped and looked around at the continuous movements of military uniforms going in and out of the government buildings. Alan had given up counting the numbers and spoke to Cameron "In a perfect world we would have an outside a street café where we could take our morning coffee alfresco, and people would come and chat to us, and tell us tales and stories, and we could go home a job well done."

"I'm not certain we need to Alan. I can feel the tension on the air."

"I'm with you there sir. I couldn't agree more and now Russia has signed a treaty with Germany I get the feeling that although the blue touch paper has not been lit, I reckon it could be closer than ever.

As you know sir I'm a great believer in hiding in full view sir but hanging around here too long will get us noticed Herr Hitler has his HQ in the Kaiserhof, and I don't believe he would see us as a welcome guests.

Here in 36 there was a certain amount of tension but now you can feel it in everyone. The ones who don't seem tense will be the ones in control, and I think they are looking forward to it all staring.

Given what we've learned so far sir I'm not certain how much more we can find out unless someone tells us what the plan is I don't see that happening somehow; I believe we are waiting for something we already know is going to happen. It has for a long time when not if and when is getting nearer on a daily basis.

I can understand why some at the embassy might be getting jumpy. I'm sure they will be, but I do hope they're staying ahead of what's going on."

Cameron and Alan, having walked up and down Wilhelmstrasse, headed back to their hotel.

"I don't know if we'll learn anymore here we might be better off getting a bit out of town tomorrow to see what might be happening around. We know there are camps and makeshift prisons about and we know that what was happening when we were last here is now on the increase. Perhaps a bus ride out somewhere and see what we can see."

"I think your right sir, shall we look at the street map and see what we can find?"

"That's about the best we can do I reckon."

They arrived back at the hotel Cameron went to the lift, Alan went for the reception desk.

"Keys to room 27 please."

"Herr Lewis?"

"Yes."

"A letter for you sir.

"Who brough t this?"

"A young woman sir. Or a girl teenager age not certain sir."

"Thank you."

Alan took the keys; he and Cameron got the lift to the third floor and got into their room before opening the note.

Alan read the letter out quietly.

"You must leave Berlin as quickly as possible ideally in the next ten minutes if that isn't possible but very soon you and your Major, go to Hamburg, an address is enclosed, which is quick and then to Copenhagen. Passage back to England will be easier from there. You're on a list for picking up as you are a known visitor and they know who you work for as we always did.

I am genuinely concerned for you. I cannot stay here now. I have had the message delivered hoping not to be seen to be involved. I consider my debt to you is paid please don't waste it. Auf Weidersen my friend."

He handed it to Cameron.

"You think this is real?"

"Yes no one else would know about the fact that he believed he owed me something from three years ago."

Cameron thought about it for three seconds. "I'll go and pay our bill I'll let you pack everyhing and I'll meet you in reception."

"Take the keys with you sir. I'll get out of the lift and head straight for the door. We can get a taxi, I know it's only a couple of miles but that's half an hour with suitcases."

The half hour walk saved had them catch a train and they were on their way to Hamburg twenty minutes after paying the bill at the Grand hotel. Another taxi from Hamburg central station and they were at the docks. The taxi driver said he didn't know the street that Cameron had asked for, so he dropped them on the main road.

Alan and Cameron were both familiar with the dock area and they didn't know the street they were looking for either. Directions from one of the locals had them close and another question and there they were. It transpired that Elke ran an establishment that catered for the needs of itinerant seamen, which was why the last person that they asked for directions, had a knowing smirk on his face. When Alan explained what he was looking for and mentioned Otto, Elke's attitude changed, and she became super-efficient and helpful. 'There was she said a boat leaving tonight about nine, a cargo boat, Danish, named the Alabaster. It was originally white till it showed too much rust and over the years had been painted black. She was single funnel registered Copenhagen. Tonight, heading for Harwich. She took passengers. It wasn't full there were possibly only three berths still available. Hurry they will shut up and leave early if they can.

"If you come back here in the future you should try some of the other things I have on offer. I don't only supply information, but lots of entertainment too." Elke possibly couldn't resist an attempt at a sales pitch.

"when I'm back Elke, I promise to come and see you. We are most grateful for your help."

She smiled and closed the door.

Alan and Cameron headed for the Alabaster it was nearly eight, but still no time to be wasted.

The ship was almost ready to leave when Alan and the major arrived at the dockside. They'd got there before the walkway had been removed and managed to talk their way on board passed the seaman at the bottom to speak with the deck officer at the top of the gangplank.

"We have room for only one more passenger."

"I thought you had three places."

" We did until a short while ago two other people arrived just before you. The company will not let us carry any more passengers than twelve. Therefore, I can only take one of you. I don't mind which one it is but only one. I'm sorry."

"Do you have a full crew?" asked Alan.

"What do you mean?"

"I have a lot of experience crewing on fishing boats working out of the river Mersey, so I can join as extra crew and not only will I not need to be paid but I will pay my passage and work as well so you are getting the best of both worlds."

"How do I know you are not lying just to get aboard?" Alan went into the top of his suitcase and took out a small leather bag. He opened it carefully. He took out a leather wallet opened the wallet and gave the deck officer a smaller hard backed leather book.

"Show this to your skipper." Alan said.

"I shall speak to the skipper wait here if you move I won't take either of you."

"Are you sure about this Alan?"

"Yes sir."

"What did you give him?"

"I still hold a seaman's ticket that dad got me when I worked the fishing boat for him. Stopped any issues with the union. And as we've been told to leave, I can see no point in not taking the advice offered."

"you've not worked on boats for a while."

"They don't know that and according to my ticket I have. Dad fills it in whenever I go back home to see them. Fingers crossed it works."

"I hope so." Cameron said, "There's obviously something happening for Otto to have sent that note. It's all part of a bigger picture, I'm certain but as yet I can't see quite where it's going as there are some pieces missing. We'll see assuming we get our passage."

The deck officer came back out from the bridge. He was followed down the staircase by another man.

"You have a deal. This is the bosun. Find a bunk for him and give him a job, if you need him. He says he's experienced."

The bosun beckoned Alan. "Come with me." he said.

"And you follow me." Said the deck officer.

The Major asked "What about the cases?"

"First job bosun deliver the luggage to cabin 4 same as the Norwegians."

"As I'm sure you heard your friend will be in cabin four." The bosun told Alan.

"How big is the cabin?" Cameron asked. The deck officer replied

"There is room, but not enough to swing a cat. We don't really do passengers after eight number other than for occasions like now, but we keep four extras in case people are not getting on, or there are snorers. You don't snore do you?" He laughed.

"Don't know." replied the Major "I'm always asleep if it happens."

"You pay in cash?"

"Yes."

"Follow me," he said to Cameron

"Good man Alan."

"Have a good journey sir I'll be fine."

The bosun took a suitcase, Alan grabbed his own and his duffel bag with a few bits in and followed the bosun,

The crew were on the deck level officers one deck up at bridge level along with the passengers now numbering twelve with the major.

They followed the major and the deck officer up the staircase and while they went straight into the bridge Alan followed the bosun along the deck to a second iron door. The bosuns spoke to him in German he asked him if he spoke Danish. "

English French and German.

"OK, He said we'll manage. So you're a fisherman?"

"No my father is a fisherman. Before the Great war and during a after the war, he sailed for Blue Funnel as a mate, in 1923 he bought a fishing boat and I crewed for him and do when I'm there."

"Fishing is a hard life. How big was his boat?"

"Just over forty feet."

"What's that in metres?"

"Thirteen."

"Tiny. Dangerous. You got big balls."

The major was sharing with the two Norwegians who didn't speak much English and only a little German. They apparently had got a warning too about impending hostilities and decided it was safer outside Germany rather than inside. Although Denmark and Russia had both signed non-aggression pacts with Germany. Norway, Sweden, and Finland had all refused, and even though Harwich was a long way from home it was probably going to be a safer place in the immediate future. Norway was nearer to Hamburg than Harwich especially if you got yourself first to Copenhagen. It would be straight forward to go North from there but this was the first boat leaving, so they caught it.

The deck officer was right about one thing it was cramped there were four bunks, a double and two more side by side in a line against a bulkhead, a small gap between each of the bunks would just allow enough space for a person to get out of the bunk and walk to the door. Except there was no need to walk far if all you wanted was a wash or a shower as next to the end berth was some sort of a curtain behind which was a rusty looking shower head, and at the opposite side a wash basin with two brass taps and rust streaks on the porcelain.

The three bunks away from the wash area were all taken and when Alan put the suitcases on the bunk he could feel the blankets and the damp.

After Alan had taken some things from his case and put them in his duffle bag, they headed for the crew quarters.

"Throw your bag on that bunk there. The guy in this one here is a bully. If he gives you trouble it's up to you what you do. Back down or fight. If you incapacitate him you'll have to do his work. He's a pain in the arse but a hardworking and an experienced sailor and he's German so you will understand each other."

"What do you want me to do?" He asked the bosun.

"Nothing at the moment. Maybe nothing all trip. If it goes well, we'll be in Harwich this time tomorrow. Depends if they have a berth for us.

You will be in the way until you are needed. Later I will introduce you to the others . They have their jobs and they know what to do. Sit tight, later we eat. You are only here a day at most two, don't worry too much about work you have paid your passage too. Any work you do is a bonus for the company or letting another man shirk."

Alan was reading when some of the crew returned to the quarters.

"Who are you?" A big man asking.

"Alan. Who are you?"

"I ask the questions."

"You English?" Alan had that here we go again look but continued with the game.

"Why?"

"Because I want to know."

"Half English Half Swiss."

Maybe I beat both of you up." Then he laughed . Not the laugh of a joke but the laugh of arrogant bully.

"You'll be lucky to beat either of them." Alan told him and laughed at him as the one of the other hands arrived with the bosun.

"Who he?" the German snarled at the bosun.

"Someone working their passage by sleeping rough with you lot." The bosun told him. "No more room with the passengers so he's here till Harwich. He'll work in the engine room greasing tomorrow, he's here one night maybe two. We dock on flood tide tomorrow evening or following morning if we have to go slow. Depends when we get a berth. In the meantime make him welcome."

The German shook hands and leaned in to Alan and spoke quietly in German. "I don't like English. I just beat up the English half." Alan felt him trying to squeeze his hand to hurt him, all to no avail. Alan had a trick of folding his hand so it became like a tube. It worked unless the other one was too strong; this wasn't the case which saved the German getting his nose broken, when he got nutted in the face. Perhaps Alan thought that might happen later.

"Food time," said the bosun, "let's get cleaned up and eat".

Hans, the bosun, introduced Alan to Viktor Schroeter the chief engineer. He wanted him to work to keep him away from the German down in the engine room away from trouble trying to keep the peace.

Then having crossed the North Sea and heading south towards the Channel on Friday 1st September Germany invaded Poland.

The skipper for reasons only known to himself decided to announce the news to all aboard. The bosun made his way down into the engine room to let Viktor know what had occurred.

"I will leave you two together if you have problems with Horst maybe he won't try anything with two of you here. We are not docking until tomorrow morning tide. I will try to keep him away from you. Mr. Lewis go up to the bunk room grab your stuff. There is enough room down here for you both to sleep. I will be in the galley at mealtime and I will send for you.

When Alan went topsides to get his kit he came across Horst on his bunk. "Good news eh Englander maybe you die soon."

I wouldn't suggest it you are going to dock in a British port soon police would be happy to lock you up. Or is that what you're hoping for? Avoiding getting involved with big boys fighting back safe in a British prison cell, being a big man's girlfriend." Which was when he charged at Alan and got his nose broken. He did bleed well Alan noticed. Not that it stopped him because he took a swing like a drunk in a bar fight. Two punches on the side of his head rattled his brain and he hit the steel deck with a thud. Alan left him there, grabbed his duffle bag and headed back to the engine room.

The bosun had stayed with Viktor.

"What took you so long? We don't know where horst is."

"He is lying on the cabin floor by his bunk. He's still alive which is a bit of a nuisance but we have not long to go and then we can have him arrested if he causes anymore trouble. From your point of view it won't do you any harm he's a liability. You will pick up crew at Harwich anyway if you need them. I reckon you will have some of your people wanting to get home."

"You may be right Mr Lewis. However I need to report to the skipper what has occurred."

"Of course. I will be here with Viktor. No problems." The bosun left to report to the skipper. Alan looked at Viktor shrugged his shoulders. "May I dump my gear in your cabin?"

"Help yourself Alan. Are we going to have more problems?"

"I would bet on it Viktor." Alan left the engine room on the opposite end to access the chief's accommodation. He put his duffle bag on the obvious spare bunk and took out his small leather bag that kept his personal possessions in and lengthened the strap hung it over his shoulder and fastened up inside his boiler suit. He went back to the engine room to find Horst prowling around on the middle level walkway. He was slowly working his way along towards the far end. Alan suddenly realised where he was going Viktor was at the other end and was facing away from Horst. Just at that moment Hans arrived on the gantry above he looked down and saw the German going for Viktor. He shouted but couldn't be heard above the engine noise. He took his whistle and blew as hard as he could and both Viktor and horst looked up at the same time. Viktor realised he had a problem Hans was heading along the gantry but the German had lost his senses and drew a knife and started again towards Viktor. It was then that Alan who had sneaked up to the middle level and followed the same path directly behind Horst shot him in the back of the head. He just slumped again onto the floor but this time he wasn't getting up.

Hans arrived as Alan was putting his Beretta back into his pouch and closing his overalls over again.

"You'll have to go and speak to your skipper again." Alan said

"I didn't get there. Horst wasn't in the bunk room so I did a quick about turn and headed back here."

"Just as well saved Viktor."

"I didn't save Viktor ,you did."

"I think it was a joint effort. Though you best tell your skipper soon cos we need to move him and when you do get my boss in cabin four please to come down he'll need to know too.

Ten minutes later the skipper, Cameron, Hans, Viktor, and Alan were standing looking at what had happened. They are having to shout to make themselves heard which added to the understanding of how difficult it had been to stop what happened. "Are we all happy then with what took place? You three know what happened because you were witnesses." Cameron said. "I'm happy with the explanation. What about you Captain?"

"I have to report this to my company and to the police in Harwich as soon as we land. I cannot let anyone leave until I have permission form the British police."

"Of course you can't." Cameron said, "do you have ship to shore?"

"Of course."

"Then I shall call them as soon as you let me and we'll have them meet us as soon as we land. All I will add to that sir is we are not your standard passenger types."

"I can see that looking at the state of him." He nodded towards the dead German. "I imagine I will see a lot more than him before this war's over. Come with me Mr Cameron you have calls to make."

"I wondered what you had in that bag Alan."

"Mr Conway would have blocked it so I dint ask him."

"Good move Alan, well done I'll see you later."

"Before we move him," Alan said, "we must take a couple of pictures in case there is an inquest, which I doubt, but we should log it some way."

" I have a camera in my cabin." Viktor said. "How do you want the pictures?"

"As he is and the location. A couple will do but three or four would be perfect."

Cameron returned to the engine room and beckoned Alan over towards the door.

They stood outside in the evening just going steady as they y weren't going to dock tonight but tomorrow morning.

"I got hold of George and gave him instructions to contact Mr. Conway and tell him what's happened. We still haven't got a direct number for him, and with all of this kicking off, it might be difficult to get hold of him. He's got every number we have, so he's on it until he gets it done. Problem of course is everyone is going to be trying to get themselves prioritised. Fingers crossed let's see what happens."

"Could be worse we could still be in Berlin explaining to the Gestapo why I shot a German national."

"They're feeding me soon Alan so if I hear anything I'll get back in touch."

"It will be fine sir."

Just after midnight the ship engine rhythm changed, and Alan came awake to the different sound. He'd been asleep in the engineer's cabin and when he sat up in his bunk there was enough light to tell him that he was alone.

He figured the chief was engine watching. The slowing down was done down below with a request from top sides. The second had taken over r for four hours after the German's death but then gone back to his bunk in his own cabin.

Almost as soon as there had been a shift in the engine sound it returned back again.

Alan got up only to find the engineer returning to his cabin.

"Just juggling " he said. "We are stationary, waiting for a pilot to take us in. We can't go any further without a pilot but tide has just turned so we just tweaked it all to hold her steady. Everything is normal go back to sleep. I am on watch now till second comes on again. I'll wake you if your people arrive."

Alan had packed his bit of kit and was eating breakfast the crewmen were tying up at Harwich. On the quayside was a police car and what Cameron hoped was Mr Conway's Humber. A narrow gangplank was lowered and as it had its top tied and a seaman walked to the bottom two plain clothes officers left the police car and headed for the gangplank. Cameron watched form the deck as one of the twins left the vehicle showed his card to the officers and spoke to them. They got back in their car and waited.

The other twin opened the rear door of the Humber Cameron noticed they had another driver today as well. Mr .Conway followed his man up the gangplank.

Cameron saw a two more vehicles arriving one of which was driven by George Robinson. Who stopped and waved to Cameron. He nodded a hello to whichever twin it was and looked to see what sort of mood Mr. Conway looked to be in.

"God morning sir."

"Good morning major. I hear Lewis has started the hostilities early."

"Self-defence sir and saving the chief engineer's life."

"Where is he?"

"I believe he's eating sir. I don't think he knows you're here."

"Where's the skipper?"

"On the bridge." The officer of the watch told him.

"Take me to him."

"I can't leave here sir I'm sorry."

"Do you know where he is Cameron?"

"Yes sir."

"Let's go I haven't got all day."

"Martin come with us. We'll need your warrant card otherwise we could all be actors from the old Vic."

Cameron knocked on the side door of the bridge. Skipper waved him in.

"Captain this is Mr. Conway."

"Good morning Captain. I don't do waffle. My name is Talbot Conway. I represent his majesties government in a number of roles. I believe one of my men shot one of your crew."

"That is correct."

"I am also told that the reason for this was to save the life of your chief engineer."

"That is also correct."

"I also am told there are witnesses that confirm all of this."

"That is also correct."

"As far as I'm concerned case is closed then. The police will confirm this later. Show the Captain your warrant card please Martin." The skipper looked at it

"I'm happy to let your men leave my ship."

"The detectives will come aboard and take statements, which will cover you with your company. Thank you for your time we shall leave now."

"One thing Mr. Conway."

"Yes."

"Thank your Mr. Lewis on my behalf. He saved my engineer's life of that there is little doubt."

"I shall pass on the message good day sir." They left the skipper on the bridge and headed back down to the gangway.

"Cameron go find Lewis; then get yourselves back to Woolwich. Sit tight, listen to the radio tomorrow morning at eleven am. I will speak to you as soon as I can get there. I need your reports in writing and signed and they are to be given to me only. No one else is to hear anything. Clear?"

"Yes sir."

On Sunday morning at 11am 3rd September 1939 Britain declared war on Germany. Woolwich was not exactly quiet on a Sunday but this afternoon activity raised the sound levels beyond the normal .

"Well if nothing else," Cameron said, "It proves Mr. Conway knows more about what's going on, than anyone else we know."

"I think I'm becoming a yes man sir, as you don't say anything I can argue with."

On Monday morning just after nine Conway arrived in his normal hurry. He read both reports which were almost exactly the same. "One looks like a copy of the other.

We decided it was prudent to stick together when we there sir as we weren't sure how volatile it was."

"Is that why you took your instant problem solver with you Lewis?"

"Yes sir."

"Not asking me about taking weapons was a smart move."

"Yes sir"

"The Captain of the Alabaster sends his thanks. Right gentlemen. Shortly the academy here will be closed and it will all be run from Sandhurst. Sort of, as that's for other people. Your team Cameron will stay here and work as you have been doing with Salisbury Plain, and your instructors there to continue to train and develop small specialist teams and individuals. I will be sending as many as I can down to you, assuming Sandhurst have passed them as good to go. Any conscripts or regulars with extra talents may also turn up on your door step. I hate to say it but you will have to vet them yourselves. They will have all done the basics but athletes with a foreign language might just be someone we're looking for some time in the future and I can't afford to miss them. We started conscription earlier this year and quite a lot have already done their six months but the numbers will increase again shortly as we'll take everyone over eighteen. Normally I've sorted the wheat from the chaff long before they land with you so I expect the failure rate to be higher than usual. If they're no good send them back to unit as quick as you want to."

"We'll need more instructors sir" Cameron told him. "We can only just manage with what we have at the moment."

"Pick your own take any you want from the regulars already down there as a starter. Any problems speak to Colonel Haslet. I don't do pep talks but we are at war, we need to do what we can in order to win it. I might not be easy to contact so get Colonel Haslet focused on any problems and hassle him if you need to. He will have a massive increase in his workload and I will increase the officer staff numbers down there. If needs be, take control of your part, do a deal with him to bypass his need to approve. I do not want unnecessary delays. Any questions?"

"Not yet sir."

"Hopefully not at all." and then he left.

"He seems to be moving even quicker than usual." Alan remarked

"There is a certain urgency about him. Better get George in here and sort out a game plan. We've got a lot of work to do."

Chapter 7   General Harrer

The phone call as usual went through the order of command. Mr. Conway phoned Colonel Haslet at Salisbury. The colonel organised a car and Alan was chauffeured over to Woolwich. Every time it happened he suggested that he could go on his motor cycle, and every time he asked it was vetoed by Mr. Conway on the grounds that he couldn't afford to lose anyone by riding a motor cycle; they were dangerous.

Alan had to agree with him. He had, after all, got the motor cycle after his granny had died on it. But it wasn't that happening that caused the ban; because no one knew about it, but the accident that killed T E Lawrence in 1935. He was a friend of Winston Churchill's and also known to Mr. Conway. Go by car it's safer.

The other good thing of course was that when he got there he was clean, fresh, and not tired, which was just as well as Conway was there and waiting for him. Whatever was happening was definitely being taken seriously.

"Right Lewis glad you're here. I've given the major here a basic brief outline of the job. I assume that you remember helping a lady and her family to leave some trouble behind; well her husband would now like to do a similar thing. Do you think you would be able to put together a plan in order to sort out this problem?"

"In what way sir?"

"General Harrer wants to leave. He has issues over the killing of Jews and everything else going on in Russia and Yugoslavia."

"Where do you want me to get him to?"

"I would like to get him here, to the same place as you got his family, but I think onward travel may be refused, and some time in a restricted area may have to happen before any other options might or might not become available."

"What if he's not happy with this arrangement?"

"The short answer is I don't care. The diplomatic longer answer is I think that his personal circumstances, and the problems he is encountering at this time are sufficient for him to be happy to take his chances somewhere else and here is better than where he currently is."

"Where is he?"

"As far as i know he is at the moment In Germany."

"How are we communicating with him?"

"That is privileged information."

"Sorry sir. I thought we were on the same side."
Cameron was horrified. Conway took it in his stride.

"Touche." There was a long pause then Conway continued. "I'm thinking how much I should tell you."

The room was quiet for a short while. Conway was strangely deep in thought. Neither Cameron nor Lewis had ever been in his presence, when nothing was being said.

"I don't tell people things just because I don't trust them, it's because people don't need to know; and normally I don't trust anyone anyway.

A brief intelligence lesson. In our embassy in Bern in Switzerland we probably have as many spies and agents as we have anywhere else in the world. They have been collecting and dealing information, refugees, foreign agents, various indefensible activities, since before this war started. They also run various trade deals and other pieces of business that would, with a war taking place, one would assume couldn't be done. We have a communication system in operation which allows us to talk to foreign governments mostly via other countries representatives acting as intermediaries. When you moved Frau Harrer and her family I told you that the information came from a legitimate reliable source. The information that we have now comes from the exact same source and I have been dealing with this person for enough years not to question the authenticity of the information.

We can't do instant question and answer what we have to do is put together a set of questions, which can be replied to, and then take it from there to where it goes next. So what you do gentlemen is work out what you need answers to and we run with it. That's it get on with it I don't have more than ten minutes and I need to leave to speak to others."

Cameron took a foolscap sheet from his desk and the top off his pen. "Alan when you're ready."

"Is he mobile ? Is he able to travel without hindrance?

Can he move around the country without being followed, and without attendants, or hangers on? Is he physically fit? can he walk okay? What sort of distance? That will do for me sir."

"What was he like when you saw him in 36?" Conway asked. "Overweight deteriorating a bit mostly age and fat problems."

"Are you always this blunt Lewis?"
"No sir sometimes I just answer the question as well and as accurately as I can. If you'll excuse my apparent rudeness? And thank you for my promotion sir."

"You made a valid point about position. I promoted you because I want you to have enough clout to get what you need. I doubt you'll ever make general but if this war goes a while you will get higher I can assure you of that. Are we done?

"Cameron?"

"Yes sir. I've added 'is he coming on his own?"

"Lewis remain here and work on plans for a variety of possibilities." And as was usual he left at speed. One of the twins was outside the office door. Alan thought he had seen them in the Humber when he arrived.

"Touche." Cameron said. By Jove Alan, I thought you were going to end up in the tower. Didn't seem to bother him though did it."

"He's human and he knows we are too. Let's get coffee and order lunch. We have some things to guess at."

After lunch, Alan and Cameron were looking at some small maps they had of Western Europe.

"How far is Germany?" Alan suddenly asked.

"Why ?"

Because we're planning things and we don't really have an accurate mileage or a decent map. These are way too small."

"I think there's one in a cabinet in the outer office."

Cameron returned with the biggest map of western Europe that he had, He pinned it to the notice board and they had a look at what they had.

" What difference would a couple of miles here or there make?" Cameron queried.

"It might make the difference between success and embarrassing failure, if you were in an aeroplane crossing the English Channel."

"You have an idea Alan?"

"Half a one, at the moment, depends on a lot of things."

"Such as?"

"How far, when, if, etc. What my idea is to fly in and pick him up. We can't go to Zurich like we did with Frau Harre we need something swift and simple as we've always worked at. I think I need to speak to someone at the RAF."

"What about?"

"Aeroplanes."

"What sort?"

"One's that don't need a lot of space to take off and land, and can carry enough fuel so they don't have to refuel for whatever distance we need."

"It's called a Lysander," said Cameron. "Pilot and some cargo which could be human. I often wondered when all the bumf that kept landing on my desk for me to read would finally come in useful."

"What details do you have on it sir?"

"Probably not a lot. And the original paperwork has almost certainly been sent on to someone else. It was more of a news item information for storing purposes. But what I do remember is that they had a base near Chichester on the south coast between here and Salisbury but down to the sea rather than straight across."

"It's a start." Alan was getting excited. "I need to know how big, payload, ceiling, range, etc.. "How do I find out sir?"

"I don't know exactly but I do have a pal who will tell me."

"We'll write down what we need and I'll go see him. It'll get me out of this office for some fresh air."

Straight after lunch Cameron took the list to a man he knew . He borrowed a bicycle, caught the Western Ferry across to the north side and rode just up the road to Berking, where in a back office in a non-descript building, his pal from the RAF was based.

Less than two hours later he was back at Woolwich with Alan's information.

Cameron had all the specifications for the Lysander but they fell short of what was required for the plan that Alan was thinking about.

"There is some extra available possibilities." Cameron told him. "The story is that there have been some additions tested on the plane that increases its range significantly."

"How significantly?"

"The possibility is that it will increase the range for m 600 miles to nearly a 1000."

"How do we get one of those?"

"Walter the pal of mine at Berking is going to find out and will phone me when he has an answer. So, tell me what's the plan?"

"When we picked up Frau Harrer and drove from Switzerland into southern Germany and near to the Black Forest. We went through a wooded area as you would expect at the edge of the forest, over a small rise and through some magnificent gates and onto a long drive up to the estate house. I do of course have the advantage of having been there and seen it. The driveway must have been at least a quarter mile long flat as a billiard table and wide, up a slight hill. There is a fence either side and fields in both sideways directions that go on a very fair way. The fence isn't very high its purpose is solely to keep the animals in the fields."

"So you are thinking of landing a plane on this drive and then flying out again."

"Yes sir."

"It's mad Alan but it might work."

"I have it locked in my head as plan A. It has risks as you would expect but there is no plan B at the moment that would guarantee anyone surviving the exercise. Ball is in with Mr. Conway. Answers to our questions will take us to the next step or a complete rethink."

Cameron's pal phoned back just after lunch confirming the extended range of the Lysander and the location of the nearest was at Tangmere near Chichester, where the CO has been good enough to offer a meet and view to see if we can work a way between us all to solve your problem. 'Come down anytime but tomorrow will be ideal because unless something changes there will be one to look at'.

"Tell him I'll be there, if that's alright with you sir. And then you will be here to tell Mr. Conway what our plan is and save me from a trip to the tower."

"How will you get there Alan?"

"There's a delivery every night now over to Salisbury. I'll get a lift with them and then get to Tangmere tomorrow morning."

"Right organise it and we'll keep it moving and try to stay ahead of the game."

Alan went to speak to the corporal clerk in the outer office and got him to organise his lift to Salisbury.

Three hours later down at Salisbury he was at the quartermasters office, for a great coat, two woollen sweaters, two pairs of gloves, and a pair of waterproof mitts. "Can I have a job reference please sir."

"General transport to Woolwich"

"Very good sir I don't understand but it will do for our purposes."

At 0600 Alan had raided the officers mess kitchen, made tea and toast and two fried eggs, and was on his way to Tangmere, on his motor bike . He was wearing an extra woollen sweater, woollen gloves, a pair of water proof and therefore windproof mitts, and an army great coat. His beret was tied on with a headscarf. The sentry on the gate wasn't certain whether to salute him or shoot him and wisely looked the other way so he didn't see him leave.

At 0750 hrs and just over sixty miles Alan arrived at the gate to the Lysander base at Tangmere. The guard on the gate finally managed to contact the duty officer and the strange man on an old motorbike was allowed in.

"Captain Lewis, good morning. I'm Flight Lieutenant Bob Lomax, would you like breakfast or do you wish to watch us eat ours? We are in our sort of mess here, but food is ready and we are hungry."

"I'm more than happy to join you thank you."

There was a small group of officers eating breakfast. They gave Alan a look hello and got on with their food. Alan took off his top coat and hung it on a hook on the wall near to the door.

"Do you hide your officer status for a reason Captain?"

"Not really. I don't normally wear any insignia, half the time I'm not in uniform, and I grabbed a couple of extra pullovers from the stores to ride down here this morning. I'm sort of attached to Artillery, officially I'm in Kings own Yorkshire light infantry, but I also have paratrooper wings and I'm senior instructor for the army on Salisbury Plain. I work for a man who would tell you I'm General Lewis, if it suited him, and it was the only way for me to get my hands on something. Hence my visit here. But if we're eating. I don't wish to spoil your meal. I will brief you after if that is ok."

"Perfectly enjoy your meal."

After breakfast, when they had walked outside a short way Alan apologised for being a bit rude and abrupt. "I'm sorry about shutting down our conversation inside before. We are a very limited number of people who need to know. My boss would shoot me if he thought I was being too open mouthed and I'm not joking. I'm not suggesting that your chaps are going to tell everyone everything down in the pub later on but if people don't know they can't say anything."

"I understand. Thank you."

"You can ask me anything you want if I can tell you I will."

"Well we're here now come and take a look at what we've got and then you can tell me what you want us to do."

Alan was shown the Lysander aircraft. He had a picture of the Harrer residence and the long smooth drive locked in his memory; and he could visualise the landing, and the take off, and how it all would work. Seeing it in your mind and getting it to happen were two different things and leaving a broken plane and an RAF pilot in pieces too on the ground in Germany had no appeal at all.

Alan walked around the plane. He could see that the wings were probably as wide as the drive if not wider but the height of the wings was so much higher than the fences they would almost certainly clear them . The turning up at the house was big enough if someone helped to turn the plane around.

"I think I've seen all I need to see," he told the Lieutenant.

"Now you tell me what you want to do, and I will tell you if we can do it."

"I want you to fly into the south of Germany pick up a passenger and fly them back to the UK."

"Too far."

Why I though t you have extended the range to about 1000 miles.

We have but that's over 1000 miles.

It is from here what about from the east coast. Around Dungeness.

"As far as I know we have got a base there. We can land if there is a landing strip there but we would need to make arrangements for mechanics and refuelling."

"That would save a hundred miles each way. Are we starting to look like feasible?"

"Yes. We'll look at the map show me exactly where you want to go."

Alan was keen on the idea of robbing the map, but decided their need was possibly greater than his, so settled for a long discussion with Bob Lomax on the feasibility of the job he wanted.

"So we are thinking Lympne?" Alan asked.

It was fleet air arm but we've taken it over now. I don't know what they have down there yet, but it would be ideal as long as it's operational and can fill us up and check the plane over."

"Next question then Bob is how long do you need to put this plane in the air with pilot, maps, and ready to go there and back?"

"Within 48 hours. Plane won't take that long. I'll need to get right man to fly it. He'll need to rest before he flies. Depends what he's doing at the moment."

"Do you have someone in mind? Because if you do I'm going to suggest you get him here and primed and ready. If we get the go ahead and I'm certain we will then it will be ASAP."

"What about Lympne?"

"I'll get them sorted for you."

"Seriously?"

"Yes just give them a courtesy call. Tell them who I am and I will see them tomorrow or the day after. Please also tell them that there is minimum number of people to know what we're doing and they don't need to know where we're going or anything other than fuel, mechanics, and when."

"I Understand."

Either me, a major Cameron or a Mr. Conway may speak to you about it. No one else is to know apart from the pilot and your CO if he needs to. But please impress on them that it goes no further."

"Perfectly clear, Alan."

"Excellent. There is now nothing I can do here other than drink some tea go to the toilet and get myself back to Woolwich."

As Alan arrived back at Woolwich. He could see Richard, Martin and Mr. Conway's Humber. He parked around the side of the building, took off his gloves, greatcoat, and extra pullover and sneaked into the building by the side door.

"Ah good there you are Lewis." Conway was still in the outer office, so either he had just arrived, or was about to leave.

"Cameron's in the mess apparently just finishing lunch so I'm told. I hear you've been to Salisbury."

"Yes sir."

"Why?"

"To speak to some chaps at RAF Tangmere Sir. I've just got back."

"And?"

"Should we wait for major Cameron sir? Or at least should we go into our office."

"In the office then and get on with it. Cameron could be at least ten minutes getting here."

"I went to Tangmere because we had a plan that we could land a plane in Germany and fly it back out again on one tank of fuel."

"And?"

"Yes we can if we stop enroute somewhere near Dungeness."

"Where are you going to land it in Germany?"

"On General Harrer's drive sir."

"You are obviously being serious, so what do the RAF boys think about it?"

"They think that it is doable sir."

"What do you need to make it work?"

"General Harrer at his place in southern Germany. Some landing lights, a windless night, dry weather, permission to go ahead, and a bit of luck."

"So you want me to get Harrer to his house, and permission to go ahead. How long do the RAF chaps need?"

" Two days and we have to find an airfield to refuel in or a straight piece of road with no high hedges or fences which might be more difficult."

"I have here the answers to your questions for General Harrer," which Cameron timed perfectly by walking in.

"Just at the right time Major, I was telling Lewis I have received the answers to your questions. I shall read it as written."

'I am a well-built German officer I can walk but I don't run I am not hampered by attendants and as a General I am free to wander anywhere I wish. I will be travelling alone. I am about to spend a short time at my estate.' That's it."

"I wonder what a short time is?" Alan asked.

"That might be, how long is a piece of string?" Cameron offered "Which I know isn't an answer, but we must also be conscious of the fact that others might join the equation even if they weren't expected or invited."

"You are completely au fait with this idea then major?"

"Yes sir, though I'm not completely up to date as Captain Lewis and I haven't yet manged to speak. I am assuming that as he is back and discussing it with you that it is feasible and that is the path we are hoping to be working on, sir."

Conway was looking at the map still pinned on the office notice board. "Show me what you're proposing Captain."

"Tangmere is here, near Chichester, where the Lysander is based. It's had an extra fuel tank fitted that extends its range from 600 to 1000 miles . The pilot will fly it from there to here in Southern Germany near to the Swiss and French border near to the black forest." Alan was showing Conway where everything was as he was explaining the plan. "That journey is 1050 miles which is too far . Therefore we need to find an airfield that's operational to land in near the coast at Dungeness. Here the pilot could land and take on enough fuel to get to his destination load up turn around and fly back again with his passenger who he could drop off there when he needs to pick up enough fuel for the final 100 miles back to Tangmere. Flying in and out of Dungeness would reduce the aircrafts continuous part of the journey to 850 miles meaning the fuel requirement would be covered by its carrying capacity with a bit of extra, just in case of indeterminate factors, a bit of headwind, a slight detour, slow turnaround, it allows for a margin of safety."

"I've seen worse ideas work" Conway remarked. "What if you can't find an airfield?"

"We have one that is ideal sir. It's near Dungeness name of Lympne. Was fleet air arm till quite recently . RAF have it now and I left the duty officer at Tangmere trying to make contact with them to let them know what we wanted and that I would be down to see them as soon as I could get there."

"I'll send a vehicle for you. Keep it here you and Major Cameron can share it. What do you want me to say to General Harrer?" Conway opened his pad and leaned on Cameron's desk.

"Would you like a seat sir?" Conway looked at the office chair.

"There are front line troops that I believe are not living as near to death or serious injury as I do when I sit on this furniture. I will send three new chairs over here as soon as I get back to my office. In the meantime I shall remain standing I believe it's safer. And while we're on safety Captain no more motor cycle. I spotted you coming into the yard, and Colonel Haslet told me you'd already left when I phoned you this morning at Salisbury. You have a car now."

"Yes sir. Thank you sir."

"Right, message for Harrer."

"I need to confirm the airfield and I need a weather window and then I can put timings in it. Message at the moment would be proposed pick up from house details to follow how long can you stay there? I don't know if major has anything to add."

"I agree Alan. Until we get the airfield and the weather we can't plan anything but I'll get straight onto my pal at Berking and see if he knows the place and we can try and contact them before you go down there."

"I expect Major that you will spending more time on your backside than you are used to but I need a good planner. I will get you an assistant. Captain you will remain on the sharp end. I gave you a couple of chaps in Hamburg before this started where are they?"

"They're with me at Salisbury sir training the instructors."

"Is one of them any use to you Captain, as an assistant?"

"Both are very good sir but I'd prefer George Robinson. He looks ordinary nondescript so blends in like he's camouflaged because he looks insignificant."

"Is he?"

"Is he what sir?"

"Insignificant."

"No sir he's extremely competent; understands German. Perfectly fluent in French, teaches all the instructors the same course that I did."

"Break him in then, he's your man now. He can cover your back."

"Yes sir."

"That it?"

"Yes sir."

"I'll be back when I have any answers."

Immediately Conway left Cameron phoned his pal at Berking and to confirm the operational readiness of Lympne and to get a contact number for them to arrange a meeting. Then he phoned colonel Haslet and asked him to send sergeant Robinson across to Woolwich. 'Permanent transfer sir Mr. Conway's request sir'.

"George will be on the morning truck from Salisbury. All we need now is your car. He's given you a car Alan; this is serious stuff matey, even Colonel Haslet hasn't got his own car."

"Be interesting to see what he sends us."

"A Ford or an Austin. Don't see you getting a Humber yet old son."

"I need to eat soon sir I've not eaten since breakfast. I'll go and see what I can scrounge from the mess. Do you want anything?"

"Yes tell them we want a coffee and tea system over here. We can't affords to be leaving the office every time we need a drink or sending someone over for one. Dougie's got his set up in the armoury see him if you don't get anywhere with cooks."

When Alan got back to the office Cameron was on the phone he gave Alan a thumbs up. He put the phone down

"Good news RAF have got the base Lympne nearly fully operational. Did you get your food?"

"Chef's special sandwich," said Alan, "two sausages, two slices of bread. I don't think that man can cook anything other than sausages and chips. They're bringing a tea urn over and the makings within fifteen minutes, they promised, we'll see."

The tea urn turned up at the same time as three new office chairs; followed as they were drinking fresh hot coffee, by 'a car for Captain Lewis, please sign here sir'.

"When I've seen it corporal. Have a go on that old seat outside try our new tea and coffee service by all means while I drink my coffee."

The corporal had delivered a two door, black, Ford Popular reasonably clean, started ok, no dents or any damage, nearly full tank of fuel, spare wheel, tool kit, starting handle, and two keys. "Thank you corporal."

"Do we have the name of the CO at Lympne yet sir?"

"No names yet. Why?"

"We need to get in touch and get them up to speed."

"I have a telephone number. Do you want to call them ?"

"No. Will you do it please sir. Even if it's a small place it could still have a minimum of squadron leader in charge which equals to Major so you're on level terms. If you tell him you're sending me to speak to them about a job I'll go down. He'll pass me to an underling and if I have a problem I'll have Mr. Conway speak to them."

"When do you want to go?"

"First thing tomorrow, it's about a hundred miles there and same back again that'll be a day done for. Ask them for lunch as well please. They gave me breakfast at Tangmere which made me wish I'd joined the RAF."

Cameron spoke to the CO at Lympne. "Duty officer will sort it out with you. You are welcome to lunch with them any problems get in touch with him, otherwise he hopes to meet you at lunch time tomorrow."

"It's coming together sir; will you get George settled in until I get back? He is clever by the way doesn't say a lot but when he talks he makes sense."

"I'll bare that in mind yes leave him with me. I've got stuff for him anyway he speaks and reads French probably as good as me. He can work his way through some of the accumulating bumf."

Alan arrived back from Dungeness at 1600 hrs. "Yes they can land a Lysander there, yes they can refuel it, yes the mechanics can give it a quick look over, yes they can work with our Military Police to take away a passenger. Yes they can refuel it for return to Tangmere. No one will speak to anyone about what has taken place. Yes just get Tangmere to let them know when it's going to happen. Yes lunch was very nice and not a sausage in sight," was the report from Alan to Cameron.

"Up to the General now. And I see what you mean about Sergeant Robinson. He is a bright chap isn't he. Reads and speaks French at a hell of a speed. He's way quicker than me and nearly cleared all my back log. I've sent him for his meal early and got him into the sergeants mess and he's been and spoke to Dougie White so he shouldn't get any irritation from anyone, if Dougie puts the word about."

"They'll only do it once I think he hits as hard as Joe porter which causes almost as much shock as damage. Idiots who try rapidly lose interest in continuing any further."

"These are decent seats at last." Mr Conway arrived at 0830 without warning. "Our man is staying put for another week at his residence. Meteorology boffins tell me that we have a high pressure area moving across us at the moment going eastwards which will, as long as it maintains its projected path and speed, be over our required area in approximately 48 hours. The embassy at Berne are aware of our interest and are keeping an eye on the weather there for us. They tell me it's been stable there at this time and they agree that it should remain so for a while. Assuming that we have the high pressure staying there we will have little wind clear skies but currently as we have a new moon we have little if any moonlight. Which according to my chap from the air marshal's office will suit the pilot perfectly."

"I have spoken to the RAF at Lympne They are primed and ready to go. Assuming a successful transfer all that we need is a welcoming committee and some transport for the passenger to his next destination."

"It seems we are about ready then. It is Saturday when will we be able to go?"

"Tangmere asked for a couple of days to be certain they would be ready though I'm sure they could do it quicker than that. They want to be ready not trying to catch up. The pilot will fly in the dark. I think Monday sir"

"Monday will be better than Sunday to make certain our passenger has the necessary details. Right then gentlemen I need a written instructions from you as to what Harrer needs to do. When can I have them?"

Cameron handed Conway a sheet of paper. "Already done sir."

"Excellent." Conway read through the details.

'A small suitcase or ideally soft holdalls, and if so, it can be a couple but not large ones. The pilot will land on the driveway. He will taxi to the house and turn around. There will be a ladder to climb into the rear seat. He needs warm clothing and a head cover that won't blow away. When the pilot lands and taxis up to the house somebody will have to help turn the plane through a half circle by pushing the tail round so the aircraft is pointing back down the drive again. If the general can't do this, his batman or someone else will need to do it for him.

The pilot will not want to hang around he will not stop the engine nor will he wait any longer than necessary.

Today is Saturday. on Monday at 2100 hours local time three white lights in a straight line centre of driveway approximately fifty yards apart first one around a hundred yards from the gate at the roadside. House lights on.

When the plane lands house lights turned off and get ready to go.

If weather conditions are against us on Monday, that is it is too windy, it will be called off and we will try again in next weather window which might even be Tuesday. If it's clear then you do it again until picked up. We will get a forecast in England and can only hope that theirs is accurate enough to get the job done.

Flight Lieutenant William Turner sat waiting for the order to go. The Lysander was warmed up and sounded fine. He and the duty officer Squadron Leader Ashley had meticulously gone through the whole programme and tried to find anything they'd missed. This was going to be a long one. Normally with a range of six hundred miles this one had had an extra tank fitted which increased its range to around a thousand. Tick

Just in case that might not enough. He was flying from Tangmere near Chichester to Southern Germany and back on one load of fuel. His flight plan was to fly to an airfield RAF Lympne a couple of miles north of Dungeness where he could refuel and take off and land back there again, fingers crossed. Tick. This would give him a hundred extra miles with full tanks and probably the edge needed between success and failure. Tick. The rear compartment had been stripped out by the mechanics and the armourer had removed the second pack of machine guns normally operated by a gunner. Tick. This trip he was travelling as light as possible to get as far as possible, and importantly, as far as Bill was concerned, back again. Tick. He was as happy as he thought he could be all he had to do now was get an all clear to go.

First he had to get to Lympne. He wanted to do it in the daylight. What was keeping them from giving him the go ahead he didn't know. He knew he would be landing in Germany in the dark and taking off in the dark in point apart from the flight to Dungeness all of it was at night. But something to eat and drink before he left Dungeness and a trip to the toilet would make him a lot more comfortable if it was going to be a long night. He kept looking over at the timber shack staring at the window hoping to see something going on inside that would give him a clue on what the delay was. Suddenly the door opened and duty officer came out he climbed up onto the wing strut and William opened his side window

"Sorry about the delay Bill been waiting to get it all coordinated. Fuel's sorted at Lympne or will be by the time you get there. They were checking mixing the fuels because you run on low octane they wanted confirmation that what they had was ok as it's higher octane. weather forecast is good for next twelve hours so it all systems go. Good luck see you tomorrow morning."

"Thank you sir. Is my tea sorted?"

"Yes."

" I'll get off then I'm clear to go now?"

"Yes get going they'll be waiting for you. And remember there is to be no mention of any part of this job to anyone. Top secret is not quite how I'd put it but it's not for discussion any time with any one understood?"

"Yes sir."

Turner shut his window. He opened the throttle and the plane started to move. It shimmied in to some sort of a straight line and he opened up the throttle further. The nine cylinder Bristol engine purred into that almost quiet exhaust sound. Bill Turner loved flying and the Lysander was his favourite little plane. 'Lympne here I come.' About forty minutes flying time later and Bill had parked the plane. He'd had a meal and was drinking a last cup of tea and smoking a last cigarette before take-off. It was dark, nearly. He'd had a wash and toilet visit. And now he was going flying what could be more fun than this?

He'd checked over the plane after landing but gave it another once over by torch light. All the panels were screwed up tight. They'd left the machine guns and ammunition in the wheel pods just in case. If it got to that with a German fighter plane he knew he'd have to be lucky to survive that encounter. But you never know, there's a first for everything but not tonight please. The headlights in the wheel pods were working fine. Apart from when those lights were on the plane was almost invisible. Painted a flat matt black all over it was difficult to spot in the dark night sky and the sweet sounding engine was quieter than most other planes and as a result difficult to hear.

The mechanics had refuelled the plane topped up the oil reservoir and readied it as best as it could be. They knew this was in many ways a tester for them all adding an extra fuel tank and stripping out the weaponry from back of the plane to create more space and give it a greater range came at a cost. Tonight would tell them if the cost might be worth it. He probably wasn't the first to test these modified Lysanders out but he knew he was pushing its range to the limit. Every flight was different wind speed direction altitude any of the variations could create the difference between failure or success.

Tonight, in theory, had the added advantage of no wind at the destination

Bill turner had a couple of maps, a watch, a torch, and a local arrival time of 2100 hours. Time to go. He opened up the throttle again and the Lysander was up and away.

At the Harrer farm near the southern edge of thee Black Forest General Harrer sat quietly with his man, Ludwig, once his batman, now part friend ,confidante, manservant and minder. They had eaten together a practice occasionally happening after Frau Harrer and the children had left. They had toasted each other and chatted through the evening about old memories. The lighting had been turned off , the dining room lit now by a couple of candles,

" We have been together a long time my friend and one day if everything works out, we will see each other again. I will leave you to manage the house and do what you can with the farm. It is nearly time just a few more minutes and we must be ready. Now I will do the house lights as per instruction and if you will swich the lights on in the drive.

At exactly 2100 hours General Harrer switched on the main light switch and all the house lights went on the generator responded instantly and roared in the garage which told Ludwig to do the same for the three lights on the driveway.

At 2102 the Lysander landed on the drive and after a bounce or two at its 80 mph landing speed it stopped snaking and ran a lot smoother than even Bill turner thought possible towards the house as it did so the house lights went out and Bill switched on the lights in the wheel pods to light his way along the drive. As he got to the house he saw two men coming into view. One spherical chap which he knew to be his passenger and another carrying two holdalls from what appeared to be a garage. The smaller of two men pushed the back of the airplane around in the direction Bill had started to turn when it came to a stop. The bigger man climbed the ladder on the side and got into the rear seat. The other man climbed up twice each time with a bag. They shook hands. The helper stood back produced a beret from inside his jacket and stood smartly to attention as he saluted his General.

Bill shouted into the back, "let's go my friend, we can't hang around we don't know who's seen us."

General Harrer dropped on to the seat and Bill aimed the Lysander down the drive. Fortunately, the Lysander doesn't need much room to take off as long as it goes in a straight line. Bill didn't like the look of the fence. His wings were higher than the fence but there was no wind shadow available which was why they'd needed a clear wind free night for the pick-up thank goodness someone knew what they were doing. The plane was a great plane to fly but a wilful beast to drive around on the ground and any drifting to either side and they might be ending up in the local hospital if they were lucky. Shimmying around in a field with plenty of space at the sides is one thing, but drives and fences don't leave too much room for error.

Bill squeezed his mike button. "Get comfortable. Strap yourself in two to three hours let's hope none of your pals want to shoot us down. will speak to you if I need to, otherwise let me fly this. I've got a bit to do and I need to concentrate. Understood?"

"Yes carry on young man. I am strapped in and in your hands now. I shall be quiet."

Bill had taken the Lysander right up to nearly twenty thousand feet very close to its ceiling height. Figuring that the further away from everyone and black in a dark sky would be enough to avoid any unwelcome confrontation. He didn't see another plane over France. The channel crossing was quiet too and as he got closer to the coast, by his dead reckoning, he called the team waiting at Lympne. He had crossed the channel with a quarter tank of fuel still showing on his gauge. He asked for twenty five gallons comfortably enough fuel to definitely get him back to Tangmere

Duty officer met him with a driver and a jeep escort. The general stiff but happy to have landed, insisted on shaking Bill by the hand, and thanking him personally. His two bags and he, along with two Redcaps, were in a second jeep and driven across to the main building.

" Well done lieutenant. You look knackered."

"Glad to be back sir. It was just time consuming in the end. No issues at all. But it does take it out of you."

"Well let's get you topped up. Is twenty five gallons enough?"

"Yes sir should be plenty .I'm still showing I think enough to get back to base but it'd be a shame to spoil it all by running out now."

"It would I'll leave you to carry on . I'll give your base a call and let them know you're on your way."

"Thank you sir and for your help tonight."

Bill finished his journey and in less than three quarters of an hour later he was back at Tangmere.

When he landed he drove over towards the workshops and parked. Within a couple of minutes a jeep was coming across and Duty officer appeared. "Welcome back; do you need a drink?"

"Could do with cup of tea please, sir, and a fag, been a long time since I went that long without either a fag, or a sleep."

"You've probably earned both tonight. Glad to see you back."

Another jeep came along the perimeter road. Two boiler suited men climbed out. The driver started a slow reverse towards the Lysander.

"Shall we go and park it sir?"

"Measure the fuel that's still in it and we can see how much we got extra. Check the oil tank level too and condition of the whole aircraft." The mechanics connected a rigid tow to the Lysander and gently towed it over to the workshop.

" I think you've helped proven their worth tonight Bill for extended journey times. We'll go and do a debrief now I'll get you tea and some ciggies. Are you sure you don't want anything to eat or stronger to drink?"

" No thank you just tea please."

Debrief covered the refuel at Lympne and the reason behind crossing the channel there. Being the fact that as no one was aware of the mission ditching over the sea was unlikely to get them home and they weren't certain about the range of the Lysander due to it being on its limits and unknown factors like avoiding German patrols or a sudden change in the weather

"Are you happy enough to volunteer for more jobs like that one?"

"It's fine by me sir. I'm not certain what the failure rate might be, but I'm happy enough at the moment to keep trying."

"Good man. We've got a training programme going at the moment with some of these secret service types. All hush hush stuff, seems they need transport on occasions like tonight, go in behind the lines, drop someone off, or pick someone up like tonight, or maybe one in one out, that sort of thing . Do you fancy it?"

"Sounds okay sir. Gives me something positive to do."

"Jolly good. Then We'll speak again tomorrow. When you've had a sleep on it."

"Don't need to sir. I'm game for another go."

"Excellent. I'll let the MOD chaps know. Now drink your tea and get some sleep and that's an order. And very well done again."

Shortly after 0900 Talbot Conway telephoned the CO at Tangmere. "It was a good job your man did for us last night."

"He's a competent and experienced pilot and he's up for more if you need him."

"Send him over to Woolwich next Monday. Get him there early and we'll give him some specialist training. We don't want him disadvantaged unnecessarily. He'll be with a Major Cameron. I'll let Cameron know he's coming. He'll be away for a week to a fortnight depending how quick he learns and how good he is."

"Will do"

"Keep me posted on how you're progressing with your pilot training programme I suspect that we'll be doing a fair bit of business together. Things don't look that good at this time, and our leader believes in using any devious underhand ways, if needed, at winning, which is where we lot are going to come in.

Alan was sitting in the bar he had a whisky hardly touched on the table with a coffee pot almost empty and a packet of cigarettes opened and a box of matches. He was getting too deep into staff training he preferred the sharp end and thought he could be getting stale with not being active. The door to the lounge bar opened' The lady stood just inside the door and looked around when she spotted Alan she headed straight for him. She gave the impression of being a working girl and sat at the table.

"My friend said that you would give me a light if I needed one." Alan smiled he did not expect to have this happen in Woolwich. "My friend also said he would be sorry to bother you when you are quietly enjoying the evening. He asked me to give you a couple of messages one is that I am only a messenger and you should never shoot the messenger they can be useful. The second is to thank you for the task you undertook and successfully completed. He is also sorry to tell you now that given his current circumstances he believes that the link that you share with him is probably no longer able to continue and that he wishes you many thanks and all the best.

 I have another message from a different source. Henri and Marcel have requested a visit. It isn't urgent but whenever you can." That last sentence intrigued Alan. Be assured that not everything is as meets the eye. When you first saw me your initial thought might what do we have here? There is a reason some of which may only be available to those who need to know. Perhaps I should carry a business card explaining my services."

She seemed to be clever and articulate but also talking in riddles. Alan didn't understand. She looked like any other woman in any pub or every pub. The strange conversation had left Alan slightly bewildered but not as much as the message from Henri Murcia had.

Alan smiled again. it nearly became a giggle.

"Have I offended you?" The lady hardly looked worried if she had.

"Not at all. I don't know how you relay your messages back but thank your friend for his appreciation of a job well done and let Henri and Marcel know I will come and see them as soon as I can."

"We may meet again Captain until then goodbye." She had a funny little laugh She took a light, stole the matches, and was still laughing as she left. A man just leaving held the door for her, and she slipped quickly through. He seemed in no rush to follow her and as he was blocking the doorway Alan bemused saw little value in pursuing her or doing or saying anything. If as she said the link with Otto Witzell was now broken, then so be it. She was right no point in shooting the messenger. She was more useful at large and free than locked up in a jail. But what would you lock her up for? And how did Otto link in with Henri and Marcel, and what is a different source? Then he realised how stupid he was. The message from Henri had thrown him off track. She had been telling him that she played the same game as he did she was hiding in full view. She didn't look out of place in the pub she looked completely like she could have been part of the furniture or the decorations He looked at his watch early enough to give the major a call and let him know what had happened. But he did wonder who the lady who stole his matches was.

The following morning Alan has a plan to go to France with a motor bike strapped to Lysander. Having spoken to Cameron the night before, the message from Henri had given Alan the excuse to go and visit the bar in Paris. He was a Swiss national after all so no reason why he should not be there. Under the Germans the Swiss, as neutrals, were slightly better off than the French citizens, who were still considered as the enemy albeit a n invaded and defeated one. Alan couldn't see a problem capitalising on that and he decided, "I'm not going to ask Mr. Conway for permission to take a motorcycle to France as he doesn't have any jurisdiction there."

"Are you being serious? No jurisdiction." Cameron managed the incredulity look again.

"Well I wouldn't say it to his face but he's too busy to bother with minutiae."

"What are you going to take?"

A DKW motor cycle with Swiss plates.. And radio equipment as it's more difficult to hide but you know when the message has arrived you can't ever be certain with the bird until you get a response, by which time it could be too late.

And where are you going to get that from and how big is will it go in a Lysander?

"I've worked it all out sir."

"Keep talking Alan."

"Some of the guys in the pub last year were talking about motor bikes and when one of them mentioned this bike is so small you could pick it up; my ears pricked up and I bought it."

"Well that's good then."

"Well sort of it was stolen from a German cargo ship that was here in 38 in the hold when the dock workers accidently loaded it into a net and off loaded it into a warehouse. So it's not registered here which is fine because I'm going to get some Swiss plates made and then I can ride it around in France sort of legit."

"Do you not think that's asking for trouble?

"I do sir but given what else we're doing there I don't think that's something that's high on the danger list."

"Have you spoken to them at Tangmere?"
"Not yet. I need your permission to do so."

"Carry on don't tell me anymore about the motor cycle."

"Thank you sir." Alan continued with his preparations to travel to France. The message said there was no hurry so he would have time to get it right.

At lunchtime Cameron told him that Mr. Conway was due to visit this afternoon, usual time after two.

"I've given you a call Lewis as you had a meeting last night with a lady in the lounge at the Crown pub."

"Yes sir."

"Under no circumstances are you to ever tell anyone about this meeting or any other meeting you may have with her in the future."

"Yes sir."

"I spoke with her this morning she gave me the same information she passed to you last evening. I presume you are now thinking of going to find out what is happening with our Paris project?"

"Yes Sir."

"I will leave that with you. Keep me posted."

"Will do sir." Conway departed at the same speed he arrived.

"Whoever the lady was she was important enough to get Mr. Conway to leave his office and speak to us and not just give us a phone call. Maybe one day we might find out, but before then I need to get to Paris."

"How long do you need?" Cameron asked.

"I don't know. I need to get someone to make some kind of frame I can fix to the ladder on the side of a Lysander. Then I can attach the motorcycle to that. Doing that could take a quite a few days and then we'll need to test it which means I have to get access to a plane. Don't want it dropping off over the channel. Could be two weeks before I go. Is there anything you need me for?"

"Yes I was going to go home for the weekend. I sent Clarissa a message that I'd be home on Friday evening."

"I can mind the shop sir as the bike's here and the engineers here are just as good as any others anywhere else."

"Wonderful thank you."

"Just leave us a telephone number in case and an address please and enjoy your weekend."

Chapter 8

OTTO WITZELL   STALINGRAD   RUSSIA

This part has been put in here as it fits in to the chronological order of events as we know the dates of what occurred in the second world war. The original is in German and was translated by Alan Lewis for Adam Lewis.

Translated from the notes given to me by Anne Marie. They were passed on to me after a visit I made to the Swiss embassy in London in September 1949. Contact with me had been lost but this letter along with a journal that Otto Witzell had kept was later passed to Anne Marie before he left Europe for the final time. They were then attached to a file the embassy kept on me and when I made an application for renewal of my Swiss passport these papers arrived with my new documents.

Dear Anne Marie.

Plans, as I am sure you are aware as I am, frequently don't always go as one might wish. I find myself in conflict now with myself and my beliefs. When General Harrer left, for me to save family face, I was about to return to my old unit. The credit of the family name was stretched beyond reasonable lengths and I'm certain that had my father not been a general with a voice still listened to It might have been a dangerous one sided time for me. The chance to return to my regiment, still as a captain, was a my only real option that would satisfy the authorities that I had nothing to do with his departure and subsequent arrival in England. The fact that when he escaped or deserted depending on where your sympathies lie I was at the family residence near Hamburg with my father and a number of other still serving senior officers was probably the only thing that tipped the scales in my favour. During the following weekend, whilst I was still awaiting orders on where and when I was to go one of my father's visitors was Herr SS Ober Fuhrer Hermann Schmidt. He is the commander of a new Panzer tank regiment of the Waffen SS. He insisted that I join with him as his intelligence officer, essentially the same job as with General Harrer, but with a different uniform. I would have to learn how the SS rules as I progressed but given the time, the situation as it is with the war on the front lines and the fact that I was a career officer. It would be a straight forward transfer to his unit. Transition would not be a problem with his endorsement. Father seemed keen that I should return to a fighting unit as all of my family had been in the past and a Waffen SS tank regiment was after all an elite unit. An opportunity not to be ignored. I was almost without any doubt blackmailed and pushed into this situation. Not only by my new chief but by my father and the obligation to protect the family name. I am relieved that at least I am in a fighting regiment. Army against army is what it is all about. I have no love for the idea of fighting civilians with tanks and machine guns. But as has been pointed out to me on numerous occasions recently I am a professional combat soldier and so I now find myself faced with the probability that we will be travelling north and east against the Russian army and on a road paved with the dead who came searching for only glory. My father I'm certain doesn't wish me dead, when glory is still an option, but as long as I don't bring shame on the family name, I will have done my duty.

You must let our mutual friend Herr Alain know that our line of communication is now closed, that I hope he survives this war and that one day we shall shoot deer in the black forest and grow old and fat eating venison.

Thank you Anne Marie and Auf Wieder Sen. Otto signed the letter sealed it in an envelope. He wrote a six number code on the front of the envelope which he knew would eventually get it delivered to the right person. There was no urgency in this delivery, He would travel down to Berlin tomorrow on the train and dropping off the envelope at the Embassy, before his appointed time, would not be a problem

Otto had travelled to Berlin from Hamburg to report to military headquarters and receive his papers and swear his allegiance. As an officer in the Waffen SS, he was in a different league now. His uniform signified a power that he had never experienced. Previously he had wandered about and no one or hardly anyone took any notice. Now he saw people viewing him with a reverence or some would look away unsure about eye contact. It was interesting shift in his social standing and in one way or another he was going to have to live with it.

Otto reported to his new commanding officer at his office in Berlin. "Do you know what General Harrer was working on Otto?"

"Not specifically sir no. He had me looking at some work that he had done in the Balkans. Which is why he suggested that I go and visit my father as he had been in the Balkans during the first war and he was a possible source of ideas and information. Basically it was a typical talk and see what comes of it."

I think that had all been finished some time ago. He was working on another huge undertaking on the eastern front but instead of going north to Moscow he was planning going South to Stalingrad.

I'm not aware of any part of that sir.

Good because if he didn't tell you he might not have told anyone else. It is not common knowledge at this moment. But we are looking at the opening up a second front to run alongside operation Barbarossa. We need to get fuel for our ongoing objectives and Russia has it. If we can get down into the south and take Stalingrad then we can control the oil supplies and give us the fuel to carry on destroying the enemies of Germany. Are you with me ?

Yes sir.

That is our objective. We are going to go and have a look see down there and see what we can find. We will take a fast run and see what gives. I will be surprised if we don't encounter some serious hostility from the red army and I will be surprised if we all return . However that is the order I have been given and that is what we must do. Understand?

Perfectly sir.

Do you have a billet?

No sir. I have reported as per instructions and I have not received anything else.

Your father was good enough to provide food and shelter for me when I visited him the very least I can do is return his generosity to his son. I have accommodation here in Berlin and I will be leaving here around eighteen hundred. Ask the corporal at the desk to get you something to drink and to eat. Take the spare desk in the outer office there and have a read of this.

A large, packed folder, tied both ways, with heavy tape, was handed to Otto. You will probably recognise the writing. It was done by the traitor Harrer. The report was compiled in late 1938 before the war started of course but not before the planning started and at that time Harrer was considered to be a worthy General with wisdom and a logical mind. See what you think, though I doubt you'll get through it all before we are ready to leave this evening. The file does not leave these offices under any circumstances.

A couple of hours later a message to deliver the file back to Scmidt and report on his findings from what he has managed to learn from it.

"General Harrer sir is a very clever man. His assessment of attacking Stalingrad is that defeat though not inevitable is too unpredictable. Too much relies on good fortune and the capitulation of the Russian people which given the brutality they have experienced in operation Barbarossa is unlikely to happen. I suspect that due to his desertion and fleeing abroad that his words are probably going to be ignored. He was my fathers intelligence officer and I worked for him for nearly four years. Knowing how accurate his understanding of how during war transport weather and terrain numbers and weaponry all effect the difficulties and possible outcome his assessment doesn't look promising and his proposal that Ukraine could be a better holding place for consolidation has significant merit. Sir though given the time lapsed since the original evaluation and now. I would not be certain."

"Interesting, and what do you personally think Haupt Sturm Fuhrer? Do you think his assessment is right? If you had to make a decision with only two choices do we go or do we stay what would it be?"

"Knowing General Harrer sir I believe that he thinks he is right. I think sir and I believe that what he thinks is that we are almost certainly going to lose against Russia. The consequences of that would be devastating and as I have only his notes to look at I think he may be right. Sir and with the limited information I have at my disposal sir my advice would be that we should not attack Russia on the eastern front at this time."

"I asked you a question as my intelligence officer and you gave me an honest answer that would not have been appreciated by other staff officers. I might not agree with you all the time but at least you'll give me an honest answer to a question. You remind me of your father not a bad thing to do.

But we have orders Otto and so we will see what happens but first we eat and then we sleep and we see what tomorrow brings.

Three days after joining his new regiment Otto Witzell is in a Kubelwagen. He has a driver and two soldiers. He is now considered important enough to have bodyguards, or the vehicle is. He didn't question why they were there but he did get the feeling that his commanding officer would not want to explain to his father how he'd got killed. They had flown south from Berlin to an unnamed military airfield in eastern Romania, where they had picked up their vehicles and the soldiers who were ready and waiting for their arrival. They were in a group of six vehicles two Kubelwagens one for Otto and the other for Schmidt. One troop wagon two APCs and a service and food truck towing a gulashKanone, their mobile kitchen.

"We are only a small group Otto remarked when they stopped en route are we meeting others?"

"Most definitely so . This is about a tenth of the size of the group waiting for us. The troops were Wehrmacht, regular army. Schmidt introduced Otto to his other officers. There was a Captain and two Lieutenants. The captain was the leader in the front APC and the other APC had a lieutenant while the troop platoon was officered by the third officer an extremely young looking man. Schmidt told Otto his father is a staff officer. His young son is a disappointment to him. He was hoping for a big strapping monster and he has a young 'litter runt' his words not mine. I feel sorry for him I don't think he's cut out for either war or aggression but he is an officer in the Wehrmacht and up until now I have no complaints about either his attitude or his performance. Let's hope he doesn't fail at any time.

They travelled steadily over dirt roads for most of day one. Muddy ground, leafless bushes, and equally bald trees signified a hard winter coming up. A cold wind and high humidity made for an uncomfortable journey. The soft top of the Kubelwagen was useless at keeping out the wind. The only consolation was that it wasn't raining. Otto reckoned rain was unlikely but snow probably wasn't. Sometime before the afternoon they stopped for a drink and a leg stretch. The cooks got hot water sorted and although there wasn't any hot food available sausage bread and hot coffee filled a gap.

Whilst they ate and drank Schmidt addressed his officers

"We are still in Romania so camp tonight should be quiet and trouble free but that isn't guaranteed. Romania may be our staunchest ally, especially where we are on the eastern front, but we are not as popular with everyone, so there will be guards and a sentry rota. When we came through here earlier this year we found a small wood that this track goes through we will camp there hoping to keep out of this wind. The men can find as much dead wood as possible to supplement the cooks fuel store and to the side of the road about three to four hundred matres is a running river that will allow us to top up our water supplies. We are making reasonable time so I expect to be there before dark which will make getting water and wood a lot easier. Start with the water as soon as we arrive. We can survive without wood if necessary."

At nearly fifteen hundred hours we arrived at the wood that Schmidt had chosen for the night camp. Most were happy to get out and move about and quickly a detail with buckets and cans headed to the river for water. Lieutenant Boucholtz the blond boy organised his troop into a guard detail. He split the members not gone for water into four groups proposing to add the others when they returned with the water. A couple of field tents were erected followed by a couple of others smaller and slightly further away. Officers as usual separated from the enlisted.

Ten minutes or so after we arrived we heard a single gunshot from somewhere in the woods we thought but direction wise we couldn't work out. We assumed someone shooting crows possibly. But five minutes later and our water carriers are not back. We need to investigate. The lieutenant has got a couple of his men with rifles and is about to go down to the river. Otto stopped him.

"Have you done this before?"

"No Sir."

"I shall accompany you."

"Tell your Captain where you are going."

Otto looked at the two privates. "Have either of you done this before?"

"No sir," they replied in unison. The Lieutenant returned slightly breathless.

"Captain says I should take my orders from you sir."

"Are your weapons loaded?"

"Yes sir."

"Do you have one in the chamber ready to fire?"

"No sir."

"Put one in there, put the safety catch on." They did.

"Does the safety come off easily?"

"Yes sir."

"If we need to start shooting remember to take it off quickly. Do not shoot each other, your friends, your Lieutenant, and especially me, I will get annoyed." They smiled. "It is probably nothing but let's be careful."

"Yes sir." Otto had relaxed them he hoped but not to get them too sloppy.

They moved swiftly but quietly down into the wood. Otto led. They could hear the stream and the sound of running water but no sound of birds or voices of men. Something was definitely not right and Otto took out his pistol, safety off ready, his instinct was telling him something was wrong, time would tell him if he was right. He slowed down there was no rush. Whatever had happened was over for now, and adding to the problem was not going to do any of them any good. The pathway opened up the river was narrow between the banks here and its speed increased. He could see down to the fast flowing water and he could also see two legs and the soles of a pair of boots. The top half not visible to him seemed to be hanging over the edge of the bank as though it was getting water by reaching down. Otto held his hand up and signalled them to spread out as far as the path would allow and stay low. He motioned for the lieutenant to move behind a tree and watch him as he made his way down to see what was happening at the bottom by the bankside. He kept a careful eye on the opposite bank looking for any sign of movement. The trees showed no sign of anything or anyone hiding Otto had tracked across the path from left to right and back again giving him a better view of what might be trying to hide but there was neither any sign of movement nor noise. Whatever was wrong with the man at the river appeared to be permanent there too was no sign of movement. Issue now was where are the other three soldiers. He squatted onto his heels and waited.

Then it happened a head appeared just in front of the body that was hanging over the bank and as it did so he spotted Otto squatting waiting and when the rifle came over the top and started to aim Otto shot him through the head and all hell happened in seconds two more heads and rifles were in the process and coming into the attack and they too were dispatched just as quickly each shot once in the head. Otto waited again. He swapped magazines in his pistol for a full one carefully stood up and moved towards the edge. As he got nearer he could see that there was below the bank a shingle lower bank and in a state of disarray six bodies. The three German soldiers and on top of them now t given the clothes they wore to be three dead Russian soldiers.

"Lieutenant." Otto called. He signalled him down. "Your missing men. Take one of the men make your way back to the camp carefully there is no rush. Report to your Captain in a controlled manner what has happened here. Tell him we will need a burial party and some assistance to sort out what we've found. Understood?"

"Yes sir."

"Send the other trooper down to me I want someone to watch my back while I take a look. I don't think there is anyone else about but let's both stay safe we have lost too many today already."

The lieutenant took one last quick look over the edge of the bank and moved swiftly up the hill. He spoke to the two troopers, one of which fell in behind him, the other one moving down to where Otto stood looking out across the other side of the river trying to work out what happened.

"What do you want me to do sir?"

"Keep watching from where we came this side of the river I will do the other side I doubt there is anyone else out there but we can wait our people should not be too long."

"Yes sir."

Commander Schmidt himself arrived five minutes later with six riflemen and carrying his sub machine gun.

"What do we know Hostuff?"

"Haven't checked the bodies yet sir but looking at the amount of blood on the stones down there I expect to find that their throats have been cut in some sort of ambush."

"What are the others?"

"They look like Russian uniform but no insignia so it'll be guess work."

"Then guess."

"My guess is that the three; we shall call them Russian. Were surprised either by the sound of our vehicles arriving, unlikely because that would have given them plenty of time to get away from here. Or more likely by the sound of the troopers coming down the path. But not so surprised that they didn't have time to set an ambush in the event that they were spotted. The troopers had left their weapons at the camp expecting only to be carrying water back up the hill. Whether one was shot first or last

I don't know but the three onto three fight was done very quickly and cleanly. Whoever these people were they knew how to deal with their enemy. From a professional view they were very good."

"Until they met you. Let's have a look eh." He handed his weapon to one of the troopers and dropped over the side onto the lower bank where Otto joined him. They searched through the clothes of the Russian soldiers.

"You're right about no insignia. Why I wonder?"

"If they are captured or found they can claim just to be a private nobody. And just end up as a prisoner of war if they got lucky. If they are a colonel of an elite regiment, Gestapo would be keen to interview them using some primitive methods that they always assume work."

"Find anything in the pockets?"

"Nothing sir."

"There isn't even a label in their shirts."

"No sir, but the caps look Russian, and so do the rifles."

"They aren't carrying side arms. Which if they were would make them officer material too."

"Probably what got them killed sir. My pistol works a lot quicker than a rifle. If they'd started with pistols I might not be talking to you now sir."

Schmidt was looking over his soldiers bodies and checking them carefully. Knowing full well they were dead he still checked for any sign of a pulse.

"Don't sell yourself short Otto. We heard three shots, three dead enemy, all shot through the head how long? A few seconds, five maximum. That's why you were Harrer's bodyguard. Normally a body guard is a corporal or a sergeant not a Captain in intelligence. That's why he made you his assistant. I can see you were right in your assessment, Harrer was a clever man." Schmidt was finished checking over the bodies.

"You were right too about their death. Throats cut and other stab wounds too. I don't think it matters which order it was but the trooper hanging over the edge was shot and stabbed too. Maybe he didn't die quick enough for them."

"The fact that there was a shot gave us an edge, cost the Russians if they are Russians, their lives."

"I've seen enough. We can't do anymore here. Lieutenant."

"Sir."

"Throw the foreigners up the hill in the woods somewhere out of the river. Find more buckets and get the water up to the camp. Get the water from a bit further upstream. Then get a couple of stretchers and carry our men back to camp and we will bury them tomorrow morning. We don't have much daylight left now."

Back at the camp Schmidt told Otto to join him at his tent.

"What do you think that was all about?"

If you are asking me to keep guessing sir. Then here goes. We are at least ten miles inside the border of Romania. The Russian front is even further away. If we have just killed three Russian soldiers. Who were they?

what were they doing there? How did they get there? Where is there base? They were all clean shaven freshly by the look of them today. Where did they do that? Do they have a camp somewhere within easy reach? The river there is too fast to cross. Were they heading for a crossing point somewhere when our men came upon them? If that's so then the crossing place or their camp must be up stream otherwise they would have hightailed it downstream. My thought then it might be worth a look further to see if there is any sign of a camp or anything that looks like it had been used as one such as a camp fire or anything like a shelter on either side of the river."

"I like the freshly shaven observation. That's something I hadn't appreciated until you said it. Everything else such as location and transport and general lack of equipment and nothing that would identify them was in the equation. But now you have me thinking about what I should do. We are about thirty miles from our rendezvous point with the rest of my regiment. My radio man has attempted to make contact but so far has been unsuccessful. I think because we are so low down here we are in a hollow and distance added to the terrain has limited our signals. That's what he says anyway. I'll assume he knows what he is doing as a regular and a corporal. Most of these troops are green. If I thought about it which is very easy in retrospect. We would not have gone down there without weapons. These soldiers need to be told about everything what we would do automatically has to be drummed into this lot. Maybe todays lesson will waken them up to the fact that there's a war going on.

Thoughts Otto."

"I think we should have another look at the Russians. I also wonder if there is a basecamp somewhere handy and someone is there What will they do when their comrades don't return or if they heard gun shots."

"What do you think you might get from the bodies?"

"I don't know. Something hidden in the lining of the clothing but currently we can't even confirm they're Russian we are guessing because of the cap and the weapons which could have been stolen. I have my issue pistol sir but they were shot by my Beretta that doesn't make me an Italian does it?" Otto suddenly realised how his offhand remark had sounded.

"Careful Hostumf Witzel insubordination will irritate me."

"Sorry Sir. It didn't come out as I meant it."

"Forgiven but remember it well."

"Yes sir."

"Take a flashlight and two troopers with you and see what you can find on the bodies. They will be easier to examine off the river edge. Then depending on what you find. Tomorrow morning first light take the young Lieutenant and four troopers and investigate further upstream returning in one hour which means you will be in time for breakfast and the funerals. If anything, significant comes from the body search report to me on your return this evening."

"Yes sir."

Otto saluted his commander, and left, thankful that he hadn't got a dressing down for that silly slip up in his statement.

Lieutenant Bucholtz provided two troopers and a flashlight from the stores box. And smiled quite broadly when told he was to accompany Otto first thing tomorrow morning along with four troopers. The ones who had taken the first sentry shift and therefore should be the freshest available. "Rifle and extra ammunition and drinking water. Out for an hour travelling fast and light."

"We will be ready sir."

Otto was certain without any doubt that there would not be another ambush but nevertheless he approached the area very carefully. The bodies were up the hillside not too far into the woods. Access was reasonably easy. He worked quickly feeling through the material and checking hems and seams in the clothing feeling for anything extra in thickness or texture that might give a hint as to who they were. He removed the boots. Which is when things started to develop. The leg of the trousers covered the tops of the boots . when he lifted the trouser legs he could see that the boots were made from something other than leather and there were no nails on the boot sole. He compared the boots with his troopers boots. There was no obvious similarity and all three dead men's boots were the same. He removed the trousers completely from the first soldier. There was no label in his underwear even but there were some marks where the stitching had been. There was a definite deliberate non-identification planning here. Then not knowing why maybe because he was a man but he noticed something.

He moved quickly to the second man and took down his trousers and underwear and again for the third. He pulled their trousers back up again as best he could fastened what he could.

"We are finished," he told the troopers. "Same thing applies now, rifles loaded safety on don't shoot me. It's dark now going up the hill you can slip accidents happen."

They returned to camp, "Ask cook for some coffee please and I shall pick it up when I have spoken to the boss."

A sentry at the front of his tent told the General he wanted to enter.

"Yes Otto find anything?"

"Yes sir, I believe the boots are Russian. Strange imitation leather that they use and all three of the men had been circumcised."

"You were thorough then."

"I checked the other two when I spotted the first one had been done."

"So what have we learnt?"

"I don't think that we've learnt anything at this time sir other than the possibility that they might have been Russian jews but that might be totally off course without anything more substantial to back it up."

"Agreed See what tomorrow morning brings."

"Yes sir."

"You're very thorough Otto you will go far in this army as long as you don't get killed."

"Thank you sir."

"Now go eat. Report when you get back tomorrow morning."

"Yes sir, thank you, good night."

When Otto left his tent on the following morning Lieutenant Bucholtz and four troopers were waiting outside. The air was cold and humidity was still uncomfortably high. "Have you briefed your men Lieutenant ?"

"Yes sir."

"Good, then let's get going. We will take the same path as yesterday, down to where we were. Then we will find a way to work our way back up the river. Keep your eyes peeled gentlemen Anything that looks out of place or unusual, different, strange, not normal, speak, understood ?"

"Yes sir."

Otto led them back down to where they had been yesterday. He checked the bodies from the path. They hadn't been disturbed by either people or animal. Then following the bank they slowly worked their way through the bushes and stunted trees. Lack of leaves gave them a clear picture of the opposite bank and although there had been a couple of places where crossing may have been possible, the banks showed no sign of any boot marks on either side.

Lieutenants Bucholtz called to Otto. "Sir you asked me to tell you when we had done half an hour. We have now been out half an hour sir."

"Thank you Lieutenant now tell me when we have done ten more minutes."

"Yes sir."

"We have less distance to travel back we will not be searching and it's downhill we take less time to return."

"Yes sir."

"Sir we have done another ten minutes."

"Thank you Lieutenant remind me in five more minutes."

"Yes sir."

Otto had decided that it was too strange not to find anything. Three men were dead in a remote area no sign of transport shelter or any camp, too many unanswered questions. The trees were thinning here and up ahead Otto thought maybe five more minutes. His commander did not know exactly when he left. He moved quickly although the trees here had thinned the access to the river had gone for the last five minutes the ground had risen not steeply but steadily and it looked as though the river was now inaccessible down a steep gorge. And there in front of them in a small clearing was a canvas shelter stretched over what looked like a motor bike with a sidecar attached.

"Lieutenant I think we can justify being a little late for breakfast."

"Yes sir." That boy did have a nice wide smile.

"We can see because of the wet ground which way the motor bike came in so if they rode it in it should be able to be ridden out. Therefore, one must assume that somewhere in that direction," Otto pointed in the direction of the motor buke tyre tracks; "there is a road, and I would think that looking at the direction is where we were travelling yesterday and we know where the sun rose this morning then we cannot be too far away from the road we came in on yesterday."

"Yes sir. Are you going to check their camp sir?"

"I will do so shortly but first I'm going to study it from here."

"Why is that sir?"

"They left all their kit alone unguarded, for whatever reason. If I did that Lieutenant, I might booby trap it first, so we will do this slowly and carefully. Take two men and see if you can see anything five minutes maximum that way. I don't think they would want to bring this lot too far from the road getting it back would be too difficult.

Go carefully Lieutenant"

"Sir."

Otto watched the young officer making his way along the line of the tyre track made by the Motor bike. He called the other two troopers over.

"Walk around to the other side don't get too close, watch where you are walking, and look where you are putting your feet. Don't walk without looking where your feet are going to land. Understand?"

"Yes sir," in unison.

One went left and one went right. Otto took his field glasses and looked at the camp they could focus in tight and he could see underneath the tarpaulin basha and everything looked clear. He moved in very slowly there was nothing obvious as a trip wire and he grew in confidence. Within five minutes young Bucholtz was back. He stood off staying on the path.

"You were right sir just to the side of the hillock there is where there is a road."

"Which way does it run Lieutenant?"

"East west sir."

"So as we have walked in a westerlie direction should we assume that our camp is along that road in an easterly direction?"

"I think so sir."

"Good so do I."

"Right gentlemen breakfast beckons we will all head to where Herr Bucholtz says our road is then we shall turn left when we reach the road and I think we will be back at camp in less than twenty minutes without rushing. Let's go."

When they reached the camp he gave out his orders.

"Get your men fed Lieutenant ,feed yourself. Well done. Keep it up keep learning, we are at war, trust nothing and nobody, don't do anything unless your certain, and at the same time don't spend too long thinking about it. Confusing isn't it?"

"Thank you sir, and Yes sir."

Otto headed to Scmidt's tent.

"We saw you coming down the road Hostumf what news?"

"Motorcycle and sidecar, they had a tarpaulin for shelter over it. Presumably to hide it from the air and provide some cover in the event of rain. Doesn't look booby trapped but I'd like to pull the tarpaulin away so I can see it better."

"How long, and what do you need?"

"Two troopers and my Kubelwagen and driver not too long."

"Get some food down you and then get on with it. But don't take too long we have to make a rendezvous today."

"Understood sir."

"Most of the troopers had eaten breakfast drinks were still available and there was still enough hot water in the goulashkanone."

"You can have an egg sir."

"Did everyone get an egg?"

"No sir just the usual bread and sausage or cheese. Tea or coffee."

"I will have bread sausage and coffee please cook."

"Very good sir, though you are welcome to an egg too should you wish. I would normally give out eggs on a rota depending on supplies. We may have more when we join the rest of the regiment though I will be surprised if they have any left."

Otto had sent a soldier to find his driver and his two troopers with instructions to bring his vehicle to him. They had been primed and ready to go.

He got into the front seat.

"Slowly along the road driver. Back the way we came in. I don't wish to have my coffee anywhere but in my mouth. Pull up here on the right driver. Gently this coffee 's still hot.

Trooper get a rope and a hook out of the back and follow me driver stay here."

They made their way down to the camp. Otto uncoiled the rope tied the hook on to it and gave one end to one of the troopers. When I tell you to pull I want you to pull the rope steadily no jerking just a steady pull. Stay as far away as possible by grabbing the very end of the rope I don't know if it's booby trapped. I will give you directions from the other side of the camp.

Otto slipped the hook into an eyelet hole and then standing back signalled the trooper to pull the tarpaulin slowly off the motor bike.

"Stop." The trooper stopped. "Get as far back as possible, lie on the ground and pull gently."

Otto got down low and as the trooper pulled the tarpaulin again the motor cycle exploded and the whole machine burst into flames. The petrol tank had blown up and what was probably another container of fuel.

"Stay down." A minute they stayed down for.

"Let's get up you stayed down in case ammunition went off. There's still that possibility but we can't stay around here for ever. We're not going to find much information here now most of what was here is burnt not that there happens to be much here to start with. The tarpaulin had Russian markings on it and they took it with them as they returned to their vehicle. Just as they got back Schmidt was hammering along the road with a couple more troopers.

"Report."

"Was booby trapped, was Russian as is the tarpaulin, but very little else there. I think there's more of them about at a guess I'm going to suggest that they are part of a bigger group and there's always the possibility we'll meet them on our route. They looked like a recce team as they had only a small amount of kit."

"What about the booby trap?"

"Their comrades would know about it they would all do it the same way."

"Let's get back. We have buried the four dead troopers I don't want to bury anymore today."

Scmidt put the APC at the head and tucked in behind it.

Towards evening having moved over bad ground throughout late afternoon and just after sunset they arrived at the rendezvous with the main force.

"Something is wrong. There are nowhere near the numbers who were supposed to be there." Otto's driver had pulled up next to Schimdt. A Wehrmacht major arrived and saluted. "Where is everyone?" Scmidt demanded.

"Orders have been received that sent most of the regiment north to Barbarossa leaving just a token group to wait for you sir. I have here sir a new set of orders from High Command and General Hadler directing us to do a survey of the route to Stalingrad."

"Tell me major where did I fit into this crazy idea of Hadler's?"

"I'm sorry sir, I don't know."

Gruppen Fuhrer Schmidt is not happy. And less so when he was told of an incident with a group of four motor bike and sidecars.

There had been a surprise when they had just stopped where they were. The motor bike group suddenly and definitely accidently ran onto the camp.

"You had not posted sentries Major?"

"Yes sir, but there was no warning from the sentry, and I have not been able to find who was responsible."

"As it stands you major because you don't know how you r chain of command. How could a group of Russian motor cycles suddenly come upon you by accident without being heard?"

"I think it is because we had only just arrived here sir and our motors were still running."

"Continue with your report Major."

"A small skirmish ended with the capture of two of the Russian teams. One escaped by turning around and going back the way they came. one escaped going forward through the group, who were unable to shoot them down in case they hit our own people. Two of the six Russians from the other two machines had died of their injuries. Two had been beaten to death by the troopers when captured. One is now in such a poor physical condition having been subjected to torture and the last man is singing and telling everything he could about what he knows which isn't very much."

Otto listened to the officers report to Scmidt without making any comment. Scmidt asked the questions and the officer addressed his answers directly to him but Otto noticed him periodically taking a quick look in between questions but before making eye contact he would look away again.

"Where did you leave the rest of the regiment?"

"About fifty miles back that way sir they were heading north sir as fast as possible. General Halder sent the change of orders himself, demanding threequarters of your group to join him in the north to attack Moscow while we assess Stalingrad. I have no radio working hence no communication from me to let you know. My radio man can't fix it as he has no spare parts they have gone with everything else to General Hadler."

"Tell me major then what do I have left of my promised command?"

"I think looking at what you have brought sir you have slightly more than double what you have brought with you. I have two APCs with crew, two lieutenants two small platoons of twenty men in two troop carrier, one field kitchen two medium machine guns and a fuel truck."

"We won't get even halfway to Stalingrad."

"I was told to forage sir and take from the enemy."

Scmidt said no more but was lost in thought. "Let us get tonight sorted first. Organise your camp Major I have a Captain two Lieutenants and my intelligence officer with me twenty men four killed yesterday by the motor cycle trio that got away going through you. They too are dead. Get the camp sorted get the men fed organise a guard rota. Give me a fuel situation. And I shall think and plan. Carry on. Hostumf come with me."

Otto walked with Scmidt as he looked around at what he had shaking his head and muttering. They walked around the camp spoke to a couple of sergeants who were less than complementary about their troopers.

"Politics will be playing a part Otto. General Hadler is Wehrmacht we are Waffen SS that's enough for some to hang us out to dry. No good whining about it. When we get a look at what we've got tomorrow we'll make some decisions and see what we can do. General Hadler is in total charge of Operation Barbarossa at the moment he will be allowed to have anything he wants."

On the following morning Schmidt called a meeting of his officers.

"Hostumf you will take one Kubelwagen a driver two troopers and a machine gun. Lieutenant Bucholtz you will follow behind with a driver and two troopers and enough fuel to return us all back to here. Major you will remain here in charge until we return. I will lead at the front in an APC. The fuel situation tells me that I don't have enough to get back what men and machines we have here home again. We shall see how far we get and see what we can find. You must also remember gentlemen that one of the motorcycle tams escaped yesterday. We have to assume that if they didn't crash and die shortly after they left then the Russians are aware of our presence and will be considering what to do about our arrival. We will leave in thirty minutes."

Otto was sorting some food and water to drink when he was approached by the major.

"Hostumf were you General Harrer's adjutant?"

"I was major."

"I was in Berlin when you shot at the shooting range against he Englander. I thought I recognised you."

"A long time back major you have a good memory."

"I think your shooting skills may well be required before the day is out Hostumf. I hope I'm wrong but keen amateurs are no substitute for even a small number of professionals."

"We all started somewhere major."

"We did Hostumf but Russian armour on Russian soil is not a good place to start learning your trade. I wish you a safe journey."

We had travelled around fifteen kilometres when we came upon a small group of buildings. Scmidt's driver pointed the halftrack towards them and then stopped half way across the road. The general signalled Otto to join him. Then he sent me to go look see. "Don't endanger yourself." I got close and stopped my driver to one side My view through the glasses told me nothing but given what occurred with the motor bike and sidecar a booby trap would not have surprised me.

I returned to my general and reported.

"What do you think Hostumf?"

"If it isn't a trap it would be a miracle. It's too tempting . I would have planted something."

"Maybe you are more devious Hostumf." He leaned into the cab and told the gunner to shoot the front door, which he did. The door, or what was left of it, moved on its hinges and swung like it was in a gentle wind. "Perhaps Hostumf we were supposed to think that so we didn't check it out." At which point the building blew up and the ones either side followed seconds after. "Or Hostumf our enemy is just as devious as you are. Well they know were on our way one wonders where they might wait for us."

Three kilometres it was where they waited for us around a tight bend through a cutting . The APC should not have been in the lead. A Kubelwagen possibly could have turned and got out.

When the Russian tank appeared in front of them on the road Otto new they were done for. The APC lasted for one shot it may have hit the tank but to no avail. The tank fired and the APC died as did the crew inside it. Scmidt was hurt jumping from the halftrack but he could still move and he made it back to Otto's vehicle.

The driver got the Kubelwagen turned and they headed off in retreat away from the tank. Around a bend in the road Otto pulled over to one side. Lieutenant Bucholtz pulled his vehicle up beside Otto.

He said nothing there was a confrontational conversation taking place between his General and the intelligence officer.

"They are T34 Tanks sir. The only thing we have that might have stood up to them would still be in Germany having broken down for the third time and stuck on the roadside waiting for parts. I'm sure you don't want my advice sir but at this moment we are going to die without achieving anything. Achieving our objective and dying is one form of death and glory. Getting killed and failing hopelessly already knowing that we will fail is death and stupidity sir."

"I am not a man who runs."

"You won't run anywhere shortly sir because you will be dead. Accept the fact that you are not running away but regrouping and my advice sir is that regrouping and returning to Berlin with the information you have and the knowledge you now have is more likely to bring success in the future, if that wherever possible here. It is better than finishing as a corpse without a voice in a muddy battle torn field. We can't even send a message as the radios won't work. The only possible advantage available now is to get back home and tell the high command what we have learnt. Sir."

"You are your father."

"We need to move sir while we still can."

"How will we get back we were stretched too far already/"

" I don't know we've been sucked into a trap they have let us come in. There is no food or fuel in the empty villages because they have run and taken it with them. Soon we will not be able to retreat even to the Romanian border. If we keep chasing the enemy across land. We have no heavy weapons, little food, very little spare fuel, and no element of surprise. They can pick us off whenever and wherever they want."

"Put the lieutenant in with you I shall take the lead in his Wagen."

Bucholtz got into the back between the troopers and Schmidt had his driver turn the vehicle and they headed back onto the road. They were nearing the abandoned farm that had been booby trapped when machine gun fire hit the Generals vehicle.

Schmidt was shot in the leg the driver was killed instantly and the vehicle because it was already moving into a bend then overturned. The troopers with our machine gun took out the Russians and Otto stopped near to the other vehicle. He could do nothing for the driver. Lieutenant Bucholtz got Schmidt under his arms and dragged him over to Otto's vehicle. They got him into the back with the two troopers who were firing the machine gun at a tank that had now arrived from in front of them. The tank wasn't returning fire but it was aiming for us I got the Kubelwagen turned and we headed off at speed. The tank was out of control. The drivers hatch was partially open. Had the periscope malfunctioned was the hatch jammed whatever it was the tank was out of control. It hit the General's vehicle and the vehicle exploded the tank was still going in a straight line something had happened in the Russian Tank. Otto didn't know what but he wasn't hanging around to find out.

General Scmidt had finally given in and stopped arguing with Otto. He was now damaged enough to know he was no longer capable of being in command. They got him out of there, he had two bullets in his leg and he had number broken bones from when his Kubelwagen overturned.

They got back to Major Vorg and headed back towards Romanian border. What was left of Schmidt's command took up a defensive position near to the water supply where the troopers and Russians had been killed.

Otto took Bucholtz, one driver and a trooper with a machine gun in a Kubelwagen and headed for the nearest town about sixty kilometres away where he got a fuel truck a medical team and food supplies.

They made Schmidt a staff officer when he got out of hospital and posted him back at his office in Berlin and Otto was promoted to SS-Sturm Bann Führer and sent to join another SS Tank regiment on the Russian front. He had by his actions redeemed himself, even though the initial attempt to survey a way to Stalingrad had turned into a disaster.

They had learnt that trying to take Stalingrad was not going to be easy. General Harrer was right but no one took any notice

I have been a witness to barbarism that has left me feeling nothing but loathing for the people I thought were my comrades and friends who had honour and principals that the world would envy and respect. Instead of this we have been involved in the butchering of innocent defenceless old sick and weak. Women and children versus the machine gun or the club shovelled into mass graves without consideration of mercy. Prepared as I was to fight man against man or war machine against war machine I could find nothing other than abhorrence for the act of killing non-combatants just to satisfy the thoughts and ideals of some madmen and to see how high they could climb up through the hierarchy by committing as many atrocities as they could. I could not stop any of it happening but I could bear witness to the fact and tell what happened.

I am classed as a criminal now an officer in the wrong organisation the army has been saved General Hadler is with the Americans most of the army butchers have escaped some of us though not innocent in all cases will carry the blame and pay the price. For the crimes of others.

Chapter 9 France

It took the best part of ten days for Alan to get everything prepared. He had already taken his motorcycle to Tangmere where the mechanics adapted the frame for a flying flea to fix the bike to the plane. The engineers at Woolwich had managed the first part of the adaption but not having access to what it was going to be fitted to, could go no further. They hadn't a plane available when he arrived but they did have a spare side ladder so they made the frame to fit the side ladder knowing that it would fit when they could trial the idea.

One morning Bill Turner flew in with his Lysander looking for a Captain Lewis. The duty officer found Alan in the mess as normal working his way through food and or coffee.

"Bill this is Alan, he 'll tell you what he wants."

Good morning Bill. Do you know of any other Bill Turners flying Lysanders?"

"Not that I know of."

"Then I know you, but you don't know me. Do you want a coffee?"

"I'll get a tea after thank you."

"What is it you want then?"

"Where's your plane?"

"Outside I got told off for bringing it in last time."

They were still laughing when they went outside and walked down towards the mechanics shop.

"You know you're carrying me and a motor bike to France."

"I do now first I've heard of it."

"That's normal. You flew a German General from by the black forest a short while back."

"I was told that was top secret."

"It is. I organised it. That's how I know you. How was the landing on that drive?"

"Wonderful one of the best strips I've been on."

"The next one won't be so good but it's just outside Paris and a field on a farm but there's no big holes and no animals at this moment in there. We have three landing fields in the area we rotate them . I don't think you've done any of these. A couple of the others have been flying in weapons and radios for me. This time it's a motor bike and with a bit of luck another one fairly soon. We'll see. Next question is when can we go?"

"Tonight if you have decent location details and a map."

"What about a test flight?"

"Put it on we'll go up now and if for any reason we're not happy we can go via Lympne if we have any issues stop there have a check; if there's a problem we can always stopover there anyway. I wouldn't normally fly that rout e it's a lot shorter to go in a straight line."

The modified parachute frame of the flying flea was strapped to the ladder on the side of the Lysander. Alan lifted the motor bike and hooked it onto the frame and strapped it on tight. The hard part was then getting in but a short ladder got him in the rear seat and climbing out was be careful and jump the last bit don't break an ankle.

Alan was in Bill was now in charge and off the y went. They flew around the airfield did a couple of low level passes to check it flew level and then landed. They checked the straps and the buckles. Decided to increase the number and settled for a go tonight. Alan took the motor bike off the side and let the mechanics check it all over. They improved the fixing of the adapted frame by bolting it to the ladder, which left only the motor cycle straps as a weak point. Doubling the straps would reduce that to a less than worrying level.

They decided to fly direct and avoid Lympne.

Marcel had organised the lighting. They put the motor buke into Marcel's van and were leaving the field almost as quickly as Bill Turner who was heading back to Tangmere another job done.

Alan stayed with Marcel overnight. When he queried the message he had received Marcel told him there had been some problems but he didn't want to tell Alan about them as he was only able to provide some of the information as it was to do more with Henri though Simone who knew more than he did.

Henri was according to Marcel doing some business somewhere of which he knew nothing. It was not one they shared.

Alan decided to called at the bar before heading to Fatima's house. The bar was closed. He scribbled a note asking for Henri or Simone to get in touch.

Alan was out in Pigalle on a people watch, avoiding the ladies but watching the pimps and the clients, when Simone left a message with Fatima saying that she was at the bar but better would be to meet her at the park later as it would be a better place to talk.

Alan was sitting on his own easily spotted when Simone arrived. As he expected Simone came by bus, though mostly unreliable due to fuel shortages it was without Henri her only form of transport. She told him there had trouble at the bar.

"Two German soldiers drunk and stupid have hired Justine for a top and tail session but part way through something has happened and they start to beat her up.

Jacque has heard the commotion and left the bar to find out what was going on.

They were not upstairs but in the back room what was fortunate for Justine was disastrous for Jacque he runs in to two half naked drunken German soldiers who got lucky and he is stabbed with a bayonet in his neck. He died almost instantly.

Henri arrived just seconds after Jacques was killed. They had started back on beating Justine again. As old as Henri is he has learnt how to stay alive and consequently he is still a dangerous man. He clubbed both of them and knocked them out. He carries a lead truncheon now as well as his knives.

After he'd tied them up, he gagged and blindfolded them, then he gave them one hell of a beating. I've never seen him so mad. He kept beating them. I think he was breaking their bones while keeping them conscious. He left me sorting out Justine. The Germans he left tied up gagged and blindfolded and nearly dead .

He covered Jacques 'Oh my friend I will make them pay more later.' Was all he said. Then he shut and locked the doors to the bar and left me to take care of Justine and mind the place; while he went for some help. He came back a while later with two men I had never seen before but I think they work with his brother or at the orphanage. There's not many people you can trust in the circumstances and he and his brother are very close when they run businesses together. The Germans were conscious again and making grunting noises. They were given a kicking and then put into laundry bags and taken out to a van in the street.

It was a lot later when they all returned around ten o clock. Henri just said he had put them through the band saw and the mincer machine and into the pig food. The pigs were now about to produce real German sausage. It sounded like a joke but he didn't laugh and I really believe he was sorry to see Jacques killed. First time ever I've seen anything close to remorse or sadness in Henri in all the years I've known him.

The two men who came with him helped me clean the place up. They did some painting on the walls to make a reason for the bar being closed as well to hide the smell of blood and thuggery.

The following morning when it was still dark the two men took Jacques away in another laundry bag to the undertakers. They gave him a decent burial early in the cemetery. I think it is not the first time that Henri and his brother have done jobs like this. I sometimes believe it is better not to know what goes on."

"How is the girl?"

"Sore but alive."

"I assume she is not working."

"She can't at the moment they beat her badly."

"Pay her a wage from my takings until she is well again. I am not in a hurry for money. Thank Henri for me. What else is happening?"

"Henri has gone off somewhere to do some business. He didn't tell me he just said he would be away for a few days and I was to do whatever I could on my own if there was a problem to phone Marcel.

Henri has been doing Jacque's job at the bar for the time being until it all settles down. Marcel says he can have one of his men or he can find him a man to replace Jacques unless you want to."

"Tell him to pick his man he has to deal with him. No good me sending someone he might not get on with."

"He told me to tell you what happened and what he did about it. He said to tell you he didn't do it because he was afraid of you but because he felt that he owed Jacque."

"Fair enough. Tell him if he needs more muscle let me know."

"Thank you for Justine's money."

"She's welcome. Let her get fit again before she needs to go back to work but don't let her take the piss."

"I understand thank you Alan." They sat quietly together on the park bench .

 "My bus should be here soon; I dare not miss it. The driver told me he would be doing the return journey the next bus after that was anybody's guess."

Simone turned slightly in her seat. Alan seemed like a sweet man but if Henri was frightened of him there must be a reason even though when they first met she treated him like any other punter now there was a fence between them and she knew that if she looked too closely on the other side it might see things she did not wish to see.

"Then do not miss your bus. Our business is complete for now you are feeling ok?"

"Yes thank you."

"Then continue to do so and let me know if any other problems occur or more firepower is needed."

"I shall pass on the messages."

She put her cigarettes and matches back into her handbag, closed the clasp, kissed Alan gently on the cheek, and headed off for her bus.

Alan watched as Simone walked away towards the bus stop. She seemed better on her feet than when he had first met her. The heels were lower and her hips were getting a less impactive exercise. After years of working on the streets the change of job was doing her some good and she even sounded nicer, the hardness, bounding the edges was easing off and softening. He waited until she had caught the bus then went to get his motor cycle parked just along the street.

Alan is living in the top floor of Fatima's house. He managed to get the room again that he and Cameron had when they first arrived in Paris. The war has reduced everyone's income and food and money are competing to see which one can runout first. The Germans are deliberately crippling the French franc to make it difficult for the people to buy. He is living there as a Swiss national. His plan is to keep the room long term to leave his kit there. He also has access to the rear of the house where there is a shed where he keep the DKW and a small store of petrol. This way it's locked away and there are still a few Moroccan heavies staying there that won't let it disappear. There is a radio he has left with Marcel, hidden at the orphanage. Marcel checks in for him from various places dotted around his area.

Having made contact with Henri and marcel and found a place for the radio and motorbike, he asked for a lift back to England and at the same time to bring another radio.

Two days later Henri drove Alan to the pickup point this time put four lights the field one in each corner the plane landed Alan passed the radio to Henri and climbed aboard and was flown back to England.

Chapter 10   Paris Almira

Marcel took the call himself, at the orphanage. He had been talking to Father Jonquet about a small party he was planning for a member of the district Council, when the phone interrupted him.

"Marcel?" a man's voice familiar but not quite put a name to it yet.

"Yes."

"Good I am surprised to catch you, but we are in luck. I thought I was going to have to leave you a message, but this saves us time and time may be more important. This afternoon there was a meeting of some of us from the local council, nothing formal just a get together to keep each other up to date. There was talk that Madame Almira may be picked up and interrogated for reasons I am not privy to, but it is likely that people are talking to save their own skins and will incriminate anyone they can to do so. I am not certain, but I have heard that there is a business link between your brother and Madame

Almira; and I thought if I do you a favour, you will probably do me one sometime in the future."

"I'm not totally aware of what my brother's business links are, but I will pass on the message to him. And even if there is no thing for us to concern ourselves with I will still be happy to do you a favour should your need arise."

"Well thankyou Marcel, that is very good of you."

"The phone went dead."

"You must excuse me father. I am sorry I may need to rush away but I must contact my brother just in case there is a problem. I will try to phone first."

"As you must Marcel."

It would take twenty minutes to get to Henri's bar. He should be there by now. If he phoned first he could leave a message if he wasn't there yet.

Simone answered. "Simone, Marcel, is Henri there?"

"Not yet, he is on his way."

"Tell him I am on my way over. He must stay there till I speak to him."

Henri was serving a drinker when Marcel arrived. Simone was

sitting at a table smoking a cigarette a glass of red on the table with her but no customer.

Henri motioned her to take the bar while he went out with Marcel.

"I have had a message from Pierre Chevalier, one of my clients telling me sometime soon that Madame Almira is going to be picked up by the police or someone else Possibly tonight or maybe tomorrow but soon. I think your friend Alan would prefer her not to be damaged by people keen on extracting information.

I have my car here we could go to the restaurant and see if she is there. That is a first place to start. And if she isn't then we rethink and ask questions."

"I will speak to Simone then I am ready."

The two men on the door to the restaurant recognized Henri and wouldn't let him in.

"I need to speak to madame Almira," he whispered to one of the men. "I am not here to cause trouble; if she is not here is Charles here?"

"Wait outside do not try pushing in."

"I won't." Henri lit a cigarette and paced along the pavement outside the restaurant. He could see through the windows, as usual the place was mostly ful;l soon the floor show would be on, if they were having one tonight. They were never advertised or guaranteed but every night there was one whether it was a singer a pianist or a dancer, something would generally happen, hence this time of the evening it was always a popular place, Henri could see to the far side to the kitchen door then he saw Charles come through the door next to it and make his way across the room towards the street. The door man came out first followed by Charles.

"Good evening Henri How can I help you?"

"It is how can I help you Charles." He got close into Charles and whispered to him.

"I have been told that Madame Almira is on a list of people to be picked up for the purposes of interrogation to find out what she knows about what goes on in its simplest form."

"Who told you this?"

"One of my brothers clients told us this about an hour ago. We have no other details but there is no reason to suppose it isn't the truth; heaven knows she has people working all over Paris for her. It could be a business competitor trying to get rid of her. I don't know and neither does the person who gave us the information."

"Well thank you for telling me Henri. I will pass the message on when I see her. Is there anything else?"

"Yes tell her I am at her service. We have a mutual friend who would expect me to help if I could. You know where to find me Charles. I can at this time do no more than I already have."

Henri nodded to Charles and joined his brother, who had waited in the parked car engine running.

"And Henri?"

"Take me back to the bar please. The rest is up to other people, but I must send a message to Alan."

When they got to the bar it was quiet, which suited their purpose this evening.

Henri wrote a note for Marcel to take back to the orphanage which he would send on the radio to Alan.

An hour later he got a coded message back.

ETA142330Z3AL

Marcel took the message to Henri.

He is coming in tomorrow night. Message is 14 tomorrow's date followed by time. I shall meet him at agreed location.

Henri closed the bar at ten and was about to drop Simone off at her lodging "You don't want me to come with you?" she asked. "We look like we're going for sex if anyone spots us."

"Good idea we'll still get shot but we might stay warm while we wait."

Simone wasn't certain about Henri's humour, but the idea of getting shot didn't have any appeal and she was regretting making the offer. Perhaps she should learn to hold her tongue and not make rash suggestions. Tonight, hopefully will be a warning not a lesson.

They drove out of the suburbs and down into the country lanes. There was little moonlight coming through the clouds and the road dark and twisting wouldn't allow for anything going too quickly. Henri too had little appetite for the thought of dying and he knew that even driving quite steadily he would be in plenty of time to arrive at the field were Alan would land. Around eleven fifteen he slowed his car the gateway he knew was near and he turned his lights down and started to crawl slowly partially to see if any other lights were a bout and partly to extend his journey time. After five minutes he was at the gate and turned into the field he turned off the engine and waited for a couple more minutes. At five minutes to ETA he climbed out went to the boot of his car and took out three large lanterns. He took them to the other side of the field and lit them as he heard the plane overhead back at the car he started the engine and shone his lights across the field in a straight line towards the light. The plane made a slow low circle and landed. He left the engine running and got out to meet Alan and see if he needed a carry with anything. He had with him two loaded Bergans. They ducked down and the Lysander took off. They squeezed the Bergans into the boot with the lights and headed back to Marcel's house next to the orphanage. Job done.

The following morning Simone is helping prepare breakfast while Alan is trying to come with a plan to get Madame out of the restaurant or wherever she is and get her away and safe. The discussion is with Henr, Marcel says he will help if he can, but he isn't certain if there is anything he can do. He has a delivery to do today at Madame's restaurant and three others. He does the others first and then finishes at madams.

"I deliver vegetables, chickens and eggs. Standard order from them same basic order twice every week."

"So, you are expected?"

"Of course, we go before lunch on Monday and early morning Friday."

"I will come with you this morning." Alan decides. "I will take the labourer's place and do the delivery and carry the goods inside.

Henri you will go to the restaurant and tell her what we are going to do. I will go and deliver the stuff with Marcel and one of the other guys to the other places. Then join you at Madame's place if that is ok with Henri and you too Marcel?"

"It will be ok with us." Marcel nodded his agreement.

"I will put my stuff together and leave you to do what it is you have to do. Just be careful, if your contact is right this could all be happening soon; let's hope we are not too late already."

Alan had put what he needed into a box and joined Marcel outside at his van. "Has Henri explained exactly the plan?"

"He has. Seems straightforward."

"it is if it works. If it goes wrong it isn't but keep things simple and they should always work. Where do we load up?"

"We have loaded the vegetables already just chickens to pick up from slaughterhouse and we're ready."

The four sets of deliveries were all separated in the back of the van first lot first restaurant hen the same with two and three. The first three were done. Madame's would be a five to ten minutes away depending on traffic and hopefully Henri would be there and inside by now.

Henri had dropped Simone off at the bar and left her to manage it while he was speaking to madame, if she was there, if he could get in.

Henri arrived at the restaurant. It was only just opening, but there appeared to be a number of people hanging around outside that didn't look like clientele. There was no one on the door so Henri walked in. Right by the kitchen door stood Madame with Charles. She was deep in conversation. she looked up and Luigi was saying." I'm sorry sir we are not open yet." Henri ignored him. And made a beeline for Charles and Almira.

"You are being watched," Henri told them.

"We know," said Charles.

"We have a plan."

"Why should I believe you?" asked Almira.

"Because our friend is here, and he is coming with a delivery of food as usual for the restaurant. You will take his place and leave with my brother who will take you away from here."

"The question is still. Why should I believe you?"

"Monsieur Alain said if I did you any harm he would cut my balls off and make me eat them. I have no reason not to believe him. Now I have passed the message on I will wait and try to cover any problems if they occur from outside. Get a move on Almira you don't have time to waste. My brother will take care of you." Henri turned and walked outside.

"Do you think he's telling the truth?"

"We will know soon enough. It is nearly time for Marcel to deliver. He is always here just before lunch. Get your identity papers and remove your make up, make sure you're completely clear of lipstick and any rouge and powder. And change your shoes. You need to have some working footwear. Try one of the junior chefs if you don't have any."

Almira went up to her apartment.

A short time later Alan arrived at the back door to the kitchen carrying the first of the parcels with his own box on top. He was hoping to see Charles and frantically searching, looking around time was limited the were more people standing outside than usual. The chef was shouting at him, but he ignored him he didn't like people wandering through his kitchen when cooking was happening. Charles hearing the shouting came through the kitchen door and Alan spotted him instantly.

"Is Almira here?"

"Upstairs, removing clothes and makeup."

"Good can we go up? We need to keep the schedule. Marcel is outside with the van. Henri is watching. If we stay too long the spies may rumble us."

"Follow me then." Charles let himself and Alan into the apartment. Almira was dressed in slacks and a shirt her hair tied up in a bun and stuffed inside a hat. Alan took the overalls off.

"Put these on and go out through the kitchen. Marcel will take you to his place. Hurry I will catch up later."

"What will you do?"

"I shall have lunch here." Alan emptied his box a shirt tie and shoes and two piece suit were wrapped up inside. "I shall borrow your bathroom if I may, but you have to go now, hurry, I will see you later.

Take this empty box with you and walk out. Don't speak to anyone. Get in the van sit in the middle and keep the hat on until you are at Marcel's place."

She kissed him on the lips. "Thank you," and disappeared. Alan got quickly into the bathroom picked up Almira's clothes and hid them in a cupboard. He got a quick wash and was just finishing dressing when Charles returned.

"They are away," he said, "do you have a plan?"

"Not yet."

"I understand."

"Good."

"Thank you Monsieur Alain. What would you like to eat?"

"Two crepes, lemon, sugar, and a a pot of fee please."

"On the house."

"You are most kind. The washing is hidden in the cupboard."

"I wonder if it will ever get worn again."

"I shall eat in the restaurant."

Alan was eating his crepes, when a uniformed policeman came into restaurant. "Papers Monsieur."

Alan gave his Swiss passport and after a quick look was immediately given back the officer saluted and checked the others in the dining room.

Luigi offered the policeman a cup of coffee which he declined. He appeared to be about to leave when he suddenly spoke to Alan in English.

"Are you staying here for long Monsieur Alain?" Alan replied in French. "Do you mean at the restaurant or in Paris officer? If you wish to practice your English I need to change inside my head. I am fluent in German as well as French. An advantage of being a Swiss from Bern. Bern is bilingual and English is taught as a language in most good schools. I am reasonably proficient in English, but I have to concentrate. But to answer your question, I shall finish my coffee shortly and then I have some calls to make, and I will be in Paris until possibly sometime next week."

"I shall not bother you any further. My apologies for disturbing your lunch monsieur Alain."

"Not a problem. Lunch was finished and shortly the coffee will be." He saluted again and this tome he did leave. Alan took a couple of deep but gentle breaths and would swear he could feel his heart beating. Simone and Almira had taught him a lesson; he kept his fingers crossed that it had worked.

The dining room was quiet, food shortages and a partial evacuation from Paris into the countryside or anywhere away from the Germans left the lunchtimes at the restaurant less busy than the staff were used to. Waiters tended to hover more still not used to the reduced clientele.

Alan lingered over his coffee, and it was nearly cold when he finally finished. Having hung around a little longer than he intended, but now ready to leave, he headed to his lodging house. The shortage of petrol and goods in the shops meant that the once busy streets here were now short of the hustle and bustle that used to be.

A trickle of traffic was normal on the minor side streets and if it not for people selling everything on the black market, Paris would have ground to a halt months back. He had planned to continue to keep his room here on a more or less permanent basis and though he was pretty certain he wasn't followed he sat outside in a chair for a short while before going in.

Fatima was in the kitchen. "Ah monsieur Alain coffee?"

"Why not? Please. I maybe away for a short while. I will give you three months' rent in advance, if you will be kind enough to take care of my room for me and my motor cycle. If at some point you need more money then do speak to Charles. I am sure he can sort out anything you need. Should I be away too long and there is a problem ask Charles to send me a message via Simone."

Alan went up to his room after the coffee, filled a bag with every piece of warm clothing he could find and having paid the rent in advance as he said, he headed for Henri's bar.

Wearing a suit and tie and carrying a couple of duffel bags made him look too obvious, he should have changed to his work clothes. Tension was rising he didn't want to be stopped now. He imagined what the police might make of his luggage, it's a donation to the orphanage made him feel more comfortable. Why are you going to the orphanage so late? I have been busy. You know there is a curfew. I was not aware of any curfew. You are nervous sir. Do you have a problem? Alan couldn't understand what was happening all he knew was that when he got to Henri's bar he felt relief. First time in his life he had felt not in complete control. His fear was imagined not real his imagined interrogation almost like a walking dream. He got the feeling the policeman checking his slightly doctored, forged papers had rattled him more than he had realised. It could have been him that blew the mission to pieces. He felt shaky when he arrived but here now it was disappearing quickly. Henri was serving again tonight.

"Monsieur Alain how is everything?"

"All fine thank you Henri." The customer took his wine and sat down at the table in the far corner. Alan leaned in towards Henri. "Do you know him?" He whispered. Henri followed suit, "He is a regular, but know him, no."

"I need a lift to your brother's place and the use of your car and its lanterns."

"Certainly. When?"

"Tonight. I'm sorry to rush but I have a trip to do tonight. It will arrive same time as last night at number two field."

"Simone." Henri shouted in to the back room." She isn't working just cleaning up."

Simone came through from the back rooms carrying a mop and a bucket. "Dirty pigs." She was muttering.

"I am going out monsieur Alain needs a lift.

I will not be back I will stay with my brother tonight. If none of the girls are working close up and go home before curfew otherwise stay here."

Henri changed his jacket and took a hat from behind the bar.

"Let's go Alain."

In the car and Henri asks.

"You played this very close to your chest. Did you not trust me?"

"Nothing to do with that. I had to make certain it all worked and if it went wrong then no one would know anything they could tell to anyone else. It won't take long to get to the field I know but I need to pick up Almira from your brother first. Don't be offended Henri It is the safest way to play the game."

"Perhaps, but one feels untrusted."

"If you don't know Henri you can't tell anyone anything. It's as simple as that. I have that all the time with the people above me. Same programme if I don't know I can't tell anyone. Now accept it and let's get on with each other again."

Henri said little on the drive to his brother's house. The road was quiet now, what rush hour there was hardly extended this far out as around here was mostly agricultural with little in the way of domestic housing. During the day it was not unusual to find a herd or a flock travelling along the road between one field of food and another but this time of night and this time of year then even the farmers had called it a day andgone home.

Henri drove into Marcel's drive and as Alan grabbed the duffel bags Henri headed into Marcels. He met Alan on his way inn. She is next door at the orphanage. I will go for her they don't know you. "Of course they don't, and they don't need to. Close to what I was talking about before on the way." Henri kept on going he took a small gate close to the houses that split the wall in the front gardens. Alan went inside.

"Marcel thank you for today. Did you have any problems from anyone?"

"No everything went as planned."

"Good I will take Almira away tonight so there should be no trace of her being here if someone decides to check on the delivery people."

"That's why we put her next door. It wouldn't be a problem to hide her in there she could pass for one of the staff, unless someone knew her."

"Henri has gone for her. Do I owe you anything for today?"

"No. A favour in the future will solve it. It is easier than trying to put a price on deeds."

"Thank you. I'll be away for a bit but if there's a problem send a radio message. It worked well this time; you found me just in the right place to get it all done quickly. Any later and we would be trying to get her out of jail. That would be a different game. Also remember to send signals away from here."

Next door Henri was waiting for Almira, one of the children had gone for her.

"Henri you need something?" Almira asked.

"Yes you're wanted next door."

"I spoke to Alan briefly. He says he didn't say he would cut your balls off."

"No but I needed you to do things."

"Maybe I misjudged you Henri."

"No madame don't ever think that. Now let us hurry the man is waiting and we still have things to do."

Almira followed Henri. He was in a hurry, what for she wondered.

Alan was waiting, "Time to get dressed again. You will need to get as many layers as you can There are gloves and hats and there is a leather cap with a chin strap to keep your head covers on whatever they happen to be. We are flying out tonight if we get there in time and there isn't a problem.

Tis hurry up time Dress in the other room if you must but please be quick."

Almira was quicker than expected and soon with Marcel sitting in front with Henri, Aalan and Almira in the back, and Henri driving way too fast for the roads they headed for drop place two.

There Henri turned into a gated field at a tee junction and dropped off Marcel, Alan, Almira, and the lanterns from the boot of his car. "Stand here Almira. Stay just inside the gate out of sight of the road. It is not a great drop place, but we knew we could get to this one, the other option is too far away. Alan and Marcel carried the lanterns across the field. Two minutes before ETA they lit the lanterns and almost instantly they heard the plane overhead. Henri's car lights shone from the other side of the big field lighting up a fresh cut grass runway, and the Lysander made a circle and then landed running up towards the lanterns Henri's car lights went out and shortly afterwards so did two of the three lanterns at the other end. The Lysander came up the hill using its pod lights and the one lantern for direction. Alan carried two lanterns back and got Almira.

"Let's go." he called. He grabbed her hand. Marcel had turned the Lysander around and engine running, ready for takeoff. Almira was helped up the ladder.

She was wearing so much clothing restricting her movement. Alan followed and after they 'd squeezed in Alan put on the headphones.

"Ready pilot."

"Thank you sir, welcome aboard about to take off." They gave Marcel a wave, but he was on his way back with the other lantern. Henri had left a fourth one down where he'd been which gave the pilot an aiming point and a next stop is a hedge warning, but the Lysander was well away and in the air before that point would arrive.

"I can see why you wrapped me up. This is so cold."

"The heating is on sir," the pilot said when asked.

"Where are we landing?" Alan asked.

"Lympne s sir. It was decided that it would be quicker and easier than getting you from Tangmere tonight. The time you would have landed in Tangmere you should be half way to Woolwich. If that's where you are off sir."

"You know more than I do."

"Major Cameron organised tonight sir." He said. "To tell you Woolwich and Mr. Conway was interested in what was going on. That's the reason for taking you off there."

George was waiting for them. Alan did the introductions put Almira in the back, still rattling with the cold and wrapped her in the only blanket they had.

"Go to sleep," Alan told her, "at least two hours from here and that's if it goes well."

It went sort of well. Three hours and they were parked up outside their office. Inside Cameron had left blankets pillows and three mattresses. They drank tea showed Almira where the toilet was and went to sleep.

Cameron arrived at eight and left them sleeping. At nine he woke them to let them know Mr. Conway was on his way and would be there at ten. The officers mess sent toast and fried eggs there was tea coffee and still everyone apart from Cameron looked knackered. The corporal had found a place to stash the bedding and right on time Mr. Conway arrived with both twins and still with a driver.

Cameron did the introductions, and Mr. Conway was bordering on sweetness and light when he spoke to Almira.

"You must be very tired my dear. This is Martin he will take you to stay at a nearby house with another member of my staff. They will take care of you, find you some more usual clothes and sometime over the next day or so I'll give you a phone call and we'll meet up have a chat."

"As you wish Mr. Conway. Thank you Peter, Alan, George. I am extremely grateful." She shook hands with Conway. "Right then Martin lead the way." That's what he did, and Almira followed him out.

"What an interesting person. Right Lewis from the beginning tell me why you are flying your private airplanes around France and picking up people like you're on a jolly holiday. Major Cameron filled in the basics, now I would like the whole."

Alan gave Conway the whole story. How they work as an agency for them and send information which was collected and then passed on. Partially now superseded by two radio sets he has taken over there. This has kept the system running now given Almira being moved. They also are the muscle and back up when required which will run without Almira there as it can be done as and when needed. Alan spoke for a while and Conway give him his due listened carefully to everything he said and made the odd note.

"So, what you are telling me is, you picked up a Moroccan national and transported her to England. The question why is because she runs our projects in Paris, and she knows too much. Could you not have shot her?"

"If I had to answer that question sir it would be if the Gestapo had picked her up I would have done to save the torture."

"But you didn't and the word for that is splendid. I have always considered myself as good planner Lewis. If I wasn't I probably wouldn't be where I am today. Major Cameron here is the same he has been providing training programmes that I have asked for and done so extraordinarily well. Planning as I'm sure you are aware requires a problem, and careful thought, a good idea, a team, and a certain amount of luck. You, in your usual style, Lewis have gone about things in a totally different way. Before you even knew there was a problem you have solved it ahead of its existence.

You don't of course no anything about what I'm on about. Later this year we and our American allies are proposing to land a huge force of green U.S. troops onto north African soil. We are hoping that the Vichy French will join us rather than fight us and for that we need to negotiate effectively a surrender and then a change of sides. Which means we could blood the green troop s and get them battle hardened without counting too many bodies.

Now knowing how useful madame Almira's father could be for us, do you think that he would be grateful for the safe return of his daughter?"

"I do believe so Sir."

"Splendid again because sometimes things can work even better than I could ever plan them."

"I'm glad it worked then sir."

"It's not quite there yet, there's still a lot to do. It's a good start, I will speak to her in the next couple of days; after that we can plan the next phase. In the meantime, the number of people who know about this is extremely small, I expect it to remain so.

Stay at Woolwich for now Lewis with your sergeant too. I don't know where you are going to sleep, somewhere off site might be a good idea, as the Germans are quite keen on blowing up the arsenal. There are Anderson shelters hereabouts and I'm certain you can get your hands on one, and that gentlemen may be your best option. I shall be in touch when I have more to say.

Almira got to the Queens pub early. Cameron had said they'd be there by seven. It was quiet she sat at the table away from the other customers who were gathered around the other end of the lounge, nearer to the bar.

She hadn't been there long when she caught the eye of a young lieutenant. He walked over to speak to her. "Good evening miss would you like a drink?"

"Thank you for the offer but I am waiting for a friend he shouldn't be much longer."

The young man accepted the answer and returned to the group he was with. There was a short conversation, and the group carried on drinking.

Almira checked her watch five to seven. Hoping they wouldn't be late. Another man, possibly a little older, but part of the same group left the group and walked over. He sat down on the seat opposite Almira.

"Your friend, if there is one hasn't arrived, so I thought I would buy you a drink."

"That's very kind of you but I don't want one thank you."

"No need to play hard sweetie."

"I don't drink." Almira told him.

"Then a kiss just to say thank you for the offer." Almira looked at him.

"What is it you want? A kiss to impress your pals?"

"That could be about right." he said, he had a smirk, slightly drunk, maybe he couldn't hold his alcohol. Almira pursed her lips and leaned forward across the table. The Lieutenant leaned towards her and pursed his lips the same, and as he did so, Almira raised her hands to touch the side of his face. He closed his eyes, stupid man. Almira grabbed him by the ears and smashed his face onto the top of the table. The third time his face hit the table his body had gone limp and as his head flopped down onto the marble surface. She stood up and hammer punched him twice in the side of the head.

She sat back down again as the others were coming from the other end.

They looked at her, and then the mess of their friend, still sitting in the chair head unmoving on the table. Almira pushed the chair with her foot from under the table and all of it went over backwards the other three were still looking at the mess of their friend now lying on the floor still trying to work out what they had just witnessed, when Alan arrived With Major Cameron.

"What 's happening here? Are you alright Almira?

"Fine thankyou major." The three lieutenants were stiff at attention.

"A man's unwanted attention. Wouldn't take no for an answer had to explain what no meant."

"Is he still alive Captain?" Alan knelt by the heap on the floor and stuck two fingers into the side of his neck.

"He has a pulse sir, and he is breathing."

"Not bad then, can't ask more. You lot aren't from Artillery what you doing here? Cameron asked."

"We're on a language course sir."

"Where?"

"At the annexe sir."

"Doing?"

"Arabian language and culture sir."

"Why?"

"Future operations in north Africa was as described to us sir."

"You three might be alright. He is to be returned to unit.

Almira?"

"Would be interesting having him on the course. The messed up face might keep everyone else in line."

"You may end up beating him again; better returned to unit. These three will explain to everyone what happens if they get out of line. As if you haven't already realised gentlemen Madame Almira is your instructor in basic Arabic language and culture. The idiot has picked on the wrong person. If your pal doesn't wake up soon I would call an ambulance. When he does tell him he's RTUed orders of Major Peter Cameron. There will be no discussion, and no appeal considered. Clear?"

"Yes sir."

"I will see you three tomorrow morning." Almira told the three young men. "Please don't be late."

"No Madame." The very polite young man had done all the talking for the three of them. The other two had spent most of the time with their mouths open and nothing coming out but warm air.

"Right then that's sorted," said Cameron. "Now that I have you both here I shall buy you dinner, and we can celebrate your new job."

The following morning, Alan is with Cameron in their office. Almira has a small group of junior officers on a learning Arabic course in a makeshift classroom along the corridor.

She wasn't certain if teaching was going to be something she could do successfully. She had taught French to some of her people and some English but never the other way around. In theory it should be easier but in practice when you spoke your own language you used words and spoke in a natural way. Not is this an adjective? should it go in front or after? is that an adverb? should I say that when I mean? She'd voiced these concerns and questions to both Mr. Conway and Peter, and both had said why don't you give it a try and see what happens. She had a certain concern about getting her message across but whatever was happening in the classroom when Cameron checked on her through the window that was in the corridor what she did have was a class of eleven students concentrating on her every word. Either the news had got around of how she dealt with issues of and problems or she was a better teacher than she thought she might be.

"Mr. Conway is here later Alan. He wants to speak to us both about Morocco."

"How do you mean?"

"I haven't got a clue, but he said he would be here as soon as possible after two this afternoon, so I suggest you get back here for about fifteen minutes before, and we'll see what he wants."

Just before two pm Conway's Humber pulled into the parking area next the annexe. One of the ubiquitous twins opened the rear door and escorted him inside.

Cameron had let Alan know he was here and as he came through the door to the outer door Alan opened their office door and Mr. Conway walked straight in.

"Shut the door Lewis. Richard will wait outside. Right gentlemen. Yesterday morning I spoke to Madame Almira about returning to Morocco. I have asked her to do introductions to her father in order to facilitate the landing of a force of American and British troops in Morocco.

I know you are aware of the proposed objective well it's getting a lot closer now and we need to get on with it. As is normal you won't be alone, others are working towards the same end and we have previously accessed useful collaborators in country, but belt and braces is how we want to do this. What we want to do is forge a link inland towards the center of Morocco as well as heading north towards Rabat, Tangier, and the straits of Gibraltar."

Mr. Conway opened his briefcase, took out a map and spread it out on Cameron's desk. "Take a look at what I want. Here is Casablanca, here is Marrakech near where Almira's father is based.

The nearest coastal drop off therefore is a fishing port here name of Mogador it's around fifty miles from there to Marrakech. Brahim, her father lives in a small village before you get to Marrakech.

We want to offer Brahim a business opportunity similar to the one the embassy and you both had in Paris with him. Are you with me so far?"

"Yes sir."

"I will keep you posted on that as we progress. When I spoke to her yesterday we had an interesting discussion about what I want so she is fully conversant with our requirements. I can understand why you allowed her to run the business side of our operations. She is a hard negotiator and she knows what she is talking about, but were trying to win a war not make a profit.

Shall we get her in here now. If you will go and get her please captain, send her students for a half hour tea break."

Almira joined them in their office one of the twins in his usual position actually opened the door for her.

"You wanted to see me again Mr. Conway?"

"I hear Madame, that you have been depleting my officer corps. Apparently he went in an ambulance in the end or so I heard."

"I assume he's still alive."

"He is. He has lost a couple of teeth, a broken cheek bone, and concussion. You are very rough Madame when you want to make a point."

"I am gentle, my brother would have killed him for doing and trying what he did. My father would not have killed him, but he would have punished him and done it slowly and savoured the time spent."

"Well, as I understand, he wasn't that good looking to start with so I doubt when the bruising goes down anyone will notice anything unless he smiles of course, and he hasn't got his teeth in.

Now tell me how did the lesson go today?"

"From my point of view, it was straight forward. Simple words and simple sentences. We are on day one. It is always difficult for the student to start with. They need to get a list of useful words plus some extras in their vocabulary they need to conjugate a verb but probably not every tense. More importantly, I think they need to learn what is useful. Learning to conjugate the verb to love is unnecessary. Telling someone to kill someone else and not be misunderstood is more useful to them. If you want my opinion, that is?"

"Anything else you think is relevant?"

"A class of twelve is too many. The best way for you to learn a language is by communication whilst living there and listening all the time. One to one is ideal but not a practical solution. If you want speakers you are better living with us. Find competent French speakers and you will have a possibility of a common language and then you can teach them in our country."

"I think that is very relevant that's a job for these two gentlemen to solve with you. Now, I need to discuss some other things with you. When we spoke yesterday morning and I suggested that a return to Morocco could be available you were quite happy for this to happen. Can I assume that nothing has changed, and you are happy enough to go back home and explain to your father what I want."

"Nothing has changed I am more than happy to speak to my father and tell him what you want. Whatever decision he makes though is entirely up to him. Other than explain the details I cannot predict his answer, but business is business as far as my father is concerned and if there is a profit without harm to either his people or his name then he probably could be persuaded to go for it. However, he will not want me to be passing on the request. I don't represent your side of the deal I am his child, and he will expect to deal with a person he can ask questions of or make requests to that is responsible enough to guarantee delivery of your promises."

"Would Captain Lewis be a suitable?"

"Yes. My father will like him. He likes different people for different reasons not all of which might be immediately apparent, but he is a shrewd man and when you know that you learn from him. He would get on with you all for different reasons. The fact that Alan brought me out of Paris and got me here will stand him in good stead with my father. His gratitude for what he did will give him credibility."

"Major I want you to plan this with Lewis leading the team to Morocco. You will need to consult with Madame

Almira as to how you get from Mogador to Marrakech. I will get Lewis and his team to Mogador, or the Royal Navy will. I don't think jumping Madame out of a plane even if I could get you there and them back in one is a good idea. I'm thinking Royal Navy is a more realistic bet. I will speak to the Admiralty, and we shall have another meeting to finalise our plans. Questions?"

"Numbers?"

"Sort it out with Madame. Remember we have to accommodate them get them there and get them ashore."

"That's it for now sir. Unless Captain Lewis has anything."

Alan shook his head. "No sir, my questions may come later, but for now I'm okay."

Let's get on with it. I need to be ready if the navy come up with a plan."

"What about my students? Almira asked.

"Are any showing signs of being ahead of the others?"

"Three or four are ahead of the others."

"Keep them. Get rid of the rest." Conway told her. Cameron butted in.

"If I may sir. Do the better ones speak French?"

"All bar one who speaks German."

"He might be handy as well. Thank you madame."

"Contrate on the smaller group. Captain Lewis will sort out the others. Major you have your planning head to get on and I will be off to the Admiralty. Good day to you all."

Two days later. Mr. Conway phoned. "Eight persons maximum. You will be canoeing in at night, a distance of less than a mile but with equipment. I have spoken again with Madame, and she has told me what her father will expect.

He will want a similar format as you have it in Paris. We provide the officers, and he will supply the men. Pick your team. Madame Almira Lewis and sergeant Robinson plus five others. The other five will remain there in command of the local personnel. Lewis and Robinson will return back to Britain. I will bring dates tomorrow after lunch. It will be soon. Got that?"

"Yes sir." The phone went dead. Cameron picked up his cap and his cane and went in search of Lewis. He found him standing outside Almira's classroom watching proceedings through the corridor window.

"Are we lusting after the staff? Alan or becoming obsessed like a schoolboy for his teacher?"

"That's an interesting thought sir but neither is the answer. I'm watching how comfortable they are.

Sometimes you can see them getting slightly flustered and that doesn't bode well when something might be developing in another country."

"An interesting observation. I'm not thinking we could do a paper on it but analysing how students react to problem solving might give us an insight into how they might react generally to all of the problems they may encounter. It's a thought, more importantly we have to find five men to accompany you plus George and Almira. Almira will stay of course and so will the five men. I'm thinking three officers and two sergeants or three sergeants and two officers. Thes e officers here are too green to be let loose without a minder. The question ids do we send an extra officer or an extra minder?"

"I would go with two officers and three minders. Two best Arabic students three sergeants one of whom speaks fluent French."

"I only know of George." Cameron replied.

"There's a man name of Tim Forester he was in a batch of new instructor trainees. He's a corporal get him promoted and he can join the band."

"And who else?"

"Tom Logan and Phil Green."

"Phil Green's not right. No one likes him and he's married with four kids."

"What about Barry McHugh then?"

"Yes he's better."

"What about the student officers?"

"Almira can pick them. I shall speak to her after the lesson. Have you seen enough here?"

"Yes."

"If you have I'll wait here for the class to finish which won't be long now and ask you to phone Colonel Haslet and get the men sent down here today."

"What if they're on the Plain?"

Ask him to get them. It's now not tomorrow if he baulks. Any problems Mr. Conway's orders."

The following morning in Cameron's office with half a dozen borrowed chairs were Alan, George, Almira, two officers and three nco's. Cameron had the floor.

"I will tell you what I know and after if there are questions I will answer if I can and if I know. Very soon you are going to be picked up and you are going to Morocco courtesy of the Royal Navy. Madame Almira will show you the way when you are in Morocco. Captain Lewis is in overall command. His back up will be George. You two lieutenants will have Tom and Barry as your back up.

Tim is going to be floating until you establish yourselves in Morocco and then it will play it by ear. Nothing is cast in stone we start with a plan. Bare essentials and busk it and make it work as we go along. Tim will close protect Madame though you all have responsibility to keep her alive. I hasten to add that without Madame this mission won't work. We will have everything planned up to the landing in a fishing village name of Mogador. Madame knows the mayor there and the whereabouts of his house and we need to make contact with him or any of the family. Thereafter we are in a certain sense a hostage to fortune. How am I doing? Are you all with me so far?" There was a general murmur of understanding. "There will be about a mile of open water canoeing at night to get ashore. How many canoeists have we have. Captain Lewis I know, and George, Tim, Barry and Tom.

I did expect all the instructors, secretly i had hoped all you but that was wishful thinking. How do you want to split them Captain?"

Each of the Lieutenants with their sergeant Tim with me, George will take Almira. Tim and I will lead and then we can cover the rest landing."

"That's all we have so far."

"I'm guessing sir then we don't as yet have travel sorted?"

"Nothing. As soon as I know I'll let you know. I will add that the way this is being put together you might not get told anything until it's happening. The mission is currently not for discussion outside this office or with any person not involved with the nine of us in here. Is that completely clear. For that reason, apart from madame, we all will be sleeping in Anderson shelters from now until we go. Questions?"

"How are we getting fed sir?" asked Barry.

Either the officers mess or the sergeants mess will feed us. The barracks and the academy are closed now but there is still a facility we can get a cook or two to put enough food together for us all. We have a tea urn in the outer office, and we'll see what cookie can knock up for us for tonight. Anything else?"

"Can we go to the pub?" Barry again.

"Captain?"

"No stay out of the pubs. They're dangerous around here one Lieutenant got a hammering in one only a few days ago. I want you all staying sober and I want to know where you are all the time. We are as of this moment on standby. We stick together and mind each other. Lieutenants go and sit with the Barry and Tom and see which of you fit better together. Tim come with me let's get your stripes sorted out, Which reminds me sir you should have Joe Porter here."

"Good idea. I'll get Colonel Haslet to send him down as soon as you are away. There won't be any left up there shortly."

"They'll manage."

"They'll have to Captain."

Almira was back in the Queen's again. She hadn't been there since that time when she'd poleaxed the idiot. Was that only a week ago she realised seemed like it had been lost in time so much had occurred recently.

Alan had arranged seven again and this time he was early.

"I have booked a table for a meal at a restaurant just around the corner from here maybe five minutes' walk at the most, but there is no hurry we have to seven thirty before we need to sit down."

The evening was warm and comfortably so. They walked along side by side occasionally making contact when negotiating others but generally filtering through the walkers enjoying the warm evening.

The restaurant double fronted glass shop sized windows bright yellow lights illuminating the street. There were a number of tables outside waiting for customers, a Maitre D at the door.

"Good evening sir."

Good evening I have a table for two booked for seven thirty Alan Lewis."

"You do sir. There is a choice you may go inside or if you wish there is a table available outside."

"Almira?"

"Inside please Alan. As much as like being here this country is still not warm enough for me." The Maître d beckoned a waiter over.

"Table for two for Mr. Lewis. Bon appetit sir and you too madame."

They both had a mixed grill. Almira remembered one from her days in school in the England many years before, Alan had the same wondering how many sausages might turn up. Coffee afterwards finished the evening off.

"You haven't told me to what do we owe this pleasure? Almira asked in her heart she craved a night of passion ideally with a man rather than a woman.

"We are leaving tomorrow getting picked up about mid-morning. I thought a celebratory meal might be nice. Last one before the off."

"That's very good of you thank you." She thought to herself that's not what I wanted to hear. I wanted to be taken out and have a nice meal and have you take me to a hotel and make wild passionate love to me all night like that time in Paris. Now it will never happen. When we get home it will not be allowed in my father's house.

"It's my pleasure I never paid for any meals I had at your place the very least I can do is return the favour. Especially when you look so smart."

"I got a lot of help from a lady that Talbot said would help me. She was very nice. She took me clothes and shoe shopping got me into places that might have been a little more difficult on my own, I don't have the wardrobe I had in Paris but it would do for now."

"You look good."

" She asked me how I got here and when I told her that you got me out of France in a mad rush which is why I had very little in the way o gf clothes . She told me that she knew who you were. She said she offered to make you a lamb roast."

"That will be Marcia Jonson."

"You remember her then ?"

"Yes we were in Spain in 37."

"Well you missed a fine meal. She cooks a really nice lamb roast. I haven't eaten one that good since I was at boarding school years ago. So I paid her back by doing her Moroccan crepes for breakfast with semolina flower."

Alan wasn't sure where this was going but he kept listening.

"Over breakfast we compared notes on you. Apparently she told me her notes weren't as comprehensive as mine.

I told her that an offer of a lamb roast with trimmings and a supper desert being turned down was almost a criminal act and I would find some way to punish you for neglect of a lovely lady."

Almira was laughing; her personal laugh that Alan had never quite worked out if it was humour or sinister.

"She said she wanted to talk to you about getting drunk when you were in Spain. She says she did something she'd never done before and it made her feel incredibly sad. She didn't elaborate but she wanted to speak with someone who maybe knew more about it than she did."

Alan thought back to the time at the airport at Reus when Marcia shot the Spanish soldier and then the other four got shot as well. Marcia may have killed her first and possibly only one, but it had also been a baptism of fire for himself and Cameron. He'd killed three automatically without thinking even though he had taught trainees how to do it, until that moment, he had never had to do it himself and the same applied to Cameron. The difference by the sound of it was that he and Cameron had pushed it into their learn from experience box and thought of it as job that had to be done. Marcia seemed to see it as murder or something akin to it

"If you knew how many people I had let down ,disappointed or unintentionally neglected Almira you would question why I hadn't shot myself already. It's a bad habit and I don't know why it keeps happening but it does. I'm glad you had a pleasant time."

"Is that all you've got to say?"

"Probably."

Almira seemed to be getting either annoyed or irritated. Alan wasn't certain where it was going. Almira then felt a need to continue.

"I told her I was working in the same building as you and Peter Cameron as you were probably going to be the ones who would take me back home to my father. She didn't know where you were as she hadn't heard from you. She appeared to be a bit sad about it. But she is OK now as I explained what you've normally been doing for the last couple of years and she didn't in the end feel too bad when I told her you were working as a children's pimp in Paris running a bar and brothel. I said it suited you. She said she couldn't argue or disagree as it was a long time ago when she met you. So you see you are now persona non grata with her and no longer missed, so everything is fixed. Or broken beyond repair." She had that laugh again.

"You look sad Alain. Have I made you sad?"

"I'm disappointed in what you have just said."

The evening had gone pear shaped what was supposed to be a pleasant evening between two friends had now developed in to an unexpected savaging that had left Alan totally bewildered.

"I'm not surprised. Do you honestly believe I would say anything like that to anyone. I'm tormenting you Alain."

"You might be only tormenting me Almira. But you are right, the truth is your statement itself is hardly inaccurate and being reminded of what I'm doing all be it for a cause and a reason does not dispel the distaste I have for my part in it. I might feel that I am the cowboy wearing the white hat but can I honestly take the moral high ground given the game I'm playing?"

"I'm sorry Alain. My attempt at tormenting you has gone wrong my sincere apologies. It was meant to be a joke albeit a slightly cruel one but only a joke."

"Unfortunately the joke is too near the truth and you probably might consider that my reaction lacks just cause but the damage is done and the business will keep us together but what you know about me and what you appear to be happy to use as a lever in a n argument or a discussion means the personal bond is possibly beyond repair." Almira's eyes had filled with tears. They weren't running down her cheeks yet but they were just holding in the bottom lids.

"Excuse me please I won't be too long." Almira stood up, took her handbag and disappeared into the ladies room.

Whilst she was away Alan paid their bill and stood waiting at the desk, near the exit door. She had her composure back when she saw Alan waiting for her.

"I have delivered the information that we are off tomorrow. Arrive in warm clothes trousers, boots, pullover and topcoat. There will be kit for you at the annexe before you get there. Be there by eight please. Now I will walk you back to your lodging."

"There is no need Miss Jonson's flat is now only a hundred metres or so along the street from here, you have nearly walked me back already.. Thank you for my meal I will see you tomorrow morning." She kissed him gently on the cheek and left.

Woolwich to RAF Northolt then Lisbon.

At 0900 hours nine people were sitting drinking tea and eating toast. Eight were dressed almost exactly the same. Major Cameron was the odd one out and earlier he had confessed to Alan that he was disappointed in not going with them. Not because he wanted to lead but the fact that he enjoyed being in the fight not planning it and watching from the outside.

Without warning Mr. Conway's Humber arrived in the car park and in typical fashion He came into the building in his usual rush. Alan got the door while all bar Almira stood to attention on Cameron's order. Good morning gentlemen and to you too madame. I hope they have been taking good care of you." He looked around. "The body count tells me no one has irritated you so they must have been kind. Possibly the rearrest I've ever got to a joke. We will probably never meet again thank you for your assistance on behalf of his majesties government. I wish you all a safe journey." He passed the usual brown envelope to Lewis. "Captain your orders. To be opened when you arrive at Northolt. There will be a truck here shortly to pick you up. There is some kit to be taken with you in the truck. There is some at Northolt and there is some already with the Navy. The rest is explained in your orders Captain. I shall see you when you are back. I shall be back tomorrow major we have some more planning to get on with. Goodbye." George opened the door, one of the twins walked out ahead of him as they left the building.

"We have our orders a truck soon." Alan told everyone. "I'd take a leak now or certainly before we go. It's forty bumpy miles in a truck you have been warned."

At RAF Northolt they were given lunch after they had loaded the kit into the plane. At 1600 hours they were given sandwiches and tea. At 1630 they boarded the Lancaster bomber carrying a full crew and gunners and took off for a five hour flight to Lisbon in Portugal. They landed in the dark as planned at 2200 hours off loaded their kit and went into a brick built building on the airfield and after a cold supper and hot drinks went to bed.

They had eaten breakfast when two men in civilian clothes arrived at their base.

"Captain Lewis?" one of them asked.

"That's me."

"Your orders will tell you sir who we are and the guards on the base I can assure you would have arrested us if we weren't supposed to be here. We are here to get you aboard a fishing boat just down the coast, away from too many preying eyes. Not guaranteed perfect but if we take all day which we expect to, you never know. We will keep it moving. Two men is our first run then one man and half the kit. Then another man and the other half of the kit. Then two men and then two men. I have you down as eight men I know one is a lady I would suggest Madame goes last. However that choice is yours sir."

"I'll assume you know what you are doing."

We do sir but we don't normally have to fit eight in. More often than not it's one or two occasionally more, but eight is a first so we are doing it a bit differently. If you are carrying weapons sir remember we are in a neutral country and any shooting could cause problems. There is no reason for anyone to think that there is anything suspicious but Lisbon is loaded with spies from every country in Europe hope fully no one spots anything that they can use against us. We are ready when you are sir."

"It's Alan."

Colin Simpson you come first with me. Barry with first lot of kit. Tim second lot of kit. Clive and Tom. Almira and George last pair. Got it? Good. George you are in charge. We don't do ranks with our teams. Only Major Cameron or other senior officers. First names Colin get your kit bag and we do what these men tell us to do."

"Yes sir."

"Alan."

"Yes Alan."

Alan and Colin followed the two men outside . they had an old black painted long backed van. The two men took the front seats after putting Alan and Colin in the back. A twenty minute drive took them to an isolated road with a parking bay near to the shore.

The back doors opened.

"We are here we will walk down a path to the beach. You will sit on the beach. We will leave you there and go back to the base. About five minutes after we have left a rowing boat will arrive, pick you up and take you onto a fishing boat a short way out to sea. The skipper will then take you to a different location where we will meet you with your man and some kit. We have it timed and planned it will work please do as the skipper asks. We'll see you later."

Alan and Colin sat as directed and waited and five minutes later a fishing boat came into view. It looked to Alan not dissimilar to many of the fishing boats he'd seen when with his father. It was around forty foot long wooden with a wheelhouse at the stern giving a working deck forward of the coxswain. Almost immediately a wooden dinghy was being rowed towards the beach. As it arrived Alan took the painter and Colin put in the two kit bags and climbed aboard.

"Climb aboard sir I'll push us away with an oar." A couple of minutes later they were aboard the fishing boat and inside the wheelhouse where a man was looking through binoculars at the coast side. The dinghy was tied astern.

"Good to go boss" the deckhand told the man with the glasses.

He spun the wheel to starboard and increased the revs and headed off out to sea.

"Good morning gentlemen. My name is Gordon Wishart originally from Peterhead in God's country. I am your host for the day make yourselves comfortable and cross your fingers. We have had some winds for a while here. They've not been blowing hard but they have been going a while and later on I expect it to get bumpy.

You can pray if you wish but my feeling is that it doesn't do any good, anybody that can do something about it isn't listening. Who am I talking to?"

"I'm Alan and this Colin."

"You are Alan Lewis then; Captain Lewis and you are in charge?"

"Yes."

"Down below there is just about enough room to sit down for most of you. You will also find down there four folding canoes which we can bring out later. But for now we are heading away from the port area a little further North where we will pick up our next passenger."

It was late r in the afternoon when everyone was aboard. When George and Almira arrived it was creeping towards dark and Gordon's forecast of it getting bumpy was proving uncomfortably accurate. They headed out to sea towards their rendezvous and at the same time hoping that the deeper water might provide a gentler swell reducing the effects of the rising tide.

It was dark when Gordon called Alan up to the wheelhouse.

"It won't be long now and we'll be saying au revoir to you all. Transfer will be just a wee bit dangerous. You'll need a good man on the other deck and Angus my crewman will mind my bow. I can manage the boat and as long as it doesn't rain and that's the only thing not forecast, I will be able to see everything happening from here. Angus will handle the lines you need one person passing, one receiving, and you need to take care. The navy guys will tell you what to do when you get on board. Just do what they tell you to do they too have done all of this before. Good luck whatever you are doing I'll ask you to brief your team and sort out the luggage transfer. You have about five minutes to contact so as soon as they are briefed get them topsides and get your life jackets on. I've not lost anyone yet let's not start tonight."

Alan did as he was asked and three minutes later everyone was out on the deck. Alan was by the wheelhouse door. Gordon was holding the fishing boat steady.

"It's nearly here. I can feel it. Tell them to get hold of something."

"Hold onto the rails." Alan shouted to everyone.

The skipper called form his wheelhouse. "Brace yourselves," and seconds later it turned into a fair shake when the conning tower of a submarine rose out of the water, followed immediately by the forward deck

"Sacre bleu Alain you did not tell me it was a submarine I will get claustrophobia." Almira looked horrified.

"Better than German hospitality I can assure you."

The forward hatch opened on the sub and a small crew climbed out. Angus on the bow and nearest the sub threw a line and one of the navy seamen lashed it quickly to a deck cleat.

"Do what the man on the sub tells you to do." Alan shouted to his team.

They moved quickly to towards the bow. George was on the bow with Angus and the rope was holding them but not properly,. Wave action was making the step from boat to sub vary too dramatically. Gordon could see what was happening. He called Angus to the wheelhouse. He gave the rope to Alan to hold. Gordon returned to the bow and told Alan what Gordon was about to do. Alan relayed the message to the deck officer who gave him a thumbs up. As the bow of the fishing boat lowered again down the side of the sub the skipper slipped it into forward gear and used the large circular rope fender to push against the sub side. The rope to the cleat was tightened as a slip line and Almira moved swiftly over the side and down onto the deck where strong hands moved her along the wet surface and down through the hatch. George sent all the baggage down and Alan had gone back to the wheelhouse.

"Thank you skipper, until we meet again my fiend good luck."

The skipper nodded he had both hands busy on the controls Alan patted his shoulder and just behind George got aboard the submarine.

He spoke to the deck officer. "You can let him go when you're ready we are finished here now thank you." The deck officer signalled Angus on the trawler. Angus released the tension on the line the rating on the deck let if off the cleat and as he let him loose the trawler gently reversed away and turned to head back to shore. Alan was down inside and savouring the smell of sweat and diesel fumes warm air and heaven knows what. The forward hatch was shut and the officer from the deck party joined him. "There is a certain aroma on submarines sir. It gets in the clothes and in the skin and the after a while you get used to the stench and after a bit longer you get used to it so much so that you hardly notice it and eventually you don't even notice it at all. Then you have been on submarines too long. Welcome aboard sir most of us don't notice it at all. You better come and meet skipper.

Sir this is Captain Lewis.

Commander Swinson

Alan shook hands

Thank you for the pickup sir.

"You're welcome. Your boatman did a good job. If you ever see him again pass on my complements. Is he Portuguese ?"

"No sir Peterhead."

"Was that Gordon Wishart?"

"Yes sir."

"He's got a new boat. Glad he's still around. Chief show Captain Lewis where he's living for a while and get the rest of his team sorted. We'll speak later Captain when I come off watch. We've got them in the wardroom for now but they can't stay there as I run my ship from there and we all eat in there as well."

"If you will follow me please sir." Which Alan did.

Throb of engines, electric motors, cramped passageways, wardroom, sweaty bodies, why is everyone else going the other way? They were bashing along underwater, driving blind at between ten and fifteen knots no windows in front, can't see where you're going; they must all be mad. They were in the Atlantic and heading south. Trust them. They reached the wardroom. An armed marine stood at the door. Unnecessary but standard procedure. He knocked and a voice from within just hearable above the noise of the boats workings shouted come in. The marine opened the door.

"Thank you Chief."

"You're welcome sir."

Alan stepped inside. Skipper was right it was cramped even by submarine standards. At the far end in front of the stove and the cupboards extending outwards back towards the door was a single refractory type table, four seats down each side, one at the door end, and just enough room for a skinny person to get behind each of the occupied seats.

"How long are we on this submarine for Alan?" Almira asked, she sounded shocked and unhappy.

"I'm guessing two to three days. Skipper will be here when he finished in the control room."

"Why didn't you tell me it was a submarine."

"Because I didn't know. All I was told was we would be picked up from a fishing boat and I found out that after I left you this morning when I got on the fishing boat. When the skipper joins us I'm sure he'll give us a better idea of our journey time but given that there is a war going on I suspect that could be changed if circumstances do. We have to wait and see."

"And it stinks." She said. She was getting in a mood. Hopefully it wouldn't last long.

"After a while you get used to it I'm told."

"I don't want to get used to it I want to get off it" at which point there was a knock and the door opened and in walked Commander Swinson. "Don't jump up gentlemen as the crew started to stand there's no room in here for dancing. About fifty hours from now miss to drop off assuming we can continue at this speed. We have nothing like the issues with the enemy here that we have in other areas it's definitely a lot quieter so we will when we can surface and you can get a bit of fresh air if it's quiet. Food will be here shortly. I will ask you to eat and when you've finished I would be grateful if you will vacate so my officers can eat as well. You have bunks for the duration. Normally they are shared but as you will not be on watch I will ask you to try to stay out of the way of my crew. We are down on crew size to fit you and your equipment in. Do exercise but be considerate. Anything else you need to know?" Alan looked around at the team.

"It appears not sir."

"I will keep you posted of any changes. Food will be here shortly."

Two days later His Majestie's submarine Falcon was sitting below the surface approximately two miles from the coast of Morocco pointing towards the bay area of Mogador. They had crept in as close as they could during daylight and then sat until darkness, at which time they moved in another couple of miles. They were still two miles offshore.

Skipper was at the periscope. "There is more going on here than we expected he said but at the moment there is no rush tide is on the ebb paddling canoes against it will leave you in mid Atlantic not on the shore.

Our tables tell us it will start to flood in about an hour or so. By which time it will be darker and we can relocate. Ask Miss to join us in here please Alan."

Alan collected Almira from the wardroom where she was sitting and waiting with the rest of the team.

Right Miss Almira I need a decision. We are sitting directly in front of the village where there is a lot of boats and activity I need to drop you off as close as I can to where you want to get to. Which side of the bay is the better.

"As you are looking at it go to the right hand side. The beach is sandy and the man I want to contact has a house on that side."

Thank you Get yourselves ready Alan you and your team will be out of here within the hour. Lieutenant Hardman will supervise the deck crew take your orders from him. Good bye and good luck."

"Thank you sir."

The darkness improved by the lack of moonlight, the turn of the tide, Alan and Colin took off first taking some kit and ready to use sub machine guns. Almira and George were covered front and rear by the other two pairs. Almira was not a canoeist so most of the remaining kit was split between the others which allowed George to concentrate on the one job get Almira ashore safely. It all ran without a hitch. The tide did most of the work and quickly they were on the beach . The problem there was they were exposed with little cover. They dragged the canoes up the sand emptied them and hauled the empty canoes into some small sand dunes and where they themselves regrouped and took a breather.

"How far to the house from here Almira?"

"Five minutes." She had put her cloak on and covered her head. "Are you ready to go?"

"Yes."

"What about the kit bags Alan ?"

"We carry them now. The canoes are a giveaway but let's get away from here as a starter. Lead on Almira and let us hope it all works as planned."

Almira led them across the sand dunes and after a short distance they came to a white painted wall. She moved to her right and they fell in behind her. "Wait here." She told them. "I will go alone to the door. If he has moved then I can speak to the owner and find where he has gone if they see one of you they may not be so helpful."

A minute later she was back. "Come follow me. Be quick he is here." They tucked in behind her. Alan in front with a Sten gun then three pairs carrying kit between them. A narrow staircase only four steps fortunately mercifully short awkward with two men carrying a load side by side. They crossed a flat sandy piece of ground heading for an open doorway, a feint yellow candle showing the way.

Almira told them where to put the kit bags. "Come meet our host his name is Hicham."

Almira made the introductions.

Hicham spoke to them in Arabic. Almira translated. "As you have brought Almira back home and you are her friends you are welcome in my house. There is only the floor to sleep on but you are welcome to sleep here."

Alan asked Almira to thank him for his hospitality, which she did.

"The toilets are outside through this door here. They are Moroccan toilets. I have shown you all how it works now you get a chance to see for yourselves. I have a bed you have candles to show you the way. Thank you for bringing me this far; time for sleep. We can do nothing before tomorrow. The front doors are locked. Sleep well."

Six men in sleeping bags and remainder of kit filled the room floor. They would do an hour on watch, then wake the next man. The order was first name alphabetical. Alan took the first watch.

Almira joined them in the communal room shortly after first light. She brought pots of boiling water. She knew they had brew kits that suited them. So all they needed was hot water.

"My friend Hicham has gone to speak to another man name of Hassan. Someone he trusts who has a truck. He will get him to come and pick us up and take us to my father's house. I don't know when until he comes back. In the meantime we wait. He does not expect to be long.

Hicham returned with his friend and two other men. The two others left the truck and headed for the beach. Hassan had partially backed the truck towards the end of the boundary wall. A few minutes later the two men returned carring twocanoes between them. They put the canoes down at the back of the truck and then went for the other two. Hicham and Haddan started loading the truck as Alan and the team were carrying the rest of their kit out.

It wasn't the biggest truck in Morocco and cramped as it was everything was squeezed in and in less than fifteen minutes after Hassan had arrived the truck was on the way to Almira 's father's house and a homecoming that he was unaware of.

The man was elderly, how old was anyone's guess. He is Almira's father and Almira is only a bit younger than Alan. His beard was white almost as white as his loose clothing. The tagelmust his head covering was indigo blue, the colour of the Tuareg. He had removed it as he came into his house. Almira had spent some time alone with him while Alan and the team had sorted themselves out into rooms and washed and cleaned the travel dirt, sorted their kit, hidden the canoes and generally spruced themselves up because they could. Brahim and Alan had been left to make small talk while Almira organised some refreshment.

The door opened Almira wearing a long black over garment and a head covering followed by a man, white cloaked, with a small red fez. He was carrying a silver tray with glass cups and two steaming pots.

Almira joined them sitting on another pouffe ready placed between the two men. "Mint tea Captain Lewis." Brahim told him.

Unsure if it was a statement or an offer Alan didn't instantly reply. "Business can be conducted while we drink." The servant poured three cups of tea lifting the pot into the air as he filled each cup. A practiced art, no spillage at any time the three cups all containing exactly the same amount. Almira passed Alan one as Brahim took the other. He spoke in Berber to Almira.

"My father has said you may make your proposal now. I will translate, and he will speak to me in Berber, and I will translate again do you want to deal in English or French?"

"I don't mind but to make certain I too get it right I shall do it in English. Do I need to go slowly your father seems to speak English perfectly well and you were with Mr. Conway and the Major when the plan was outlined do you wish me to go through it all??"

"Yes, just so I don't miss anything and so he realises that the words come from you."

"Okay." Alan shifted his position slightly in order to look directly at Brahim.

"I am not so much a negotiator as a deliverer of a message. Mr. Conway who represents our government is interested in the possibility of your help at a similar amount of costs per man as is in place in Paris. What he wants is ears and eyes telling him who, where, why, when, and what is going on, and possibly some unknown extra assistance at a future date to bring an army here with a view to removal of the Vichy French and any Germans. He is more than happy to put funding in place to assure of our intentions and so you are not financing this out of your own pocket. He is also happy to arm your people with pistols rifles submachine guns and ammunition. At our expense.

Currently our assessment of the situation here is that everyone in Casablanca has at least two jobs. The first being their normal trade and the second being as a spy for one group or another. Your knowledge could save us getting involved with the wrong people."

As Alan was talking he would stop momentarily when Almira put her hand up and after her translation continue.

"I think I've said enough for now I don't think I've missed anything.

In an ideal situation we would prefer the French to join us rather than fight us. They will lose and costs and casualties would occur to both sides. If we can do a deal which suits Morocco and both us and the French all the better."

"Father asks why should the yoke of the allies be any more comfortable than the one attached by the French."

"We are passing through not staying here. Your issue later on will be with the French government as per the 1912 agreement. Personally, I believe that if we don't win this war, you will find that It will be German yoke not a French yok e that you will be suffering under. The German regime will remove the Vichy French when it suits them to do so. They have no time for anything other than Germanic culture and control of the world. I suspect that removal of all foreign peoples and religions will be part of their ideology."

"My father asks are you trying to frighten him?"

"I am not. I am trying to look at where it may go in the long term.

But if it frightens him then it may do so because of its accuracy and plausibility."

Almira spoke some more to her father. "More tea Captain while I go and think."

Almira picked up the pot and poured two teas same way the ritual of the mint tea she said it is a sign of respect and of welcome. The further away the tea is poured the warmer the welcome.

"My father will be back. He asks for some private minutes. He will pray in his room, on his mat then he will come back and speak to us."

He returned.

"I have had my thoughts and sought advice.

Captain Lewis. Thank you for bring my child out of harm. For that you will always be welcome at my house."

He had taken the second pot and started to pour it went nearly twice as high as the first pour and Alan was instantly grateful for Almira's explanation.

He handed the teas around as Almira translated.

"Two questions how many people do you want and how many fighters?"

"If you tell me what you can do I will take the numbers back to my government and after that it's a question of maths and transport of weapons all of which are able to be worked out when the numbers are known."

"Give me an about figure and I will tell you if it would be possible."

"If I may think a moment." Alan looked at Almira her face was looked more beautiful than ever before. Relaxed and back with her family had lifted her from tension and stress in Paris through her escape to being wrapped in warmth and friendliness. It had done her good to come home.

If I said 60 good fighting men able to shoot and move quickly and the maybe 25 keeping an eye what is happening in Casablanca and possibly the same number in Marrakech."

"Both places?" asked Almira.

"Yes as they both have airport facilities. Quickest way to get from one to the other. Quicker than the train."

"True."

"I don't have as many as 25 people in Marrakech, that maybe too many anyway unless you spread their range to include Mogador. But the ones I have are already working on supplying any information I might find useful. I can extend their range.

Casablanca. You are right about. I think there are more spies in Casablanca than the rest of the country put together, including Rabat and Tangier even. Who knows? Nor does it matter. Again, numbers are not a problem nor is sixty good fighting men. I will give you the same rates as you're paying in France, but everything is from day one. I will put together your private army with some French speakers. You will provide the officers. Your officers will train them to do what you want them to do, and I will relay information to your officers as and when I get it and they will act on it or deliver the information to your government by whichever means they want to do so. That way they can see that I am keeping our end of the deal and as long as they don't do anything stupid it should all work. Your opinion Captain Lewis."

"What we want to do is use the information that we can gather here. Ideally as I've said the best plan is to get the Vichy French on our side and working with us."

"I believe the French will be keen to join us rather than fight. I am not suggesting that they have no stomach for a fight, but I think they are smart enough to work out what the best survival chances will be."

"Then personally, sir, I think that is a workable plan.

We need to set up a way of communication. But I think that will come as part of phase two, which will be when we get some more staff organised here."

"Good, Almira will write it down, and We will read it together and I will sign it and when you leave you can take it with you to your Mr. Conway who can then do with it as he needs to."

"Mr. Conway did say that he would as a good will gesture send weapons and ammunition when I get picked up to act as a starting point."

Brahim finished the tea pouring again as high as it had been when he poured the second cups.

"Business is concluded. We must find a way to get you back to England now. Tell me where are you being picked up from?"

"According to my orders sir, I will be picked up six days from my drop off, which is to give me enough time to speak to you and settled my men here before I leave and I will be picked up from the same place we were dropped off and at the same time the submarine will bring weapons and ammunition for our combined fighting force. I will require the use of something like a fishing boat to drop me off at nighttime and one that you can unload safely somewhere that suits yourselves. My men will of course provide any help that you require."

"You will not return some time in the future?"

"I go where they send me sir." Brahim nodded his understanding.

"I imagine someone a lot higher than me will take overall charge and then he will do what they see as the best way to achieve our objective."

"I think our business for now is done until we have a read of what Almira puts on paper for us. I will let you get on with putting your men in the picture."

Alan left them. Almira had said nothing in all the time she was there since she had done the translating.

Brahim looked at her. "You should have formed some sort of an alliance with him. He is a dangerous man, but I don't believe he would ever harm you."

"I think you are right. I don't think he would ever deliberately do me any harm. However, I was stupid. He had some wounds that somehow he'd fixed himself. I tried to be clever and made a pathetic attempt at being the villain and then the savior. The problem was the villain cut too deep, and the wound opened and bled, and I couldn't stop the bleeding. The bond was broken and not repairable. It was a bad mistake, and I only have myself to blame."

"A shame."

"Yes. I shall go and write this contract for you.

Alan and George went to see Hassan about getting a fishing boat and crew to take them out to sea in three days' time. Almira went as translator. Hassan had a friend who knew Brahim as well as Almira. A deal was struck and yes they could get the truck again to move some more kit over to Brahim's house.

Alan spent the following day planning the programme and the training plan for his team and how to develop strategies to contact the French and keep an eye on what was going on. Late in the day before the evening meal Brahim asked Alan to join him for a private talk.

"Sit down Captain." Alan did as he was asked and Brahim's man filled a cup with mint tea and passed it to Alan. After the servant had left Brahim refilled the cups.

"We have some business to discuss, or more accurately I am going to offer you a proposal and I'm going to ask you to do a job for me which you will think about for a length of time that suits us both. Then you will give me an answer and thereafter we will never speak of it again. Are you with me so far?"

"I believe so."

My two children went to a private school in England possibly one of the worst errors of judgement I have ever made. We shall see. Almira found the attention of young hormonal males and their attentions on a sweet innocent or not so innocent child demanding but satisfying. Almiras brother Kareem developed a level of violent protection that I though t if they were to remain in

England to learn English I may even need to buy them a school. I solved the problem by sending over my friend Ibrahim. Who you know as Charles. His influence with the headmaster and the other teachers settled everything down; the children also knew that if Charles said something the rules came from me. It remained mostly peaceful there was the occasional damaged child which Charles would fix, and Almira did have moments when opportunities were never going to be wasted. Almira became a very popular pupil which compensated for Kareem's level of protective violence towards anyone stupid enough to hurt Almira. After their lessons in England Paris compounded the problems Charles stayed with Almira and another of my people took over minding Kareem and teaching him about the business.

Did you ever go to an English private school Monsieur Lewis?"

"No sir."

"But you have been promoted to Captain and still a young man."

"I am slightly above a junior officer. It gets me access to upper echelons normally denied to the more junior officers and other ranks."

"Which then allows you to bring a proposal to me on behalf of your government."

"Yes sir."

"I digress forgive me. One day all of this." He opened his arms wide and swivelled his body as though he was showing off his house. "Will belong to someone else. My desire is that Almira, as my elder child, should own this place, the land, the business, and control of the staff for the benefit of all of us. Typically the heirs to all of this would be all of the family. My wife does not care to take any part of it. Hence the whole would be shared between Almira and Kareem. It is not possible to split the business into equal parts which is the first problem and the second problem is that Kareem will want to be in charge and have it all. There are a number of problems with this. Kareem will be prepared to kill Almira to take control and the second part is that he no longer sees me as having any say in this business or what my wishes for its future might be. He has already brought shame on the family by dealing with the drug smugglers and criminals in Marseille. He controls a lot of the movements of people working at the docks as he often provides the labour to load and offload the cargoes. But he has found a more lucrative sideline and some of our people have been sucked into his business. He has polluted them with the lure of easy money for the risks are minimal as all seem to be in league with each other, and in receipt of generous payouts. I am told there are significant sums of money involved, but I am extremely grateful that the family has not received any part of this illegal profit nor do we wish for any. We are not as pure as the snow that will fall on Jbel Toubkal but wholly criminal acts is not part of our business. Which may sound as hypocritical. You can judge that yourself on how you have conducted your business when one does as one needs to do.

As I understand it any relationship with Almira is unlikely to occur or continue depending on where the time line has been drawn. And when you leave here and your assignment is complete there is no need for us to meet with each other ever again. So, I have decided to ask you to do one job for me.

When I reflect on family relationships Kareem once upon a time would damage anyone who even annoyed Almira or any member of the family but now he is totally the opposite. Now with hatred where there was love and despise where there was respect. This doesn't apply to just Almira but the whole of the family and everyone associated with us." He was quiet for a moment perhaps choosing his next words carefully. Alan said nothing and waited he knew Brahim had not finished.

"I want you to kill my son Kareem; no pain one shot instant death. I do not want to see him suffer but as he has brought shame on the family and has isolated himself from us, he is a liability to the status that we hold as being conscientious, reliable and honest. And he will try and kill Almira when I am gone. I do not wish for these things to happen."

Brahim paused again. He let what he had just asked for sink in.

"In taking on this task you may incur expenses that would be expected. I will, should you agree to do this, deposit in your bank the sum of one thousand pounds which as I understand is over two years' salary for a British Army Captain. There is nothing to discuss with anyone about this. Should you be prepared to take this on. You will give me details on a piece of paper of your Bank account in the UK. I will accept that as your answer. I will do business the same as you do with me. Half up front rest on satisfactory completion. When you give me your bank details I will give you a picture of

Kareem and his most up to date address in Marseille. If you are clear in your head with the task and prepared to accept the terms we will shake hands on it and never speak of it again. Then when you are ready to leave here and are prepared to commit yourself to this for me your statement of intent will be the bank account details and thereafter I will consider we have an agreement and a contract and as honest men we shall fulfil our obligations."

Alan thought back to earlier on when he looked at Almira and watched as she talked to her father. He remembered the night in Paris the escape to Britain then coming here. He'd worked to keep her alive perhaps it was destiny that he would have one more chance at making certain the job was completed and Brahim could live out the rest of his life here with Almira in peace.

He leaned forward and shook hands with Brahim. Brahim poured the remainder of the mint tea. The pot was as high as Alan had ever seen it go.

Alan had a couple more days to finalise a training program with his team. He split them three and two. Colin only spoke German as a second language Barry's French was inadequate so logically he put Tim Forester as the third team member then there shouldn't be any loss of communication

The other team with the young very polite Lieutenant in from the Queens was fluent in French and the best of the Arabic students he'd have Tom Logan to mind his back. The sergeants would knock there groups into shape but what they needed to do was create a force that would back up a negotiated joining of forces with a view to have a united front against any possible opposition. Time only would tell and co-ordinating the whole program with landing allies when they did land would be the measure of its success or failure. That's in the hands of others.

On the morning of day six Alan met with Brahim and Almira. They signed contracts Alan handed over a significant sum of American dollars for which Almira gave him a receipt.

He told Brahim, "The rest goes to Hassan and his friends for transport to the submarine and to bring the weapons and ammunition here. Almira negotiated the price for that I thank you. I will speak to my men then we will head off to pick up our transport. Thank you for your hospitality and the loan of your vehicle and driver. The truck will pick up my men to carry the guns back here. They know what is expected of them and will do as the situation dictates." Alan passed a small envelope to Brahim who gave him a larger envelope back again. Almira looked at the exchange but said nothing. Alan shook hands with both.

"I wish you both well." He said and left to do a final run through with his team. Knowing that they needed to leave in mid- afternoon. One final team talk and a small float to give them some spend money for cigarettes or sweets with a promise of something more substantial when the cavalry arrived.

It was nearly three hours later when Alan, George and Marcus were on Hassan's friend's fishing boat. The evening tide was on the ebb and they let it take them out about three miles offshore. They had a rendezvous for just before slack water. They would off load the weapons from the submarine and then Marcus would travel back to meet the rest of the team along with a couple of Brahim's men on the beach, where they had originally landed six days before. They would then move the guns to Hicham's house stay the night there and the following morning load the truck and return to Brahim. Alan knew that was out of his hands. The one thing he was happy about was that Hassan's friend spoke French so there was no communication issues with Marcus. Trust your team you trained them and picked them.

Alan thanked the fisherman shook hands with Marcus and said hello to lieutenant Hardman as he climbed aboard HMS Falcon.

Now he was again in someone else's hands and heading for home.

Four days later, Alan and George were picked up by Cameron at Northolt and driven back to Woolwich. Their arrival there was almost instantly followed by Mr. Conway and the twins.

Alan handed over the paperwork that he had brought from Brahim apart from his personal envelope.

"Well done Lewis. We know it's a deal in principal and it will almost certainly fluctuate probably on both sides but it is a deal and we can always thrash out the niggles when and if they occur. Do you see any possible problems ?"

"None that can't be resolved sir."

"What do you see as an issue?"

"As part of the maintaining the balance of power with Brahim and Almira I have been asked to do a job by Brahim."

"Go on Lewis. I need to take these papers to the minister today."

"He wants me to assassinate someone in Marseille."

"Keep talking."

"He has a son who is involved in criminal activities in Marseille and given the chance he will kill Almira to get his hands on the family business is roughly how he described it to me. He will deliver on what we have asked for but he wants to be able to sleep better at nights and the family name having been dragged through the mire by his number two child is another factor. I believe he sees this alliance as a start to Morocco being free of German French and Spanish and in the hands of Moroccans. To be certain of keeping this on track I told him I would do what needed doing."

"Are you aware of the consequences of getting it wrong?"

"Yes sir."

"How do you think you will do it?"

"Brahim has asked me to shoot him one shot, no pain instant death."

Mr. Conway was quiet. The room was quiet. George and Cameron were also hearing this for the first time but both knew to say nothing whatever was going to be said was going to come from Mr. Conway and until he said something the room was going to remain silent.

"I think that making a promise to do what he has asked was the right move. You three come up with a plan. Sergeant you go with him and watch his back. Captain go and see Dougie White ask him for two sniper rifles and ammunition to suit and anything else you think you might need. Tell him I've approved it. Major I'll leave you to approve the plan. Keep me posted. I don't know how long this will take you so get me another team to cover for these two while they are away. Good luck I will see you when you are back."

Even after Mr. Conway had left the room remained silent. No one knew quite what to say and to whom. Alan broke the silence.

"Well that'll keep us busy for a bit. Be nice to see Dougie again."

"You do get involved don't you Alan."

"It seemed like the right thing to do sir and even Mr. Conway agrees and that almost feels like a first for both of us."

"How are you going to do it?"

"Haven't got a clue at the moment, sir. We need to make a list of what we need and see where we have to get to, because we know it's a long way because we weren't that far from Marseille when we did the Spanish trip."

"No you're right. Coffee time I think. You're very quiet George even by your standards."

"I just thinking what's the next job. Which is coffee for three. I'll be mother." George went to get the coffee from the outer office.

"I do try to avoid swearing Alan but that was close."

"Almira's father is convinced her brother Kareem will try to kill her. He's involved with drug smuggling and various other forms of crime. Do you remember talking to the man at the embassy in Paris about the orphanage?"

"Yes."

"He knew what was going on in Marseille. A chat with him without going into details might be useful."

"I'll speak to Conway about it and see if he knows how to get hold of him. So what's the big deal with the drugs?"

"Apparently it comes in on the ships and then gets routed to America after it's been processed in places in France."

"What is it?"

"Heroin."

"And it's big business?"

"Huge so I'm informed, with massive profits."

Where does it come from?"

"Turkey. It's grown legitimately for medicinal purposes but there is always a surplus and that's when the big bucks are made." At which point the coffee arrived.

"Can you ride a motor bike George?"

"Yes."

"What are thinking?" Cameron asked.

"Nothing yet creating options. We need good maps of the area around Marseille."

"I better start making some lists." Cameron got paper and pencil from his desk drawer. "If George is going to be mother , I may as well be your secretary. I'm getting a belly and a bottom from sitting down so long I'll need a wheelchair soon. I do hate being stuck in here."

"We worked well as a team sir but the advantage of you being in here is that I can trust you to deliver what we need when we need it."

"You flatter me Alan. There's a lot of people who can do what I do."

"Yes sir but I know you will do it. Trust is built we've built it and that makes it work sir and I'm not certain I would have the same amount of confidence with anyone else doing your job."

"I'm going to stop you there Alan I need to get my head through the door."

"Don't sell yourself short sir if you weren't the right man for the job Mr. Conway would have removed you."

"Okay, I give in. I'll do the list."

"George have you done a parachute training course?"

"No."

"Sir can you get a George into jump school please.?"

"When?"

"Today."

"You're not thinking of jumping in are you?"

"No still increasing options and in the future even if we don't jump now we made to in future. Jumping in is relatively easy jumping back out is a bit more difficult. That's my problem. I can get in but how do we get out again?"

"Do we have a time scale on this? Because I need to get a couple of people to cover for you."

There's no urgency in it doesn't have to be done tomorrow. But it shouldn't be sat on indefinitely. Let's get George on this course then we can always get in, all we have to do then is get out again."

"I'll give Ringway a call. How long do you need to get yourself ready George."

"Where is Ringway sir?"

"Manchester."

"Ready in ten minutes."

"We'll aim for tomorrow morning. I'll see when they can fit you in. It won't be long they have a continuous program running now. You'll be away a fortnight the course is twelve days and a couple of days travelling. So pack what you need for a two weeks away and come back here at 0800 hours tomorrow. Do you have anything to add Captain?"

"Have a good time you'll get another beret. In the end you'll get so many berets you wonder why you've only got one head. Thank you for the last couple of weeks. Now go chill out for a while and I'll see you when you're back."

"Right then Alan, George is off to Ringway what you up to now?"

"I'll go see Dougie White and find out about these sniper rifles and get a decent pistol organised for George for when he's gets back. If he's going to stay as my back up and that looks to be how it's going to remain for as far as we can see then we need to get him properly kitted out. I'll see what Dougie's got for him and if you can get him some Swiss identity papers then that's another thing. Get him papers using his date of birth and the same parents as mine and we can go as brothers."

"I'll do Ringway and sort out the papers. Anything else?"

"No that'll be it for now except food I realise I've sent George off but without a meal for tonight. If you can get a meal for us from the mess that would be the best idea, the war can wait."

The mess was no longer a mess more of a feeding station for those still here or passing through. They got a table and three servings of beef stew with chips.

"Major Cameron will get you some Swiss identity papers for when you're back and you will be my younger brother. That's the first thing. Number two is if I was to get you a semi auto pistol which one?"

"Don't mind."

"Would you be happy with anything then?"

"I've shot all sorts as long as they 're stoppers it'll be ok."

"And one more. Are you any good at woodwork?"

"Did it at school made bookends and simple stiff though other than put floorboards down for me mam I haven't done anything for years."

"When did you do floorboards for your mum?"

"About ten year ago."

"And you still remember?"

"She reminds mee every time I go there to see her cos they still squeak in the same place when you stand on them."

"Are you coming up with a plan?" Cameron asked.

"Maybe sir when I see what Dougie's got tomorrow, he's not here today and I don't know I'll get what I want form his man Friday."

"Good I'll leave it with you. George I will see you tomorrow morning; I will get you a travel warrant and directions from the station." Cameron left them. Alan gave George some notes on his new family and they then hauled themselves off for an early night.

Chapter 11   Marseille

"Dougie, Dougie come out where ever you are."

"Sounds like Mr. Lewis."

"You know it's Alan stop removin' the urine."

"But you're a captain now I remember you when you were a scruffy little sergeant."

"Well that's the doing of our mutual friend and he has sent me down here to speak to you about some equipment scruffy sergeant's for the use of."

"Keep talking. I might understand you in a minute."

"Mr. Conway said I should see you about two Lee Enfield sniper rifles and some ammo."

"Did he now?"

"He did."

"How specific was he?"

"He wasn't. He just said see Dougie about two sniper rifles and ammunition to suit. They were his exact words."

"Okay there are different types all are good some are better than others some are even done by Holland and Holland and they are supposed to be the best and if cost was method of measurement of quality they would be ahead of a lot of the others. The scopes cost a chunk of money. I need to know some details."

"Such as?"

"Target distance, number of targets, location, and how are you going to carry it."

"Distance not known, single target, Europe in a tool box."

"A toolbox?"

"Am I right then in thinking it's exactly the same as the standard issue rifle?"

"Yes it's four feet long. Apart from the scope it looks almost exactly the same."

"So if I said I want to cut just over twelve inches or so off the stock, with the idea of being able to fit it back on again, because I want to carry it, hidden in a tool box. Then it wouldn't effect the way the rifle works and I could carry it hidden in this box."

"In theory no effect because you aren't changing the workings of the rifle. But you would need to make certain that it was a good tight fit. Or you might not get a second shot."

"We won't get a second shot hence two rifles."

"So you have a one off target, one chance two shooters and no repeat performance. I will get you the best I can and if you are serious I will take them to the gunsmiths and have them make the stock into a two piece."

"How long will it take?"

"How long have I got?"

"Two weeks."

"That'll be alright, especially if I take two of their conversions back and they can check them over after the extra work. Anything else?"

"Pistol for my sergeant with a spare mag and a box of ammo please.

"Colt 45 auto. Got a few of those in. Do I need to lose it?"

"No this is via Mr. Conway."

"Do you want it now?"

"No when I pick the rifles up please."

"Are you staying here?"

"We're in an Anderson shelter down the road a touch, Major Cameron is here permanent so if you can't find me he should know where I am."

"Leave it with me Alan. I'll be in touch as soon as they're back."

On the following morning Alan joined Cameron at breakfast, over coffee Alan explained the plan he had.

"The target is a criminal. He will be guarded by others of the same. He is not a German general an officer of Vichy France or a member of the local police. Therefore my theory is that fingers crossed there will not be any hullaballoo if he's suddenly no longer there."

"I'll subscribe to that with reservations and subject to a bit more detail."

"I have an idea of getting to Marseille by train and leaving the same way. As Swiss nationals we will be able to move around a lot easier than the French. We are going to pretend to be boat repairers. When I worked the fishing boat with dad we were forever cauilking the deck to stop the water getting down inside. The planking would get damaged sometimes take a hammering spring a joint and it would need a repair to make it watertight again. It's the only thing I know how to do on boat repairs. Because it was my job along with the fishing and I did it for two years nearly with dad. I'm not able to claim I'm a shipwright or anything like that but I can do that, so we have a trade and we are going to Marseille to get some work. It's small boat stuff not shipbuilding and they have boats like this in Switzerland, small wooden boats on the lakes. We can get away with this. And Dougie is going to get me some guns that we can fit into a woodworkers tool box. It's a keep it simple again.

There is a train that goes from Paris to Marseille and back again.

My idea is a Lysander to Paris train to Marseille do the job reverse the route. Works perfectly when you say it quickly."

"We need to fill all the big gaps."

"Agreed, I'm open to any better ideas.. Getting out is the difficult part and going on the train seems a better idea than trying to get a submarine in the Med. We know the trains will run. The other thing in our favour is that there aren't any major forces of Germans down there but there is the Gestapo and the Vichy police and they do like to work together, and again I'm banking in that being Swiss will help. Life isn't perfect but the gangsters are in some control of certain areas and large German forces wouldn't allow that."

"How long does the train take?"

"Twelve hours ,give or take. But certainly no less than ten."

"Gives you a lot of time to have problems and no means of escape."

"As I said sir I'm open to better ideas."

"I think that's something we need to think about; we do have time if George isn't back for a fortnight. What's your plan for the rest of today.?"

"I need to go to my bank and check a few things out and I want to find someone to build me a couple of toolboxes for me to a particular design."

"Where is your bank?"

"Cox and kings in Pall Mall."

"That's your day done for then. It's two hours there and back from here to your bank and finding a joinery shop will take the rest. Are you eating here?"

"I hope so."

"I'll order for two and I'll wait for you then you can fill me in and I will do what I can to turn up a better plan for the job or at least get times and details for the one we're stuck with."

Beef stew and chips again. The meat was tender so it was likely to be last night's leftovers recooked . The chips were fresh. Alan had been to his bank picked up some foreign currency all be it with difficulty but he'd got it via a friend who worked there as a cashier.

Cameron had been in touch with Tangmere and two men and two toolboxes could be flown into France in one trip. Weight wasn't a problem as long as tool boxes weren't too heavy or too big.

"How did you get on with everything else Sir?" Alan asked after he'd got the information about the Lysander.

"Unfortunately I'm almost resigned to the fact that the idea of getting a train does seem both the easiest and safest way of going about it. You could always split the journey as it stops a number of tomes so if you were getting in any way uncomfortable with other passengers perhaps or too many military people you could always get off and do a rethink. There is some flexibility but it is limited."

"I'm working on going to work in Marseille as the reason for travel and then on the way back we are doing the same from Paris we go on to Le Havre, not that we will but that's the why we are on the train and we are Swiss itinerant workers. We are not unusual."

"I'm hoping you are right Alan."

"So do I sir."

Georgee had got his parachute wings in June 1942. June had been a heatwave but autumn started early before summer had properly begun and the idea of Paris was looking as attractive as Paris could when it was full of Germans and empty of food. Just short of three weeks later at the start of July Alan and George with two tool boxes and a two duffle bags are at RAF Tangmere waiting for their lift to Paris. It is 21.30. in Paris. France is normally one hour ahead but we are on double British summertime clocks. As long as the pilot and the Henri know what time it is that will do for Alan. journey time has been set at two hours; Henri has been told where they will land and has confirmed the receipt of the message.

At 23.25 Henri and Marcel put a light in each corner of the field and right on time The Lysander landed dropped of its passengers and turned around and took off again to return direct to Tangmere. Practice makes perfect. Alan and George spent the night at the orphanage while Henri stayed with Marcel.

The following morning two itinerant shipwrights took a small ground floor room in a house, near to the railway station, run by a French lady. They expected to be here for just a couple of days at the most. Their hostess was pleased to see them; business was quieter than normal and every bit of income helped.

They stayed two days with her and having picked up their tickets they headed for Gare de Lyon; they got the train and put the two tool boxes side by side and after the train filled up en route they took to passing on their seats and sitting on the boxes for the remainder f the journey. They arrived in Marseille just as the Germans decided to take over even more of the city in order to stop the refugees escaping and the resistance resisting.

The ticket collector gave them directions to the Rue Du Pasteur where they managed to get a room not unlike the one that Alan had with Fatima, top floor four story house. The double solid timber doors here appeared to be just on a latch though Madame assured them it was reasonably secure. The room had two beds, wooden floorboards, a washbasin, a window that was open but would not properly close, no curtains and a candle and box of matches on a rickety bedside cabinet. At the end of the two beds was a runner, four yads long by one yard wide. Alan rolled it out of the way looked for some loose floorboards found one cut another and then hid two two-piece rifles two scopes and three boxes of ammunition, a colt and a beretta. He screwed the boards back into place and covered over it all again with the very dusty piece of carpet. They locked their room and downstairs they looked for their landlady to give her their key.

"Monsieurs, how long will you be staying?"

"We don't know madame it depends on work and if we get it. Prospects may now become a bit more difficult if the Germans arriving. Why do you ask?"

"Perhaps some more money in advance."

"I have given you money madame."

"That is a deposit in case of damages. I hear you cutting things already."

"I was repairing my hammer ready for work if we get some."

"I will refund you if nothing is damaged or broken."

"Can you feed us too. Breakfast and dinner."

"Yes of course."

"What do you want to eat?"

"Crepes or bread and meat, and coffee for breakfast. Whatever you do for dinner as long as it's substantial."

"I can do those things. Shall we say five thousand francs per week for you both.

No let us say for two, three thousand,

"I do you both for four thousand per week. I will feed you well and good food is in short supply."

"Deal."

"In advance." Alan took a small bundle of notes from his pocket and counted out four thousand.

"Thank you madam. If we get work and we are still here I will pay you again next week."

"Good luck monsieur if you get work it will be a miracle. Only street girls, gangsters, and the police, and I think they all the same, have full time jobs here."

Brahim had provided an address for Kareem. MI6 pal of Camerons had shown where that was on the map and Kareem had based himself near to the docks as was practical. George and Alan had got themselves roughly in the right area. The start of the docks were only a ten minute walk from the railway station; their lodgings were off to one side between the two and Kareem's base was less than a mile away from their lodging house. Transport was not going to be a problem other than a getaway. The streets were narrow some only one vehicle wide a clear shot on a target might be difficult to find and carrying two rifles through the streets might be nigh on impossible.

They had located Kareem's office. The ground floor had a concierge the first floor was Kareem's. Across the street from Kareem's office was the warehouse of an importer exporter dealer in whatever they could buy and sell at a profit. His name was Manny Epstein and he wanted to leave Marseille at the earliest opportunity. Alan asked him if he had any fireworks. No but he had a friend who possibly would. Perhaps he still has some. He will find out. If Alan will wait outside he could go and see his friend and get them and then Alan could pay for him for them.

"I shall return tomorrow but I shall leave you a deposit which will assure you of my return." Manny was happy with this and promised to have fireworks here tomorrow morning.

George walked into the opposite building while Alan was inside the warehouse across the way. Alan needed to see if there was a place from where he could see what was happening and where it was in relation to Kareem's office. Manny wasn't keen for Alan to see any other part of the building's so he didn't get a chance to see across the street.

 There was no contact with the concierge when George went in and so he took himself up the stone staircase to the floor above. He knocked on the door and got no answer . He knocked again got no answer and tried the handle. It was open he walked in. It was a single room office. It was dark inside, just a small amount of light filtering through the dusty glass. There was a bed against one wall and on a table next to it was a small stove with a kettle and a coffee pot on top. There was no one here. Then he heard along the corridor the sound of running water and realised that whoever was responsible for the running water sound was probably the person from the office. George shut the office door and went partway up the next flight of stairs. He squatted down in the darkness of the staircase and pretended to tie his boot.

Kareem came out of the washroom and went straight back to his office switching a light on as he went in before shutting the door behind him.

George mad his way downstairs and walked straight past the concierge who was about to speak to him then as he was being ignored kept his mouth shut. George spotted Alan and on opposite sides of the street they walked back towards their lodging.

Back at their room George started the conversation. "Small single room come office, not much more than fifteen foot by the same one window that looks out onto the street. I could see the doors of the building you were in from the small window in the room. I also noticed with bed and cooker there's some sign of occupation but it's not living accommodation so I think he may live somewhere else. That's a guess but there were no clothes about no food just a kettle and a coffee pot a desk and a couple of filing cabinets. To be honest I could have shot him there and then as he seems to have no one in the office with him. Maybe his people are out collecting or what, I don't know."

"What about the caretaker. He would have heard the shooting."

"I saw him on the way out he wanted to speak to me but I ignored him and walked straight past and he went straight back inside his cubby hole under the stairs. Perhaps he avoids associates of our man."

"You could be right and that is another tick in our favour."

"Did you get anything from across the way?"

"Yes, I'm going to buy some fireworks. They might provide a disguise from gunshots."

"Could do .What you thinking?"

Day after tomorrow is Bastille Day; fireworks going off might be a bit unusual but not totally out of place."

"It doesn't go dark until late."

"Makes our target easier to see."

"Tell me the plan."

"In our tool boxes is a coil of fuse cord. A couple of bags with fireworks in; you leave them on the pavement down the road, having lit the fuse off your cigarette lighter. When I see you do this I will go inside and then upstairs when the first fireworks go off and I will open the office door and look in and shoot him as the second lot of fireworks is going off in the street. I will walk out of the building and head off towards our room. We will pick up our tool boxes and head off to the train station for the overnight train to Paris. Say it quick it works."

"I think you're right Alan. What gave you the fireworks idea?"

"I've always thought bonfire night was a good night for shooting someone, and in the Warehouse across the road I spotted a poster from a few years back about Bastille Day. Which is day after tomorrow."

"Well I reckon it will work. I could have done it today exactly the same way. What are we going to do with the rifles?"

"Leave them here under the floorboards just use pistols and hide them where we had them in the tool boxes on the trip back to Paris."

"Are you not worried about the Germans finding them?"

"They're no better than the ones the Germans have so what the hell. One day we might get back and retrieve them. You never know. But no I'm not bothered I'd be more bothered getting caught with them. Let's see what our Landlady has done us for dinner."

Alan and George retrieved their pistols spare magazines and ammunition from under the floorboards and slid the rifles a lot further underneath so that they might not be easily found and screwed the boards down tight again. Alan cut some lengths of fuse cord that had been hidden in their materials box.

"The longer one is ninety seconds or thereabouts and the shorter one about forty-five seconds. I reckon time to get up the stairs and the office door open should be less than a minute. So the shooting should happen as the second bag of fireworks goes off down the road."

"Is there nothing to hang them on?" George asked.

"Nothing just put the bag on the pavement. We are not going to do it until the road is clear. I don't want to attract attention just having fireworks going off is to disguise the gunfire. We will walk down the street together and when we know he's in his office then I will give you my bag. I will go by the street door and wait. You will set off the fireworks. My signal will be the first lot going off that will give me forty five seconds to go upstairs open the office and do the job during the noise of the second lot of explosions. You will continue walking up the road and back to our lodging house . I will either catch up or meet you there a bit later depending on how quickly I can get away. We will then tell the landlady that we will be off for a couple of days but keep the money and we will see her when we are back. A short walk to the statin and then the train back to Paris."

"It now depends on the dealer turning up with the fireworks."

"It does but he buys and sells that's how he makes a living. He says he thinks his friend may have some. I reckon he knows where there are some and I will [pay a premium price if he is lucky. And if he doesn't have any we have the rest of tomorrow to find some."

"It's starting to sound too easy Alan."

Rehearsal and practice, repetitive it might be but we will talk it through a couple more times and tweak as we're going if it needs it.

At ten o'clock, opening time for Manny Epstein Alan and George arrived at Manny's warehouse. Just as they were arriving a black van came up the street, stopped outside the door on the opposite side of the road. Kareem got out of the front passenger seat and went straight into his building. The van drove off and just as Manny opened the door to his warehouse the light went on in Kareem's office.

"Monsieur I have your fireworks Come in please come in. They were more than I expected."

"Oh there is a surprise."

"Monsieur do you think I would tell you a lie?"

"Shall we say that how you see the truth and how I see it could be different."

"That's an interesting way of putting it Monsieur. Is your friend coming in too."

"No need, he will wait outside for now."

Alan got the fireworks; gave Manny some advice on getting away from Marseille before it became like Paris, and he and George walked back to their lodgings.

They primed Madame about the possibility of their probable imminent departure due to a no work forecast but gave her no details of their planned travel directions.

Not having a fuller picture of Kareem's daily rituals they decided that all the y do was go with what they knew and the guess was this morning would be the same as yesterday and Kareem would arrive at his office around ten and everything would be as predictable and as simple.

Alan and George knew that it might not happen like that and if for any reason that Kareem wasn't in his office and he didn't arrive while they were there waiting they would abort and go back to the drawing board.

This morning it was nearly eleven and they were about to return to their room when the same van as yesterday drove up the street. Kareem got out and went into his office.

The plan they'd talked through, tweaked and changed at least ten times kicked in. Kareem' s office light went on. George took both bags, the street remained empty. As George walked down the street Alan crossed the road and stood near the door. When the first lot of fireworks went off Alan went inside and walked up the stone steps to the first floor. He got to the door as the second lot of fireworks were about to go off. He opened the door, Kareem looked up as Alan went in. The fireworks started and Alan put one shot through his head and two into his heart. He switched out the light, took the key from out of the door lock on the inside, and shut the door behind him. He locked the lock and put the key on top of the architrave. He wiped the door handle put the gun into his pocket and walked slowly down the stairs. There was no movement from under the stairs.

Outside, down the street were a couple of bags nearly burnt out on the pavement with a small amount f smoke still hanging around. George was way up the road. Alan looked at his watch pretending not to be in a hurry. He hovered but when he saw the door to Manny's warehouse start to open he figured it would be prudent to make a swifter exit than he had until then considered necessary. Ten yards up the road with only his back visible, speed was no longer required, so he settled for a gentle saunter. It was after all Bastille Day. A day for celebration and relaxation.

George was waiting outside the guest house. He went up to the top floor picked up their tool boxes checked they had left nothing while Alan spoke to the landlady and settled for a discount when they returned.

Fifteen minutes got them to the station.

"There is a long wait Monsieurs before the train perhaps six hours before you can board."

"You have a café here?"

"We do. At the far end past the long waiting room."

"We can eat and sleep six hours is okay."

They got lunch and one read and kept watch until they got their train. The overnight was quiet and twelve hours after they left Marseille they arrived at Gare Du Lyon in Paris.

Two smelly Swiss non-Jewish, boat repair workers, were of no interest to the French police.

Alan and George walked to the house, where they had stayed before they left for Marseille. This time they carried their tools to the next floor, hid their pistol and ammo took the dirty clothes off, washed, climbed into their beds, and slept the clock around.

"If you are hungry gentlemen I can offer you some food. I have some chicken and rice that needs eating. Some small recompense would be appreciated. If I try to keep it I fear it might go off in this heat and it will be wasted."

"That is perfect thank you madame."

"You are both very polite and I wish I had more like you two here. I shall serve it now if that is ok?"

On the following morning they made their way over to Henri's bar and got a lift to the orphanage. Alan took a radio and organised a pick up for George and himself. Henri did the honours that night and the morning after Mr. Conway arrived at Woolwich.

"Report please."

Job completed straight forward, kept it simple, worked fine."

"Another splendid effort. Now I will give you the good news. For your work on our Morocco project you have been promoted to Major. The major has been promoted to Colonel. Sergeant Robinson will be made Warrant Officer. On behalf of his majesties government I am asked to pass on the promotions along with their thanks. Good to have you back. No doubt I will drop you in the mared again in the future. Thank you gentlemen. I shall be in touch. Have a beer relax and day after tomorrow if you haven't heard from me Major take Mr. Robinson and check on training at Salisbury.

"Congratulations to everyone. I shall buy you both a beer as soon as the Lion is open." Cameron said the instant Mr. Conway left.

Alan went to see Dougie White in the armoury. "First off thank you for those two rifles. I have to be honest and say I didn't use them we couldn't get anywhere we could fire from. I also had to leave them there . They are well hidden and maybe one day I'll get them back and return them. They did fit well in the tool boxes so the plan itself worked except I had to go and eyeball my target it was a close action hit. Which is why I'm back here. George let a load of fireworks off to hide the sound of gunfire. We were lucky we could.

"Alan are you after pistols with silencers?"

"Dougie you're a mind reader."

How many?"

"Two please with spare mags in case we need to do more than just a hit.

"Two Walther PPK's and mags and silencers." And a couple of boxes of ammo. Do you want them now?"

"If they're here yes please."

"I've got a case full of them. S.O.E. have taken to using the Welrod that is quiet but you can't get into a firefight with it. It's a bolt action pistol so it ain't rapid fire . It is quiet but it's like having a single shot shooter."

Douglas put Alan's new guns into a duffle bag.

"Thank you Dougie."

"You're welcome Major. Congratulations again."

"How did you know? I only just found out half an hour ago."

"I saw Talbot Conway after he left you. He keeps my supplies topped up. I'm providing all sorts of weapons for all sorts people like yourself. He reduces the paperwork to bugger all. Without him I'd be a clerk not an armourer."

"You spoil me Dougie. Thanks again."

"Just keep coming back in one piece Alan."

"We're going to the Lion for a quickie at lunchtime you are welcome to join us."

"Another time I'm even eating lunch in here. My customers don't do normal shopping hours as I'm sure you're aware, and my man Friday's been reallocated somewhere else."

"We're off to Salisbury tomorrow morning. I'll see you when we're back."

George didn't fancy a beer too early for him. "Too early for all of us." Alan told him, "That's why we we're just having one and then lunch."

"I'll organise food then shall I?"

"Can do ," said Cameron, "Give us an hour. The walk there and back and a pint will be about an hour."

Alan headed for a table at the far end while Cameron did as he promised buy the drinks.

"Your very good health Major."

"And the same to you Colonel."

I have to say Alan Mr. Conway does take care of us in more ways than one."

"He does sir. Dougie was saying how he makes his job run smoother than anyone else could. I doubt if we'll ever know how much stuff he's run and developed over the years."

"Probably not. You know he once said to me that sometime in the future he will be asked by his wife or his children what did you do in the war? He said he would have to lie to them, as he honestly could not tell them the truth to what he had been a party to."

"The same thing may well apply to you sir." Alen replied.

"I doubt it to be honest. Children are very unlikely and my marriage came to a stuttering halt during the honeymoon. I haven't seen her now for a couple of years.

You covered the office for me the last time I went home for a long weekend. I don't know if you remember?"

"Yes that was when I realised you had your car here which is why you didn't need the Ford to go home."

"Well I arrived about Lunchtime on the Friday. When I got there the house was shut and the dog wasn't there.

Mrs. Hodgkins my nearest neighbour, about fifty yards along the lane had our spare key. The dog was with her. I don't know which one I was more intimidating Mrs. Hodgkins or the dog. Both were snarling at me neither with just cause. Though the dog probably had more entitlement than she did, as he had originally been mine and it probably felt neglected.

'She's left you a note on the dining table, in case you actually turned up.' I took the key and walked back to my home.

She had gone off for a long weekend to the Lake district with the local country club group. Should be back Tuesday or possibly Wednesday weather dependant. So the note told me. That in itself left me a little disappointed; but the straw and the camel's back was finding someone's leather cased shaving kit in the bathroom and the Gibbs shaving soap was still wet.

I returned the key to Mrs. Hodgkins and I stayed two nights at the pub and I came back to Woolwich on the Sunday."

"I am sorry to hear that."

"It was a marriage of convenience in many ways. I got free accommodation and Clarissa got a husband instead of being known as spinster of this parish. She really wanted to be the same as her mother."

"In what way sir?"

"A widow.

Both of her parents had died, her father a long time before her mother, and this was the family house. She's always been a part of the country club people group, in the village there. If I ever make General Cameron she might let me back in her bed but I'm not certain I'd want that doubtful privilege. I was an only child who went to boarding school. I learnt from an early age how to survive on my own. My wife refined it."

Alan didn't know what to say.

"I can't imagine being able to find any interest in her . Though I must admit I found those 'ladies' who were friends with Almira a lot more enticing than my beloved."

"Some of them come with parts that your wife doesn't have sir."

"Well while we 've still got ours too. I suggest we get a move on or cookie will be wanting to cut them off for being late for lunch again."

Chapter 12

The following morning Alan and George filled the Ford with all their gear from the Anderson shelter and drove over to Salisbury and took overall charge of the specialist training program which would put two more instructors back into the mix again.

Near the end of 1942 the combined US and UK force landed in Morocco, met some resistance from the Vichy French but quickly there was an armistice signed and the Vichy French joined the US and UK troops as a combined force against the Axis armies in North Africa.

Alan sent George home in the Ford to spend Christmas with his folks while he manned their office on the Plain.

While Alan was doing that Cameron was working on plans and ideas with Mr. Conway.

There was success in North Africa where the power had shifted towards the allies and in February the German s surrendered at Stalingrad. The German forces though a long way from being defeated were losing some of their power and their forward momentum.

Mr. Conway was keen to keep the allied forces forward momentum going and a phone call to Major Lewis to bring himself, his pal George, and all their kit down to Woolwich seemed like a good odea to him.

A couple of days after they arrived they had reestablished themselves in the now again shared office, even though the walls were covered in pin board, notes, and various maps of various portions of the world, and a number of the Colonel's assistants periodically were in and out of the place it still felt like home.

Mr. Conway completed the picture when he arrived at the usual time of just after two P.M. or as everyone else preferred 14.00 hours.

"Don't get too comfortable Major. I want you and Mr. Robinson to go back to France. Shortly there will be a concentrated effort we shall call it for now in Western Europe. I want you to improve the fighting capabilities of the French resistance. I don't even know if it's possible but we must make every effort to do so if we can. Once again you are not doing it on your own, but you do have an access already established with the slightly more unruly elements of Parisian society. That is the area where I want you to apply yourselves. We established this a long time ago. It has proved useful in a number of ways, but soon it could prove itself to be an even better investment than it has thus far. We have weapons to distribute, we may even have some funding, but that's a path I'm reluctant to go down, given some of the reprobates we are dealing with. If they've managed to stay in business through this war, they've almost certainly been up to no good at some time or another.

When you both went to Marseille you managed to do so on forged Swiss passports, which I'm told are very good as long as no one has access to the Swiss records. I am about to get you and your new younger brother I believe some real ones, that will actually stand up to serious inspection.

You will get a phone call and meet the lady again that you met quite a while back now that I told you never to speak about. Same thing applies. She will organise a meeting place. Go there do what she says give her both of your forged ones with the family details on a note inside and then wait until you are told what else you need to do. Is that clear?"

"Completely sir."

"When you have the passports ask Colonel Cameron to contact me and we'll then go from there. Usual any questions?"

"No sir."

"Right I'm off. I shall be in touch when I have any more to say."

On the following day Cameron took a phone call asking for a meeting with Alan in the Crown pub., lounge bar, 18.15.

"I believe you have some documents for me Mr. Lewis."

"I do mam." Alan handed the lady a small brown envelope which she slipped into her handbag. "All I can say is I will return these to you as soon as I can. Not long just a couple of days. They will possibly come with some other information that you will have to learn. It won't be difficult.

Our friend Talbot says you are a solver of problems mostly by removing the problem in a final unlikely to occur in the same form again way. He says he has given you almost free rein to do this and although he is not entirely happy nor comfortable with your methods he is extremely satisfied with the results. He says therefore I can trust you completely and there aren't many people he has ever said that about. You are held in high esteem Alan whatever it is you have done you have earned the respect of a very powerful man. That is just a piece of information for you. I am going to go now. Is George going to follow me out?"

"He may do. Do you want me to stop him?"

"No let him follow I'll have a chat with him he can walk me to my car."

George followed the lady outside. She had walked four or five paces along the pavement. Stopped and retraced her steps. George had stayed put outside the double doors clearly visible in the vestibule light . He wasn't comfortable there and even less so when she had turned around.

"George," she said, "Walk me to my car. It will put my minder's minds at ease even though they know who you are. I am about a hundred metres or so along the road. She linked his arm. A man followed out of the doorway and a second man appeared across from out of the shadows across the street.

We spotted you when you got to the pub before Alan. I will be gracious and suggest that Alan sent you to mind me rather than follow me to find out who I am. It feels so much better when you have people watching over you. We'll walk slowly. Alan asked if he should stop you. I told him no you can take me to my car.

The man who had walked along the pavement on the other side had crossed the street as the door was unlocked by the driver from the inside. The man following from behind arrived at exactly the same time. He opened the rear door while the other man took the rear seat on the roadside. The lady sat next to him.

"Take care of yourselves George." George stepped back and the man shut the door. Just a nod of respect or politeness and he was in the car. He had taken the front passenger seat, shut the door, and they had all left.

Alan bought George a beer. Neither mentioned what had happened and nor would they until they were with Cameron later on.

The following day mid-morning. Alan again looked at the card the lady had given him. Very simple a name on it 'Anne Marie' and a London telephone number nothing else.

He dialled the number and waited it rang a while and he was about to put the handset down when it was answered.

"Embassy of Switzerland." accented English speaking voice.

"Anne Marie please."

"Who is calling?"

"Alan Lewis."

"Hold please."

"Alan how are you?"

"Fine thank you. "And you?"

"Busy but I have some time to talk later. Perhaps a coffee this afternoon?"

"Okay."

"There is a tea room called Lucy's, near the embassy, it is safe and my people will mind us there."

"I'll find it."

"Three o'clock ok?"

"Yes I will be there."

The phone connection broke Alan hung on to see if anything else happened.

"Embassy switchboard can I help you?"

"I'm done thank you."

Alan hung up checked his watch and sat wondering what was happening now. He had four hours to fill. Half hour to get there half hour for lunch possibly same again with the Colonel to keep him up to speed.

Lucy's tea rooms was in a small group of similar sized shops. Centre single widish door, glass window either side, peeling paint on all the woodwork. The minders were at the first table on the left as the door hinged on the right let them know instantly rho was coming in. Anne Marie sat on the far end on the right.

"Alan how nice to see you," she greeted him like a long lost friend rather than an arranged meeting. "Please join me," she continued. "Tea and cake?" she asked, "my treat, and I do recommend any of the cakes, they're all delicious. Our friend Otto has been called away. He got in touch to tell me he was going south and east. Circumstances left him with little choice if he wanted to stay in one piece. Apparently he has been put in charge of some heavy vehicles the likelihood he believes that it's a dead end job with very limited prospects. He tells me it all might hinge on the quality and reliability of his men. He doesn't expect to return soon but lives in hope that he might be at some time in the future able to get back again. Unfortunately I have not heard from him for so long now I fear that our contact may have been lost forever."

A little fragile lady waitress arrived .

"Tea for two Alan?" Anne Marie asked.

"Yes that's fine please."

"And a tray of cakes please."

Alan got a word in

"And what are you doing yourself?"

"I have this sort of liaison job now. It doesn't even have a title. They just give me a little card and I introduce people to each other and pass on messages. Such a long time since I've seen you I should stop talking but it's so unbelievable that I'm sitting here and you appear.

And what are you up to are you still going home to Bern. You should contact them at my work place they can organise any transport or paperwork you need. That will be easy knowing who your mother is and her parents. You should try us some time. Oh dear I am sorry I'm rabbiting on and you haven't manged to say a word please forgive me. Tell me what are you doing now."

Alan was still absorbing and deciphering information that had been shot at him in such an unusual way whatever this lady was she was extremely bright and articulate and sounded so real. Alan was still reeling from the verbal onslaught. Anyone listening would have assumed exactly what she had intended which was one old friend greeting another. The lady returned pushing a small rattly trolley with a tea pot, sugar, milk, and a plate of cakes. She carefully placed it all on the table.

"Just call if you need anything else."

"Thankyou."

"I'm doing a bit of selling. It's a bit quiet at the moment not everyone wants pest control equipment. Don't suppose you have any contacts in pest control or personal protection equipment sales suppliers do you?"

"I might have, I'll have to speak to my boss and see what we can do. Where are you thinking of selling them?"

"Western Europe."

"And buying from where?"

"Possibly home in Switzerland."

"Tell you what, leave it with me, and I'll ask around, very least I can do after letting you off the hook a while back. She laughed that laugh again.

Now we must drink our tea eat our cakes and I must return to my office or they might send people out looking for me.

Here is my card. Phone me in a couple of days and I'll see if we can be of any assistance."

Alan took the card. It was exactly the same as the one handed to him previously he put it in his wallet.

"Please let me pay for the tea and cakes."

"No it was my insistence. It was so nice to see you again. I must leave in a minute." The two guys near the door had paid their bill and they moved towards the exit when they heard Ann Marie say she would leave. She put a half crown and a sixpence on the table. "A tip for our waitress" she said.

"Do take care of yourself." she whispered as he started to stand pushing himself up from the table. She stroked his hand.

"No sit, finish the tea, there's another cup in the pot. Maybe one day we'll meet again who knows what will happen in the future."

She left then. She was right, who knows what will happen in the future. Alan never saw Anne Marie again, but he never forgot tea cakes and the very clever lady with an infectious giggly laugh.

Two days later Alan phoned the number on the card.

"Anne Marie Please."

"Who is calling?"

"Alan Lewis."

"Will you hold a minute please."

"Mr Lewis," a male voice. "Good morning sir. Anne Marie is on leave sir, but she has asked me to help you with your requests. Can you come to the Embassy before lunchtime today say eleven o'clock?"

"Yes."

"Good. When you get here reception will be expecting you and they will contact me." The phone went dead Alan didn't wait but hung up and went to see the colonel.

At the embassy later that morning Alan was given two passports one for him and one for his younger brother George. The two passports were issued three months apart so as not to look the same as they went through customs together.

The following day Alan and George flew to Paris.

Henri left a message with Fatima for Alan to give him a call.

"We have had an offer for the business. It is not as generous as yours was. If we don't leave they will come and take the bar and kill us."

"Do we know who it is?"

"Yes. His name is Dom Olise he owns a few bars and other businesses. There is talk that his strength is down to his collaboration with the Germans. He gets away with things that most others don't. Only gossip nothing proven of course. They are just French gangsters. On their own probably not that good, but they do have numbers and Germans have been seen at his house."

I assume then you have a location?

Yes they are based in a large, detached house in Nanterre on the outskirts of Paris in its own grounds with a high wall all around and only accessible, as far as we can see, via front gates which are watched all the time. The house is right on a 'T' junction.

I think they have more clout than just a few bullies with machine guns, maybe police as well, but definitely some military. We have seen an occasional German staff car going in and out of the gates with high rankers in them. I get the feeling that the Germans are robbing stuff and shipping it out and the local crooks are a way to do business so I suspect that the robbery that's happening is not going to the fatherland but possibly to feather the nests of others."

"How bloody interesting is that then?"

I think they are doing some cleaning out of undesirables for the Germans probably too. Taking assets, money, jewelry, and anything they can get their hands on promising to help then sending the poor buggers off to camps and prison."

"Get me an accurate exact location and I'll get it sorted. When is all this to happen?"

"He says we have a week."

"Tell him your partner is in Switzerland won't be back for ten days."

"He 'll tell me he doesn't care and he'll deal with you when you get back."

"See what happens. Just keep talking unless it gets too dangerous to."

"What else do you need?"

"Nothing at the moment. Just avoid the area and make certain everyone else does."

"Pardon."

"As I've said stay away and leave it with me."

"My brother delivers vegetables and meat to the house. There is enough people living there to make it worth his while. We're not thinking about money here but he goes there legitimately so he could keep a watch for us and if he stopped they'd want to know why."

"Okay then Ask him to continue to keep an eye on the place until I say stop number s in there and food amounts will give us an idea of numbers as well."

An hour later Alan was back at Fatima's he picked up a radio and along with George headed off on the motor cycles to do some calls.

"It's simple Sir. I want someone to drop some fire bombs on a house near Paris.

It has multiple advantages to killing off the group in one fell swoop.

You're taking a sledge hammer to crack nuts Alan.

That's the point sir the nut won't survive and the lesson to others should be obvious."

"I told him we need a couple more days until you were back from Switzerland he said seven days is what I said seven days it is. But he will give us the full seven in return we will provide a virgin sacrifice sort of. He wants a young girl to entertain him while he eats a meal in two days' time at his café Chez Dom. She is to be there at seven thirty, fresh, clean, and looking smart like a private school girl pupil."

"Perfect," said Alan. "Now I need to speak to Charles about some additional drivers and a bit of back up too."

"Perfecter, if such a word exists."

"Why is it so good?"

"I know Chez Dom. I know the manager, who used to be the owner, and I now know who Dominique Olise is."

The woman who manage the ladies washroom at Chez Dom, swapped her shift and a substitute took the Thursday evening for her. The chef and the manager were in attendance; a trainee waiter hovered. Two men with a cup of coffee each sat at two tables one either side of the dining room. The café was nearly empty apart from the staff and the two customers. There was no one at the outside tables the afternoon had an edge with the wind even though it had stopped raining the wind hadn't dried the water just moved it around on the table tops and the cobbles.

A young lady maybe not quite a teenager came in through the front door. She looked intimidated and apprehensive. She stood just inside the door looking around. About five feet tall oriental, skinny, tinted skin, black hair, in two plaited pigtails, one either side around her ears the joined with a ribbon, tied with a bow at the nape of her neck. The manager walked over to speak to her. Her voice was quiet, no one but he heard what she said.

She followed him over to a set table and he gently eased the chair in behind her as she sat down. He brought her a glass of water which she drank followed quite quickly by another.

She had nearly finished the second glass of water when Dom Olise arrived. He looked around the dining area saw the other two customers and the walked over to the table where the girl was sitting. He sat down next to her. "Good evening my little Chinky one, my name is Monsieur Dom. What is yours?"

"My name is Sonja, monsieur." Her voice was quiet and slightly squeaky.

The manger arrived with a glass of water for the girl. "Good evening sir ,anything to drink?"

"Not yet. What is she drinking ?"

"Just water sir."

"Good, I might get her drunk later, but first I want you to entertain me. Come sit nearer. Her bottom lip is starting to quiver. "What are you shaking for girl? There is no need to be frightened, well not yet anyway. Where you from China?"

"I'm from Tonkin."

"Where is Tonkin?"

"French Indo Chaina Sir."

"That's what I said Chinky."

The manager and the waiter were hanging around in front of the table.

"What are you two waiting for? I'm not ready to order yet. Dom put his hand on the girls knee and she started to cry. What you crying for it's your knee that's all and he moved his hand further along the inside of her thigh. "Your wet," he shouted. "Have you wet yourself?" She was crying properly now. "Go to the restroom and get washed and dry. And you two go away." The manager moved the girl's eat backwards to let her out. The waiter moved out of the way. The girl ran to the toilet and as the manager moved back Alan sat down on the other side of the table and put his Beretta on the table in front of him. As Dom looked for his two minders he realised that neither of them were there. The manager and the waiter had blocked his view as someone had removed them.

"If you move your hands off the table I will shoot you now." Dom put his hands flat ion the table clearly visible.

"I'm glad you didn't hurt the girl. I did have to seriously think of a way to solve the problem you created for me and I know it sounds like poetic justice but almost exactly the same way I saw you do the same thing here a few years back. And that only happened when you picked here to indulge yourself." Alan knocked twice on the table and George the trainee waiter shot Dom Olise three times with a silenced Walther PPK he had out of eye shot behind his tray.

The manager returned followed by two men dressed as ambulance drivers and carrying a stretcher. They put Dom Olise on the stretcher and carried him out through the kitchen into the rear service yard behind the café. They put him in the ambulance with the other two bodies that Alan had put in there earlier on when the Manager and George were blocking the view.

When Dom Olise was out of the way. Alan knocked on the ladies washroom door. Simone opened it and looked out to check it was Alan.

"How is the child?"

"The child is a nineteen year old woman and she is fine. She is good actress."

"She looks like a twelve year old."

"When she was twelve she probably looked nineteen. When I was nineteen I'd been on the streets three years and looked thirty five. Sometimes I think there is no justice in this world. Can we leave now?"

"Yes you are all finished; go out the back way through the kitchen, the way you came in. There is a car waiting.

You have half hour to curfew should be plenty of time to get home. Thank you both."

The three men in the ambulance had neither wallets nor identity papers. Alan removed their guns and put them in the Citroen that Dom owned. They took the ambulance to the general hospital and parked it at the far end of the car park, leaving the keys inside. Alan then drove the men back to their lodging house. He asked them to mind the guns overnight and take them to Charles on the following morning. He parked the car near to the park and then cut through and was back at Fatima's house just moments before curfew time. George was sitting with Fatima chatting and as usual they had a coffee with Fatima before retiring to bed.

The following day a raid on the railways around Paris specifically aimed at the trains and goods yards had an extra wellington bomber with a fighter escort. The two fighters showed the way and the Wellington using the straight line that formed the leg of the T junction made a very low pass and dropped near two tons of mixed high explosive and incendiary bombs on an isolated detached manor house at the end of the road. The sledge hammer worked and nothing and no one survived.

Colonel Cameron is having his mid-week meeting with Mr. Conway in one of the spare offices at Woolwich.

"Do you remember Your deputy head at boarding school?"

"Yes, Mr Wilkinson, maths teacher, nice man taught me to row with the school club."

"When you were about fifteen, He recommended you for military training to us, He's sort of ex-army but never really left, always scouting for talent, and he thought you had prospects as a leader and officer material. So you became one to watch. Deviously you were almost certainly shepherded discreetly in directions that would test you and to be honest until a short time ago when we sent you to Berlin we were still testing you. Now we don't test but continuously assess and evaluate. You had a degree of autonomy not afforded to most officers of your previous ranks, in fact that there is only one person above you which is me. You have almost carte blanche to do as you please. If it goes wrong there will be no second chance though and the consequences for your career will be devastating.

My possible issue is with Major Lewis and how to explain to Our leader who gets fed information and other titbits that are more politically motivated than are necessary to the cause. I am on too many occasions having to justify procedures because someone is after my budget or my position. There are people who still believe in using the troops as cannon fodder they'll dig trenches at Dover thinking no one will dare to cross the channel but if they do we'll be ready for them. They worry me more than the Germans do they are potentially more dangerous than the enemy.

So, I ask you. Do I risk losing one man or half a company say?"

"Forgive me sir. I was up with you until the last question."

"One person or half a company. The fraction or the numbers are not relevant I won't lose a war losing one person but I could lose a battle with dire consequences if I lost a lot of men because a plane on a planned bombing raid decided to change its target because of a request from a colonel. My job is to help win the war effort, using whatever means I can, or see fit, to make it happen. There are people who believe they were put on this earth to make my job difficult. Welcome to murky world of muddy waters Colonel.

What do I lose if I get rid of Major Lewis?"

"I think if we lost Major Lewis it might be as bad as losing a lot of good men. He wears numerous hats surprisingly well."

"Explain like you need to satisfy my curiosity."

"Heavan knows where to start; He is liked by some, respected by most, feared by many, but he would never be described as popular, that implies a level he is never likely to attain. In many ways he is more unpopular than popular and often as welcome as a dose of anal warts. He isn't a team player and is never likely to be. Solo or him and one or two others, that's why you and I put Sergeant Robinson with him. He will trust and rely on George and

George will do the same and that's the size of team he works in. Two men shared objective same level of ruthlessness and able to totally trust each other. The two together are greater than the sum of the parts that's what makes them as they are. I trust his judgement completely."

"That's high praise for one we originally promoted for purely appearance purposes."

"He's my junior in some ways, but I'd follow him into hell knowing that whatever happened he'd be the one to get us out of the damn place in the end."

"You authorised the bombing of a building just outside Paris."

"Yes at Nanterre."

"Why?"

"Major Lewis believed that we only had one chance of stopping our information supply chain breaking and that was to smash the problem in one go. Escalating as the situation is developing always leaves you in a situation of reacting to a problem as you have allowed it to develop. The longer the problem continues the more likely it is that you will lose as you are continually allowing the enemy in this case, French gangsters with German assistance, to regroup and come back at you with a stronger force. We don't have the where withal to accelerate as required. Therefore, if you wipe out the opposition in one go the problem goes away. If it doesn't go away and you've hit it with the most force you can muster in one go then you need to get out and start again you aren't going to win this one."

"And?"

"The problem has gone, our information supply chain is intact, as is our share in the property and it's business as usual and long may it continue. You advised me to read The Art of War by Master Sun many years ago; I can't say that's why I approved the bombing raid but given the people who were trying to take over our business believed that we were weak hitting them with a pile of bombs from an aeroplane, having executed the gang leader as well, proved the situation to be significantly different even though no one knows how it happened they are no longer even in existence let alone in competition and everyone else will not think about trying the same move."

"What a good answer Colonel, a fine answer. I shall speak to our leader later today and pass on your information. File closed then thank you anything else you want to tell me?"

"Yes sir. We've still got a spy in the camp or more accurately you still have. Someone is passing information to the Germans. We are getting info from them before you are giving it to us."

"Interesting, we found one by feeding junk to him. He is locked away now. So there is another then."

"I don't suppose you have any names?"

"No even our contacts couldn't give us one."

"Ok we'll have to try and winkle that one out as well. In the meantime, careful what you send and to whom and keep the fingers crossed it hasn't gone wrong already. That it?"

"Yes Sir."

"Good well done Carry on."

"Thank you sir.

Cameron saluted about faced and left Mr. Conway in his office.

Long term suspicions about his boarding school and un requested help from teachers now exposed as a form of grooming for benefits other than just his own.

Cameron headed down the corridor past the NCO who jumped up to open the door but not quick enough . "Sit sergeant."

"Sorry sir."

" I doubt anyone will be looking for me if they are I'm in the canteen, having lunch, then back to my office."

"Very good sir."

Chapter 13   GUNS FOR MACQUIS

It was nearing the end of 1943. Alan had a full complement of instructors and even some admin staff. His brief had extended from specialist training to encompass raiding with small teams and working deep behind the lines on a self-sufficient exercise that included living off the land and foraging. The pigeons once upon a time used purely for communication often unsuccessful provide the occasional filling meal along with hare rabbit and any game bird; shooting dates no longer considered applicable or enforceable.

With all these new skills fresh in their minds they were dropped into western Europe with arms and ammunition both for themselves for the partisans and then if they could put a group together create a landing area and the RAF would send in a Lysander with a top up and enough supplies to keep it all running.

Alan and George ran the Paris area having all the contacts and a distribution process organised by Henri and Charles both accepting that although they might not like each other they were on the same side.

Fatima kept the room open for Alan as she had done almost for the whole of the war so far. The income that came via Simone more than sufficient to pay for everything that had occurred between Alan an Charles as well.

They had been coordinating deliveries for the last few weeks it was getting warmer it spring of 1944 they were staying at Fatimas as usual when the message came from Simone.

She needed to see Alan as soon as possible. She was at the bar according to the young girl who delivered the message. Alan grabbed his jacket and let George know where he was going.

"Simone you need to speak to me."

"Justine has been beaten again."

"They came here beat her, shaved her head because someone said she has been associating with the Germans and is a traitor."

"Does Henri know?"

"Yes, he is looking for them."

"Do we know who they are?"

"Yes they are Macquis."

"But Which group?"

"Justine says it was led by a man named Paul Boret."

"I know him I supplied him with weapons not a month back. He fancies being a leader. I suspect he wants to make a name for himself maybe."

"Does Henri know it's him?"

"Yes that's why he's out somewhere now. You know Henri will kill him."

"Seems like a good idea to me."

"People don't realise that you are behind Henri and they will make an attempt at revenge if he does kill them."

"Put the word out and get Henri to contact me."

"Thank you."

"How is Justine?"

"Sore and nearly bald. They were rough when they shaved her head and the worst part was they laughed as they did it. They locked me in the backroom but I could hear them."

"How many were there?"

"Six including Boret."

"Six men to beat one woman."

Alan returned to his room at Fatima's.

"George we're going out matey."

"What do I need?"

"Your pistol, spare mag, both fully loaded, a killing knife and a couple of grenades."

"In a bag or on my person."

"We'll be on the motor bikes so put a big coat on and stuff your pockets."

"What's the job?"

Remember last month we dropped a load of guns off with a guy by the name of Paul Boret?"

"Creepy little backstud, talked like he was going to save France."

"That's the one well so far he' and five mates have managed to beat up one of my lady employees."

"And we are going to exact payment ?"

"That's about it."

"Am I on crowd control then?"

"Yes whatever you need to do. I am going to make certain that no one decides they can hurt my people. I would have thought the last lesson should have taught them that but some will never learn so maybe lessons in meritorious violence might get the message home."

Fatima made them a coffee each, then let them out of the kitchen into the shed, where Alan kept the motor bikes. He topped up both with petrol and pushed them down the garden path and into the road at the back of the house.

"It's about thirty minutes or so I would think. Ready?"

"Lead on McDuff?"

George tucked in behind Alan and they headed off towards the outskirts of Paris. They took the road that leads to Marcel's place but about halfway along that road they took a right hand turn and headed up towards some low hills. A couple of miles up hill and it plateaued out and though only slightly higher the wind blew freer up at this level with nothing to protect you from the chill effect. Paul Boret had a cottage off to the left with a lengthy winding drive to it. What Alan found a bit disconcerting was seeing Henri's car in front of the house. When he got to the cottage there was no one in the car. Where was everyone? he was asking himself when the front door opened and out came a man shot gun crooked over his arm looking to stop anyone from entering.

"Who are you?" he asked.

"I'm a friend of Henri's and I thought this was Henri Murcia's car thought I'd stop and see him."

"He isn't seeing anyone, he's doing business."

"Oh I'm certain he'll want to see me." Alan said as he crossed in front of George who then when unseen by the man with the shot gun., drew his pistol and shot him in the chest.

Alan was going through the front door pistol in hand and heading for the main room. He remembered the layout of the house. There was a small hall with a door at the far wend which opened into a large living room with a kitchen on the back end.

The living room was empty and as Alan was on his way across towards the back of the cottage, past the staircase to the upstairs, when the kitchen door opened and another man and another shotgun came through. He lasted as long as the first one then Alan heard shots coming from the kitchen. He smashed down the door and into the room. He took in everything in one sweep of the room.

 Henri was nearly naked on the kitchen table gagged someone had been cutting him up a bit. Boret was standing at the window aiming his pistol outside. Alan assumed his target was George. Two shots in the back of his head and one for luck in the backway to his heart.

George came through the kitchen door.

"Alright?" Alan asked

"Ther's another dead out the back."

Alan took the gag out of Henri's mouth. George started undoing the ropes. Tying him to the table.

"How many were there Henri?

"Six of them Alan. How many you done for?"

"Two each that right George? When were the others here?"

"Only a couple of minutes ago. They went into the living room."

"They couldn't have gone out of the front door we'd have seen them going down the drive."

"Staircase. They have to be upstairs. Finish untying Henri George, I'll invite them down." Alan went back into the living room. He stood out of direct line to the upper floor.

"Come down and I won't shoot you."

"You're lying."

"If I have to come up I will shoot you."

"Then come on and get us."

"George."

"Yes"

"Is Henri ready to go?"

"Nearly."

"As soon as he's ready tell me."

"What do you want ?"

"A gallon of petrol and two grenades. I'll burn them to death. Drag the other two bodies in I thought these two might be able to pass on the message not to mess about with us maybe we need to find a medium and the other idiots can have a séance with six in the afterlife."

"Do you promise not to kill us."

"I do."

"What about the other man and Henri?"

"Can't speak for Henri. Did you do any of the cutting on him."

"No we got away the others did it we weren't involved."

"Henri do you hear that."

"I did."

"And."

"Blow them up and burn them out."

"Sorry boys." That's when they ran down stairs firing their shotguns. Alan shot the two of them as they were trying to reload.

George and Henri came in from the kitchen.

"You know what bothers me George is we supply these people with guns and how useless they are. Six of them properly armed and they're all done for. Henri you do look a lot better with your clothes on." Henri started laughing, the laugh of a man who knew he was nearly about to die.

"Can you drive?" Alan asked him.

"I think so my friend." Then he grabbed Alan in a bear hug kissed him on both cheeks and hugged him so hard Alan thought any harder or longer he might feint.

"Alan, George, thankyou is not enough."

"It'll do for now let's get going. It will be curfew soon we need to get back before then."

Alan enlisted Charles to assist in putting out the information that Henri was telling to pass around too. Any more damage to our people and the next deaths will be slower and a lot more painful.

On the 6th of June 1944 most of everything changed again.

Chapter 13   Hamburg 1945

Cameron landed at Orly airport on a RAF transport plane where Alan was waiting for him. "Good to see you Alan."

"And I you sir. Hearty congratulations too sir on your promotion."

The message had been clear and simple. 'Meet me at Orly 07.00 ready to travel, away indefinite time. Brigadier Cameron.'

"Sorry to get you out this early but we've got a little job in Hamburg from our very good friend Mr. Conway. It's possibly nothing but you never know. These chaps are dropping some people off here and picking you and a few others up and then we're off again."

"Goes with the territory sir."

"I don't have anyone else and I don't actually have anything else but at least it'll keep us busy for a short while. Your part is to sniff around and find anything that doesn't smell right. I am going to be working on the admin side trying to glean any info via the other people up there."

"What's my brief sir?"

"In one sentence apprehend escaping war criminals."

"That sounds like a job for someone else."

"It may well be but till something more your style comes up and we both know it'll come up normally when we don't want it too. At least you'll be employed and get paid. People are being sent home now, no longer needed, admin are moving in, the lawyers, the engineers, and the trades people. Mr. Conway is keeping our department open at the moment but he tells me it might not last much longer with the change of government this summer. If we're not careful we'll have won the war again but lose the peace."

"Are we getting that close to a finish?"

"We are not quite redundant yet but it's when not if; in the meantime though we need to keep an eye on the Russians especially, but personally I don't trust anyone. As we've always said the Americans prefer to fight wars in other countries, the French will be looking for reparations, and it maybe they'll be competing with us for the valuables. The Germans haven't even paid for the money from the first war yet so it's anyone's guess as to who's going to claim what and from whom.

So what I need you to do is set something up on the base in Hamburg. Charlie Jordan is CO on one there; he'll give you what help you need and fill you in on what's going on. I'll get George there with you just in case you need some back up but I don't think anything is likely to cause you any problems. Where is he by the way?"

He's training a group of junior officers on a climbing course in the Alps. That course finishes a week on Friday."

"So he'll be more than a few days behind you. He'll definitely be with you by Monday week so try and stay out of trouble till he gets there.

They'd walked back and boarded the RAF flight which took off again. They landed on a military airfield in northern Germany where they parked up for the rest of the day. The following morning Cameron arrived at the officers mess where Alan was eating breakfast.

"I'm staying here for a couple of days getting filled in on who's who in the hierarchy up here. I'll get a lift for you organised how long do you need to be ready to go?"

"Ten minutes I didn't unpack anything."

"Good, there 'll be a vehicle of some description to take you to the camp within the hour. I'll have the orders for you with the driver and I'll give Charlie a call let him know you're on the way and to leave you in peace to get on with your job. He's a good man he won't bother you. Try not to hurt anyone please Alan. It's all changing now and we need to be seen to following the rules. Just over an hour and Alan is thinking he should have got some more to drink when a three tonner arrives near the billet.

A pretty Wac climbs down from the driver's seat. "Major Lewis sir?"

"Tis I." Alan replied.

"Brigadier Cameron said you'd be waiting; paperwork took longer to type; he extends his apologies and wishes you bon voyage.

It'll take most of the rest of the day to get there. If you will get yourself comfortable we'll get going when you are ready."

"Are we stopping en route?"

"Only to take on fluid or to dispose of the same sir."

"It's a big truck for a trip up the road."

"I have vehicle spares for our transport depot so just the one drop same place I'm to drop you off sir. It's my regular run so I know the times and the stopping places for a drink and a bite."

The girl could drive. Alan took off his cap put on a woolly hat and with a blanket wrapped around himself went to sleep.

A long way down the road they joined a queue to get through a road block; creeping forward one vehicle at a time.

Alan awoke. "Is this usual?" he asked.

"It's not unusual, but it is taking longer than normal."

" Hello pretty lady," said the guard at the barrier. "Now if we'd known you were coming through, we 'd have invited you up to the front, quick search in the office and you could have been on your ages ago."

Alan peered out from his blanket. "Tell that man if he doesn't shut up and lift the barrier I'll get out and batter him."

There was no need for the WAC to repeat it. Alan had said it loud enough . for him to hear. Like a red rag to a bull the corporal came round the other side of the 3 tonner and yanked open the door.

He was met by a pistol barrel ready to go and the sight of Major's crown on the shoulder just behind the Beretta and an unshaven irritated man who seemed perfectly happy to shoot him.

"I'm sorry sir."

"Before I spoil your day completely corporal get that barrier up. And, corporal, if this ever happens again, especially to any of the female drivers, I will come back and shoot you."

"Yes sir I'm sorry sir."

"Don't slam the door. And get a bloody move on man." Alan switched on the safety, returned the Beretta to its holster and went back to sleep.

The WAC looked at what appeared to be a bundle of rags, with his two boots jammed into the footwell to stop him falling off the seat, and decided there and then, if there was ever a chance in future to be promoted to an army major, she would grab it with both hands.

They gave Alan an office and a corporal clerk to do any necessary paperwork. Report after report after report was all he did, nothing but read and comment. Alan figured the C O had shifted all the reading assignment from his desk to Alan's. Mostly it was intelligence reports and ideas about escape routes information, and just about every possible piece of useless information as well.

Having never spent more than a day at a desk in the last ten years, Charlie, the CO thought Alan might be glad of a rest time, do some paperwork, that'll give me a chance to disappear for a couple of days myself. Brigadier Cameron who was in charge of Major Lewis would soon be around as well.

Paperwork and Alan were not an ideal relationship and all he felt was tired and segs developing in places he didn't want. Three days of reading tea drinking and he was ready to climb walls or fight someone. The corporal had been given advice not to irritate him. The WAC driver had let it be known that he could be a very angry man when annoyed and apart from delivering tea and sandwiches and emptying the ash tray and the waste paper basket he sensibly stayed out of his way.

Wednesday morning just as Alan was about to drink his mid-morning tea he saw a young lady coming through the door into the outer office. The lady was young but the clothes looked older than her. The top coat and hat probable hand downs from an aunt or mother contribution, almost like she was in the school play. His office door wasn't quite shut and he could hear the conversation with the clerk in the outer office.

"I'm sorry Fraulein I cannot pay you. Only the colonel can do that."

"The payment is way overdue. We have bills to pay too."

"I don't dispute that Fraulein but I cannot make a payment even on account, only the colonel can do that as well."

Alan got a small case of nose disease and decided to enquire. "Tell me corporal what is going on?"

"This young lady's father is our coal merchant sir and they want us to pay the bill."

"Is it due?"

"Yes sir has been for a while. Colonel seems to keep missing it out of the must be paid file."

"Are we burning the coal from this merchant in these potbelly stoves and that's what keeps the place warm?"

"Yes sir."

"Then pay the account corporal. Any problems refer the colonel to me. If I have any problems he can deal with the Brigadier."

"Yes sir."

"Right out my order to you corporal and I'll sign it. I think I may have finally done something useful here."

The young lady looked at Alan, like she wanted to remember him. "Thank you major I am extremely grateful."

"Your welcome Fraulein. If you will excuse me I shall return to my tea."

That Monday afternoon George arrived with an envelope from Mr. Conway which he had to deliver to the Brigadier on arrival. Alan had acquire d a jeep and having got a message form the Ops room headed out to the train station to pick him up.

"I've been here only a few days George and to be honest if they said you're no longer needed thank you very much goodbye I don't think I could shed even a small tear.

"That bad?"

"Unfortunately yes. Perhaps there is some better news in the Brigadier's mail for us."

Cameron had managed to acquire an office at the Hamburg Zoo and almost immediately regretted it.

"Welcome gentlemen. I'm glad you're here George somebody has to keep our companion under control."

Alan gave the 'who me look' Cameron but said nothing.

"I had Charlie on the blower apparently you paid a bill that he was hanging on to till the end of the month."

"I did sir."

"Well don't worry about it . I told Charlie it was his own fault for buggering off and leaving you in charge. I doubt you'll hear any more about it. Now let me see what George has for me and after we've had some tea I'll tell you what 's happening as far as I know."

"Our boss, Mr. Conway, says pretty much what he told me last time I spoke to him. I'm in here as a liaison officer. I have a typical brief, open ended, no budget, look like you're doing something, see what stinks, report back to me. Your brief Alan and now you George is as I said a few days ago arrest any war criminals."

"No chance unless they come into the office and surrender."

"Well Charlie's back on the paperwork. You have no need to have it dumped on you again. Avoid Charlie for a short while, he will be smarting.

Mr. Conway is trying to keep his team together. He's sending some of the instructors over from Salisbury to give you a hand, basically trying to get the unfinished work completed. They've shut down Stirling's mob, one wonders how stupid and short sighted that might be.

Anyway back to our job. Around the docks basically and we did the same thing just over six years ago. It is to start with a snooping exercise. It's going to take more than ten minutes so get George a bed somewhere and another seat in your office and do what we did a lot of times in the last ten years . Good luck is all I can say. Now let's have some tea, the coffee is not that good."

The first thing that Alan spotted was an empty American jeep, parked up on the left hand side. Most of the houses were no longer buildings but piles of rubble. There was neither a window nor a roof in sight. The British and American Airforce's had demolished just about everything this close to the docks.

Further along the road he spotted the soldier standing just inside the wall of another pile of rubble. As he passed he noticed the old lady's coat and hat he saw the other day on the young German girl. He didn't slam on not certain what was happening or if it had anything to do with him. But when he got to the junction at the crest of the hill he did a 'U' turn and headed back down.

He stopped on the other side of the road and watched . The soldier he had assumed was American looked to be wearing a Russian uniform, which gave him enough reason to get out and investigate.

As he crossed to the other side the man turned his head and spoke to him. He is Russian thought Alan but what did he say?

Alan spoke to him in German "I don't speak Russian," he told him. what did you say. The Russian spoke again. Alan went to English, "I don't understand. Do you speak English?"

The Russian answered again in Russian.

The girl said. "He said you go second Englander; he's first, stand in line."

He made a move then towards the girl. Alan said to the girl "Tell him to look behind him. And as she did so the Russian went for a pistol inside his tunic.

"Not on my shift Ivan." Alan said as he was turning. He took one in the head and two in the heart and just became another casualty of war. Alan took the pistol from the Russian's hand, Webley British Army issue and put it inside his tunic.

"What are you doing here?" Alan asked

"I wait for my brother in case he comes back."

"I am none the wiser."

"My brother went to Russia in late forty one. We have never heard from him again. This is where we used to live before we were bombed out. We had another apartment not far from here that we used to let Grandmother have and we moved back in with her which is where I live now with my parents. And then later I was evacuated to the mountains."

"Come I'll take you home."

"What about him?" she asked.

"Do you want to take him home too?"

"No I didn't mean that."

"Don't worry about him he's dead. Come on let's go, it's too cold to stand around talking."

"I can walk it's not far."

"And if the Russians arrive before you get home."

"Okay."

"How good is your Russian?"

"I studied languages at school. I speak German obviously, English, Russian, French, and some bits of others. We learnt Russian in case they got here before any of the Allies. You just saw what they're like with us."

Do you want a job?"

Doing what ?"
"Teaching basic Russian and translating any bookwork that we might need a hand with especially if it's in Russian. I assume you read Russian?"

"Yes."

Alan stopped at the American Jeep. On the passenger seat was a Sten gun and wrapped in a white paper bag a loaf of black bread. Alan took the Sten gun the girl opened the bread wrapper, smelt the bread rewrapped it and put it in her pocket.

"I'll drop you at home now and pick you up at eight tomorrow morning."

"I have to ask my parents if it's ok."

"How old are you?"

"Twenty two."

"No you are not how old are you?"

"Seventeen, why did you not believe me?"

"Because you have to ask your parents."

"In my house the boy could do as he pleased when it suited him. I will have to ask my father for permission until I am married and if that's when I'm thirty then that will be the way."

"I'll still take you home and pick you up tomorrow morning. If you don't come to the jeep I will accept the answer is no."

Alan turned the jeep around and drove about half a mile.

"Pull up here, please. Our flat is on the first floor above the café."

"My name is Alan what's yours?"

"Katarina Kohler. I hope I see you tomorrow thank you for today." She slipped easily out of the jeep and quickly crossed the road. She looked back from the entrance, waved, then went inside.

Alan and George were studying a map showing the streets around Hamburg docks when the Brigadier arrived.

"Alan apparently a Russian soldier was murdered by a person that was a major that looked exactly like you. A senior Russian officer approached me today at our daily get together. Any knowledge about this?"

"No sir. But I do know of a Russian soldier carrying a British Sten gun and a Webley pistol just about to be pointed at me, having arrived in an American jeep, who was about to attack and rape one of my staff and was adamant that was what he was going to do. If the officer who requested the information finds his behavior acceptable tell him that I will come and shoot him too."

"Is she one of your staff?"

"Yes she is my interpreter, and she is teaching basic Russian to the people in our section until we can get a full time fully qualified teacher. She is doing what we got Almira to do a while back with basic understanding a vocabulary and pronunciation. She is currently preparing a series of lessons in the outer office. Would you like to meet her?"

"Not necessary at this time no doubt I will be enlisting her help shortly and as you are also taking care of my staff too, I shall relay a message to him tomorrow. I may alter yours slightly, unless he becomes difficult, in which case he'll get it verbatim; So, leave it with me for now.

After Cameron had left Alan introduced George to Katarina. "One of us will pick you up and take you home. Only go with one of us unless we tell you differently."

"OK."

They left her getting on with a teaching plan while they went back towards the docks.

"What are we looking for Alan?"

"A brothel."

There's more her than Paris. Well, there's none in Paris now De Gaulle closed them. Someone suggested it was because he was a do it yourselfer or words to that effect."

When we here just before war broke out we met a lady who actually told us about the ship we managed to escape on. Her name was Elke, and I promised if I ever got back I would visit her again. I hasten to add this will be a non-contact social call to see if she has any information that might help us in our search. The problem is that last time I was here all of these piles of rubble were buildings with street names and people about you could ask. I don't even know which part we left from as she was only a short distance from the quay where the ship was.

"You don't recognise anything then?"

"No, it's all different and the other problem is we were dropped somewhere by a taxi then we walked. There were streets and houses, and it was dark as well. I could be at the right place, and I wouldn't know. What we need is a working girl who might know where we might find her."

"We could work from the docks outwards."

Alan headed the jeep down towards the water side and suddenly realised exactly where he was he was on the same place they'd got the Alabaster from. He turned the jeep around back to where he knew the street was where he had met Elke, Like everywhere else it was another bombed out building, nothing left but broken bricks and concrete; the windows and doors burnt for warmth and cooking a long time back.

"Dead end again. We may as well head back nearly time to take Katarina home. Drop me off and you take Katarina home. Take directions from her it's not far nor complicated, and a lot easier in the daylight."

The Brigadier arrived just after lunch.

"I have done a deal with the Russians. He's to be buried here and being hailed at home as a hero of the country shot while trying to keep the peace and I have organised another job for you back in England.

"Pardon."

Two reasons the Russian accepted the explanation too easily no concessions no problems. The first reason is, I now believe they will try and shoot you to prove a point. The second reason is that there has been some intelligence that says that there has been some traffic out of here and Denmark over towards Greenland. Go and have a look and see what you can find out. The RAF have seen small boats in and out of the islands North of Scotland most of which are owned and run by the Danes.

Mr. Conway is completely au fait with what is happening here and it's his suggestion as to how we proceed. He is effectively bringing you home. His words not mine. On the way home you are to go to Paris, which can be made to fit in nicely with proposed travel plans and sell your share of the bar.

 The embassy will do the paperwork again. The money you get for it is to be deposited back in the government's coffers no one is to know about the sale or the original purchase. The embassy will handle the money via the lawyers."

"Is Mr. Conway aware that De Gaulle closed all the brothels which is how the money was made. The bar is possibly not worth a lot especially if Henri is having to buy it back."

Speak to Henri then the Embassy then Mr. Conway. It will happen the same as when we bought it because enough people wanted to do a deal the same will apply. Henri won't want anyone else in there.

George can manage things here with me it doesn't need all three of us and It'll fit nicely for you I need someone who knows about boats, and you're the only one I have. I know you did bits with your dad and a lot more since and you did the stuff on the Danish boat out of here six years back. And you'll be back at home in Birkenhead. It's non-negotiable Alan it comes down from the one above me. In theory the war is over and the likes of us now are surplus to requirement and to some of them we're nothing more than an embarrassment. They're the ones with a chest full of medals when their arses have spent the whole of the war behind a desk in London."

"Very good sir When do I go?"

"ASAP and to be truthful I wish I was going with you. Diplomacy is starting to irk me. You're entitled to some leave you may as well take it at home in Britain. Just book yourself in and out at Woolwich and Alan please stay out of trouble. Enjoy your leave. Your orders will be at Woolwich."

"When?"

"Why what are you thinking?"

"How much leave can I have?"

"Keep talking tell me what you're thinking."

"The Germans have exited, and De Gaulle has been back a year, it's all gone quiet. I want to go to Marseille, then Paris, then Woolwich."

"If I gave you two weeks would that work for you?"

"I think a week to ten days depending on travel times."

"We do still have this job to do. Don't let it take more than it needs to and if you can get it done earlier even better."

"Will do I'll keep you posted. Now all you have to do is get me to the South of France."

In the end it had been a long day Alan was tired but his mind was hammering along out of control. He had left Katarina working in her office. If she worked late she could share a bunkroom with the other girls. He had told both George and Katarina that he was being transferred and as of tomorrow morning it would be George picking her up unless either George or the Brigadier found another minder for her.

The peace process was providing too much deviousness and intrigue. Never quite certain where or who was the enemy now. He had shared the bar with two newly commissioned lieutenants, who had left the bar slightly the worse for wear.

Hopefully, they would be capable tomorrow morning. Charlie Jordan wasn't going to be too pleased, if they couldn't function on day one. Alan was working his way through the remainder of the bottle of scotch. Not normally a keen drinker but he'd got irritated by politics and diplomacy, which was never his forte and he was uninterested in partaking of the black art, perhaps going home via Marseille and Paris might be a good thing to clear the taste he was finding here. The bar had emptied mostly when two more late arrivals appeared. Alan had had enough he beckoned one over. And gave him the remains of the bottle of scotch.

Wished them goodnight bid farewell to the steward and headed for his bed.

His room was small but it was his alone. The single bed against one wall a small mat covering nearly all the floor with the added luxury of cleaning his teeth and running water was something not to be missed; a wet flannel and a stand up wash left him feeling cleaner than he was used to, but something he was getting to enjoy again. The sheets were fresh and clean cotton cold a little stiff the army issue blankets heavy on his naked body. Soon he would be warm and sleep would follow.

He lay in the darkness still wide awake unable to clear the thoughts from his head. He came instantly alert the second the handle turned on his door. The light outside in the passageway told him that the intruder was Katarina. The door closed and she was inside. The sound of a zipper and smell of perfume was enough to dispel any fear and seconds after the entrance the young nubile body slipped between the sheets. She had removed her outer clothes and her pants, her hand groped between his legs it didn't take long and he was ready.

"I waited for you," she whispered. "I want to thank you for helping me and not expecting anything. For that I will give you everything I can."

As she kissed him she rolled her body over the top of him and slid her body over him taking what he had riding him slowly and seductively. Her tongue searched through his mouth saliva dripped Alan remembered her age realised it was so wrong. Eisenhour had sent out a pamphlet about fraternisation but it had been so long since anyone had shown him any affection he was lost in the heady smell of her perfume and the seductive writhing on his body. She maybe was only seventeen but she knew more about love, passion, and the seductive sex of a female, than he did, so he did all he could do and live for that one wild passionate moment, which was all too soon in its arrival.

Her body squeezed and milked him dry and sometime in the night whilst he slept she slipped quietly away. For the first time in a long time guilty as he was, headache gone, he slept the sleep of the innocent.

Alan got himself a screwdriver from a local junk shop. He got a train from Hamburg to Berlin then managed to get on an RAF flight to Paris. He called on Charles and Henri and then got a train to Marseille. The lady where he stayed recognised him but was not happy to see him, until he told her that he didn't want any money back and he would give her some more if she would let him retrieve some tools he had to leave when he was here.

"There are no tools in the room Monsieur. The room is occupied at the moment by some other men, it was cleaned a long time ago and nothing was found."

"Good then they might still be there. Are the people in at the moment?"

"No. they are all out."

"Then will you let me into the room so I can get my tools if they are still there. If they are I will give you five US dollars."

"OK."

They went upstairs and the landlady having confirmed non one was in the room let him in. He rolled up the carpet removed the floorboards and took out one small wooden box and two long narrow ones . He screwed the floorboard back, unrolled the rug, thanked the lady, gave her five US dollars, and headed for the train station and back to Paris. The return journey was almost as disrupted as the one from Paris and when he finally got back to Paris he had been travelling for over 36 hours. Bed beckoned and Fatima found him somewhere to sleep.

Chapter 14

The Brigadier had told him that Mr. Conway had developed a habit of arriving unannounced and he did it just after two pm. He was as usual accompanied by the twins . The war was over his driver now chauffeuring another senior civil servant perhaps. Alan spotted them as they arrived. One twin driving one doing the door opening and the minding. Alan had just finished his phone call. One single bang on the office door and Mr. Conway walked in. The door was closed behind him. The routine rehearsed a thousand times.

"Good afternoon Lewis."

"Good afternoon sir."

"Sit down. I will talk for a while." Alan did as asked and Conway took his seat at Camerons desk. "I hear that you are still fighting the war Lewis. You started it early and now you're extending it. You are right by the way. It's a long way from being finished. Having won the war we will now set about losing the peace. I can almost guarantee that we will be worse off as victors than if we were the vanquished. Colleagues call me an old cynic. Other apparently old cynics call me a man with sixty years' experience. History will tell but no one will realise or learn from it.

I'm going to give you and Brigadier Cameron some advice and some more clout. You both have about a year and this new government will dispense with your services and you will go on the scrap heap as will a lot of good men. At some stage in the future they will regret it but they will have cut the umbilical cord and thrown out what I always thought of as my baby. Between us all we trained a lot of good men. We didn't win the war on our own but we did play our part to the best of our abilities.

I'm sending you up to Scotland. Your orders are in this envelope here. You might get a year out of it especially out of reach of the politicians, civil servants and senior officers on a pruning mission.

For what you have done for the last ten years you have never been given medals or any awards other than promotions, whatsoever. There are officers who never left the comfort of their office chair unlike you and

Cameron have and they'll be the one's who'll want to get rid of you.

I may last another year too but they will consider that I am too pally with the previous management, and that my departure though not immanent, is on the cards. They will give me a knighthood, probably, a token, doesn't cost a lot, and it might keep my mouth shut. Official secrets act of course does that. It would save them a knighthood, but I'll take it you never know, it might prove useful, if only for invitations to dinner.

 Now some advice. If you both get together I'm going to suggest a business venture. There are a lot of good men who will be on the scrap pile with you both. You trained them you know who they are. Some will be happy to do close protection ,maybe some foreign government work, maybe even some British government work. Get a base get yourselves some business cards and some letterhead. I will improve them from now, as I have already made Cameron a Brigadier I will make you a lieutenant Colonel.

Work might not roll in to start with, but it will build. Sometime after I've been chucked out someone will remember what I used to do and will ask me for some security advice and maybe a company to do some work for them. War is a big business, if you are careful and survive, your talents will always be on demand. You have been very quiet Lewis so I presume you are taking all this in?"

"I am indeed sir and thank you again for my promotion. Up until now sir I hadn't considered what I was going to do after this. I.ve been army since I was eighteen I'm thirty seven. I've been in it over half my life."

"Well it's not finished yet. Before you go anywhere you have to go back to Paris. I believe the brigadier will have already told you but I shall do so again. There is the ownership of a bar and brothel to consider. I'm certain the press and others would love to find that we were supplementing our war effort with the proceeds from a Parisian brothel which was providing us with a place of refuge a staging post and a source of extremely dodgy information gathering."

"It's not something I've ever been happy with sir."

"Neither have I Lewis. But I'll tell you now the critics will be the same people who were happy to condone the brutal torture to extract often worthless pieces of information from poor unfortunate prisoners in a dirty dark underground hovel. I can't justify any of it but I can say that you took care of your people and they're all alive. Just remember it that way."

"Thank you sir."

"General de Gaul for whatever reason has shut every brothel in France. This is useful as the bottom, if you will excuse the unintended pun, has fallen out of the market you can sell it cheap and we are out of it. We know it's in your name and in theory the government is in the clear but gone completely is best. The embassy is open let them do the paperwork. If there are any complaints they can take it up with the French government and then explain to them why Britain was operating a brothel. No one will want to go down that path. You may, if you are devious enough, even make a profit. If you do I suggest you keep it. I will not be checking the accounts."

"Yes sir."

"It may be the last time. Any questions?"

"No sir."

Mr. Conway did something that he had only done once before some ten years back. He shook Alan's hand. Then he left in his usual hurry.

Lieutenant colonels can get flights a lot easier than other ranks and the RAF were happy enough to drop him off at Orly airport the day after he spoke to Mr. Conway.

He took a taxi to see Charles. "Monsieur Alain how are you?"

"Alive and well Charles and you?"

"Likewise I am pleased to say. It is good to see you I'm glad we are here to say that to each other. Now what can I do for you?"

"I think Charles that we have come to the end of our business relationship and I have been instructed by my superiors to shut up shop here in Paris"

"All good things will come to an end one day sir and if it is today then so be it. Come into my office and see your account.

Alan followed Charles into his tiny little cubby hole of an office.

He took out a large hard backed thick book and opened the book somewhere near the middle.

"During the seven years we have been minding your account apart from payments to us for services rendered and Fatima for food and accommodation you have not taken any money from your account. If I said to you there was a significant balance it would be an understatement. My only question is how do you want me to pay the money to you?"

"A cheque will be fine thank you."

"Perfect I can right one for you now." Charles wrote the cheque passed it to Alan shook his hand.

When you are here again come and have a meal it will be nice to see you. In case the question was in your head; Almira is in Morocco. Brahim is alive but not as active as he used to be and Almira now runs everything from there. Almira's brother was killed they believe over drugs and trafficking by persons unknown. I wish you well Monsieur Alain you will always be welcome here."

"Thank you Charles now I must go and see Henri."

Alan took a gentle amble over to Henri's bar, not knowing if he would be there or not. The bar was open a young man behind the bar serving if there had been a customer. His face lit up when Alan came through the door.

"Yes monsieur what can I serve you?"

"Is Henri about?"

"No monsieur."

"Where is he?"

"I don't know monsieur."

"Well phone him and tell him there's a man who wants to sell him some shares in a business that in the right hands could do well for him."

"I'm not certain I have a number for him."

"I can give you the number if you can't find it. It used to be written on the pad behind the bar." The young man made the phone call. "He said he would be ten minutes and you better not be messing him about."

"Not a lot's changed then."

It was a quarter of an hour when Henri almost burst through the door to the bar. The bar man pointed down the room to Alan sitting in the seat he'd sat in seven years back.

"Jean go into the back and bring me the best bottle of wine we have."

"Red or White Henri?"

"White there isn't a red good enough; and our very best white will still not be good enough for this man."

"Alain my friend it is so good to see you. We have survived and you look well." Alan had stood and Henri hugged him and kissed his cheek. Jean had never seen Henri like this before. He made certain the glasses were polished clean before bringing them with the bottle to the table.

"You are looking well too Henri. How is Marcel Simone and Justine all still alive I hope."

"They are all okay. How come you are here?"

"I have been told to sell my share in the business, and I want to see if you want to buy it back again or if I should sell it to someone else."

"Alain you would not do this to me after all we have been through together.

"Make me an offer."

"Let us drink some fine wine first."

"No we have been here before. Make me an offer."

Business is slow my friend; it is a struggle, everywhere is closed and no one is buying anything."

"Business is not that bad I have seen Charles and I know what Somone has been taking to him every month."

"That would explain why my money is down she is overpaying you."

"She pays in what you give her Henri. Now make me an offer.

I'll help you Henri pay me what I paid for it originally." That got Henri thinking.

"Seriously?"

"Yes but you will have to do me a favour."

"What is it?"

"Collect and hold all the weapons we have distributed that you can safely get your hands on and keep them for me until I need them."

Henri offered his hand Alan shook it.

"We have a deal now I will try some of your wine."

"How do I pay you?"

"I will get someone from the embassy to come and speak to you. You will pay them. Any problems you contact me. I don't know where I'll be but I will sort it out for us."

"You have always been good at that." They touched glasses. "Sante."

"Cheers."

CHAPTER 15 Scotland.

They had got a boat for Alan. An ex-Royal Navy MFV. The phone call from the Admiralty told him it was waiting for him at Lerwick in the Shetland Isles. It had been decommissioned a couple of years back but there was a group of mechanics checking it over and it would be ready for him when he got there. They would send a sailing crew to manage it for him and take him wherever he wanted to go.

Alan got the RAF to fly him up there from Woolwich and then a water taxi took him up to Lerwick form the airfield at RAF Sumburgh at the southern end of the island.

Waiting on board for him was a lieutenant, a petty officer, and two ratings.

The introductions were made, Alan told them where he wanted to go and showed them an old map with a grid reference.

"It's a bit like treasure island sir." The lieutenant suggested.

"The island is small even by the standards set by all the others up here. The RAF tell me if we're going too fast we might miss it in a light mist. It's not even marked on most maps though there is a reference on this old admiralty chart. Its ownership has been in dispute for years. Its nearest neighbour is the Faroes. It's currently administered by Denmark, which is no surprise, as it has been for as long as anyone can remember and most of the population are Scots or of Scottish decent. It has at least three different names depending on where your allegiance lies. The locals call it Lysternoy."

"We shall try not to miss it sir."

"That'll please me no end lieutenant . What sort of range do we have on this boat?"

"Ten days two thousand miles, roughly sir."

"More than enough then."

"Yes sir and as long as you don't want to chase anything; She isn't very quick just functional."

"Hopefully she'll do what we need this trip."

"She'll do that sir and probably loaded to the gunwhales with fish. She's got plenty of power just a bit slow."

It took a couple of days to get there. The lieutenant was right fast and this boat would never go together. But they got there and Alan watched as the crew manoeuvred the MFV close into the stone sided harbour wall. They were in a big, sheltered bay not completely enclosed plenty of sea room to get in and out but a very sheltered anchorage almost completely surrounded by high hills and solid cliffs keeping the wind out inless it came from the south east then the thought was that it could be quite entertaining in here if there was a big blow.

There was another fishing boat tide up in front of them. There were some steel ladders hanging down from the top of the quayside and Alan decided they looked ok and as the boat bobbed high on the wave he stepped off the deck side and onto the ladder. When he got onto the quayside the ratings followed up with for and aft lines . Alan headed upwards to make contact with the lady, wrapped in a plaid, who was standing at the top of the slope, looking down at the navy boys making good the lines.

"Good afternoon sir. I am Mrs. Rosemary Cuthbertson. I am the harbour master. Who are you?"

"Good afternoon mam , my name is Alan Lewis and I am here for a short while with your permission and I have four other men on the MFV with me."

"I think you look like a Royal Navy boat; they are all dressed the same in almost standard civvy type uniform."

"You would be correct mam."

"You are very polite you address me as mam. How should I address you?"

"My name is Alan. Alan is fine by me."

"Well then Alan first off you must come into my house where I have a desk and fill in the visitors forms. I get the feeling soon it will rain. Will you be staying long?"

"That will depend on the answers to my questions mam but I don't think that we'll be here more than twenty four hours."

"My assumption then is that your visit is official."

"Yes a sort of speculatively official; a bit of a stab in the dark, see if anyone knows anything."

Alan followed Mrs Cuthbertson up the steps at the top of the slope to her cottage. From the front door she could see the whole of the bay in front of her and out to sea. From a harbour master point of view it was ideal. The door of course wasn't locked and was only on a Suffolk latch. "When the wind blows from the wrong way I have bolts to keep it shut from the inside and if I'm out I can tie the handle to the steel post. It's worked for the thirty years I've been here."

"I like the idea of keeping things simple. If it ain't broken don't fix it."

"Come inside. I will make some tea. Will you join me?"

"That would be welcome thank you."

"I shall put the kettle on. The form is on the desk there, and while your filling it in ask the questions you need an answer to."

Alan started to read the form. He looked outside through the metal framed window that provided light to the desk. There was a steady drizzle. "Does it always rain here Mam?"

"Of course not. Sometimes it snows. If you want milk and sugar I have condensed milk or goats milk."

"Just a teaspoon of connie onnie please.

Of all the people here I believe you will be the one to ask.

Are you aware of any unusual movement of boats or small ships about here or have you had any foreign visitors? It's my shot in the dark question."

"We get quite a few boats passing through. The harbour as I said is well known to the fishermen form Scotland Scandinavia Iceland. The island is of course owned and administered by Denmark even though most oof us are of Scottish descent.

Denmark doesn't cause us any problems and nothing other than fishing and some distilling for personal use goes on."

"So what does everyone do for a living?"

"Fishing and fishing and more fishing. There is nothing else to do from here. And there's not many of us doing it. We have some sheep and goats which one of the men here will butcher when we need more meat."

"Do you ever get anything that might be considered as unusual?"

"What do you mean by unusual?"

"Anything out of the ordinary. Foreign boats even fishing boats with too big a crew say, something you wouldn't expect."

"Foreign fishing boats is the norm here. We have had everything up to and including Portuguese schooners, Russian fishing boats that are really spy ships, British, Spanish, American, Icelandic. They are all normal."

"What about pleasure craft?"

"What's a pleasure craft? If you mean non-commercial yachts and things. Yes. The odd ones now and again. They if they stop don't do much more than tie up for a day or two. Take a rest buy some fish form Mr Farquerson if he has any and then move on. You ask a lot of strange questions Mr. Lewis."

"I am probably more interested than I would be expected to be but we think that there are escaping Germans, guilty of war crimes, that authorities would like to put on trial."

"Now a German boat would be unusual. Probably the one nationality of boat that we no longer get , though we did often before and during the war. You have to remember that Denmark was invaded by Germany and even though we are Scottish we were limited as to what we could or could not do. The Germans didn't bother us either. We had a visit now and again. We did have a submarine once here. In the bay there is a lot of deep water. We probably average 180 feet just offshore around high water and although there are predictable currents and a tide race there is little tidal movement between high and low water."

"So you know all the regular visitors really."

"Sort of ,though there is another one though thinking about it. Danish yacht doesn't often call in here but a few of the fishermen have seen it. Beautiful boat just under sixty feet, ketch rigged with a powerful engine as well. Sails back and forth to Copenhagen. The skipper told me once last year when they came in for a visit."

"Which way were they going?"

"Back to Denmark."

"Many people on board?"

"Only a few crew that's all anyone saw."

He stayed overnight was very pleasant and cheerful man. Told me he's just the skipper working for a charter business taking Danish officials around the islands up to Greenland sometimes leaves them there and brings others back. This time empty so he thought he'd come and say hello.

Has he just called the once?"

"He did but there was another one arrived on the same boat a couple of months later It seems they changed skippers that very pleasant man had retired and another man has it now. Not a nice man at all. I asked him all the normal questions and he started shouting at me. If Mr Farquerson hadn't heard him heaven knows what might have happened."

"What questions upset him?"

"About his business. Where from, where to, how long staying, people on board. He got very annoyed told me it was nothing to do with me.

I told him it was. I was the harbour master and in practice we both worked for the Danish government. He shouted at me that he didn't work for the Danish government scribbled in the book the crew numbers and signed it almost illegible. Look at it."

Mrs Cuthbertson was right, the boat had made just the two calls here this last year.

"He shouted at me that he was never coming back called me a nosey old woman and stormed out of here.

That was three months ago."

"They've not been back again?"

"No he kept his word and he's nor been back. but it has been seen an Icelandic boat called in with a sick crew member while he was getting seen to the skipper did a bit of shopping for sweets and things and he told me he'd seen a ketch heading south westerlie a day back lot of people on deck. He had the glasses on them as it looked really good in the water sailing nicely . He told me whoever was in charge knew what they were doing.

"Did he say where they saw them?"

"No just that they were sailing south west he was sailing south east and they were close for only a short while. He said he always liked them."

"What sail boats?"

"No this particular one, he said they were a one off type of boat, cruising come racing ketches, he thought there were about only five or six of them ever built. He reckoned they were built in Hamburg before the war and he had seen them there as he used to frequently sell his catch in Hamburg before it all went out of bounds."

"So when was that?" Mrs. Cuthbertson looked in her duary.

"Eighteen days ago the Icelandic boat was here so three weeks about. When he saw the ketch."

"Thank you very much both for the information and the /tea."

There was a knock at the door before it opened. NO one came in . A lady's voice from outside called, "Rosie it's Sara may I come in?"

"Come in my dear. What can I do for you?"

"It's not you I want to see it's Colonel Lewis."

"Oh you mean Alan. The visitor looked at her friend Rosie not certain what she meant. "Let me introduce you two. Sara this Alan. And now that I know, Colonel Lewis this is Dr Munro."

Alan offered his hand and she shook it like an army sergeant.

"What can I do for you Doctor?"

"I was talking to your crew and the lieutenant tells me that as far as he knows you are going back to Lerwick."

"We will be yes."

"Can I scrounge a lift please. John Farquerson normally picks me up and drops me off where and when I'm needed but he has a radio problem at the moment and he isn't certain when he might get it fixed."

"Not a problem for us. When will you be ready?"

"Ten minutes I'll just get my bags and shut the surgery."

"Do that, get yourself aboard. Get one of the ratings to give you a hand with the bags. I'm sure you've been up and down those ladders more times than they have, but lowering bags is easier. Ask the lieutenant who's name is Christian to give you my cabin and I'll bunk in with him. Clear?"

"Completely colonel."

"Alan."

"Completely Alan. I'll see you next month Rosie." Dr. Munro shut the door as she left.

"Dr. Munro does island hopping, her father did it before her when there were a lot more people in need of medical services. I suspect that before long they will decide that her position is no longer viable. Her salary is supplemented via a number of ministries. We will see. The other thing I will say about her and she is a very dear friend of mine is that she is a confirmed spinster by choice. You can read anything you wish into that, it won't bother her. Her father was a good doctor and she's a better one. Safe journey Colonel; landing and mooring fees waived you are picking up medical personnel."

The MFV was well over halfway through its journey back to Lerwick The petty officer had the wheel, the ratings were playing cribbage, Christian was asleep, while on deck Alan was staring almost blankly out to sea. Dr Munro broke into his thoughts.

"You seem very happy out here; in the wind getting sprayed on now and again, like you were born to it."

"My father was a merchant seaman my grandfather and his brothers too. I couldn't join the army until I was eighteen so I did two years crewing for my dad on his fishing boat in the Irish sea. It was a forty foot, gaff rigged sail boat. I don't think I've worked as hard as I worked in those first years after school life. The army was a piece of cake after that time. You are almost certainly right I was born to it it's still apart of me I can't deny it and I wouldn't wish to."

"You were lost in thought though in a different world."

"I have a job to do. I am pursuing people who we consider to be war criminals."

"Surely a worthy cause."

"It is. The part that bothers me is that, if we had lost the war instead of winning it; I suspect that I would be being pursued by the people I'm chasing for exactly the same reasons with the same provable just cause.

Peaceful moments, like these, that allow for thought and reflection are almost certainly more disruptive to my health and wellbeing than a firefight in the trenches. Back to the land of the living again.

Are you comfortable in your cabin?"

"I am thank you. It's better when I got rid of a pair of socks. I thought something had died in there. You should try and change them more often."

"I do. They weren't mine. Don't know where you found them. I didn't notice I'm used to sleeping in smelly places a self-respecting animal would not condone."

"I'm sorry. I've been rude."

"Don't worry put it down to giving out free medical advice.

It reminds me of a story. My brothers friend Alf was a young mechanic; his unit was fighting a rear guard action in France.

Alf's job was to keep the tanks running. Eventually he got to Dunkirk. He'd walked through mud and slime, in trenches, across streams, just keeping the tanks running, and staying alive. They don't know how he managed to wade through the water and get on a small boat and then get aboard a ship. But needs must and he did. In the sick bay they got his bots off him for the first time ion over three weeks. The brigadier surgeon marked him down for amputation of both feet.

After they landed he was transferred to a London hospital.

A few day later he was, in a bed ,in a ward, fortunately part of a long queue, awaiting surgery, when a visitor arrived at the hospital. The queen Consort was speaking to some of the patients. She spoke to Alf and a sort of gentle offhand question asked him if there was anything he needed.

"Yes your Majesty. I want to keep my feet, but the Brigadier wants to cut them off."

"I shall speak to the brigadier." she said

A month later he went home to hospital in Birkenhead. A year later he walked properly again, He finished the war fixing tanks in France going in the other direction still with his own feet."

"Is that true?"

"Totally. I wouldn't have told it if it wasn't. I have over the last twenty years had a number of salutary lessons most of which involved duck before you get shot, but Alf's personal 'take care of yourself' was almost as important."

Ten hours later in the middle of the night they docked at Lerwick. On the following morning. Dr. Munro was picked up by a colleague. The navy team returned to their base at Lerwick.

There was some discussion as to the ownership of the MFV. When checked it was found that it was under the control of a government department headed by a Mister Talbot Conway.

The harbour master was instructed to keep it there until Colonel Lewis or brigadier Cameron told him otherwise, and can you organise a water taxi to take me to the base at RAF Sumburgh please.

When Alan got back to Woolwich he contacted Cameron. "I don't know who you've got spare there sir, if anyone, but I could do with someone having a nose around Hamburg docks and Copenhagen too. I'm looking for a ketch about sixty foot long so it should be easy enough to spot. Unless it's been hidden behind a big one. It's named 'Foniks' registered in Copenhagen."

"Can do."

"And I need a piece of advice sir."

"Well as long as it's not matrimonial fire away." Alan remembered that conversation he'd had with the Brigadier a while back, maybe his marriage had gone completely Kaput now.

"No sir. They got a boat for me it was up at Lerwick in Shetland. Totally unsuitable."

"Go on."

"I believe I'm on to something, which is why I asked for the check on that ketch. I need a bigger faster boat with some firepower on it and a small team and a skilled crew who can do the business which could be anything."

"So what do you want from me?"

"A bigger boat with firepower."

"Hold it Alan. You're a Lieutenant Colonel. Phone the Admiralty tell them what you want; It's designated, important, approved, government business. Don't take no, don't get fobbed off, any problems threaten them with Mr. Conway. Assert your authority."

"Thank you Sir. Can I have George?"

"No."

"Well not at the moment he's on leave for another two weeks. He's got married to the German lass Katarina."

"That was quick."

"He did seem in a hurry. I did suggest he slow down but he was keen. I could have blocked it of course but I wouldn't have been sure of my motives so I let it happen."

"Give them my best wishes when they're back."

"Do I send George when he's back?"

"No I'll get one of the others from Salisbury . I just need my back covering in case. Thank you for the advice . I shall speak to the Admiralty."

Phone calls to the Admiralty weren't getting him anywhere. He couldn't remember when he wore one last but he got his uniform out, glad that he'd got it up to date and ordered a taxi to take him the Admiralty.

The brigadier was right and even better when you do it in uniform in person. Alan found himself going home to the Wirral. One of the boat building companies on Merseyside had, the Admiralty think, exactly what he was looking for.

 "Why don't you have a look at it sir. Currently it is with the company that did the original conversion work, and it's having an overhaul and a refit. We're not certain why as it was like a lot of other commandeered craft going to be either returned to their owners sold on or scrapped.

The original owner was paid for the boat. I think it's surplus so you can do with it as you please. It is almost certainly one of many now no longer required.

Please have a look at it. It fits what you have told us you need, and it's there for the taking. If it's not suitable come back to me and I'll try and find something else."

Alan headed home. He hadn't been there for over two years. It hadn't felt comfortable last time he was there. What would it hold for him now he wondered.

He took the Ford after all he was still in the army and on Government business and carrying a small arsenal of guns and boxes of ammunition onto a train would probably get him arrested of there was a policeman daft enough.

He got a meal and a bed for the night with the south Staffordshire Regiment in Lichfield, which saved him trying to drive all the way to Birkenhead in the dark and it kept the Ford safe overnight loaded with the weapons.

Home wasn't as cramped as normal brother Frank was buried in Rome three were married and moved out which left the two youngest there, Harold eighteen and Alec sixteen. He still had to sleep on the floor or share a bed and settled for the floor next to a pile of weapons. All he had to do was stop his younger brothers playing with them. Mother did that with one sentence. Not much had changed here in many ways thank goodness.

Alan went over to Wallasey jus the other side of the bridges , the two boroughs here separated by the docks. Up the lane form Duke Street bridge was the workshop of Barlow Boats.

There was plenty of noise going on in the workshop and the yard. Alan stood at the gate. It had been a long time since he'd been here. Before he joined the army he'd often got wood for dads fishing boat to do repairs. That was near twenty years back change was certain to have happened here even without the war.

It wasn't long and a man, flat cap, bib and brace, covered in sawdust, came out from the double timber doors.

"Are you looking for someone sir or just looking?"

"A bit of both . For a full complete and truthful answer. I was thinking it must be twenty years since I was here. Either my memory has gone or things have changed. I am after here to pick up my boat."

"Which one is that sir?"

"To be unintentionally difficult ,I haven't got a clue. But I can tell you that you are doing a refit on it and it's numbered 96."

"That's the Lady June and she's in Vittoria dock and yes she's having an overhaul and upgrade where ewe can. And who might you be sir?"

"My name is Alan Lewis."

"And what makes it your boat sir?"

"The Admiralty have offered it to me to do a job. They suggested I go and have a look at it and see if it's suitable and if it is I can have it and if I need something doing to it to speak to a Mr. Barlow or a Mr. Bertie Williams, who is the foreman here. Would that be you sir?"

"It is." Alan offered his hand, Bertie wiped the dust off his own and shook it.

"Do you know about boats Mr. Lewis?"

"A bit."

"As long as it's the right bit it's ok."

"So tell me about this one."

"Come into the office. Mr Barlow isn't in ,if he was he could tell you all about it without looking it up. I know most of it because I was the foremen on the first conversion."

Alan followed Bertie up the stairs that were just inside the double doors into a fairly large, untidy, drawing office, come a place of general clerical use.

 "Have a look on the second drawing board . That's your beast."

"It looks like a useful tool. Yawl rig not ketch."

"You know a bit then."

"Go on then fill in the details.."

"42 feet motor sailer. Plus another four with the bowsprit out. Small main so the mizzen balances a big foresail to reduce the work on the helm. She will sail close hauled but never feels that comfortable, or so I'm told. Wind from anywhere else and she's ok and it saves fuel and she will go quick with the wind behind the sails up and the engine running.

Engine is a six cylinder diesel plenty of horse power. Now the good bit. The engine drives two variable pitch gearboxes with propellers to match. The system was cannibalised from a between the wars lightweight tank. What were originally the slewing clutch levers now operate the variable pitch props one each side. You need to drive it and stay focussed. If you get it wrong you'll turn around in circles. I kid you not. That's it."

"When will it be ready?"

"For what?"

"To go to sea."

"A week. It's in the water now we're just putting the last bits back on it and sorting both the standing and the running rigging out. Sails are what we're waiting for they should be back this week just a case of checking all fits after that."

"How many can I sleep on it?"

Six at a time at least. If you do it in shifts ten would be cramped but workable."

"Galley?"

"Yes paraffin hob and grill no oven."

"Can I live on it now?"

"As long as you can put up with the guys working on it while you're there. The forward cabin is ready kitted out and the heads work but the dock board don't like you sending solids outside into the dock there are facilities on the dock itself if you give the stevedores a dropsy."

"Can I go there now?"

"Yes. Do you know where Vittoria dock is?"

"Yes."

"There are two men working on it Brian and Peter. They are the riggers so there on the outside. Tell them who you are and that I know all about it. Your boat's at the far end just before you go into the East Float.

"I know it. Thank you for your time Mt Williams. I shall go and see my boat."

Down the hill, over the bridge, turn left before the policeman on point duty, down past the fishing boats, and a small pretty wooden yacht, to Lady June. Alan parked the Ford and went to meet Peter and Brian.

They worked until four thirty. Tomorrow they would be here at eight am. Yes you can lock it from the inside.

"I'll be staying here tonight . I'll live on board from now on. If I'm in your way let me know. I shall be back by four with my food and kit from my folks house. No thankyou I won't need a hand."

After the riggers left for the night Alan onloaded the Car and hid all of the weaponry under the kiss berths in the forward cabin. Put some food he'd picked up from the shops on Laird Street into the cupboards in the galley. He fed himself visited the dock workers rest rooms and then went to bed. Sleeping on a boat in a gentle swell is one pleasure that's free and legal.

A couple of days after Peter and Brian had finished, Bertie Williams turned up.

"You wanted to see me Mr Lewis?"

"I need a job doing Mr Williams."

"What might that be?"

The drawings are showing a frame on the deck in front of the wheelhouse front screen with the sort of Houdini hatch turned in the other direction."

"Yes , the specs changed when the war finished and the Admiralty decided it was an unnecessary cost even though it was part of the designated budget and costings with a view that any money saved could either be spent elsewhere or reduce the cost of the refit."

"Has the money that was allocated been spent elsewhere?"

"No."

"Then can we have that original work done as soon as possible please."

"I need someone to authorise it."

"I shall do that for you."

"Do you have the authority to do so?"

"Have your typing person do an order. I shall sign it. Do the order from Lieutenant colonel Alan Lewis on Behalf of the Ministry of Defence."

"Even Mr. Barlow will be happy with that sir . Thank you very much I'll ge tit organised and conform the extra works and sort out the structural timbers we need."

"I'll leave it with you but please be as quick as you can."

Brian and Peter had finished all the rigging the sails had arrived and been run up, taken down, folded, and put in the forward cabin. Alan had moved into the portside cabin which left a starboard cabin with two spare bunks in and one in his. They had space for another three plus there was a a possible quarter berth each side and a pilot berth over the dining area come chart table. There was enough room but given that most of the bulk had come form a small tank there wasn't a great deal of spare space available.

Barlow's had sent a man down to put some decent locks on the wheelhouse, so Alan went shopping for food leaving the joiner with the order on no circumstances should he let anyone on board while he was away. Which is why he found George Robinson sitting on one of the steel bollards on the quayside waiting for Alan.

"George, what on earth are you doing here?"

"My job sir."

"I told brigadier not to send you. You've just got married."

"Well I asked the Brigadier to find you and here I am."

"He's happier now, and so am I we all know each other too well Alan. And I came because I found your boat. Or more accurately Katarina did. We went for a walk. About ten minutes and we found it. It was in Hamburg docks, just sitting there, no one on board, no signs of any activity. The brigadier has some of the boys keeping an eye on it.

"That's good and okay I'm not arguing I'm pleased to see you. Good job I went shopping. Come aboard. Where's your kit?

"It's with your ma. We had to start the search somewhere and Woolwich said you left for home."

"Do you need any of your kit tonight?"

"It would be handy."

"If you mind the boat , I'll go home say bye to mum dad and the boys, then I need to go and see someone at the TA depot; and then I'll be back and we'll eat and you can bring me up to date. Help yourself to anything you want to eat or drink. Okay?"

"Of course."

It was nearly two hours later when Alan returned. He brought George's two bags another of his own and a large metal tripod.

"Where's that going in the cabin for now but hopefully when the shipwrights arrive on top in front of the wheelhouse, we need some structural work and then a hatch turning. First off what do you want to eat?"

"Anything. But quicker the better."

"Bacon and eggs?"

"Spot on boss."

Later, after dark, meal eaten, tea drunk, gossip caught up. Alan could hear a vehicle coming down towards their boat.

"Perhaps our delivery." They went outside to look.

A nondescript unlettered Bedford van had rattled along the quayside. It stopped by the boat. The driver got out and walked around to see them.

"I have a number of parcels for the Lady June. A Mr Lewis I'm told will show me some identification." George climbs out of the boat and shows the driver Alan's ID.

"Sorry sir the guys at base they just told me Mr Lewis."

"Don't worry as you're in civvies too, you'll realise why they told you that."

"Yes sir, and do you have any light here? We've got no lights inside the back of the van."

George produced a small torch from his pocket and handed it to one of the two helpers who had climbed from the passenger side of the Bedford. George went to help . One man was inside. The parcels were strapped tight to the wooden ladderwork for parcel security. The manifest said four wooden crates and as that was all that was in the back George assumed they were all for them. Alan used the boom off the mast swung across the quayside as a derrick and the parcels though not really heavy were easily shifted aboard in a net and down through the hatch way in the centre of the wheelhouse. George signed the drivers sheet, took his copy, read it, and passed it to Alan who folded it and put it into his breast pocket.

They unpacked the boxes and put it all into the forward cabin.

"Where did you get that lot from?"

"The TA here are attached to artillery and were throughout the war. They got loads of it about some still with the original grease on. At least they sent what I asked for. Let's hope we don't need it.

On Sunday second of September Japan surrendered. They were still unsurprisingly still talking about it when the Radio man got all of the electrics and the electronics finally working on Lady June the Wednesday after. All that was needed now was a bit of woodwork and a cox and trials could begin.

When Aalan got the radio working he made contact with what was left of the Western Approaches Team in Liverpool to get them to act as a link with the Admiralty and the MOD. It worked and a message system got set up that on day one let him know that the yacht 'Foniks' had left Hamburg with a full crew destination Stavanger. The following day an RAF reconnaissance plane on a flight from Oslo to UK saw Foniks a lot nearer to the North East coast of Scotland than a line to Stavanger would normally take.

Alan got back in touch with the admiralty to see if they had found a Coxswain for him.

"We're doing our best sir. There aren't many who have worked on those boats who sail as well."

Just before lunch so that everything would stink of diesel a shell truck arrived and filled the tanks of Lady June.

Late on Saturday afternoon a message came over the radio that

"A CPO Lewis would arrive at Woodside station on the overnight train from London. You have your coxswain Will someone pick them up?"

"We will be ready to go tomorrow George; all we need is the man to put the timber in, and when we drop him off pick up some others."

Another message arrived late on to say Foniks had been seen by an RAF plane flying into Sumburgh. Her sails were down she had a bit of a list and was under power. Stavanger was one place it wasn't going.

"Whether we are ready or not we are going tomorrow. I need to get the shipwright here now. I'll go to the boatyard and see if there is someone I can contact."

Alan drove up the hill to Barlow's. Only the name over the front gates and a works telephone number.

'Come on Alan think. Police station. Who would they contact in the event of a fire or a break in. The desk sergeant wasn't to helpful until Alan's ID produced all the information and a salute when he left with Bertrand Williams's address.

Slightly isolated from the main camp on the Royal Navy base at Portsmouth is a long single story building housing in slightly cramped conditions a contingent of lady sailors.

Roughly in the middle were two single rooms CPO's for the use of.

Chief Louisa Lewis had one room with Chief Lizzie Evans in the other. On this Saturday evening in CPO Lewis's room with them was a sweet young thing from the valleys Tara Hughes. Although Lewis and Evans had Welsh sounding names neither could find anything other than their names that would link them in any way to the principality.

When keen young Tara arrived on the base and her gentle soft voice had the two chiefs secretly drooling at the prospect of another potential conquest it seemed only logical to have her join them as part of a Welsh group on the base.

This, they assured her, would get her some additional training in such things as seamanship, navigation and boat handling.

The lesson tonight would include all three disciplines. The young miss was sort of half lying down on chief Lewis's bed. Chief Evans was on her knees with her elbows on the top blanket, while on Tara's left was Chief Lewis who was telling her how the movement of large warships worked.

"Now Tara imagine we have to move a number of warships let's say from the Med into the Atlantic. Right uncross your ankles and open up your legs. That's it .

Now imagine your right leg is the coast of North Africa and your left foot is Italy and your left leg is the Riviera and the east coast of Spain, Now, what we will do is move the fleet through the Med trying not to rub up against the coast of Libya and the same thing on the Riviera side."

As the fleet brushed against the opposite coastlines of Miss Hughes's legs, she appeared to be enjoying the dangerous part of coastal navigation and boat handling. Her eyes had closed slightly and her breathing was just a bit faster. Perhaps boat moving could turn out to be an exciting time.

"As we gently slide as tight as we can to the coast we get near to the rock of Gibraltar," Chief Lewis lifted Tara's left knee until it was high in the air, her foot still on the bed, her uniform skirt now around her hips, her breathing quiet but faster, her eyes almost shut tight. Now then both lines of ships will be heading for the narrow gap that is the Straits of Gibraltar and as the chiefs hands steered the two halves of the fleet heading for the gap, there was a bang on the door. Tara shot bolt upright on Lewis's bunk, eyes wide open, in a state of panic. Chief Evans whispered, "Shh it's locked.

"I hear you." Chief Lewis said.

"Chief, boss wants you, Ten minutes her office. As long as you're dressed come as you are."

"I'll be there."

Tara was lying back down on her back she'd gone a bit pale

"The doors locked everything is ok, there is nothing to worry about." Lewis told her.

"A piece of advice for you," Lizzie said. "The boss here is married and had two near teenage boys, but she is partial to the taste of another girls lipstick. Don't be blatant be careful and all will be ok.

I wonder what the boss wants you for Lou?"

"Haven't a clue but we'll know in around six minutes from now.

"You wanted me Mam."

"Yes sorry rush job just come up. You have an hour, civvy clothes, train to London, overnight to Birkenhead, they need someone to drive a boat for them for a couple of weeks."

"Why me anyone can drive a boat.

"It's a converted motor sailer has sails for economy and one engine two gearboxes and variable pitch propellers, same as the one you were playing with a while back but better."

"Surely there is someone else mam. I finish in two weeks."

"If there was I'd send them. There's two men, but they're somewhere in the middle east at this time, and who knows where.

Sorry about your evening what were you doing?"

"Just about to eat supper mam."

"With a bit of luck they might have a canteen on the train. Clerk is doing your travel warrants sorry to hurry you. There will be a taxi here to take you to the station, have a good trip, see you when you're back."

As the chief left commander Sermon smiled to herself everyone on the base knew what Chief Lewis ate for supper. I wonder who that was she thought.

When CPO Louisa Lewis was getting somewhere near Crewe railway station, Jimmy Myers had noises banging in his head. He was having a strange dream ,like it was the blacksmiths steam hammer. Then he started to wake up; it was his front door; he got up crossed the small mat onto the cold lino drew back the curtains and peered into the street.

'Bloody hell he thought I've overslept' it was Bertie Williams, Barlow's foreman. Hang on its Sunday I don't work today. He knocked on the window to let Bill know he was up, grabbed his trousers and pulled on a woollen sweater, which he tucked into the waistband, and pulled over the braces to hold them all together. Jimmy wasn't a big man and the oversize second hand work trousers weren't pretty but they were practical. They let him climb in and out of jobs, even with a boiler suit on as well.

He opened the front door. "I'm not comin' in" said Bert, "We got an urgent job on and your body is needed down at the yard post haste. That means like now".

"It's Sunday I don't work Sunday what's wrong with tomorrow?" "Tomorrow you won't be here, and neither will the job."

" What are you on about?" There's some alterations needing to be done on a boat not difficult but you'll be at sea doing them. There's about three days' work and when it's finished they'll drop you off at the nearest place to a railway station, and you can then make your way back. So get yourself packed for a week away. You'll only need some wash kit and some travelling home clothes. Food is not a problem; you'll get fed on the boat. Train and travelling will be sorted for you when you leave them ok?"

"No it's not ok, my mum is going to be furious."

"Let me talk to her."

"She's not here."

"Where is she now?"

"She's gone to church. It's Sunday."

"What time is she back?"

"About seven fifteen."

"OK I'll come in. You can make me a cuppa, before you get your gear ready, and I'll speak to her to tell her how important it is, and how much extra you'll get paid."

 "What you mean extra?"

"You'll get paid for every hour you're on the boat, flat rate, but even when you're asleep you'll be earning."

"OK, you speak to her, but don't mention money, stick with how important it is."

Jimmy was packed by the time his mother got home. He and Bert had emptied the teapot, and Jimmy had breakfasted. He'd refused to leave without eating. Bert figured as is Mrs. Myers wasn't home yet, there was no rush to leave; they would still be in the yard by 8 am.

Bertie was about the same age as Jimmy's mum and she listened to the shop foreman as she well knew that Jimmy's apprenticeship; and future work, may well be dependent on her acceptance of Jimmy going away for a few days.

Bertie shook Mrs Myers's hand, Jimmy kissed his mum on the cheek and they went out to Bertie's motorbike .Jimmy put his going away kit into the sidecar and climbed on behind his boss and they headed off to the boatyard.

It was 7.50 when Bertie Williams pulled into the boatyard.

"Right first things first. Get your clock card and clock on. When you get back you clock off and that's what you'll get paid for. That put a smile on Jimmy's face for the first time that morning."

"So why such a rush?" asked Jimmy.

"The boats sailing on the night tide. We have to get the timber cut today and on board by this afternoon. You'll need to get your tools onboard, and everything you'll need to complete the work."

" Where are we sailing?"

"As far as I know northwards, up the Irish sea, and then when you've finished you'll get dropped off somewhere."

"You mean you don't know where I'm going to be put ashore." "Depends when you finish the job."

" What am I doing?"

"You are beefing up the deck head to carry a chunk of weight. What weight, I don't know, Mr. Barlow will give you drawings and a design for the conversion; all you have to do is build it. Straight forward."

"Why me, any of the other lads could do this?" They asked for someone single in case the job overran and needed you to stay longer. That was why you got it; all the other shipwrights are married with kids. You're single Jimmy."

"I've been courting for a year now."

"But you ain't married you ain't got any kids, and Mr. Barlow says you owe him six extra weeks that you didn't do as an apprentice because you went off to army camp when you should have been at work."

"I thought we was going to war."

"You're in a protected trade."

"That doesn't mean I can't volunteer."

"But it means you're not likely to get picked, especially with how much work we've been doing for the government.

Right then get yourself into Mr Barlow's office and see what he's got for you. I'll start putting the wood together. After we cut what we need to by then I reckon it'll be pick up your tools and head off down to the docks. As far as I know the boat is still in Vittoria dock. Some of the guys have already been aboard working on it and have been finished few days.

The workshop was quiet. It felt spooky. Sunday was never worked as far as Jimmy knew. It may have been during the war but Sunday was always Jimmy's day off. He worked five and a half or six days a week except when he used to go sick to disappear on army reserve exercises. The war was over now no more than a few months but Jimmy had just missed it and was not happy about it at all.

George got a rough map from Alan showing him where Woodside station was while Alan waited for the shipwright to arrive. Because there would possibly be others on board, Alan had asked George to brief the coxswain before they got to the boat. That way they'd be up to speed a lot quicker than talking in whispers or being careful what was said.

Chief Lewis had slept badly and not eaten anything of any description for over twelve hours. There was neither canteen nor cafes open anywhere. Feisty was a good word so George took her to the truckers canteen near the Blue Funnel yard where only some late finishing, lady, night workers were un attendance. Tea and toast and she felt more alive. 08.00 Sunday September nine Chief Lewis took charge of Lady June.

"Are you serious sir?" she asked when Alan gave her the starting keys.

"My name is Alan this as you know is George. We will be your crew it's your boat until the jobs done. A couple of weeks back I was in Lerwick with an MFV. I crewed for my dad on a fishing boat for two years. George and I go canoeing on occasions two of which are in the cabin until we need them. We have limited full time experience. So why have they sent you?"

"I'm nearly forty I have two weeks left and I'm finished. My father and Grandfather are both master mariners I have been sailing since I was eight. I joined the navy when war broke out and oddly for the navy they let me drive the boats from the day I started. I'd worked tugs since I was a teenager so I got put on them pushing big ships around inside the harbour. High ranking lady friends in uniform helped. Then I spent nearly five years on coastal patrol. In theory non-combat but no one told the Germans. The men didn't want me at first but then they found I could drive better than them and then I became a bit of a talisman."

"Nearly five years on Coastal Patrol you're lucky to be here; and so I think we're lucky to have you. Welcome aboard."

"Thank you, sir."

"Alan."

"Yes sir.   Alan."

They were drinking tea chatting like old friends when they heard the sound of a motor bike coming along the quayside. As it stopped outside Alan had left the saloon and was out on deck.

Bert Williams with a young man in an oversize boiler suit now taking curved and straight timbers and then a box of tools a bag of tools and fixings and an army Bergan.

"Give us a lift with these please pal."

"Jimmy this man is your boss mind your manners." Bert told him.

"I said please." He started passing down the timber. Alan took it from him. "Do not worry Mr. Williams. Thankyou for bringing him here. I have a favour to ask. Can you bring a driver down here tomorrow or later today take the car to them and ask them to mind it for me. I'll pick it when I get back."

"Of course."

Alan passed him the keys, "We have emptied the car and it is locked."

Bert took Jimmy over to one side. "Do what this man asks Jimmy and behave yourself. Any bad report and Mr Barlow will crucify you. And I will pass him the nails. Do you understand?"

"Yes."

"Then get on with your job you are being paid ."

After Bert left Jimmy joined them for some tea and toast then got on with turning the hatch around.

"You know it's safer the way it is you know its less likely t o leak opening with the hinge forward."

"Don't worry about it Jimmy just turn the hatch please." Alan spoke gently and George started to get worried for Jimmy's well- being.

"Why don't you show Louisa the way out Alan. I'll give Jimmy a hand if he needs one."

"I know the way out of here I could show you later."

"You've got a job top do. Alan likes the fresh air."

Louisa followed Alan out and onto the quay and they walked in silence down towards the East Float. Alan stopped when he reached a large bollard big enough for the two of them to sit on.

"What will George do?"

"He will explain that I know what I want and that I need neither advice nor to discuss it."

"Does he have to do this very often?"

"No it's normally just me and George on our own.

"What is Jimmy actually supposed to be doing?"

"He's turning the hatch and beefing up the foredeck in front of it so I can mount a Vickers machine gun, water cooler, and ammunition boxes, and shoot things, if I feel a need to."

"Do you think we'll need to?"

"I hope not. But a worst case scenario is that we have to and we can't because I haven't got them mounted and ready to go."

"Where do we pick them up?"

"I have Sten guns, Bren guns, pistols, sniper rifles, and the Vickers in the forward cabin. Between you me and George. Come on we'll go back. If I have any problems after George has had a word I'll get a taxi and drop him off at Bert's house."

Jimmy was out on the deck in front of the wheelhouse. "George is pushing the bolts out to me sir. With a bit of luck the hatch will turn without drilling more holes."

"Fingers crossed."

"Yes sir."

The hatch turned Jimmy got it sealed and bolted down tight. George held the spanner on the outside while Jimmy worked the inside . It was nearly dark. Alan and Louisa had cooked the meal. After Louisa had been on the radio to the harbour man at the dock board. They moved the canoes and sat down at the table to eat.

"Where did you get your Bergan Jimmy?" George asked.

"I'm in the TA," he replied ,"One of the lads brought it back from Norway and he was selling it so I bought it."

"How long have you been in the TA then?"

"Three years plus some."

"Come on," says George ,"Don't make me ask every single question tell us about your time in the TA."

"I joined when I was seventeen, but they wouldn't let me join up properly because I was working in the boat builders. I went to camp every year and I did qualify as a medic which is why Mr Barlow let me go as it fitted for first aid man at work. But he's holding it against me now says I owe him six weeks of my apprenticeship still which he's going to add on at the end. That's about it really. Apart from I've shot all sorts of things. The local TA is artillery so I shot Ack ack, machine guns, rifles. I used to hang around the batteries at night when the air raids were on. Think that's why I'm a bit deaf sometimes."

"That explains how you got a Bergan then." George replied "Thanks for telling us. Anyone want tea?"

"Yes a quick one then we have to make a move." Louisa gave her first order. We can move soon they are going to lock us into the last dock an around thirty minutes and we'll get locked out later with a tramper. We'll be a bit before high water so I'll run up river see what she's like then I'll run out wit the ebb. Saves beating ourselves up to start the trip.

From Vittoria dock they motored almost silently across and towards the bridge through the first lock gate which closed behind them. They tied up next to a black tramper and waited for high water on the river. The last tide had been high and the dock was full. Water probably needed to empty to level off so the lock gates that would let us out into the river could open. Only the two going out tonight Lady June and the tramper, its engines were up and running.

Both the deck hands on the tramper would work the ropes looped over the dockside bollards and when the gates opened we would cast off from the tramper and leave first to get out into the river.

Lou had the helm, she was ready for a sleep, but there was a job to do. Alan had the front line and George had back rope the lock gates were opening Louise opened the wheel house door.

"Jimmy put your life jacket on. Don't dare argue." Jimmy came into the wheelhouse got his jacket and put it on. Lou looked at him. "Outside at sea keep it on."

"Yes mam."

"Are you having a wind at me?"

"No mam. George told me what everyone's rank was. You're a Chief Petty Officer; George is a Warrant Officer and Alan is a Lieutenant Colonel. I am way out of my depth here mam."

Lou thought to herself you are not alone. "Right get yourself back on deck and remember that jacket and properly fastened."

"Yes mam." Whatever else George said to him seemed to have worked Jimmy was settled like someone had given him a pill or a very severe warning. George didn't appear to be a pill man.

Lou had told Mersey Docks and Harbour board what she was going to do. When they left the dock she took a diagonal line across the Mersey then let the tide take it on the flood for a short way. Then as the tide turned she eased her around and let the ebb take her out. The boat moved nicely the engine was smooth the gearboxes and clutches behaved as they were supposed to.

"Do you remember enough of this Alan?"

"If you mean the river and the channels I didn't till I saw the charts again and then it started to come back."

"Are you happy taking a first watch. I've been awake since yesterday morning. I could do with a sleep."

"If there is one place I should know it's here to the Isle of Man."

Don't wait till we're there before you wake me. Four hours will do it normally does so wake me at o300."

"Are you sure?"

"It will still be dark always easier to sleep then I reckon. I'll take the starboard quarter berth it'll be easier to get me from there we perhaps might shift some bits around tomorrow. 03.00 please. Goodnight all ."

Alan got four hours and George was stirring porridge Lou was back on the helm Alan was just surfacing after 07.00. Jimmy asked, "Do you want me to spell you on the helm. I have driven this. Only in the dock but I know how it works and I can sail a skiff, cos I do sail one with a mate of mine."

"Go and eat first then when you've eaten you can do half an hour while I eat then you have work to do on the deck."

"Yes mam."

Suddenly the radio came alive calling the Lady June. Not much had been going on other than boat movements and general traffic so when Lady June got a call. It was on an open channel and Lou squeezed the mike to let them know she was receiving. Message is sighting of interest in Lysternoy end of message. "Alan did you hear that message?"

"Yes. It means Jimmy needs to get am move on with the woodwork. Next stop maybe Cambeltown or that direction."

"What's at Cambeltown?"

"Machrihanish Naval airbase. There are supposed to be some extra crew there for us."

Lou went back to bed. Alan took the helm and George gave Jimmy a hand with the woodwork. "What is going on top of this frame?" Jimmy asked. George got the tripod from the forward cabin.

"A Vickers machine gun tripod." Jimmy said, Now I know why you wanted the hatch turning around. Have you got a water cooler as well ?"

"Yes ."

"And ammo tins?"

"Yes"

I can beef this up easier from the outside than the inside. It won't look as pretty but it will work. I have coach screws and there's holes in the tripod we can lash the water cooler to the main mast and the ammo tins will fit inside the wood frame and if you need to change it can be done quick enough by throwing the tin inside or even overboard if you don't want it again."

"Do you know what you're doing ?"

"Yes."

"Get on with it then. I'll let Alan know what you're going to do and then I'll give you a hand."

Jimmy spent the morning on deck with lifejacket and tied on. George worked through the hatch and the tripod was coach screwed into place before lunch.

"Well done Jimmy. You're right not as pretty as hidden away but it couldn't stay there anyway. I'll try and raise Machrihanish, we might be able to drop you there."

While Lou had the helm Alan got through to the Naval Base. "No sir we are not aware of any requests for a naval team. We are basically fleet air arm sir and we don't have any men suitable for what you are needing . I'm sorry sir." Alan shut down the radio. "Didn't sound very sorry did he? Jimmy would you be interested in crewing for a few extra days pay?"

"Yes sir."

"Is that ok skipper?"

"It is."

You head north past Skye heading towards the Faroes. I have the Lat and Long in my kit bag. Let's get food eaten as well.

After lunch they put up the mizzen and the main. They were heading into the wind which was almost directly from the north. Having run them up they dropped them again and lashed them to the booms.. Their second largest foresail was in a sausage bag. They clipped the head to the halyard and lashed the sausage bag, ready if needed, to the stanchions.

They rested shared the helm Alan and Lou did most of it Jimmy and George shared responsibility with strict orders to wake them up if anything amiss.

At nearly 14.00 hours on the following day the Lady June gently pottered into the harbour bay of Lysternoy.

The fishing boat owned by John Farquerson was tied up where it was tied up last time Alan was here. The Foniks was on the other side of the bay with anchors out bow and stern, for whatever reason. Lou gently put the Lady June against the wall near to a ladder and Alan and Jimmy went up with lines to tie her up.

Lou shut the engines down and came up to the quay. Jimmy went back down and into the wheelhouse while Alan and Lou walked up the slope to where Alan could see Doctor Munro standing with a man wearing a dark blue woollen sweater dark trousers and what looked like German seaboots.

"Good afternoon Doctor Munro how are you?"

"I am mostly ok thank you but unfortunately we have an outbreak of foot and mouth disease on the island and we are having to refuse visitors access. This is Mr Fredericks from the Danish ministry. Alan shook hands.

"May I introduce you to Louisa Lewis."

"You are related?"

"No just the same surname. You two will get on fine you both have the same religion."

"How do you do Doctor Munro."

"My friends call me Sara. You must call me Sara."

"My friends call me Loulew. You must do the same."

I shall and when lulu's back in town you should come and see me." She took hold of both of Lou's hands and kissed her once on each cheek. "Your hands are freezing my dear you should get some gloves on or at least put them in your pocket. Lou did exactly that as Doctor Munro had slipped something to her.

"Now I'm sorry to say Mr Lewis I must ask you to leave due to the foot and mouth problem."

"Can I wait for the ebb?"

"An hour to ebb Mr. Lewis try not to overstay."

"We are nor very quick and we are sailing too close to the wind heading for Faroes but we will mange good luck to you with the problem."

Alan and Lou made their way down to the Lady June and went down the ladder and into the wheelhouse.

George and Jimmy were waiting.

"Interesting."

"Could be." Lou took the piece of rolled up paper that Doctor Munro had slipped to her when she held her hands. She unrolled it.

'We are hostages held at the school. There are three to five armed men inside with us. All are German I think.'

"Okay," said Alan. "Battle plan. First thought from me is. We have to leave. Two of us can't storm the building running up the quayside. We'd be dead before we got halfway up the path. Tide will turn in an hour and we were told not to overstay.

Sunset isn't until 18.30. If we go out and head east and then turn around, we can come back under the cover of darkness. If we stay high on the eastern side of the island we won't be seen from the bay. Then George and I will get in a two man and paddle down to the headland in the open water it will get bouncy out there but that may make for an uncomfortable ride back in but it will make any chance of spotting us difficult if not impossible.

We will climb the cliffs and tomorrow at dawn we will work our way down the landward side, make decisions as to exactly what we do as we progress.

"Pick holes in it."

"It's got more holes in it than a sieve." offered George.

"I know so let's polish it."

"What about us?" asked Louisa.

"When you've dropped us, turn North and head north out of the sight of the island.

Then you can hold up somewhere well out of sight if you can't see the island they won't be able to see the boat and then take it a bit farther. Let's put some timings on this then. Ebb is 15.00hrs which will make the next Ebb here at 0330 flood will be 09.30 then it won't matter because it'll all be over, in one way or another.

Tidal race will take you all over the place I think you'll spend all your time pushing against it. I want you to come in to the bay around 07.30 sunrise is 0530ish. You will be pushing against the ebb . It will be better because you could turn around and run like hell if you needed to.

We will either have taken over or we may be dead or something else. If you are to come back to the harbour earlier we will send you some sort of a message. Okay?"

"What about me?" Jimmy had been listening intensely but now he wanted to know.

"Stay on board Lou needs a crewman. You're going to be better doing that. We 're used to doing stuff like this. Works as best as it's going to as far as I can see. George?

"I think it's rubbish, but I can't see anything better."

"We've got to get a move on." Lou reminded them.

Jimmy had altered the ropes, looping them around the bollards, while they'd been talking to Doctor Munro and it was only a matter of undoing one end from cleats on the Lady June and pulling the loose ends back down from the quayside. Louisa had the helm and they headed off just as the ebb started.

Out of the bay they made a turn to port ,to the east which was when Alan got the binoculars onto the headland at the eastern side of the opening.

A look through the binoculars confirmed what he thought might be their best option for an ascent. Cut deep into the face was a huge fissure that looked to go all the way from sea level to the top of the cliff. Nothing else seemed to give anything nearing this potential and at least it would give them a place to start from and a lot easier to find in the darkness.

"We have three hours to sunset but even then it would be too early to start a climb up the cliff. I reckon we could be climbing for a couple of hours at least then we need to make our way over the top and down the other side to the houses and the school."

"How many kids are in the school?"

"I think there's three or four George." Alan told him. "They call it the school but it has only those few pupils. It's more like a meeting house come community centre. Let me have the helm please Lou. George is going to show you what we have in the forward cabin in case you need anything extra."

After they'd seen the stores forward, Lou put the sails up. Going east in a northerly had them cruising along steadily on a beam reach. If the wind stayed as it was they would about face and comeback roughly the same. She left the engine ticking over to keep the radio on, lights later, and the batteries charged.

At 20.00 hrs. Lou reckoned they were about half an hour or so from the island. She wasn't carrying any nav lights nor any other lighting on the boat. The canoe was on the deck and tied tight . the was a slight swell. Inside were two bags, a length of rope, about fifty yards of hawser laid hemp. It was wrapped in a bag to keep it dry. It was heavy without getting it wet. They had their pistols, one of the sniper rifles, a petrol cooker, some beans, water, a pan, sandwiches, sou westers, and waterproof trousers and jackets. They had brew kits and a couple of other bits and pieces.

Twenty minutes later they could clearly see the black shape of the island mass dead ahead. Five minutes and Alan, George and Jimmy on deck had the canoe ready to lower into the water on the port side. They had brought it to the stern to lower the freeboard height, and to keep contact with Lou through the wheelhouse door. Lou was working hard on the helm and playing with the propellers, when jimmy helped them put the canoe into the water. Lou had used Lady June to reduce the push from the tide race which was going from north to South as they knew it would. That would take them with little effort to the headland they were aiming for as long as they got tight under the cliff they should be able to hold by the fissure as they had planned.

She held it tight as she could on one spot. Alan and George were in smoothly, everything good to go; Jimmy let go when told. Alan and George let the tide take them before heading towards the island. Jimmy watched until he could see them no longer and went inside. Lou turned North east and headed away. Not something she hadn't had to do before.

Immediately they were away from the Lady June they knew they had work to do. The push from millions of tons of water that practiced every day had them fighting fiercely and paddling as hard as they could for the cliff. Lou had dropped them a way up the east coast, if she hadn't they would have been heading south missing the headland. They got there and fortunately managed to find a slight shelter inside a shallow bend in the cliff face that provided a grip on the rock to hold the canoe steady while they worked out where they were.

They were in the fissure if they'd missed it the next stop was Cape Wrath. Alan got out while George held the rock. He tied the line to his paddle jammed into a crack. It wasn't perfect but it was all he had. George held on with one hand while they got the kit out between hem and then Alan hauled George out and onto the small stance at the base of the fissure.

"We were lucky for a thousand reasons; but I tell you what any more water here and we wouldn't have had anything to stand on."

"Long may it continue." George replied. "We better secure the canoe though I don' think we'll be using it again."

They found another crack for the other paddle and tied the second line to it. Before starting to climb away from the water.

About ten foot higher inside the fissure out of the wind they sorted the rope tied it around their waist and split the kit half each into the two bags.

Alan climbed first until he found a stance and somehow find a way to tie the rope onto the rock using a spike and a tied loop.

George followed up behind went past the stance and continued upwards.

They leapfrogged each other from small stance to small stance.

Pitches of varying lengths found them slowly getting further up the fissure, and the further they got the tighter it was becoming.

One more short pitch and not only was it tighter but this one had been very wet too. Can't stop keep going.

They had worked their way foot by foot up the wet slippery rock and now above them was a solid boulder locked roof that blocked the top.

Torchlight provided some idea of its size 20 feet was a minimum it could just as easily curl around and another roof might just be around out of site. The only option was to move out onto one of the soaking wet walls and see where it would take them.

George lit a cigarette while Alan sorted out the amount of gear they had. Whoever was following would carry the bigger sack. He finished his cigarette.

"I'll lead he said you've got a good stance here Alan. And you know I can climb as well as you. If someone's going to fall off its better to be me. Given how high we are one pitch will get me to the top if I fall off I'll probably be dead or as good as. If there's a problem and either I'm not talking or I'm dead weight with no sign of life you can cut the rope and let me fall then you'll have to get out of it any way you can."

The only good thing about the wind was it was blowing flat against the rock face. George started although it wasn't as steep as he'd climbed in his life but it was wet and cold and slimy in places and loose in others. After the first twenty feet of tip toeing and slipping and sliding on the greasy surface he started to move upwards slowly and carefully he knew that if he fell he would fall at least twice the length of his run out which was now maybe forty feet and the wind changed it lifted a bit and the angle leaned forward. He felt gras in his hands and although the angle had got gentler wet grass and boots were not a good combination. He felt behind his back for his sheath knife he'd stuck this into a few people over the years now he hoped it would be his saviour again and having with difficulty got it from the sheath he stabbed it into the ground. It hit rock within the first couple of inches second third and fourth attempts proved just as unrewarding when suddenly it went in right to the hilt. He couldn't stay here much longer his legs were getting cold his feet had stopped being a part of his body a while back after the soaking he got after leaving the canoe.

 Go for it was the thought and as he did one foot found a good grip the other scraped slipped and tentatively moving it higher he found another placement. He shifted his weight, when he knew it was a solid foothold and gingerly moved the other one higher. Again both hands were gripping the knife handle, his body weight was keeping him hanging on the rock face. Friction and body bulk was stopping gravity win the contest as he pushed hard he felt his body lifting, anxiety lifted at the same time as his body moved upwards; he held onto anything he could grab and stabbed the knife in again further up. The angle was easing enough to stop the fear siding with gravity in the contest and after finding more grip for his feet together they stabbed and scrambled their way to the top.

He needed to find something to tie himself onto there was no respite from the wind here. What had kept him firmly attached to the cliff face was trying to blow him down the other side. He slowly took in slack enough to wrap around a decent sized boulder. Two sharp pulls on the rope let Alan know he was ok. He gave g himself a minute or so to relax himself and to stop blowing so hard.

Alan gave two tugs from below and George took in all the slack in the rope. He kept the rope tight without pulling hard Alan had the heavy bag with the weapons and Ammo in and also he had a traverse to make across from inside the gulley. It took a while George was glad to be here and he hoped that it wouldn't be too long before Alan was with him and they could get out of this wind. Now it was starting to rain again. They had no change of clothes but Alan had some wet weather trousers and tops in his sack which from previous experience were always too difficult to climb in. He could see Alan's head creeping over the top of the grass, his eye sight improved by the long time out in the darkness.

"Howyou doing? I don't think I've sworn that many times in less than a week. Well done George that was brilliant climbing One day I'm going to come back and do it when it isn't raining and it's daylight"

"If it isn't raining it'll be snowing."

"You're probably right. We'd have finished the top with axes then maybe it would have been easier. They'd been talking whilst working and sorting the kit.

It was sorted out into two sacks again, the sou'westers and the wet gear were on, the rope was coiled and George put it on the top of his sack.

" We better check the weapons when we can find some shelter. I'm not certain if anything is dry."

"As long as the butties are that'll do for me I think I'm happy to be alive Alan."

"You and me both matey."

They scrambled, stumbled, fell, crawled, and worked their way over the island top, until they managed to get themselves onto the lee side; dropping just six feet below the top became a different world, not warm, but there was respite out of the wind, an instant bonus, and from where they were they could see the village below them, a feint light probably from the village school just visible through the rain.

"I think we deserve a brew." said Alan. "We can't make any moves down until we can see better. It's just a massive boulder field we're going to have to cross and in this light and this rain we 'll be lucky to get through it in one piece."

He took a bearing on the light hoping that when it went out his eyes would get a night sighting. There would be a moonrise around 02.00 which should be enough to get down to the school and scout around to find what was going on.

They found some shelter, tight under a leaning rock slab, and lit a paraffin wax bar to give a bit of warmth to get the finger blood moving again. Alan dug the Coleman stove from out of his sack. Some of the petrol had leaked out, but there was plenty enough to make a brew, after he'd heated some beans to go with the sandwiches they'd made before they left the boat. There was enough puddles of rainwater to fill the small kettle and quite quickly they were enjoying a hot drink.

"I must have been wetter, and possibly colder," George said, "but not both at the same time." Alan was the same rattling with the cold.

George had spent a while at the top, while Alan had been on the belay standing still, slowly paying out the rope, and just getting colder and wetter as George had slowly worked his way to the top.

"I couldn't agree more it was extraordinarily well done. That was some climbing."

"I Didn't fancy falling off unless I survived the fall, which let's be honest would have been doubtful. You never could have got us out in the dark on your own."

"No you're right."

"We've been in worse places me and thee, but I think we're getting too old for it now. I got half way up that bloody wall of choss and thought if my wife with a little one on the way, if either of them could see me now. She means a lot to me boss and once or twice on that cliff I didn't think I was going to see her again. And that bothered me more than it should have done. That's why I think I'm getting too old for this I'm starting to see bigger pictures and you and me we've been through some troubles now for enough years and it never seems to stop."

I think we're psychic says Alan. I was standing in the dark in that gulley thinking almost the same thing. Not quite but near enough for jazz. Cocoa's ready there's some rum in the top of the bag if you want with the cocoa. It'll warm us up. Which is good enough for me, medical grounds excuses everything." They took the rum and the cocoa in silence. They'd found a dry hidey hole out of the wind and settled down for the night. It wasn't going to get any warmer but if it stayed dry that would do. They'd been in worse places and Alan went to sleep with George's thoughts running around in his head. Leaving out the brigadier at the sharp end they were a two man team. Alan didn't think that he would trust anyone in the same way he' could rely on George.

While Alan and George were cliff climbing Lou and Jimmy were moving eastwards.

"Take the wheel Jimmy, I need to work some things out. Just keep this heading with just enough power to maintain steerage I don't want to go too far, too soon, we'll need to go further then to get back, and I have an idea."

After a few minutes of working through the admiralty book and checking the chart. Lou came back.

 "Okay I have a plan. Instead of hanging around here we're going to go around the island. We'll turn north then north west then west then south then east again and well come back from the western side of the island that way we'll be hidden by the south west corner, where the backside of the harbour is. That way we'll be within a reasonably short distance, let's say a couple of miles, from the harbour, shortly after dawn. The tide rise isn't large here, but it will carry us part of the way around we will still have to pump against the ebb, but we have to do that anyway if we're going to go in during early hours tomorrow.

You get what I'm thinking. Our orders were to stay away until after daylight, so I figure this is the best way to do it."

Jimmy let what lou had said go around inside his head for a second or two.

"We're not going to get much sleep if we don't anchor or hove to."

"I think we may be better off. We're not going to be fighting tide as long as we have enough power on for steerage, the tide will take us around the island. We'll get a couple of hours each and after tomorrow morning, we can rest up when were back on the quayside."

"Okay," said Jimmy. "I can't improve on it. I don't have enough experience."

"Good, now I'm going to prove to you what a bitch I really am. Before you go to get your head down for some shut eye I need you to get a good wash and put a clean boiler suit on."

" Why?"

"No questions just do what I ask."

Jimmy did as he was asked and came back to the wheelhouse.

"I need my head in order. This is a far better way and a lot more fun. We know I'm older than you and probably not as feminine as you might prefer but do me a favour and give it your best shot please.

I've been desperate for this since last Saturday, when I should have entertaining a pretty young Welsh lass.

Beggars can't be choosers and I'm sorry to say I need you probably more than you need me.

I'll take the wheel, after I've got myself sorted. in the meantime get your hands inside my blouse . There's not a lot in there, but if you go groping around until you find something to play with. I'll imagine that you're Doctor Munro and you can imagine whoever you 'd like me to be."

Holding the wheel, Louisa undid her belt and let her trousers drop down to her ankles. She grabbed behind her, surprisingly, found Jimmy was now ready and standing to attention and slid herself back to him and slid down onto him. She murmured. A sort of noise. Part moan part sigh.

"Oh! You lovely young man. I normally crave things without an appendage but you are a better choice than either of those two hairy arsed hooligans."

Jimmy wasn't certain where his appendage was. He didn't think he'd penetrated anything but wherever it was it seemed to be well wrapped, wet and warm.

He had no wish to complain wherever it was, he was enjoying the experience and it was making him happier, given the situation, that he might be entitled to. He figured then he better get on with the job he had to do. He could feel the warm envelope and thrust his body forward into her and hanging onto her breasts, did as was asked, and gave it the best that he could. He finished before she did but she clamped him as tight as she could and milked him until she shuddered. Jimmy didn't know how much was him or the way she'd got the throbbing of the engine against her body as she'd pushed her pelvis into the helm. Neither seemed to be bothered how they'd got to where they had. Both were satisfied with the final outcome .

"Thank you Mr Myers I needed that. I need to get more clothes on she said and so do you. I'll get my kit bag you take the wheel for a minute then you can get your head down for a few hours and I'll wake you later."

Jimmy went to bed. He could smell himself inside his bedding. There was a mixture of perfume sweat and sex, He was savouring the luxury now of warmth and comfort; Lou had the boat moving gently through the water she had the speed right enough to give her steerage and gently moving on the swell of the tide. It wasn't bouncing or pounding from crest to crest just a gentle motion; and warmth, tiredness, and smug satisfaction, had Jimmy falling asleep with a smile hidden away under the blankets.

Later, much later Jimmy came awake the boat was still moving but now it was a bit lumpier and the engine noise was louder and the bow was bouncing a bit. Dawn was breaking through the deck light just a pale grey hue but definitely daylight he didn't have a watch but he knew he'd been in bed a while. He rattled a bit with the cold he grabbed his socks and then his sea boots and pulling an oily sweater on over the boiler suit he made his way up the three steps and into the wheelhouse.

When he looks out of the screen they are near the top end of the island and lou is still at the helm.

"You didn't wake me."

"You were kind to me." She told him. "I repaid the favour. And I need you to be wide awake and not sleepy eyed. First we need some food and something hot to drink. Choice is yours take the helm or the galley."

"What do you want to do? " Asked Jimmy.

"You take the helm it means I can at least move my body. It's a tad stiff at the mo and I can loosen up a bit. I'll fry whatever we've got and make some drinks. I'm going for cocoa if that's ok for you." "Anything. I'm not used to waiter service. If I'm lucky I manage tea and toast on me own and more often than not its nowt till I get into work and I get a drink and start on me carry out. It takes an hour to get to work if I miss the bus I could lose half a day's pay or even the whole day if it gets too late."

"Well you haven't got far to go to work today let's hope we're going to get paid for doing nothing."

"That'll be another first then. I don't ever get that much good luck in one go."

Time to get the watercooler out, the tinned ammo, and the Vickers. I really hope we're not going to need them, but if we do I want to be ready. I've been in plenty of skirmishes when we ran coastal patrols in MTB's during the war. This isn't anything new for me. You're going in at the deep end, if we're in a fire fight, I promise you one thing I won't drop you in the shit, and I'll run like hell if I have to ok."

"I'll be fine."

Around 02.30 Alan and George slowly worked their way down hill towards the schoolhouse. It had stopped raining. They had taken off the yellow waterproofs and sou wester and hoping to be as quiet as possible and under the blanket of near darkness save for a small moon worked their way going from boulder to boulder.

Now and again the door to the school would open and someone would come out walk around the building and then go back inside where as far as they could see was only a very dim light possibly just enough to keep an eye on the hostages.

Around halfway down they slipped the wet weather clothes back on and waited for daylight.

Alan and George watched from the middle of the boulder field. They were still partway up the hill which gave them a view over the surrounding ground.

There were known to be at least 12 people on the island. Yet no one was visible at all apart from what appeared to be three men, carrying weapons, standing around the perimeter of the school building. There were no lights on in Rosie Cuthbertson's, the harbour master's house. The village shop opened only whenever anyone needed something. Clearly there was no activity happening anywhere that could be seen. There had been some activity earlier when couple of men had left the building gone into Mrs Cuthbertson's, where they had stayed only briefly, before they set off down the track towards the harbour.

There was certainly activity visible on the boat in the harbour but to what purpose was only a guess. The engines that had been quiet when they were last here were now running. Alan reckoned that departure was possibly imminent.

If they got away now they might be lost forever. One last job maybe was all it was for everyone involved.

Walking down in full view was the best way Alan reckoned to get close enough to find out what was happening. There was no cover for at least a hundred yards in front of the school. There was the boulder field they were in before that cleared area but the last hundred yards would be suicidal to attempt a frontal assault. Perhaps walking in as though nothing was wrong, as though you had every right to be there, may allow you to get near enough to work out what to do.

What they didn't know was the strength of the enemy inside the building, how many might there be in there. What they did know from Doctor Munro's note was that everyone was being held prisoner and potentially hostage.

Bright yellow oilskins would make him a clearly visible target, so the I have every right to be here, might be implied by the sheer audacity of walking down the hillside into the village, not trying to be devious in any way suspicious.

George needed to get himself nice and comfortable. The lee Enfield they had was one that Alan got back from Marseille.

George had got himself behind a large rock and removed his yellow jacket. Peat mud had taken the white from his face; the damn stuff was soft and cold and did a simple job of camouflage. It wouldn't last long but neither was the fight planned to last long.

When no one was outside the school and George was ready Alan stood up and made his way slowly towards the entrance. His right hand was inside his jacket pocket his left hand clearly visible his body turned to the right slightly as walked.

Three men came out of the building. They stopped as Alan got closer to the school gate two were carrying rifles which they immediately raised.

George shot them, the third man unarmed ran away down the side of the school towards the quayside as Alan smashed through the school front door. He shots one at the front door and charged into the room. There was One man holding a child with a gun pointing at the boys head. The boy was small about four feet high. The man had him on a small stool. His arm was around the boys neck. He was holding a cocked pistol against his head, neither of them looked very happy. Behind them were the villagers some tied others just sitting. Near the boy was a well-built, grey haired man; his hands tied behind him and also to the chair. Whatever he had done had obviously irritated someone. It looked like he he'd punched him in the face, a lot more more than once

"Let the boy go and I'll let you go free." Alan told him.

"I no speak English"

Alan repeated his offer in German. "I'll take the boy with me the German said let him go by the boat."

"No." Alan told him the boy not understanding started to wriggle and scream. At that point the Germans gun came away from the boys head and the man tied to the chair kicked the stool out from under the boy. The boy fell out of the Germans arm the man tied to the chair got shot and the German took a bullet in the head.

"You have a patient Doctor Munro. As long as it's not his femoral artery all he might have is a limp. Thank you matey, gave me an edge."

"What about him?" she pointed to the German.

"He's dead."

"Are you sure?"

Alan shot him again. "Yes."

The Foniks was now tied to Harbour wall. The Germans who had got away were just about there. George had come into the school via a back door. "Mrs. Cuthbertson can we use your radio?"

"Help yourself."

"I'm not certain we can but Let's see." Alan slowly opened the front door to the school. Two bullets hit the door casing almost exactly the same time. "You might be right Alan."

"One thing is certain we won't get down the path to the quayside; there isn't an ounce of cover all the way down."

"What then?" From down in the harbour came two explosions. "And what was that?" wondered George.

"Can we get into your house via the back door and go out of the back door here Mrs C.?"

"Yes."

That's when they found what the two men who had visited her house had gone to smash the radio and the two explosions were probably grenades as they could no longer see the fishing boat , just the very top of its mast.

"Bad news your radio is broken Mrs C. and your boat's been sunk John."

"Mr Lewis. John says the radio off his fishing boat is in his cottage he took it off the boat because of a problem. But the problem must have been the battery on the boat not the radio as it worked on the tractor battery."

"Keep talking. Are you telling me we have a working radio?"

"Sort of but you'll need to get the radio from John's cottage and then use a battery from mine."

"We'll get it. where does John live?"

A man at the back called out. "I'll take them John you sit tight."

They switched on the radio. "Come on Mr Marconi show us how well you can work."

The radio started to hiss; Alan squeezed the mic button.

"Lysternoy calling Lady June. Lysternoy calling Lady June."

Then a voice he hadn't heard in many years.

"Good morning Colonel Lewis. A pleasure to speak to you though something tells me we will never get around to shooting deer in the black forest and getting fat on venison. Perhaps that's just as well. It would not have suited either of us. I am glad you have survived. I could see you from our boat when you arrived. We knew then that we may have a problem. You did not disappoint me my friend. It would have been interesting to meet you again, say hello, and shake your hand, but You have you're your job to do, and I have mine. Unfortunately we were on different sides colonel, but I am glad to say we were never enemies. Auf weidersen my friend auf weidersen." The radio switched off this was a short message not the start of a conversation.

Doctor Munro looked at Alan. Whatever that man meant had had an effect on him. Then his face changed back to his normal look.

"Lysternoy calling Lady June."

"Lady June receiving over."

"Lou, islanders safe. I think the other boat will try to sink you. Do what you have to do to stay safe over."

"We understand out."

"Are they up to it?" Doctor Munro asked.

"I don't know, but what I do know is that given what they did to the fishing boat in the harbour and the damage to the radio they won't want to leave any possibility of either pursuit or communication. They now have the information that if they have to fight it is only themselves that they need to worry about.

My gut feeling is that the Foniks will try and sink them. I can only give them an option to shoot first and hope they get the Germans before they get those two. My fingers are crossed Doctor Munro and I hope they survive because I can't do a damn thing to help them."

Jimmy was standing next to Lou in the wheelhouse.

"Are you and your Vickers ready?"

"As we'll ever be."

"We are wooden. They are steel hulled heavier and quicker than us. You'll get only a small sector to shoot through about nine to eleven on the clock so that's a slice of the port side; it's not very big but what I'll do is make the target bigger, and what you have to do is point it and pull the trigger. Then I'm going to turn and run like hell for the harbour.

You can see the way it's coming out now it's hugging that western side it will turn to port when we move over towards the east it will try to maintain a collision course. It has the ebb to give it a start and I hope that what I think will happen does. Okay get your head out of the hatch and get ready to take the cover off the Vickers."

Jimmy went down into the saloon got onto the table and put his head and body through the hatch.

Lou had tied some loops into a piece of thin rope and put one over a spoke on the helm and tied off the other end.

She got the binoculars and looked at the steel beast coming towards them just steady no rush. Provocation time.

There was a screen in front of a sunken cockpit she figured the helm was below the screen which allowed the helmsman to see out in front.

Left, right, or centre, she wondered, didn't matter really. She picked up the Bren gun loaded one, stuck the barrel out of the portside window and shot the screen out of the front of the opposition.

The reaction was instant. They came at a charge; they opened up their throttle and got on a collision course. Lou rapid fired the Bren into the cockpit area of the Foniks. It was moving quickly now looking good she thought whoever had it was timing it perfectly. Jimmy swears it was about twenty yards and he could see the front of the boat when Lou pushed the levers into reverse and the two propellers with their variable pitch and the ebb stopped them dead in the water. Foniks was now going in front of them and before it did so Lou opened the throttle further and it went backwards far enough out of the way, to start to pass her by harmlessly, and as it moved backwards she turned the wheel to port and the Lady June did a pirouette . The port propeller was pushed to forward and the helm was turned to starboard. Then Lou put the starboard prop to forward and as she moved away Foniks was trying to turn into her and as she did she leaned hard onto her starboard side her gunwhale close to the water and Jimmy opened fir through all the teak decking. Lou held the position as Foniks decks were shot opt pieces by the Vickers. The Vickers was empty Jimmy was changing tins and a deep thunder sound and Foniks sank in seconds. Something had blown up inside they reckoned afterwards maybe the petrol tanks it apparently ran on avgas. Lou hung around ten minutes and no survivors no one was coming up now. They decided to call it and Lou took the Lady June slowly into Lysternoy harbour.

"You alright Jimmy?"

"Yes mam."

"You did well."

"Thank you mam." And shortly after that he started laughing.

"Are you sure you're alright?"

"Yes mam. I just thought of something funny."

"Go on then tell me."

"When I go back to work. They'll say what did you do then Jimmy while you were away. Well We dropped some soldiers off on a little island in the north Atlantic so that they could rescue hostages. Then we sailed around the island at night. I had asexual encounter with a naval lady and in the morning we sank a German boat that was trying to ram us. No one is going to believe a word of that are they?"

"You might be right Jimmy I certainly wouldn't believe a word of it either."

Lou put the Lady June away from the sunken fishing boat, its mast just showing out of the water. Jimmy took the two lines up to the quayside. Alan and George were waiting.

"Never been so pleased to see two [people in my life." Alan said before he shook Jimmy's hand and both of them hugged him.

Just as Lou appeared at the top of the ladder Doctor Munro joined the group.

"How are you Lulu?" asked Doctor Munro. "You must come up to my surgery as soon as you can and I'll check you over."

"Should I come to asked Jimmy?"

"Does anything actually hurt?" asked the doctor

"Not that I'm aware of."

"Then you'll be ok. Perhaps a couple of glasses of the local brew would fix any aches and pains. The village school is probably going to hold a small celebration later when we've cleaned the mess of the floor that Mr. Lewis left."

"I could eat breakfast. Alan, Jimmy shall we go eat?"

"Come on then jimmy it's too early for anything else" Alan led the way down on to the Lady June.

They were half sleeping half in their own little world breakfast eaten and stomachs filled too high when they felt someone come aboard the boat. Doctor Munro had arrived with Louisa. Both looked shining bright like they'd had a good wash. Doctor Munro started the conversation.

"When are you thinking about leaving here Mr. Lewis?"

"we'll stay for your little celebration tonight. Our job is finished; I'm tired and I've had enough and I'm ready to go home. So the answer is soon as possible tomorrow preferably. Why?"

"The island has no transport, perhaps I could get another lift from you."

"What about your patient the fisherman?"

"I would like him to come along as well. He says he's had worse injuries off a gaff hook and he might be right the bullet took out a slice of flesh and a sliver of muscle maybe. I've dressed it and it's clean and he's a tough old guy. We need to find another boat for the island and to keep us in touch with everyone else."

"There is a boat in Shetland you will need to paint it and give at a name. All it had before was a number and we painted that out a few months back. If his leg is up to it, get a crewman, and we'll give you all a lift down to Shetland and you can take it from there."

"That's very generous of you Mr. Lewis."

"Not really Doctor. If the German had been any good he would have shot me not the fisherman. He got a bullet in the leg and he bought me half a second which is why we are having this conversation now; and I'm not that generous, I'm taking advice from my previous boss and I'm going to steal the boat for you."

Epilogue

By Adam Lewis

I was sort of moving again. The house I was originally going to move into fell through. The couple who owned it, eventually decided to not sell. My possessions, as they were, had remained in storage, whilst I'd wandered around Scotland, in a camper van and then to Alan's via Phil's and sundry other places. I put my stuff that was in storage into an auction house as it was costing more than it was worth. I'd stopped playing rugby healing was still not complete by midweek training, body warned, and advice taken. I'd kept my job with her majesties government for a while then without rhyme reason or thought of the consequences I managed to negotiate a redundancy package which opened the decision to accept an offer. Unlike most government employees I was on a twelve month rolling contract as part of a specialised team woefully overstaffed my leaving was expedited with ease and unusually mutually benefitted all.

I had a camper van the proceeds from the sale of my house a goodbye handshake pot no wife no children and no debts. Sufficient pros to allow me to change my life completely. I'd done D of E as a teenager and been a rock climbing through the summer when I wasn't playing rugby and Alan's exploits and Stevens push to get on an do rather than sitting around and waiting I had qualified as a climbing instructor and mountain leader and my degree and my masters got me into teacher training college without any difficulty.

It was early days of teaching outside of the classroom. So early it wasn't even recognised as real teaching. I was running a sort of outdoor education on the North downs for a private fee paying residential school sort of voluntary borstal for rich kiddies when I got a message, via the school switchboard, from Katarina. Alan had died from prostate cancer. They had been trying to find me for nearly a month.

I phoned the number that had been left with the school. I got an answer phone and left a message that I would be there late that evening. The course had finished, and reports written, my job was complete. I drove up to the peak district.

The place Alan had moved them all to was a lot easier to get to. He had converted his office building back to the old manor house it had originally been when they first bought it. There were no iron gates, single track gravel roads, or possessive heifers to negotiate with. Just as well I doubt the paintwork my camper would survived the experience. I parked in the drive and as I got out Bandit came bounding over, put his head against my knee, and escorted me to the front door.

Both Katarina and Steven met me at the door. Katarina grabbed my hand to shake it. I could feel her trembling as she held it.

" What good timing Adam, we're having a late dinner, early supper, however you wish to call it and we have made enough to for us all so as you were expected you are most welcome and I'm so sorry but I'm going to cry any minute we couldn't get hold of you to let you know.

Katarina grabbed me and hugged me she was sobbing her head was rubbing on my chest her whole body was trembling. I looked over her shoulder at Steven. I didn't understand it. He was smiling and even more strange he gave me a two thumbs up . He turned and walked into the hallway and left us at the front door.

Bandit had returned to his kennel on the verandah. "I'm sorry I needed that. Come let's eat you must be starving and you've lost weight I'll fatten you up. She was smiling again like I remembered her. She led me into a living room with a table set for three. Thankyou Steven you've done the plates I shall get the food. Steven shook my hand.

"Nice to see you Adam." he said and leaned in towards me as Katerina went into the kitchen.

"Thank you," he whispered, "mother needed that she's had it bottled up for about six weeks. She'll never fully heal, but the process is at least started.

Do you need the bathroom before dinner?"

"No I'm fine, I stopped at motorway services just down the road a touch to check the map."

"Then it's sit and wait."

"Does Katarina need a hand?"

Steven answered very quietly. "No! We'll leave her be. She will want to fuss over you while you're here. She needs things to do. She'll be out when she's dried her eyes and got herself back together again. No doubt she will tell you all this again but for a quick info feed. Alan moved down here because he had been diagnosed with Cancer. He of course didn't tell anyone until he'd done everything that he wanted to do with house moves and business deals. He sold everything basically but not the house on the hill. He'd relocated the offices out of here into a new purpose built set up on a trading estate. That way he had sorted the house and all the finances out for us, all totally divorced now from the business and therefore safe for us to live comfortably.

I had stayed a couple of days. Alan had sorted out some papers about the Lewis family some phots of the brothers and one of Frank's grave at the military cemetery in Rome. Katarina had kept them separately for me. We were sitting at the dining table talking. Steven had gone into town for some shopping.

"My son has lost both of his fathers. I have lost both of the men who have taken care of me since the end of the war. Alan wanted to put things straight or as straight as he felt they needed to be. He wasn't totally honest in everything. He didn't tell lies as such but didn't tell you everything. Do you remember this picture?"

"Yes I saw it when I first came up here. I assumed it was a picture of you and your husband."

"Not true it was taken by my husband it's a picture of Alan and me when we were all at the army base in Hamburg.

Alan said that when you thought it was George he let it go at that because you'd seen a similarity with Steven. A picture tells a thousand words so we say but I add not always the truth. Alan never married because he would have shared himself and he always said there wasn't really enough in him for the responsibilities he already had without adding anymore to the load. In the end it became an untalked about subject consigned to the out tray and filed in gone forever box. It has returned to its normal place of residence probably for ever."

I didn't want to say anything or I couldn't.

"Alan Left papers including a letter from Otto via Anne Marie. Do you speak German or read it?"

"Schoolboy French gets me a coffee at Charles de Gaulle airport."

"I shall write a translation for you."

I read the letter that Katarina had translated for me a couple of days later. I put the original and the translation carefully with the photos and family papers Alan had left me.

Bandit followed me around . "He misses Alan," Steven told me. "He was always Alan's dog. I think he sort of still waits for Alan to come home.

The day was dry the wind was furious conditions as requested by Alan.

Steven had driven the Landrover and I had opened and closed the gates as we made our way up the single track to the old house where I first stayed.

We parked in the yard bandit knew exactly where he was and jumped out of the back as soon as we stopped. He looked around was he searching?

"Alan never bothered selling the house." Katarina told me. "He always said he never really wanted to leave. I believe we moved out so I wouldn't have to be too far away from civlisation." She laughed but it had no humour in it.

We walked out of the drive and about fifty yards or so stepped off the road and across the turf towards a large flat topped stone. Bandit had put his head against my knee as we slowly made our way across the uneven ground. The wind was behind us cold and mean, the wind that went through you not round you. Steven and I held Katarina's hands; no desire to have her fall down here. We got ourselves to the side of the stone, the only sound the blowing of the south westerlie wind as it forced its way up the valley.

Steven let go of Katarina and I felt her other hand tighten on mine.

He opened the satchel he was carrying and took out a polished metal urn. He looked at us and Katarina nodded. He unscrewed the top and emptied the urn towards the flat topped stone, The howling wind took Alan's ashes most before they even touched the rock and scattered them, lost forever now, over the peak moorland.

I felt Katarina's grip tighten, the lady who survived the war and then the peace gripping as hard as she could. The ashes had almost instantly disappeared all gone never to be seen again.

We all stood there in silence each of us lost in our own thoughts. Bandit had tucked his tail between his legs and flopped down, onto the ground, out of the wind, and watched us. Maybe he too understood what was happening. I didn't know what Katarina and Steven were thinking, but in my mind I remembered a picture of two people taken just after the end of the second world war and wondered what might have been if as I believed the man holding his mother's other hand should have been called Adam. I as I have many times since, wondered what father would have christened me?

Now all the brothers had gone. Alan had been the last, the survivor. He'd survived bombs, bullets, grenades, and a multitude of other wild and dangerous things. Cancer had got him in the end and now it had come the full circle.

This whole thing had started many years before at a funeral and though the circle wasn't a perfect one it was joined up at the end and finishing with a final funeral and like the closed circle, I had come to the end of my story.

Printed in Dunstable, United Kingdom

75672324R00328